SOMETHING ABOUT MAUDY

by

Delinda McCann

Cover and Graphic Design by Writers Cramp Publishing

ISBN: 978-1-938586-43-9 Paperback
ISBN: 978-1-938586-44-6 eBook
All Rights Reserved
Copyright © 2013 by Delinda McCann
http://delindalmccann.weebly.com

Paperback Edition May 2013
Printed in the United States of America
Writers Cramp Publishing
http://www.writerscramp.us/
editor@writerscramp.us

SOMETHING ABOUT MAUDY

CHAPTER 1: MAUDE

I've always considered carpets, if I thought about them at all, to be rather boring. I'm talking about rugs here--not the most exciting objects in the world. We can all continue to learn, and I learned something about carpets one Monday at City People's Nursery in Seattle when a rug decided to change the course of my life and became animate.

I went to Seattle on a Monday to recover from a stressful weekend. The first sign that I was about to have a fantastic day occurred in a little store near the nursery called Missi Lu. A **SALE** sign lured me into the shop where I found a charming, trendy jacket and an A line skirt suitable for work. I checked the tags and was thrilled to the tips of my toes. They were both made in the U.S. Avoiding clothes made in sweat-shops is a high priority for me.

I gloated over my good fortune while stowing my new treasures behind the front seat of my Porsche. This whole trip was about beauty and escaping my life, my job, and my empty nest. Early this morning, I'd started my mini-quest by dressing in a short pink sweater dress with a wide black belt. I put on my makeup, which I seldom wear and pulled my uncooperative hair into a bun in the back. The shorter hair curled around my face attractively. At first, I thought about wearing sensible shoes for walking, but a pair of cute purple heels begged me to take them out of the closet. Perhaps they were aware of their role in the life-changing events of the day. They were not high heels just the cutest little spiked purple pumps imaginable. They made me feel pretty.

When I lived near the Madison Valley, I visited this nursery often. The tough plants, the trees, heathers and grasses lived in pots outside. This particular Monday, I wanted to visit the inside plants, the sweet African violets, the bromeliads, and orchids. I considered them appropriate objects on a quest for beauty.

As I wandered through the store, I looked at the violets and considered a cyclamen. Next I looked at the crystal vases. I imagined how a red crystal vase would catch the light and brighten up my kitchen. I barely noticed the small rug lurking on the floor of the gift area. I had my eyes fixed on a lovely display of glass lilies. The instant I stepped on the rug, it grabbed my spiked heel and refused to let go. It snagged the second heel as I struggled to maintain my balance. I knew. I was going down. I hoped I didn't break too many pretty glass lilies on my way.

I landed not with a crash but with an oof against the chest of someone who felt like a football player. I wondered what position he played that he was so good at catching. I thought I should behave like a proper professional woman and disengage myself, but the carpet still held my cute heels captive. I couldn't stand by myself.

My enjoyment over touching a well-muscled body caused me to blush and behave more shy than normal as my rescuer set about releasing my feet from their shoes. I stared at those strange hands on my ankle and couldn't think of a thing to say.

By this time, I'd attracted enough attention that other customers and a clerk came to my assistance. The short clerk asked, "Are you okay?"

I nodded more out of habit than any thoughts of my wellbeing.

"What happened here?" A man who seemed to be in charge asked?

"She fell" I couldn't see who uttered this exaggeration.

"She shouldn't be wearing those shoes in here." I couldn't see the owner of this cross voice either because I preferred to look at my rescuer.

"The rug is dangerous."

"She could have broken those lilies."

"Oh, I'm so sorry for your near fall."

"I don't know why anyone would wear such shoes to a garden store."

The voices swirled around me while I did my best to focus my attention on my hero. I confess I thoroughly enjoyed placing my hand on his shoulder to steady myself while he unbuckled my shoe. I wanted to concentrate on the feel of The Hero's hand on my ankle. I suspected that he was enjoying playing the hero as much as I did being his damsel in distress. Finally, he released me from one shoe, and I could put my foot on solid ground. The Hero now concentrated on my other foot. His head rested against my thigh. I silently laughed at myself for thinking this near fall constituted the most action I had experienced in years. Finally, I slipped my foot from the second shoe. Once I was set free, the carpet released the shoes as innocently as if it had never seized me by the heels and thrown me into the arms of a stranger. Its task in life was complete.

I regained my composure enough to remember my manners. "Oh thank you for catching me. I think you saved the lives of all these pretty lilies here." I looked again at the display to avoid looking into his green eyes.

His deep, soft voice made my knees weak. "I like saving lives or at least preventing some pretty knees from getting bruised."

"I'd hate to have my Day-In-The-City ruined."

He chuckled over my inflection. "You are in town for recreation today?"

"Yes. I work weekends so I take Mondays off."

"If you don't have any appointments would you care to join me for lunch? Café Flora is just a few doors down and they serve good food."

I nodded.

He steadied me while I put my shoes back on - well away from the treacherous rug. I clung to him far more than strictly necessary. I enjoyed being slightly naughty, but didn't say anything. All the topics uppermost in my mind were all the things I came to town to escape. He held the door for me as we left the garden store.

"Oh, by the way, my name is Maude." I hoped I didn't sound as fluttery as I felt

"Ralph." He flexed his shoulder muscles as he loomed over me.

Without thinking I asked a question that often plagues me about names. "Ralph? That is a name I don't hear often. How did you manage growing up with an unusual name?"

"I got used to being called barf and puke."

"Oh dear, that's not much better than mold or moldy." We both chuckled. I wondered if an attractive, athletic man could really suffer the way I had as a child over my name. "Actually, when I was little my friends called me Maudy, which I rather like. When I reached junior high the boys started with the mold and moldy teasing, and some of the girls followed along."

"Junior high boys ought to be locked up until they recover from the raging testosterone poisoning."

"Is that what causes it?" I turned and smiled at Ralph. I seemed to be unable to stop smiling when I looked at his smile that lit up the whole world.

He held open the restaurant door for me. He nodded at our hostess who called him by name. "Two please."

I smiled at his smug tone of voice as he spoke to the waitress and felt flattered that he obviously enjoyed being out with a woman.

The waitress smiled coyly at Ralph as she led us to a small table near the window. I looked around the restaurant admiring its simple yet charming décor. I realized that this place like Missi Lu's had opened after I moved out of the Madison Valley. I felt myself shudder as I thought about the house I'd lived in only a few blocks away.

Ralph's voice pulled me out of my past. "They make great soup here."

"The split pea with carrots sounds good. My grandma used to make it for me when I was little. It was my special lunch-with-grandma soup."

The lines on his forehead and at the corners of his eyes melted as his whole face relaxed. He almost sighed, "My closest grandmother was Italian. She made a meatball soup that she called minestrone, but it was unlike anything else I've ever eaten by that name."

The soft warmth in Ralph's voice when he talked about his grandmother curled my toes. We continued to talk about food and the people who walked by outside the café. I didn't want to discuss my job so I refrained from asking about his. I thought this little escape into the immediate world around us was refreshing. I tucked away for possible future use the thought about the value of paying attention to basic pleasures such as enjoying a simple meal with a companion. Toward the end of the meal my cell phone rang. I confess to flying into a state of near panic over the phone so I tried to look apologetic and checked the caller ID.

"It's my daughter." I smiled and set the phone down beside me on the table as my heart-rate returned to normal. "Why do I have the guilty feeling that she is checking up on me?"

"Is there any reason you would not want her to know where you are?" His tone sounded just the tiniest bit anxious.

"Yes, I can think of about one hundred reasons why I would rather my daughter, my parents, and everybody at work did not know I just ate lunch with a man for no reason other than that he seemed like pleasant company. All of those reasons center on the hundred questions they would feel compelled to ask me, and on the thousand cautions I'd suffer through. Which reminds me, are you a terrorist? Have you ever been arrested?"

He arched his eyebrow at me and picked up my phone. I watched as he punched numbers. I suspected he was calling my daughter, but when I heard his phone ringing in his pocket, he broke off the call and smirked at me. I tried to give him a knowing smile, but I think it ended up being boldly flirtatious, instead.

He continued in a teasing tone. "I am not a terrorist. I'm a law-abiding citizen, a widower. I don't have any debt. In fact, I'm really a very dull fellow. I've never done anything so bold as ask a total stranger to eat lunch with me." I liked the combination of little boy silliness about him and the air of vulnerability under his manner. I confess, much to my surprise, I found his baldhead very sexy.

"Hmm, it seems strange to me that having a simple lunch can get so complicated. I've enjoyed your company, really. I'm not going to mention this to my parents and children. They wouldn't understand. Earlier I was struck with how pleasant it was to just be present in the moment and not worry about who is sick, or social justice, or the economy, or the thousand other obligatory worries we live with."

Ralph nodded and turned serious. "Obligatory worries. I like that. It really describes so much of life. What do we really need to worry about? What can we actually do something about?"

After lunch, Ralph walked me to my car. I noticed his appreciative look when he saw my navy blue Porsche. I didn't mention converting the sports car to electric. I wondered what he thought when I turned it on and pulled away from the curb without making a sound. I giggled to myself.

I did have some business to conduct in the city. I needed to go to Nordstroms and buy about a dozen pairs of pantyhose. As I negotiated Seattle traffic, I got into a grump about pantyhose that goes on easily enough but then starts a slow relentless roll downward. More than once, I've felt my pantyhose rolling down around my thighs as I've sat in meetings.

My other chore involved meeting with the real estate agency that managed my house in town. I hated talking about the house I'd shared with my husband and children, the house where I almost died. I learned the current lease was up in two months and the renters wanted new carpet or they wouldn't stay.

I whined at my poor agent, "Oh dear, didn't I replace that carpet when they moved in? Let me think about this. I am not happy where I am. Perhaps I will request an assignment where I can commute from home." I shuddered as I thought about living in that house again.

I took a ferry home feeling very thankful for the ferry system that allowed me to visit Seattle when I lived in a small town named Blackfish on the other side of the Sound.

By the time my car rolled into the garage, I'd begun to worry that I would have to have it towed, but the batteries still held a charge. I plugged it back in before carrying my packages into the house.

CHAPTER 2: WORK

As soon as I came in, I checked my phone messages. I had twenty-three, all practically the same. "Pastor Maude, Joe Miller passed away this morning. Where are you?" Grumbling about my day off, I prepared to return calls. First I called Elma Miller and talked to her daughter. Elma didn't feel up to taking calls, and no arrangements could be made until her son Joey arrived. I promised to call back in the morning. Next, I called the chair of our care committee who was in charge of taking meals to families in crisis.

"Shirley, hi, this is Pastor Maude. I got your message. What have you planned for care?"

"Well, I could hardly plan anything with you gone." Her tone told me that she was convinced Mr. Miller had died because I'd left town for a few hours.

I sighed, "Did you call your committee about meals?"

"I waited to talk to you."

"Oh." I tried to ease the pain in my back and infuse patience I didn't feel into my voice. "Okay what are your thoughts on Elma's situation." I spent twenty minutes listening to Shirley complain about how much work she had to do, and how Elma was not going to be able to live alone without Joe. Privately, I thought that if Elma could live with Joe, she'd do fine without him. I said, "Okay, their son is flying in tonight and the daughter is there now. Everybody in the congregation has called me to confirm that they are aware of this death. Can you see that food is delivered to the house this evening, maybe just a dessert and some fresh fruit?"

"Well, they'll need more than dessert and fruit. What are you thinking? Delores is taking them fried chicken with biscuits and a salad tonight. Louise is making an omelet for their breakfast. They cannot get by on sweets."

Drat! I'd been suckered again. Of course Shirley had made all the necessary plans. She'd been doing this job for years. "Thank you for taking care of the food. I will be talking to the family again tomorrow morning."

I sighed again after I hung up. I couldn't do more tonight so I decided on a nice soak in the tub. I double checked the locks, wedged the back door shut with a doorstop and moved a heavy chair to block the front door closed. I didn't want any uninvited visitors while I soaked in the tub.

I could not stop myself from thinking about my congregation as I soaked. I couldn't see how this church could possibly survive. I'd never been the pastor of a church that closed down. I suspected that the previous pastor Jeffry Morgan left just to avoid the career stigma of pastoring a dying church. I thought the place would hold up for a couple years, maybe. However, we'd already had a month where my salary was late due to lack of funds. They had no hope of paying all their bills. I sank deeper into the water and wondered if there was any way to save the life of this institution.

Tuesday kept me busy despite the fact that technically it should be my study and sermon prep day. I started with some study then visited the Miller family. They thanked me for the fruit I brought and informed me that Pastor Jeffry would be doing the service. The idea that he consented to drive so far to come back for this service surprised me, but then, perhaps he loved this congregation as much as they loved him. I made the correct sympathetic sound and trudged on. "Is there anything else I can do for you? The Bates people are good at handling the details of the service. I see other members of the congregation have been here."

Elma sounded dreamy and disconnected as she talked about her husband. "Joe attended church here ever since he was baptized as an infant."

"That should be mentioned in his service. It is unusual for a person to stay in one place so long."

"Oh, he didn't live here all that time."

"Oh?" I thought I might learn of some adventure.

"No he left to serve in the war. He was in the navy."

"Ah, be sure to include that in his service. Do you have any pictures of him in uniform?"

Elma's voice turned firm. "We'll talk to Pastor Jeffry when he gets here." After staying twenty minutes I said my goodbyes and left--feeling that the family was relieved to get rid of me. I returned to my office to outline the rest of my week and make some appointments. Finally, I remembered that I had not had lunch so I walked across the parking lot to the parsonage.

When I entered my house, I screamed and my pulse jumped into fight or flight mode. Before turning and running for my life, I recognized the three people on my sofa as members of the congregation. My pulse slowed to twice its normal rate. "What on earth? What on earth are you doing here?"

"We want to talk to you about Joe's service."

"Um, I understand that Pastor Jeffry will officiate. You need to talk to Elma or one of her children."

"Oh, well that is okay then. He knows the rules."

"Rules? What rules?" I wondered what kind of rules might they have about a funeral. Refreshments? Open caskets? Length of Eulogies?

"About using the church vases and stands. Only the mahogany stands can be used because Mrs. Walton donated them for that use. And don't let the Bates move the communion table back. We've measured and there is room for a casket in front of the table. We don't want to have to move it forward when they are done." I mentally slapped my hand for immediately wanting to move the communion table. I knew that any little change would upset the congregation.

I hate confrontation, but I've learned it is sometimes necessary. "Well, since Pastor Jeffry will be here, I'm sure he can take care of the details. Listen, I have a problem with you just walking into my home when I am gone." Before I could continue with this discussion Jean appeared from my kitchen.

"Oh hi, I just thought I would clean your refrigerator for you. Did you know your cottage cheese was past the pull date? I threw it out."

"Please if you need to see me make an appointment and come into the church office where I've been for the past two hours. I need my privacy in my home."

"Pastor Jeffry welcomed us anytime we dropped in." Jean's chin trembled at my mild rebuke. "I just wanted to help you. It's my ministry, you know, to keep the parsonage tidy."

The phone interrupted this conversation. "Maude, it's Jeffry Morgan here. Elma Miller just called and asked me to do Joe's service. Is there some reason you can't do it?"

"They prefer to have you." It hurt to say these words on top of my distress over the delegation in my living room.

"Then if I refuse, you will do it?"

"I thought you'd already accepted."

"No. I just got off the phone with Elma."

"Oh dear, well that's fine. I originally expected to do it, but you know how congregations hate changing pastors." I got off the phone with Jeff and turned to my house guests. "Please leave." I held the door open.

"I was just trying to help." Jean pouted.

Trying not to feel guilty for defending my space, I didn't say anything as the delegation trouped out. I ran my fingers through my hair and decided to write a letter to the staff-parish committee about landlord-tenant law.

That night, I went to bed with only a light snack for dinner. My sermon wasn't even started. Now I had a funeral to do. I curled up in a ball on my bed feeling depressed and discouraged. My cell phone rang. I answered expecting to hear my daughter.

"Maudy? Hi, it's Ralph. I thought I'd call and thank you for having lunch with me yesterday."

"Oh. Oh, you're welcome." I suddenly felt much better. "I enjoyed talking with someone about something other than business."

"I know what you mean. Some days my job gets me down."

"Yeah, I think I've just had one of those days. You called at a good time." We chatted for a couple minutes. He didn't tell me about his job. I didn't tell him about mine.

CHAPTER 3: FIRST DATE

*O*n Sunday evening I boarded the ferry to Seattle for dinner with Ralph. Traffic made me late, so I almost missed the ferry. The crew started to lower the gate on the full boat, but because my Porsche was small, they allowed me to park crossways at the back. I couldn't get out because the nets at the back of the boat pressed right against my door.

I couldn't get out of my car, but I could triple check my appearance. I wore a basic black sweater dress. I thought I didn't look at all like a preacher. My dark hair curled over my shoulders hanging almost down to my breasts. The low cut dress showed enough cleavage to demonstrate that I am a woman. Net stockings added a slightly naughty look to my ensemble. I wore the cutest shoes imaginable. The heels were five inches high. They had a strap around my ankle and a tiny, very classy rhinestone near my little toe. I wore makeup for a change. I liked the way the gloss made my lips look full and moist.

I parked my car at Ralph's apartment, thankful to find an outlet near the front door. I plugged in my car feeling anxious over the possibility of needing to drive home over the Narrows Bridge.

Ralph came down to the door himself to escort me up. He wore black slacks and a football jersey with a gold chain around his neck. I saw his last name above a Seahawk symbol. "Do you play for the Seahawks?"

"Not anymore." He smiled at me and I almost melted into my cute shoes. "I just pulled the jersey on because you caught me before I finished dressing. I didn't want to shock you by coming down without my shirt on."

"Oh I wouldn't mind." I wondered what caused me to be so bold with this man I didn't really know.

Ralph let me into his apartment and excused himself to finish dressing.

I called from his living room, "Where are you planning to go to dinner?"

He came back out of his bedroom carrying a black shirt and naked from the waist up. I felt myself floating toward him. He took two steps toward me and held me against his strong chest. I remember thinking that his chest was as bald as his head. I liked the feel of his skin against my face. It felt smooth like satin. I wrapped my arms around him enjoying the feel of his skin under my fingers and along my arms. I lifted my face up to his and felt his hungry lips on mine.

I felt instantly desperate to be held and kissed. I wanted to touch and be touched. It had been so many years since a man had touched me. The pain of the last time my husband touched me caused a tear to roll down my cheek.

Ralph kissed away the tear and asked, "What? What is it?" He held me tighter against his chest.

I felt safe enough to answer. "He beat me. The last time my husband touched me, he beat me."

"Hush, sweetheart, don't be afraid. That was a long time ago. You are mine now. I won't hurt you. I want to heal you and make you whole. I don't want you to be afraid."

"I'm not afraid. I've put my life together again. I have a good career. I am not afraid." I wasn't sure Ralph could understand any of this because pressing against his chest squished the side of my face. His hand in my hair held me against him. I lifted my face to his and kissed him again. Hot liquid seemed to flow from that kiss to infuse my whole body.

Ralph kissed me again and I felt his satin smooth skin against my face and arms.

I woke up.

Still groggy with sleep I remembered the dream and snorted. "No wonder his skin felt so smooth, I was feeling my sheets." I thought about the dream again and had a moment of regret for the cute shoes. I'd never find something that cute in a store. I lamented the loss of the little rhinestone. I grumped and grumbled over my foolishness, fluffed my pillows and turned them over scaring John Wesley to the floor. John Wesley is my cat.

As I settled back down on my pillows, I shuddered remembering the dream. I realized that when I parked my car crosswise on the back of the ferry, it sat outside the safety nets with nothing between the car and falling off the boat. I shook my head over how strange dreams can be and hoped I could sleep without this one coming back.

CHAPTER 4: JOEY MILLER

On Thursday, we held Joe Miller's funeral. Funerals are fairly easy to do. I acted more like a director than an actual participant. The family told me what they wanted to do, and I coordinated what happened when. Elma had selected fairly common readings. I introduced each speaker and did the readings. Otherwise my job involved sitting back and letting the family and friends talk about their loved one. Oh! And I needed to remember to tell the men from Bates to move the communion table forward to its place.

I sat back and looked around me as Joe's friends talked about what a wonderful, helpful man Joe had been. I thought everything looked beautiful. The mahogany tables for the flowers looked a mess when I found them. They were dirty with dust, and water-stained from holding sweating vases. The legs were nicked and scratched from years of being handled. I found two alter cloths that looked enough alike that I could cover the tables with them. I further disguised the tables with two lace curtains from my linen closet.

On Wednesday, I'd spent an hour cleaning out the sanctuary decorations storeroom. I found some lovely things. I also threw out some ratty banners and cloths, hoping nobody would ever know what I'd done.

Before the service ended I invited everyone for a lunch in the social hall. I tied this meal in with the practice of communion. After the viewing, I expected everyone to rush off in search of food. I sat in a front pew to be silently available to anyone who needed to talk. Within seconds, I found a whole delegation that wanted to talk.

The chair of the trustees, Alva Brinks, started, "Why did you let the Bates move the communion table back? They always do that, and we told you not to let them."

A male voice interrupted, "I wanted more space around my father's casket. I'll see that it is moved forward again." Joe's son Joey came to my rescue. He was an attractive man in a tousled way. I found his smile engaging. I noticed that it had an effect on the delegation.

Together they huffed and puffed, "Oh. Oh well, if that is the way you wanted it. Be sure to pull it forward." The group slowly assembled their canes and walkers preparing to search for food. Joey stood silently waiting for them to leave. I sensed that he wanted to talk. At the same instant that I became irritated with The Delegation for being slow to get on their way, I realized they were stalling to see what would happen between Joey and me.

I took control of the situation. "Mr. Miller, I think there are a few things we need to discuss. Would you mind coming to my office?"

He smiled. "Thank you. I don't want to take up too much of your time. You have been such a help and comfort." I assumed his words were nothing more than the pat phrases one uses at a time like this. I suspected his mother barely tolerated my presence. I knew she still considered me a stranger intruding on her grief. I actually found some comfort in his sister's openly hostile attitude.

Elaine Miller made it clear that personally, she wanted nothing to do with the church and it's clergy. "I am only attending the service out of respect for my parents." She almost snarled at me.

I smiled. I really wanted to hug her and thank her for her honesty. "Thank you, I find your honesty refreshing and appreciate your willingness to attend the service despite your personal preferences." I refrained from saying anything more because I could see I made Elaine uncomfortable.

Remembering his sister's attitude I led Joey into my office while wondering what he wanted. When I moved into this church, I fashioned a small comfortable area in the corner of my office for counseling. Several years earlier, I'd purchased a love seat and two matching chairs for my counseling office. I moved the furniture with me when I came. As I closed the door behind me, I motioned Joey to take a seat in the counseling area.

I hadn't fully settled myself in my chair before Joey's concerns came spilling out. "Pastor, I want to apologize for my family."

"There is no need."

"Yes, they were rude to you." His apology made me uncomfortable, but I allowed Joey to say what he needed to say.

"My sister has been openly rude, and mother, well I can excuse mother somewhat, but she has made no attempt to cooperate with you on the arrangements."

"You're distressing yourself unnecessarily. Your sister and I understand each other" I relaxed into my chair. "I rather like her attitude. Your mother has had her world turned upside down. Few people are fully rational at such times."

"Thank you," he smiled and I noticed the dimple in his cheek. "You have comforted me. You're very good at your job." Joey's compliment sounded slightly rehearsed as if he were on stage.

"I'm glad you feel better. Don't be too hard on your family." I waited for a sign that he wanted to talk about his grief, but he seemed focused more on what I thought of his family, so I shifted in my seat intending to end the conversation.

"I want your opinion."

I settled back.

"Mom has never lived alone. She is not young. I wonder if I should relocate to be closer to her?"

"I wouldn't make any big decisions right away. Your mom has her friends. I will keep an eye on her. You know, I think your father took more of her attention than she let on. She'll be fine when she has only herself to look after."

Joey sighed, a long drawn-out dramatic sigh and tried to look solemn. "I think Dad has always taken more care than other people realize. I wanted Mom to visit me in LA. I thought it would be fun to take her to a set where I worked. Dad refused to travel, and she refused to leave him. He always had to have his dinner right on time and clean clothes."

"It might be a good idea to invite her to visit you in a couple months. When the cold sets in here, she might like a trip to find some sunshine."

"Good. I am between movies now so perhaps I'll take care of some immediate business there then come back here for a couple weeks. She can come visit me later. That way she won't be alone too long at a time."

I started getting anxious about getting back to the rest of the congregation. I saw nothing in this conversation that required the private attention of the pastor.

"I think that is an excellent plan." I stood. "I'm sorry to cut you off here, but I need to check on a few things, and you promised to move the communion table."

He laughed at this. "Yes it would not do for me to be shut up alone too long with the pretty pastor. Too many people in this town think of me as a depraved Hollywood producer."

During the next month, I made it a point to keep tabs on Joey's mom. Elma coped with her grief over the loss of her husband by immediately driving to Portland to spend a week with her college roommate. Before she left she stopped me in the social hall after church. "Just so you'll know, I'm going away for a week. I don't want anybody getting upset and thinking I'm dead just because I don't answer the door."

"Oh, thank you for warning us. Are you taking a vacation?" She walked away from me.

Later, I heard her talking to her friends over coffee. "Anne was my college roommate. We've kept in touch, but Joe didn't like her because she divorced her husband when he got some tart he worked with pregnant. She never said much to me, but I think it was not so much that she left him as it was that he ran off with the tart." When asked if she intended to make the long drive in one day she was reassuring. "No I want to visit my cousin who lives in Tacoma. I will spend the night with her. We plan to go out to dinner and everything. I want to go to the mall and get some new pants to wear to Portland."

I smiled to myself. Elma would be okay. I offered a quick prayer of thanks that she had friends and family outside of this community. I decided to let one of the trustees lock up and returned home. I thought I might be getting a cold.

As I unlocked my front door, I recognized my slightly elevated heart rate as anxiety about entering my house. My letter to the pastor parish committee had not gone over well. They argued that they did not have to obey landlord-tenant law because the house was not a rental. They allowed me to live there as a convenience to me. I urged them to talk to an attorney. The matter remained unresolved, but today, nobody lurked in the living room or kitchen.

I sat down to a lunch of homemade split pea soup and crackers, and felt my insides melt as I remembered my lunch with Ralph. He had not called again, which was fine with me. I wondered if he'd looked me up on the internet and learned about my job. Well really, if he did not want to be friends with me because of my job, that was all well and good. I wasn't disappointed. I was just curious.

A couple more days went by, Ralph didn't call me, but Joey did. "I can't get hold of Mom on the phone. Do you know where she is?"

"Yes she spent a night with her cousin in Tacoma and then planned to visit her friend Anne in Portland."

"Oh? I worry about her driving the freeway."

I tried for a reassuring tone. "I worry about anybody who has to drive that freeway. She will be as safe as anybody else."

Joey sighed, "I suppose you are right. Since she is visiting friends, I won't worry about trying to get up there for another week or so. I really can't take much time off right now."

"I thought you said you were between movies. What do you do exactly?"

He laughed, "Did I tell you that? Well that was last week. I picked up another project. I'm a production manager. I don't suppose you even know what that is."

"I have a pretty good idea. I worked in the Seattle film industry when I was in college."

"You did? What did you do?"

"Bit parts and extras. Never anything dramatic, but I kept busy and made a little money. The fun part was the free meals on location."

He laughed again. "So you know that I'm little more than a glorified errand boy. I'm usually the scapegoat when anything goes wrong. I can see you doing bit parts and extra work. You're pretty enough that you could be quite versatile."

"Is there something else you need?"

"Oh ho, I've complimented the pretty Maudy so she is going to shut me out again. It won't work you know. You are a pretty woman and I am just going to keep telling you so until you admit it."

"If that's all it takes to get you to stop making personal remarks, I'll admit it. I was a beautiful child. I was considered one of the prettiest girls in my high school class. Being pretty got me jobs as an actress. I know I'm pretty, but that is not who I am. I prefer to be valued as the person I am, rather than for my appearance."

"Ah, I didn't mean to insult you, far from it. I see beautiful women all the time. I don't compliment them because I don't find them pretty inside. I like telling you you're pretty because you are beautiful all the way through. You have depth and passion. You are an exceptionally beautiful woman, Maudy."

"Thank you for the compliment. And now, I wish to put my feet up and be quiet for the rest of the day." Joey's nonsense irritated me. It didn't occur to me to wonder why I liked Ralph's compliments and Joey irritated me.

CHAPTER 5: DADDY

R alph didn't call. On Sunday just as I came in from church, my rental agent called with the latest ultimatum from my renters. They actually expected me to replace carpets that their children stained. I refused, but I shook with anger when I got off the phone.

I paced my small sitting room for several minutes trying to calm myself. I finally plopped down on my sofa. John Wesley crawled up in my lap and gave me a kitty hug. The vibration of his purr calmed me enough that I recognized that I had overreacted to normal business demands. I took a few deep breaths and decided I needed to take some time off and think. Late on Sunday afternoon, I drove my Sentra down to Ocean Shores. I got a room on the third floor of the Polynesian and prepared to do some serious thinking.

I pulled a chair around so I could look out at the ocean. The nasty weather suited my mood. My emotions roiled as much as the ocean and the low rolling clouds above it. I came prepared for a good rest and think, which included bringing a box of my favorite chocolates. As I sat down and selected a nut filled chocolate, the rain blew in sideways hitting my windows with force.

I tried to take an organized approach to my decision making, tackling the rental problem first. The renter's demands for new carpet angered me. If the carpet was damaged beyond livable, that was their fault. Perhaps I should install laminate instead. Laminate would look much nicer with my furniture than the mustard carpeting in the parsonage. My chest tightened. Out of the blue, I remembered Henry Wilcox walking into my garage to check on the water heater and unplugging my car so the battery didn't charge, and I was forced to drive my Sentra sedan for a day. I told myself that I should be thankful for both the Sentra and the Porsche.

I remembered I needed to be thinking about my house in Seattle. I realized, "I am really more angry over Henry Wilcox than I am over my renters." I'd reached an impasse with the congregation over access to the parsonage. The attorney advised them that they should not be coming onto parsonage property and that I would have grounds to sue.

They countered that the other pastors welcomed them whenever they visited and that they were just doing maintenance. I suspected that they knew I would not sue them. I selected a jelly filled chocolate, popped it in my mouth, and rejoiced as a particularly nasty gust of wind shook the windows and howled around the building.

Finally, I spoke out loud to the storm, "Okay I have more than one housing problem here. I have annoying renters on one hand and annoying landlords on the other hand." This realization required another chocolate. "Annoying renters and annoying landlords. I have the power to eliminate both." This thought scared me. "Do I want to move back to Seattle? Do I really want to sell my house? Do I really need the supplement to my income from the rent I receive?" I looked back at the ocean barely visible through the rain and gathering dusk. "I can afford this room because of my extra income. I can afford cute shoes because of my extra income. Do I want to give this up?"

My stomach told me I needed to eat something other than candy so I decided to go to Mariah's for dinner. I ran the few steps through the rain to the restaurant. I didn't get too wet before I was inside again. The hostess seated me in the empty restaurant as soon as she discovered a real live customer waiting in the lobby. I sat down and started getting settled when my phone rang. I did the frantic phone finding dance and answered on the last note of Fur Elise. "Hi Daddy."

"Maudy, you and your fancy phone are going to give me a heart attack. You're not supposed to know who is calling until I identify myself."

I laughed.

"Where are you?"

I wondered how Daddy guessed I wasn't at my house. "I'm staying at the Polynesian."

"What's wrong?"

"What do you mean?"

"Something is bothering you and you've gone to the ocean to think about it. Now, you tell your old Dad your problem and I'll help you sort it out."

"Daddy, the waitress is here. I'll call you when I get back to my room." I hung up and ordered some clam chowder and a salad with honey-mustard dressing. I guessed right on the dressing. My tongue melted over the most exquisite honey mustard I'd ever eaten. The excellent clam chowder met my expectations for a simple yummy meal. I felt pampered by the good food cooked by someone other than me.

I returned to my room and called Daddy. He answered, "How was your dinner? Last time I ate there, they micro-waved the dinner rolls and the things were so tough I couldn't chew them. Now what did you run away from home to think about?"

"I have to do something with my house in Seattle. The renters want new carpet or they will move out. I'm thinking it may be time for me to sell the house." I rushed on before Daddy could voice his opinion. "Daddy, I know it is a good investment, but I hate walking into the place. I could never live there."

"What would you do with the money if you sell it?"

"I don't know. I think I might want to buy an inexpensive place near Blackfish."

"What's wrong with the parsonage."

"I think about everything is wrong with the parsonage. The congregation built the thing in the nineteen twenties. I'm sure volunteers who were trying to save money did the work. Every repair or remodel has been done to no discernible code. It still has knob and tube wiring without near enough outlets. None of the doors close securely, or if they do, they get stuck. Drafts actually blow the dust bunnies and cat hair across the floor. I have no idea how much it will cost to heat in the winter. It has an oil furnace that I swear spews smoke. It has drafts and ants. It also seems to leak parishioners, which is my main complaint. They come to the house even when I am in my office. One of them cleaned my refrigerator and threw out my cottage cheese and another one came in the garage and unplugged my car."

He laughed heartlessly. I think Daddy thought my car was foolish. I'd tried explaining that my principles prohibited my support of the oil industry any more than absolutely necessary as long as the environment was being destroyed and humans were being killed over oil. He may have recognized my rebellious streak in choosing a Porsche to convert to electricity.

"So you are thinking of selling your house and buying near Blackfish?"

"Yes,"

"What are you going to do when you are reassigned?"

"Tell the incoming pastor about the perils of the parsonage and try to sell that person my house. In the back of my mind I think buying will mean at least a two or three year commitment to staying with a dying church."

"Is it dying?"

"Literally, I've done one funeral already and advised another family about nursing homes and suggested they have their doctor contact hospice"

"Why can't you bring in new members?"

I sighed, "I'd love to do that, but these old folks are hostile to anything new or different. They barely tolerate me so I don't think they can accept other new people. They might think they are being accepting because they don't tell new people to leave, but they won't speak to them. They won't alter anything to meet the spiritual needs of anyone else."

"Maudy, I don't want you staying with that church if the congregation is abusive. You're too fragile to take that kind of hostility. You tell your bishop that the congregation is abusive and get out of there."

"I wouldn't call them abusive. They're just old and more than half have some level of senility."

"Yes, they're old and senile. That doesn't mean that their behavior is not abusive. They can be just as abusive as someone with an infection in the brain."

I winced. Dad never referred to what happened with my husband, Hal, so I knew he was worried about me.

He continued, "I want you to go back and talk to Doctor Dave about this situation. Talk to your district superintendent and your bishop. Those people are concerned for your welfare. I have half a notion to call your bishop myself. If you are running away from home you are sensing something isn't right."

I couldn't put Dad off with assurances that he was exaggerating because I remembered the dream when I told Ralph about the beating. "Dad, I confess you are right to an extent. I think I'm feeling threatened. Perhaps someone without my background would not get so upset over the intruding on my space, but it does upset me to walk into my kitchen and find a man in there."

"Can you change the locks?"

I wondered why I hadn't thought of this simple solution. "I think I have to. The trustees won't like it, but everyone in the congregation has a key to that house."

Daddy warmed up to his subject. "It isn't just the congregation walking in that I worry about. Who else can get a key and get in? Many people are angry with the church. Most of them have darn good reasons. I don't want them taking their anger out on you."

I understood Daddy's concern. "I seldom experience any of that type of problem, but I'm glad we talked about changing the locks. I'll make an appointment with a locksmith to meet me at the house as soon as I get home. I get so wound up in church processes that it didn't occur to me to do something without the trustee's permission."

We talked for an hour about the pros and cons of selling the house in Seattle and buying near Blackfish. Finally, we reached some agreement. "Well, honey as long as you feel the way you do about the house, go ahead and sell it. Perhaps it is tying you to a part of your life best put behind you. The market isn't good right now."

"The low market could work to my advantage. The house is in an excellent location being so close to the arboretum and Madison Street. Perhaps I can find something here that will be a good value. If I don't find something to buy, perhaps I can rent until I can move. If I buy I'll have to stay for a couple years."

"Don't stay if you are in danger. Trust your instincts, this time, Maudy. Believe what you see."

"I think I see a congregation that I can serve, if I can keep them out of my personal space."

"Don't waste too much of your life in that backwater. You're a beautiful woman. You should get out and meet men. You'll want a companion when you retire."

I felt slightly wicked so I threw Daddy a red herring. "Oh well as for men, I met Joey who is the son of the man who died. He calls me pretty more often than I like."

"Oh well then, does he have a good job and an education?"

I laughed, "More importantly, I can't stand him. He calls once a week to ask how his mother is. I can't get rid of him until I hang up on him."

"Well then, you need to get out and meet more men." I didn't tell Daddy about Ralph who hadn't called anyway. I assured Daddy that I had an action plan that would get me started on making the changes I needed. I assured him that I still loved my old Daddy and hung up feeling much better.

CHAPTER 6: ALVA BRINKS

When I arrived home from the beach on Monday afternoon, I noticed a locksmith's truck behind me when I turned onto Blackfish road. Good. I'd called from Ocean Shores and set the appointment up for 3:30.

My house didn't conceal any lurking parishioners so I instructed the locksmith to go right to work. I'd been home twelve minutes when the chair of the trustees called.

"Pastor Maude is that a locksmith at the parsonage?"

My heart started to pound. "Yes, I'm changing all the locks."

"You can't do any work on that house without the trustees permission."

"Actually, I can. You might not like it, but I am legally within my rights as a tenant to change the locks when I know that the security of my home has been compromised, and you refused to take action on the issue for months. I can even send you the bill, which I won't."

The frail voice on the other end of the phone wheezed. "You send that man away now. We have to vote on this. I'm coming over and sending that man packing. He can't work on church property without our permission."

"Excuse me, I need to hang up now." I found my worker kneeling by the front door. "How are you coming along?"

"Oh this one was easy to do. You really need a deadbolt on this door. If you are going to stay long, you need to replace the door and frame. It is almost rotted out here, here, and here." He showed me how his screwdriver sunk into the frame that holds the door. He gathered up his tools and headed for the kitchen door.

I followed him. "Um, a gentleman from the church trustees may show up here and demand that you leave because the house belongs to the church. I want the locks changed. I checked with my attorney. I can do this, and I am the one paying you."

Don, the locksmith interrupted me with a laugh. "Lady, about half the time when I change locks some man shows up and tells me to leave. It's always the same story. The gal is usually pretty, and the guy is a creep."

I laughed, "Well this guy is eighty-four. I don't think he cares if I'm pretty. He wants control over the house."

"He ain't dead even if he's eighty-four. An old pervert is still a pervert. You keep these doors locked and your windows covered. He's just trying to get a look at you in your nighty." Don wiggled his eyebrows at me as he said this, and I laughed at his silliness. When he finished with the exterior doors, he checked the downstairs windows and found them painted shut. "I'd warn you about a fire hazard, but the sills are so rotten that in case of fire you can shove one of these dining chairs through this window and the whole thing will fall apart." He looked around and shook his head. "This place ought to be condemned."

I wrote Don a check and thanked him about a thousand times for coming out. He got in his truck and left. Within minutes, the front door bell rudely interrupted me as I started to unload my groceries from Costco. I slipped out the back, locking the door behind me, being careful to carry a key in my pocket.

"Hello?" I greeted Alva Brinks from my position on the side lawn.

"You. You're there. You changed the lock. You can't do this."

"Well I did. If you wish to discuss this, we can go to my office." He turned to face me. His face had turned a mottled red and purple. I started walking slowly toward the church.

He followed along huffing and puffing behind me. "Well, all I can say is that the hospitality of this place has certainly lessened since you came here."

Anger made my tone more curt than I would normally take with a parishioner. "That is correct. I do not entertain other women's husbands in my home. Deal with it."

He huffed and puffed and surprised me with what came out of his mouth next. He giggled and stopped walking toward the church. His toes tuned inward, and he hunched his back. "We wouldn't want to start any gossip. Would we?" He giggled again.

He pranced off to his car giggling and turning to wave at me as I stood on my lawn shaking my head in shock and wonder. In total astonishment I commented to myself, "Well, Don the locksmith is a wise man." I thought about using the idea that wisdom appears in unexpected places in a future sermon.

I think the rumor of my changed locks must have been the evening entertainment in Blackfish. I went to the hardware store early Tuesday morning. I thought I would silver tape some of the areas where drafts came in around the windows. I chuckled at the thought that the silver tape would be stronger than the window frames.

Elaine Miller surprised me when she accosted me. "So, I hear you locked Alva Brinks out of your house?"

I felt genuinely happy to see her and nodded. "Men! Yeah I changed my locks. Everybody in town had a key to that house. My insurance company would never honor my policy if they knew that anybody could walk in."

Elaine snorted, "I think I'd do more than change my locks if Alva Brinks walked in on me."

"I think I need a more permanent solution, but this will buy me some time." The idea of buying my own house sat uppermost in my mind.

Elaine laughed, "Well if you need help burying the body, I'm your gal. He's a creep."

I laughed and looked at the floor thinking I just might make a friend. "Do you know a good place for disposing of the body?"

"We could dump it off of the cliff at Hunter's Point at high tide."

"Oh dear, perhaps we better be careful with this. The way gossip travels, the story of us standing in the middle of the hardware store and plotting to dispose of a body will be all over town before I leave."

"Whose body are you trying to get rid of?" asked a clerk who came out from behind the electrical parts. "Alva Brinks? I'm surprised that he's lived this long. He had a reputation as a womanizer. I hear you locked him out. Good for you."

Slightly horrified, I wailed, "Oh my! Now, I better hope he lives until I leave town, or I will find myself the chief suspect in his demise." At least five people laughed. I'd no idea that Blackfish contained a population large enough to support five people being in the hardware store all at the same time.

"What's the duct tape for?"

Elaine answered for me. "She's going to tie up the rest of the congregation and hang them in her garage to keep them from sinnin."

I laughed. "Now there is an idea. Considering the age of my congregation, I probably won't need a whole roll to do the job." I heard a few more snickers and the bystanders continued to suggest new and ingenious ways keep my flock pure while I paid for my purchase and left. As I pulled out of my parking spot, I noticed the store clerk and a couple contractors scratching their heads and scowling at my silent Porsche. I giggled to myself. I always kept the plug tucked away behind the grill to hide the fact that my car had received energy-source realignment surgery.

CHAPTER 7: SEAHAWKS VS. BRONCOS

After my trip to the hardware store, I looked on-line at real estate prices in Seattle. I spent the afternoon when I should have been researching my sermon reading comments and trying to get a feel for what my house might be worth. I snacked on cheese and crackers for dinner while I read the passages from the lectionary recommended for this week. Reading the passages involved reading them in English, ancient Hebrew and ancient Greek. The Hebrew and Greeks had many shadings and meanings for many of their words, which created a challenge for me. I needed to select an idea suggested by the different translations and go with it. By bedtime I thought I could sleep forever. My reasonable brain told me making life changing decisions and the stress of not getting along with my congregation…well…except for Joey, caused my exhaustion. My phone rang.

It took me a few seconds to realize that Joey didn't have the number for my chiming cell phone. I didn't take time to look at the caller ID. "Hello?"

"Maudy? Hi. I hope you remember me. Ralph? We had lunch."

"Oh sure, hi." I forgot how exhausted I felt.

"Say, the reason I called is that my whole office bought tickets to a Seahawks game. I wondered if you would like to come with me Sunday?"

"Oh my, what time? I work in the morning, but I'm free in the afternoon."

"The game starts at five."

"I'll be there." I got out my ferry schedule, and we discussed boats and times and dinner. When I got off the phone I remembered my dream where I was dressed in a cute dress and heels. A football game presented a different story. I'd wear polypropylene leggings under my warmest jeans and a wool sweater with my raincoat.

I dutifully wrote Ralph and the game into my schedule, then promptly forgot about it. Wednesday, I had a meeting with other clergy from my region. We all needed to get ready for our annual review known as a charge conference. I wondered what I could say about a congregation of twenty-three people. The youngest was seventy-nine. I suppose I would have to count Joey.

On Friday, Joey stopped by the church to tell me he was in town. I forgot about him as soon as he left my office.

Saturday, I finally finished my sermon and wondered why I even try. I went over to the sanctuary to practice the hymns for the day on the piano. My first two weeks in this church, I tried using recorded accompaniment, but the congregation complained so I accompanied the singing myself. Late in the day I did some cooking then went to bed early.

Sunday morning went about the same as other Sundays. I played the piano, struggling to play as slow as my congregation sang. As they coughed and wheezed their way through the familiar hymns, I realized that I loved these old tyrants. I suddenly saw them clinging to life by clinging to what was familiar and remembered in a world where life and youth had passed them by. I noticed one younger voice in the congregation, Joey. I'd noticed him when he came in. After the service, he stopped me special to tell me what I had all ready observed--he was home for a few days.

Joey smirked and dimpled at me. "I wanted to check in with Mom. She's talking about taking a tour of the Holy Land." Joey's dramatic tone conveyed alarm as he reached for my hand.

I slid my hand into the pocket of my robe. "Is she? Well good for her."

"Do you think it is safe?"

"It'll be safe enough. Everything has some element of danger, but we can't stop living because living is dangerous." I excused myself to greet other people.

Joey did a quick two-step to dance in front of me and managed to grab my free hand. "Um, Maude, Uh…what are you doing for dinner tonight? I mean would you join me for dinner? We could go into Silverdale."

I searched my brain for a plausible excuse. Then I remembered. Thank God! I remembered! I hadn't thought about it since I got off the phone with Ralph. I suspected that I sounded shocked and bemused when I answered. "Thank you for the invitation, but I have another engagement this evening."

"No you don't."

"Yes, I really do."

"What are you doing?"

I saw no harm in telling him part of the truth. "Seahawks game."

"No! You got tickets?"

"A ticket, now you must excuse me. I need to tell Mrs. Cooper that I'm happy to see she's over her cold and ask about Mr. Cooper." Joey followed me and expressed his concern for Mr. Cooper and talked about when he was a boy and picked apples for the Coopers.

I ran back to the parsonage, knowing that I had plenty of time before my ferry but very upset that I'd totally forgotten about my appointment with Ralph. I'd started crying by the time I let myself into the house. What was the matter with me? I wrote myself a note on a large piece of paper. "Make appt. with Dr. Dave!!!!" Daddy must be right about my stress if I could forget something as important as meeting Ralph.

I dressed, put on makeup and made it to the ferry in time to park and walk on with no problems. I now had an hour to sit and think and view some of the most beautiful scenery in the world. I soon slipped into a frame of mind where I just sat drinking in the world around me. I saw a bald eagle and several harbor seals. When the ferry got out to mid channel, Mt. Rainier popped out from behind his clouds for a few minutes. The top of the mountain floated barely visible above a lower layer of cloud. I warred within myself as to whether I should be just enjoying the day, or feeling guilty over forgetting Ralph, or trying to figure out if forgetting Ralph constituted a sign of a serious problem. I knew what Daddy would say. I resolved not to tell Daddy anything about Ralph.

Ralph met me as I came off of the ferry. He acted totally casual about meeting me and refrained from making an awkward attempt to hug me, which I appreciated. A cold drizzle started to blow in from the north so we decided to take a taxi to the stadium instead of walking. I didn't say anything about not wanting to walk a long distance. I didn't feel ready to talk about that just yet. I decided to start with something easy. After we settled in the taxi and gave the driver our instructions, I leaned my head back against the seat and looked at Ralph. "Thanks for asking me to the game. It feels so good to run away from home and my parishioners." There I opened the job topic. I decided to assume that Ralph wouldn't object to spending and evening with a preacher.

"Ah. So this is what you do on Sunday mornings. Do you preach?"

"Every single Sunday--not that anybody in the congregation listens. The youngest is only seventy-nine."

Ralph smiled. "It must be a challenge to work with an elderly congregation. How big a church is it?

"Only twenty-three, I don't know why our conference hasn't closed the church. I suspect that I will be the last pastor there, which is complicating about a thousand decisions for me."

Ralph sounded interested as he mused. "At least half of your congregation should have some pretty severe cognitive impairments. I suppose the best you can do is give them comfort and assurance that they're loved."

This answer surprised me. Ralph didn't shun me because of my job. He recognized the challenges of my position and made me feel that my work with this tiny congregation made a difference. I also breathed a sigh of relief that he commented on what I told him without any remarks about my person.

I agreed with his assessment. "Yes, they need to get together and visit and follow a routine and sing the same songs they've sung for eighty years. I admit to getting frustrated at not being able to vary the routine by so much as moving the communion table back six inches."

Ralph sounded like a university professor lecturing when he said, "Oh no, don't do that with a bunch of old folks. Part of the change with aging and senility is in the area of perception. If you move the table, the new perspective will disorient some of the folks who have more problems."

"You seem to know about aging. What do you do?"

We'd arrived at CenturyLink Field. Ralph helped me out of the car and started walking toward the gate while fishing in his pockets for our tickets. When he found them in a pocket on the inside of his coat, he zipped his coat and answered my question. "Where were we? Oh. I'm a forensic psychologist. I work in a group-practice here and do contract work all over the world."

"Ah, that explains how you know so much about my congregation and their failing faculties."

Ralph grinned at me. "Forgive me for getting carried away. I get obsessive."

"Oh no, I appreciated the insight. I think I'll be less frustrated if I can keep telling myself that they really do have problems. Although some, especially some of the gals, seem to be very sharp. I have one recent widow who is talking about visiting the holy land."

"Yeah, aging effects us all a little differently." He changed the subject. "I should warn you that some of the other people from my office will be here. I hope you won't mind if they get rowdy."

"Not at all. It might help if you don't introduce me as a pastor right off. I confess that sometimes I say words I should not at football games. I went to Washington State as an undergrad. The first time I ever swore was at my first WSU football game."

"A Coug?" Ralph laughed until I saw tears in the corners of his eyes. "Oh God, watching the Cougs will do that to anybody." When we reached the stands. He introduced me to the rest of the group. "Okay, she's confessed to being a Coug so she won't know what to do if we make a touchdown."

I defended myself. "I do too. I jump to my feet and embarrass myself by singing the WSU fight song."

One of Ralph's friends, Tom I think, said, "Ha! Yeah, we'll be ready to catch her if she faints from shock." I noticed that despite the banter Ralph's coworkers eyed me speculatively and tried to pretend they weren't staring at us. I looked at Ralph. His lips curled into a smug little smile as he set out cushions for each of us. I wondered if people at work teased him about not knowing any women so he brought me to the game to be done with the teasing. I could warn him that he would be subject to more questions for bringing a guest.

We ate dinner in the stands as we watched the game. Seattle played against Denver. Both teams played well, which kept the score close and the game exciting. I discovered that Ralph had a good sense of humor, or at least, he seemed to think the same things funny that I do. We watched the people when we were not watching the game.

The cold drizzle had turned into a sideways rain by the end of the game. I started getting cold. The rest of the party wanted to go out for drinks. I hesitated to say anything because I needed to catch the next ferry, but didn't want Ralph to think I was leaving for home early because I didn't like him or didn't want to go to a bar.

Ralph solved my problem. "Maudy, what do you want? What time is your ferry?" Ralph finally sent the rest of the party on their way and called a taxi for us.

"I hope you're not disappointed about not going with your friends."

"Not at all. I could join them if I want, but I want to drop you off then go home and go to bed. I'm still suffering from jet lag." We talked a little on our way back to the dock.

The taxi let me off under the viaduct and drove off to take Ralph home. I needed to cross the street in a rain that started getting insulting as it drove in sideways under the hood of my raincoat. Once on the ferry, I took a nap. Finally, back home in my own bed, I realized that I had just spent a wonderful evening. "I need to get out more with people other than church people." With this thought I slept until the phone woke me in the morning.

"Hi Maude, it's Joey. Say you weren't kidding about going to the game. You really went. I saw you on TV in the crowd scenes. Who were those people you were with?"

My end of this conversation consisted of elegant repartee. "Huh? Uh…ah…um…oh. Joey, you woke me up. I didn't get home until eleven-thirty. Can you call back later?"

"No! Wait! Will you have breakfast with me at Timmy's locker?"

"Oh, I suppose. What time?"

"It's nine-thirty now. What about ten thirty?"

"Yeah sure." I hung up and got out of bed. Standing in the shower, I remembered that today was Monday, my day off. I didn't need to meet with any of my congregation. "Damn. Oh, and Joey too, double damn."

At breakfast Joey still sounded excited about seeing me on TV.

"Um Joey, can you tell me how bad it was?" I wanted to hold my head.

He assured me, "It wasn't bad at all. You looked real pretty even with your hair wet."

"No, I mean you knew I was going to the game. How likely is it that my Dad and my children saw me?"

"I don't see how they could miss it." Joey turned around in his chair and called to the restaurant owner, "Hey Timmy did you see the Hawks game yesterday?"

Timmy called back from the front of the restaurant. "Sure. We were all surprised to see you there Pastor." I held my head.

I'd just finished ordering when Daddy called. "Who were those folks you went to the game with?"

"Oh a group of friends from Seattle, mostly neuropsychologists. Daddy," I swiveled around in my chair as if searching for better reception and raised my voice so the other diners could hear easier. "Daddy, I'm meeting with a parishioner right now so I can't talk. I'll call you back in forty-five minutes." I hung up and hoped that the gossip chain would take my meeting with Joey as business.

I faced Joey. "About your mom going to the Holy Land, I brought the topic up with my friends yesterday. They agreed with me that there are no special problems with someone her age traveling. I don't think you need to worry."

"It isn't just the trip. It's the expenses. I don't think she has much money."

"Well, what she has is hers to spend as she sees fit. I was under the impression that she owns her own home. Have you discussed this with Elaine?"

He made a dismissing noise, "Elaine is not practical."

"Oh I don't know, Elaine strikes me as someone who knows what's what."

"You've talked to her? She doesn't have any judgment. She's been married five times now. Her kids are each from different fathers."

"She's been unlucky in love. Have you been married?"

"Once. My wife left me while I was on location. She didn't like the fact that my job took me away from home so much. She was happy enough with meeting movie stars and going to parties, but our marriage didn't stand up under the realities of my career." I wondered about his wife's side of the story. Joey leaned forward. "Pastor, it's important to me that you know that I never missed a child support payment. I was a good father. My kids are grown up now. We're still close."

I refrained from asking why none of his very close children accompanied their grieving daddy to Grandpa's funeral.

When the check came, I paid for my breakfast and said goodbye to Joey.

Chapter 8: Dr. Dave

When my renters learned that I intended to put the house on the market as soon as they moved out, they delayed their departure while they looked for something else. I enjoyed the rental income, but the decisions about selling and moving out of the parsonage still made me anxious. I made my appointment with Dr. Dave.

Dr. Dave practiced outside the Group Health system so I needed to pay cash for this appointment. I wanted to get the most out of the session. After the initial greetings, I tried to get down to business, but Dr. Dave seemed determined to talk about everything else.

"How is your job?"

"Oh fine. My congregation is small and elderly. I had a little trouble dealing with their ways at first." I tried to condense my explanation down to as few words as courtesy required.

"I was surprised to see you at the Hawks game with Ralph Graham. Is he a friend or what?"

"Oh! He's an Or What and the real reason I made this appointment." Ha, I had just foiled Dr. Dave's plan to get me to talk about trivia when I wanted to talk about what really bothered me. I rushed on. "So that is his last name, Graham? I didn't know that. I'm not sure he knows my last name. I did tell him I am a pastor. We talked some about the neuro-psych needs of my congregation. I should confess that when he talked to me about the cognitive problems with aging, I felt much better about the demands of my congregation. It means the church will close within a few years. Anyway, about Ralph…"

"Why don't you think new people will keep the church alive?"

I sighed, "Because the old congregation cannot tolerate change and will not be polite to new people. I can't vary their service to meet the needs of younger people. Frankly, the music is terrible. I play the piano, and they sing so slowly I can hardly play that slow." I spent another five minutes enumerating the reasons why new people would not find my church attractive. "Anyway, I think I have a handle on the church thing. It was the game with Ralph that prompted me to make this appointment.

He called me and asked me to the game, and I wrote it down, and then I forgot. I forgot that I had a date with a very pleasant man. He is a nice man isn't he?" Dr. Dave nodded once. "Good, anyway the only reason I remembered my date with Ralph is that Joey, that's the son of the man who died, asked me for a date. When I was trying to think about how to refuse him, I remembered my date with Ralph." Tears came to my eyes. "What is the matter with me that I could totally forget a date with a man like that?"

"Oh, I think that is perfectly normal all considered. Everything worked out okay so you don't need to be anxious about it. How is your anxiety? Are you still on medication for depression?"

"Yes, I'm on a low dose. The anxiety is much, much better. I did have one dream where I dreamt I parked my car on the ferry outside the safety ropes."

"In your dream why were you on the ferry?"

I told about my dream where I kissed Ralph and told him about my husband.

Dr. Dave nodded. "Good. You mentioned that your congregation gave you some trouble when you first arrived. What was that about?"

I explained about the congregation coming into my house and how I changed the locks. I concluded by changing the subject. "Is Ralph really a respectable man? What do you know about him?"

"Yeah, Ralph is very respected. He is one of the best in the field of forensic psychology. So you changed the locks and the congregation was upset. What did they say to you?"

I figured out that getting anywhere on the Ralph issue would be tough going. Whatever happened to client-centered therapy? "Oh all that happened was the usual complaints from the pastor parish committee that I shouldn't have stated my rule about no men in the parsonage the way I did. I agreed and said that I should have extended the ban to make certain that they understood that I would not have any men in the parsonage, single or married and that women could not come in without an invitation. I'm thinking of selling my house here and buying something near Blackfish. That is, I think I might buy something close if I decide to stay in Blackfish. Daddy thinks maybe I should move back to the city so I will meet more people. I certainly had fun with Ralph and the people from his office. I'd like to do non-congregation stuff more often, if I don't offend someone by forgetting my dates."

"I think you need to tell Ralph your history and related problems. He'll understand. I can't imagine that he hasn't heard part of the story from others at work. I think the senior-partner there, Atwood, worked on Hal's case. He may not say anything because of confidentiality. You need to be up front with Ralph about this. He'll be supportive. So, you have a congregation of tyrants. What do you do to have your worship needs met? This is the part of you that kept you alive. Don't neglect it."

"I'm a pastor. That is hardly neglecting my spiritual needs."

"Isn't it? It sounds like you are not doing that which sustains you. Miracles are all fine and good, and you've had more than your share, but they're no substitute for taking proper care of yourself."

We continued in this vein for the rest of the visit. I eventually gave up trying to talk about my anxiety over Ralph and talked about my congregation. Why did both Daddy and Dr. Dave act so concerned over my congregation? Dr. Dave extracted a promise from me that I would find ways to nourish my spirituality.

As I left the building, I felt frustrated about not getting to talk more about whether I should be dating, and my anxieties about dating, and wanting Ralph to call, and being afraid he wouldn't call, and worrying about forgetting a date, and what I could do about it all. I sighed, Dr. Dave did tell me to tell Ralph about my injuries. Well, I could hardly tell Ralph if he never called. I stood on the sidewalk beside my car debating with myself for a minute or two before I realized the rain had started soaking through my coat. I got in the car and decided I could do the one thing about Ralph I'd been told to do. I found Ralph's number in my phone history and called him.

"Maudy! Hi!" He sounded happy that I called. I didn't want to do this on the phone.

"Hi, I'm in the city today and have some free time. I wonder if we could get together and have lunch or take a walk or something."

"Great, yeah sure. Where? Where are you? I have some appointments later, could you meet me at the café where we had lunch before?"

CHAPTER 9: BEGINNING OVER

Iarrived in the Madison Valley earlier than expected so I slipped into City People's Nursery for some retail therapy. I was very proud of the two potted chrysanthemums I purchased for my front porch.

I'd just finished stowing my flowers in my car, when I saw Ralph coming toward me up the sidewalk. I got a little fluttering feeling in my stomach and felt a little smug about the idea that a man who looked like that wanted to meet me.

"Those are pretty. So you like flowers?"

I nodded, locked my car and turned toward the restaurant. "The parsonage where I am now is dark and dreary. I want to move out, but I am stuck between decisions and actions. Now is not the best time to put my house here on the market so I will be in the parsonage until spring. Then again, I may decide not to stay where I am. My daddy is anxious about me being so isolated and I…" We reached the café and Ralph opened the door for me. I liked the way it seemed so easy for him to open the door. He just touched the handle and the door seemed to float open. When I open a door, I plant both feet firmly then put my whole body behind the effort of pushing or pulling.

The same hostess we met before gave Ralph the same flirtatious greeting. I thought she gave me a speculative look. She showed us to a booth in the back. I gave a little prayer of thanks to be seated away from the area where everyone walked by. We sat and studied the menu before Ralph directed my attention back to our conversation on the sidewalk.

"You said you are thinking about not staying with your current placement?"

"Yes, the pay is not that good and has not been regular. Then again, I'm not sure how long this church can continue to operate at all. The congregation is so old. It is just a matter of time before they die or become too ill to come to church. They can hardly pay the bills as it is"

"It must be rough seeing a church close its doors."

I snorted, "Yes, I think you hit the real issue here. I can survive on my income. It's painful to watch this process and feel that I can't do anything about it. I see death often. Everybody dies, but when an institution dies it seems different. I wish our churches could stay open and be a place for families to gather and find hope or peace or whatever they need to be happy and healthy. I would love to have a church full of children." Our waitress returned. While we occupied ourselves ordering, I wondered how to bring up the topic that I wanted to discuss. Would Ralph think I wanted him to feel sorry for me because of my story? Would he be repulsed? Would he find me untouchable? The waitress left with another smile and almost a wink for Ralph.

"Anyway, I did ask you to have lunch with me for a specific reason, but I'm not sure how to begin." I toyed with my fork.

Ralph stopped smiling and looked me in the eye. His tone was playful, but I noticed a wary look in his eye. "Is this the old I-just-want-to-be-friends speech?"

"Oh! Oh no!"

He clutched his heart and gave a false sigh of relief. "Whew."

I looked into his eyes and saw pain behind his guarded body language. Completely flustered, I decided to just start talking and hope for the best. "Um…uh…well…uh, what I need to tell you is that, well, I'm not expecting anything of you by telling you this. I just think that I…well… um. Oh darn, I need to start talking about this and telling people when I have a problem." Ralph looked encouraging but he didn't say anything. "The thing of it is that I…um…well…I have memory problems."

Ralph nodded ever so slightly and continued to look me in the eye.

"I…uh…I got hurt about ten years ago." Hey this sounded better than I thought. "I, um…well…I have some brain damage, and I have anxiety and sometimes I get depressed.

He nodded, "Brain injuries can do that."

"Um…anyway…um…I want my friends." Friends, that was a good way to refer to Ralph. He wouldn't think anything more if I specified friend. "I want my friends to know that sometimes my brain gets overwhelmed and I forget everything including appointments."

Ralph squinted at me and made the perfect professional response. "Thank you for telling me this. I know it was hard for you to say. Most people never admit that they have problems from a brain injury."

His non-committal response upset me. I'd had enough counseling classes to tell the correct responses from the honest responses.

Ralph settled back in his chair, scowled, then smiled. "So you're telling me you don't want me to feel rejected if you don't show up for a date?"

I nodded.

"You want to go out with me again?" The grin on his face lit up the whole café.

I smiled and nodded. Maybe I grinned. A huge weight floated away from my chest the way that doors float open for Ralph. "Thank you for understanding." Oh dear, now I was talking like a therapist, but I couldn't stop myself. "I'm still as smart as I ever was. I went to seminary after the…the…after I got hurt, and I didn't have any more trouble than anybody else with classes. It's just that I'm so afraid I'll forget an appointment. I write everything down, but then I forget to check my calendar."

"Would it help when we are going someplace together if I call you a couple times before it is time to go?"

A wave of relief flooded through me again. He understood. He didn't think I was weird or pathetic. I nodded. "Please, it would help at least to make me feel less anxious about the possibility of forgetting. I think my anxiety over my memory loss is worse than the actual problem." I went on to explain a little more about the seriousness of my previous injuries. I thought he should know. When I tried to explain how thankful I was to be alive, I used the word miracle. Ralph's response irritated me.

"A miracle, or good doctors, or your own determination?" Ralph asked.

"All of the above. Yes, my doctors were good. I call it a miracle that I had such good doctors. They seemed to care about me. They never wrote me off as too damaged to be given their best." I saw Ralph fall back in his chair as if struck. I paused.

He whispered, "That's amazing. I've been around the medical profession and brain damage in particular too long to deny that some doctors don't try as hard as others, and some are just more skilled than others. It never occurred to me that clients realize when the doctor doesn't give them the best. Okay, I might not class that as a miracle, but you were fortunate in your choice of doctors."

"We know." I shifted in my seat and addressed the subject that irritated me. We were close to having an argument. "Ralph, I'm not going to debate theology with you. I will use the word miracle when I want to. One of the reasons I enjoy your company is that I don't have to be the preacher. I felt that I needed to be honest with you about my injuries, but I don't want you to be my psychologist. I just want to be friends."

Ralph still seemed to be looking inside himself. He thought for a minute. His voice softened. "Yes, you're right. We've had fun together because I haven't felt I needed to be a psychologist, and you don't act like a preacher. You don't look like one either which helps the illusion." He smiled, a crooked little half smile that made my toes curl.

I returned his smile then chuckled, "Since I'm being honest, I admit that some of my appearance is good reconstructive surgery. I look about the same as I did before I got hurt, but I see differences that I think would be considered more attractive. Also, I don't like to walk too fast because then I limp. Usually, I'm okay, but if I have to put my whole body into a good swift walk, I limp."

I recognized Ralph's professional voice when he replied. "Limping is not a good idea because it can throw everything out of alignment." He heard his tone, and his voice softened again. "And I'm being a psychologist again, forgive me."

I tried to infuse my voice with understanding while I brushed away the dissatisfaction that tickled at the edge of my consciousness. "I understand we are who we are." I tried to smile. Fortunately, the arrival of our lunch rescued me. I'd ordered the Portobello Mushroom French Dip this time. It tasted good, but very salty. I searched my brain for another topic of discussion.

Ralph changed the subject. "Would it be off limits for me to ask you what you studied in seminary?"

"No, I like talking about school. I went to Fuller in Pasadena. I think I chose the school for the sunshine and its location near the UCLA medical school. My classes included hideous things like systematic theology and the history of monasticism. I liked the ancient Hebrew. I also took ancient Greek, and counseling classes, and of course sermon writing."

"How much of that do you actually use?"

"I use the ancient Greek and Hebrew almost every day when I study. Sometimes the rest of the stuff is a good starting point to make me think about why I disagree with previous theologians. Much of the time, I have to ask myself what do the early theologians have to do with God, or with loving God and loving your neighbor." I realized that talking about the intimacies of a relationship with God might make Ralph uncomfortable so I decided to shut up. "And now that is the end of my preaching for today. You mentioned that you travel with your work. Do you have any trips planned?"

"No. I don't usually plan to be in any spot. When a case comes up, I'll travel where I am needed." He continued to talk about a trip to New Mexico that he'd made earlier in the year.

I finished as much of my sandwich as I wanted and started nibbling on my French fries. I felt a little cloud hanging over this lunch. Ralph's comment dismissing my use of the word miracle still irritated me. I smiled as he talked about his last trip to New Mexico, but inside I felt a note of dissatisfaction and loss. Perhaps I was getting over my crush on him.

CHAPTER 10: PARISHIONERS

I'd scheduled to visit the shut-ins on Wednesday morning. At the first nursing home, Mrs. Downing said, "Maude? Oh Maude, what are you doing here?"

"I came to visit you and see how you are. Do you need anything?"

Mrs. Downing sounded surprised. "Well, no, but I heard you were dead."

"Close but not quite." I had no idea why I should have been dead.

"Well Denise must have gotten that wrong then. That child never did have any sense."

I had no idea who Denise might be.

"How's your mother? She was one of my favorite cousins." Well that explained it: Mrs. Downing was talking about someone else named Maude. I didn't try to correct her.

"Thank you. I'm certain she appreciated your friendship."

"Well, I wouldn't really call it friendship--what, with her traveling all over the country with that worthless father of yours. He never could hold down a job."

"Oh...um...well..."

The elderly woman rambled on, "I suppose he was handsome enough, but she would have been better off to marry Fred. He got a job at the bank and made something of himself. I heard you fell off of a horse or something, but look at you now."

"A horse...yes...they can be..."

"I never liked riding. I learned to drive when I was thirteen. Some men abandoned a car at our farm in Fife and continued south on the train. We learned later that the car was stolen, but I went out when my parents were gone and learned to drive the thing. I remember when Minnie went into labor two months early, and I took her into Tacoma to the doctor in that car. Everyone was so surprised that I could drive. It saved her life, but she lost that poor baby."

"Oh, that is sad, but I'm glad you were able to help her."

"Pastor Maude, do you think that baby is in heaven? It wasn't baptized or hadn't accepted Jesus or anything."

The sudden recognition surprised me, but I changed perspective quickly enough. "Yes, I believe that soul is with God. We believe in baptism and making choices, but those rules are for us. We don't know God's rules for something like that, except that we know God loves all of us." Mrs. Downing fell asleep.

At my second stop, I visited Mrs. Forest. She lived in a small house out toward the golf course. I hadn't been out on this side of town. It looked more prosperous than the center of Blackfish. I wondered if it got its vitality as a suburb of Silverdale or Bremerton. Mrs. Forest informed me that she wanted her nap, but I could come in anyway. I stayed twenty minutes until she started looking sleepy, I promised to bring communion next time I visited and left to return to the church.

I liked the small valley between two ridges where Mrs. Forest lived. It looked like most of Kitsap County except the lack of cedar trees hinted that it might be dryer. I noticed real estate signs and wondered about looking for a house out here.

As soon as I got into my office, I checked for messages. I felt pleasantly surprised to find none. I checked my appointments. I had an appointment at four with a couple who wanted to see me about getting married. I sighed thinking a wedding would be a nice change from funerals. Sirens on Blackfish road interrupted my pleasant thoughts about weddings. It sounded like more than one police car racing through town. I tried to return my attention to my appointment book, but the wailing sirens drew my attention out to the road. The sirens slowed beside the church, turned the corner, and screamed off toward the high school. Before the police sirens died away, I heard the unmistakable whoop-whoop of the aid car. My curiosity propelled me out the door just as the aid car came past the church. It turned the corner toward the high school. More sirens accompanied two more county sheriffs racing through town. I stood beside the street and watched as the sheriffs turned toward the school. By now, the volunteer medics and another ambulance had raced by.

Whatever happened, the first responders were equipped to handle it. I returned to my office expecting that my parishioners would be on the phone with news soon.

I sat quietly in my office for several minutes before I could calm myself enough to work. What had happened at the school? No fire trucks. A shooting? Please God no—not a shooting. I didn't know any of our youth, but even in a small district like Blackfish, they had the same problems as youth anywhere. I sighed and started to work on my sermon expecting my phone to ring at any moment. Nobody called.

At four the young couple who wanted to get married arrived. The bride wore an ensemble assembled from thrift store finds. For her outer garment, she wore a man's suit coat. Under the suit coat she wore a lace top. A tiger print bra completed the upper portion of her outfit. On the bottom half, she wore ratty leggings under a net half-slip. Hiking boots completed the outfit. I admired the charming little feather headband that held her green and orange hair back from her puckish face. The groom matched his bride-to-be in painted frayed jeans. He wore a pea coat without buttons over a Grateful Dead tee shirt. He wore slippers on his feet. I may have gushed just a little to meet two people who looked so unlike my congregation.

After the introductions, the bride got down to business. "Mom says you can do marriages."

"Yes."

The bride explained, "We were going to find a judge or have one of our friends get ordained on-line and marry us, but Mom says it would be easier to have you do it."

"Probably. You know where to find me. I know how to do the paperwork. I am fully qualified by the state. What are your plans so far?"

The bride slid down in her chair. "I don't know. I'm pregnant so Mom says we should get married."

"Well, that is one reason to get married. Do you love each other?"

The couple looked at each other. "Yeah, I love her." The groom looked at his fiancé, and his face lit up as if she was the most beautiful woman in the world.

The bride snapped at me, "Like yeah, I wouldn't be pregnant if I didn't love him. I'm not a slut."

"I didn't mean to imply that you are. You told me what your mother wanted. I want to know what you want." They looked at each other. I watched their silent communication.

The bride answered. "We want to get married."

I felt anxious for fear of hurting their feelings and shifted to a more neutral topic. "Will you be living in Blackfish?"

The groom answered, "We want to. I'm working on a big project here."

"What do you do?"

"Programmer for Willets-Manion."

I knew the company. They had huge contracts with the navy.

The groom shifted in his chair. "I have a house out at Oak Ridge."

I also knew that Oak Ridge constituted what passed for a country club in Blackfish. I turned to the bride.

"Are you currently working?"

"Yeah, I teach modern dance and ballet at Olympic."

"It sounds like you have a good financial basis for getting married." The couple looked at each other so I continued. "Part of my job is to help couples have the best start in their married life as is possible. I always worry about couples who do not have enough money to live on." I tried another topic. "What do you have planned for a ceremony?"

The groom spoke up. "We want to get married in my living room at dawn."

"Who will be your witnesses?"

The bride asked, "Do we have to have witnesses?"

This sweet couple was so clueless I began to worry that they might want any peculiarity in the ceremony—like the whole event performed in the nude. I explained, "Yes, by law two witnesses have to sign your papers."

"Oh, we'll have to think about that."

"What about your parents? Will they want to be here?"

The bride sounded adamant. "They're not coming."

The groom sunk down in his chair, looked at the wall to my left and growled, "They're drunks—They're all alcoholics. I don't want any part of them near my home or family."

The bride had earlier seemed dependant on her mother. I turned to her. "How do you feel about that? When you first came in, you mentioned your mother as if you value her opinion."

The bride explained, "Mom's okay on the phone. I get along with her fine when she is fifteen hundred miles away. I don't want her here."

"Do you have a date set?"

"No, we thought we would find someone to officiate first."

"Okay, do you have your license?" Again the couple looked at each other and I wondered if they knew how to apply for a marriage license. I spent the next half-hour going over with them the steps to getting a license and the legalities of getting married. "You know, many couples make a party out of getting their license. You will need a witness at the courthouse. You can bring a friend. I would be happy to accompany you." I smiled to myself when their earlier confusion left their faces telling me they were beginning to understand the legal process. I stood as they prepared to leave.

The bride smiled. "Wow, I'm glad we talked to you. I didn't know any of that stuff."

"In any field it helps to hire a professional." I refused to tell this naïve couple that they needed to counsel with me before I could perform the wedding. I figured I could fit that in as we worked out the details of the ceremony.

CHAPTER **11**: SHELLY PERRY

My bride and groom left shortly after five-thirty. As I walked back across the parking lot to the parsonage, I debated whether it would be easier to make a sandwich for dinner, or get a real dinner at Timmy's Locker. I remembered the sirens earlier in the day and wondered why none of the parishioners had called. I decided to walk to Timmy's for news.

It was a good thing I walked. Timmy's parking lot overflowed leaving no room to park on the street. My garage may have been the closest parking spot I would find. I worried they might not have room for me.

The hostess greeted me with annoying news. "Good evening, Pastor. We're full right now. There's a half-hour wait."

The assistant piped up, "Unless you want to sit at the bar. There's an opening there."

The hostess gave her helpful assistant a shocked look. "She is a Pastor!"

I chuckled to myself over people's straight-laced ideas about clergy. "I'm a very tired and hungry person. I'll be fine at the bar, really." The hostess reluctantly led me to the empty seat in the bar, looking this way and that to see who noticed where I sat. I figured everybody would notice sooner or later, and I didn't care.

"Hi, Maude." Timmy set a dinner down on the bar. It belonged to the person two people down, so I resisted the temptation to grab it and eat. "What can I get you?"

"Can I have some of your strawberry lemonade for now and whatever is quick for dinner."

"Not fussy are you."

"Nope, just tired. Oh, and what is going on? You're busy and I heard sirens earlier."

Timmy seemed to collapse in on himself as he leaned against the bar. His face sagged, and I thought he might start to cry. "Trouble up at the school. Kid attacked the Perry girl. They were doing CPR when they took her to the hospital. That's about all I know."

"Do you know the Perry family?"

"I bowl with Alex Perry."

"Would they be offended or distressed if I showed up at the hospital?"

"Well Alex's not any sort of church man. You look dead-beat yourself. You're not thinking of going to the hospital tonight."

"If it won't distress the family, I will be there."

"Just a minute." Timmy left the bar and sent a line cook out with my lemonade. He came back in about five minutes with a huge plate of steak and baked potato and set the meal down in front of me. "If you're going out. I guess you need some real food in you. This one's on me."

I ate every bite. It tasted much better than my usual dinner of crackers and cheese. As I ate, I picked up snatches of conversation. I started piecing the story together. Shelly Perry, the girl, was a cheerleader and very popular. I didn't get the name of her attacker. I learned that the assailant took special ed classes. Somebody said something about welfare kid. I wondered what that meant.

I asked, "Timmy, do you know the name of the attacker?"

"No, just that he was some new kid." Timmy rushed off to greet another customer.

I took the term, new kid, to mean that his parents were not born in Blackfish.

As I entered the hospital, I put on my clerical stole so that the staff would recognize me as official. A series of assistants, aides, volunteers and nurses helped me find the waiting room where Alex and Inez waited.

"Hi, I'm Maude Henderson. How is your daughter?"

Alex turned on me and snarled, "She's in surgery. When I catch up to the bastard who did this, he'll wish he'd never been born." Alex looked at me and my stole, turned red, shriveled into himself and started to cry.

I remained calm. "What are they doing in surgery?" I eased into a chair, mindful not to loom over others.

Inez whispered, "They need to pick some bone out of her brain. He…he…was choking her and beating her head against the sidewalk."

"I am so sorry. I know that right now you need to be here, but is there any business at your home that needs immediate attention. I understand you have other younger children. Are they being cared for?"

Inez nodded. "My mother took them home with her just a few minutes ago."

"How long has Shelly been in surgery? How long do they think it will take?"

"Bastard, fucking bastard! Retard doesn't deserve to live!" Alex seemed incapable of rational talk.

Inez put her hand on her husband's leg. "They just took her into surgery an hour or so ago. It shouldn't be too much longer."

"May I get you something while you wait? Some coffee? Perhaps some fruit from the cafeteria?"

"No we're fine thank you."

"Fucking, retarded bastard, doesn't deserve to live." Alex seemed stuck on one idea.

I sat silently, praying for inspiration, and for Shelly, and her doctors. I debated. I didn't know how much to say. Finally, I took a deep breath and spoke gently. "I think your daughter will be okay. She will need a lot of help and understanding, but I think she will be okay. She's lived this long…" I lost my voice. Both Alex and Inez looked at me when they realized that I tried to speak, but no sound came out. I took a couple deep breaths. "She has lived this long. It is a good sign."

"Why should you care? I don't want your platitudes. I want to kill that bastard." Alex's nostrils flared, and he turned slightly purple with rage.

I remained calm. I forced more words out around vocal chords that didn't want to work. "I care more than you will ever know, because my daddy knows exactly how you feel and has certainly said exactly the same things." I gulped for air and forced more words to come out. "Sometimes we girls are tougher than our daddies know."

Alex broke down and sobbed again. Inez rubbed his back looking sad.

I forced myself to continue, and the words began to come easier. "My daddy was very angry for a long time. It took him over a year to begin to sort out his anger."

"I'm going to kill that fucking bastard."

I kept talking, "I needed to be surrounded with peace and love in order to feel safe and to heal, so as soon as I felt strong enough I moved to California and started seminary. When I came home to visit, Mom saw how Daddy's anger pulled me back into all the hurt and anxiety again. As soon as she made Daddy understand how he was hurting me, he let go of his anger." I confessed in a softer tone, "He's been quite contrite ever since, but he's still overprotective."

Alex sat hunched over with his head bowed almost into his lap. Inez continued to rub his back. I think her motion comforted her as much as it did him. I wondered if either of them heard a word of what I said. I knew they would never know how much it cost me to say those words. I pressed my hands between my knees to hide their shaking. We sat in silence for another forty-five minutes until the doctor interrupted us.

"Mr. and Mrs. Perry?" He looked at me. "Pastor thank you for being here. Shelly is in recovery. I think she is going to make it. The surgery went well. She'll be in recovery for another hour, then we'll move her up to the ICU." I watched as the Perrys absorbed this new assault.

"Is she going to be all right?" Alex seemed to be doing better with his anger, but he still sounded as if he'd like to shake assurances out of the doctor.

I tried to get some more specific information. "Doctor, I know you don't like to speculate, but can you give us some idea of what to expect so we will know what to be crazy-out-of-our-minds worried about?"

Inez looked at me, blinked, and smiled. "That is about it. Isn't it? Crazy-out-of-our-minds worried." She reached out her hand to me and I moved over to sit next to her.

Inez asked, "Can we see her soon?"

The doctor suggested, "Why don't you go on home, and you can see her in the morning."

Alex shook his head and Inez protested, "We want to stay here."

"There is nothing you can do here. Go on home."

I felt awkward intervening, "Um...you know when Shelly gets home you may need every ounce of energy you can summon to care for her. Also, your other children need to spend time with you. This is as hard on them as it is on you. Do you have a car with you?"

Inez shifted her weight and looked around as if looking for her car. "No, I... uh..."

Alex shook his head. "No, Jeff Seller gave me a ride in."

"I can give you a ride home tonight. You can sleep in your own bed. Get something decent for breakfast and come back refreshed in the morning. Believe me, Shelly will need her parents to be strong in order to convince her she is safe."

The doctor looked at me as if I were some sort of space alien. "She's right. Shelly needs our care right now, but by morning she may need you more than she does us." I started making motions to move the Perrys out the door. A volunteer, the doctor, and a nurse assisted by making reassuring comments and collecting coats and Inez's purse. The doctor patted me on the shoulder as we walked past.

After I'd dropped the Perrys at their house and said reassuring things to everyone there, I got home at one AM eager for my own bed. As I drove into the garage, I barely thought about a river of mud flowing around the garage and pooling behind the cars on the garage floor.

CHAPTER 12: CRISIS INTERVENTION

I woke up around eight in the morning and checked my messages immediately. My bride and groom planned on getting their license on Friday. They'd found a friend to go with them. They suggested Saturday as a possible wedding day. I shook my head and wrote a note reminding myself to call them at a decent hour and explain about the three-day waiting period. Nobody from the church called.

After nine, I called the high school and spoke to the principal. "I called to offer my support for your staff and the students. How are all of you doing after yesterday's incident?"

"Fine."

"I hope that nobody feels guilty that the incident is their fault. Has anyone talked to the students about feeling survivors guilt?"

The principal sounded as if he wanted to get rid of me. "We have nothing to feel guilty about. We didn't do anything wrong. The students who were nearby pulled Giddens off of her."

I continued, "In other communities when something like this happens, the counselors in the community set up temporary services for any students who want to talk. Do you have such a program here?"

He said, "I've never heard of such a thing. The students are fine."

I kept trying, "Perhaps some of Shelly's friends need to talk to someone. I am a fully licensed counselor, and in a case like this, I am willing to offer my services free of charge."

"I'll mention that in the bulletin this morning."

"Thank you. Students may find me in my office after school gets out." He hung up. I had no idea if he would actually put a notice in the bulletin. I called the Perrys' house and learned that the children had stayed home from school, and the parents had left for the hospital.

Inez's mom answered the phone, "Pastor, thank you for going to the hospital. Alex can be hot headed, but he seems to be thinking of how to help Shelly get well now."

I asked, "How are the younger children doing?"

"Afraid to go to school. I didn't know whether to send them or not."

I grunted before I gave my opinion. "Oh they are probably somewhat in shock and won't learn anything at school so there is no academic reason to send them."

The older woman asked, "Um…what do you think about the afraid-to-go-to-school thing?"

"I don't blame them. Um…can you call the parents of some of their friends and see if friends can come over, or they can go visit? Knowing their friends aren't afraid to go to school may help. What do you think?"

The grandmother agreed. "We can try that for today. I wondered if I should just make them go--like falling off a horse, the best thing to do is get back on."

"Well, I suspect that your heart told you that today was not the day for getting back on the horse. Trust your own judgment. You know them best."

The woman really did sound relieved. "Oh thank you. I don't feel so guilty for letting them stay home."

I heard the decisive tone in my own voice. "The family is in crisis they can stay home." When I got off of the phone, I sat and held my head and wondered what on earth I was doing. I thought about what I'd been saying for the past twelve hours and shuddered. People seemed to depend on me--on my judgment. What did I know? "God, what do I know? Why do I say these things? I don't know anything more than anybody else. I try to comfort people, but what do I know?" I stood up and walked to my counseling area and sat on my sofa and thought again.

"What am I doing? Am I out of my mind to just babble on? These people are in real trouble, and what do I know?" I closed my eyes and rested the back of my head on the sofa. "What do I know? How can I say the things I do?" I sat there concentrating on my breathing. Remembering all the tricks Doctor Dave taught me for calming anxiety. My only thoughts became, "quiet--breathe in--breathe out--slowly—slow shallow breaths—quiet—breathe in…I know what it feels like to be seriously hurt. I know what it feels like to die. I know how hard I worked to get well. I know how bitter and angry I felt. I know how the bitterness and anger hurt me as much as the attack. I know how angry Daddy acted. I know how many years my children spent in therapy to learn to feel secure. I wondered if they would ever be able to be as close to me as other children were with their mothers. I wondered if they still blamed me. I knew how Hal's parents blamed me. I knew how the guilt and blame and anger hurt me when I needed to be loved. I knew how abandoned I felt when those people I needed were busy being angry and finding blame. I thought about how relieved I'd been to go to Pasadena. I fell asleep.

"Oho, Maude, did I catch you sleeping?" Joey's voice woke me up.

I couldn't help myself. I said, "In my gracious Lord's name I pray, Amen." I opened my eyes and smiled at Joey.

"It's no good Maude. You were snoring."

I laughed. "Ugh, I had a late night. What time is it? I need to talk to more people and say more comforting things when I am not even sure I'm right."

"It's ten. I took an early flight. Say what is that big mud puddle outside your garage."

I still felt a little disoriented. "Oh? Is some of it still outside?"

"Yeah, is it coming in?"

I rubbed my hands over my face and wished for some coffee. "Yeah, I'll have to find the source and get some straw over it or deal with it. I hope it isn't a broken pipe."

"Why don't you let the trustees deal with it?"

I looked at Joey wondering if he had two heads, or any head at all.

"Oh. Oh yeah. I see your point. If I take care of your mud, will you have lunch with me?" Joey grinned.

"Thank you for the invite. I'm willing to let you deal with the mud, but I'm not sure if I'll have time for lunch. I need to make a hospital call, dozens of phone calls, and be available for counseling this afternoon."

"Wow, what has you so busy?"

"An incident at the high school. A boy attempted to kill a girl. It sounds as if he almost succeeded. I agreed to talk to the girl's friends this afternoon, and I need to get back to the hospital. I need to find the boy's family and contact them. I may have to talk to some of the teachers. I won't know how big the problem is until I talk to more people."

Joey whined, "Why? It doesn't sound like any of these people are members here."

"They are my neighbors." I knew my tone sounded forceful. I gave Joey a look that I hoped conveyed that he should know the depth of what that statement entailed.

Perhaps he did. He shifted in his chair. "I should go see Mom then. I'll take care of the mud problem. I know what a neighbor is too." He stood up and prepared to leave.

"Thanks for the help, and thanks for stopping by." I smiled. I think Joey's offer to deal with the mud stunned me. Maybe he had more depth to him than I thought.

At the hospital, I learned that Shelly would be moved out of intensive care in the afternoon. The Perrys were obviously still in shock, but Alex was crooning to Shelley the way a daddy talks to his baby girl.

Inez walked me out. "I hope you didn't take the things Alex said last night seriously. He was upset. What were your words? Crazy-out-of-our-minds with worry."

I tried to smile encouragingly. "I know what people say when they are stressed. I never report it to anybody. Well, I really can't because I consider that it falls under the laws of confidentiality. I hope I'm wise enough to know the difference between a good man who is justifiably distressed and a man who's a danger." Actually, these words made me shudder. I had good evidence that I didn't know the difference. I patted Inez's hand and left.

I arrived back at the church in time to work on my sermon before any students showed up. I wondered if the principal would really tell the students that they could come. He didn't. He did complain to the teachers about my phone call. The cheerleading coach overheard his complaint. Shortly before three, she arrived with her squad, three girls and a boy.

"I heard you were willing to talk to some of us about what happened to Shelly."

"Of course, come in. Please, sit down. Let me get more chairs."

"No, this is okay." Three of the students gracefully melted to a sitting position on the floor. I took my chair. As we talked, it became obvious that Stan, the boy felt protective of the girls and felt terribly guilty over Shelly. The girls sniffled off and on. Stan curled into a ball with his arms around his knees as he sat on the floor. Coach Muller's anger distorted her face and throbbed in the veins on her neck. I started by trying to get some basic information about Joel Giddens, the assailant and who his family was. I wrote down the contact information. The students wanted to talk about the young man involved.

Dawn, insisted, "He was a perv."

Stan said. "Not really, well…maybe."

Cerise argued, "Oh come on, he had a hard-on every time he saw Shelly in the halls."

Stan mumbled from his curled up position, "We shouldn't have teased him about it. I think that is what made him mad, and he took it out on her instead of us guys who teased him."

I tried to keep my voice neutral and loving. "You are right that you should not have teased him about something that's natural. The more mature response would have been to help him learn to disguise the condition. However, the important thing here is that you are high school students. You're not mature and tend to be embarrassed over these things yourselves. Ultimately, Mr. Giddens is the only person responsible for his behavior. Does he have English with you?"

"No, he's in special ed. That is next door."

Mrs. Muller angrily blurted out. "Those special ed kids just run wild. Their teacher needs more help, but the administration is too cheap to hire any." She stopped and covered her mouth. "Oh, I shouldn't have said that in front of students."

I intervened, "This is a counseling session. Everything that is said in this room stays in this room. I trust you students will not betray your coach."

We spent the rest of the session talking about their feelings of anger and guilt. I talked about what is normal and how to deal with those feelings. At the end of the session, Dawn surprised me.

"Will you pray with us for Shelly?"

"Certainly."

The students and their teacher stood, held hands, and bowed their heads. I took the hands of the students next to me and thanked God for being present with us. I asked for healing for Shelly and her friends. I asked for healing for Joel Giddens. Finally, I asked God to teach us the truth. I thought the students looked more peaceful when they left than when they came in. Coach Muller thanked me.

I asked, "Please, pass the word around that my door is open. I will be here everyday after school for the next two weeks. It is important for the students to have support at this time."

The students left and I settled down to make more phone calls. First, I called Joel's foster mother. "Mrs. Cole? This is Pastor Maude Henderson from the Blackfish United Methodist Church. I am calling to see how you are and if there is anything I or my congregation can do to help you or Joel at this time."

"I don't know. We are all upset here. I have three other foster children and CPS is coming to see if Joel was a threat to them while he was here. I don't know what to think. I don't have time to talk, especially to a preacher."

"Do you need someone to bring you food?" In the long silence that followed my question, I wondered if she had just walked away from the phone.

Finally she said. "The kids like pizza."

"I will see that you get meals delivered to your house for the next few days."

"Um…I have to go." She hung up. I wondered if she found my offer of food to be intrusive.

I made my call to Shirley anyway. "We have a family who will be needing some meals for the next few days. I'll take care of dinner tonight, but if your committee can help out I think it would be appreciated."

"What? Why didn't I know about this sooner? Who is it?"

"It is the Cole family out on Dusty Road."

"I don't know them. They are not part of this church."

"Let's call this a mission. The family is in trouble. They have three children who are most likely scared. They need some decent food."

"I think my mission is to my own congregation, not to strangers."

"Shirley, we need to expand our mission field to at least include our community."

"Well all right. I can get my committee working on this. We'll do it for the children." I breathed a sigh of relief while Shirley added. "I don't want you obligating us to everybody. We can't afford to feed everybody."

"Remember, Jesus fed five-thousand. We can do this."

Shirley grumbled some more and hung up.

We don't have a pizza place in Blackfish and certainly not one that delivers. I went over to the parsonage and pulled two large Costco pizzas out of my freezer and took them back to the church to cook in the ovens there. While they baked, I ran to the store and bought some ice cream, apples and oranges.

Elaine was working the check-out and asked about my purchases. I explained about buying food for the Cole family.

"I heard about Joel. Do you know how Shelly is?"

"Last I heard, she was scheduled to get out of intensive care this afternoon. Her parents are with her and the grandmother is taking care of the other children. I should see if they need meals brought in too."

"Their youngest is one of my son's friends. I'll see that they get something."

"Oh thanks. I'll check with Inez and see what else they need and call my care committee." I shuddered at the thought of telling Shirley to prepare meals for another family. I knew my congregation couldn't afford to feed too many extra people."

Back at the church, I called Joel's special ed teacher. When she answered the phone, she sniffled as if she'd been crying. I soon realized that she was crying and most probably well on the way to being drunk judging by her slurred speech. "This is Pastor Maude Henderson. I have been talking with several people about the situation with Joel Giddens. I wanted to know if there is anything I can do for you. I used to teach so I know how upsetting this must be for you."

"I don't need anything. Thank you for calling."

"Have you had dinner? I'm taking dinner out to the Coles in a few minutes, but I can drop something by your place later if you don't want to cook."

"You don't have to do that."

"I suppose not, but that's not what matters."

"Thank you. I would appreciate something to eat. I'm not feeling too good right now."

"I'll be there about seven."

"Yeah sure."

I made yet another phone call. "This is Pastor Maude. Is Timmy available?" I waited while someone went in search of Timmy.

"Timmy here. What's up? How is Shelly?"

Again I made a report on the last I'd heard from Shelly's doctors. "The reason I called is that I promised to take a dinner out to the special ed teacher, Mrs. Stevenson. She sounded distressed on the phone. Can you package up something To-Go for me to pick up about six forty-five?"

"You got it."

I got off of the phone, wondered whom I was forgetting and loaded the pizzas into my Porsche. I used my GPS to find the right address on Dusty Road. When I got close, I was horrified to discover that I didn't need it. Picketers carrying signs that read, "Get out" and "Keep our neighborhood safe" lined the road outside the Cole's house. A sheriff's car sat parked nearby. I tried to turn into the drive, but the picketers blocked my car. The sheriff got out of his car so I rolled down my window. "Hi, I am Pastor Maude Henderson from Blackfish United Methodist. I've been invited by the family to be here."

The officer grunted, "Just run these people over if they don't get out of your way."

I called back loud enough for the picketers to hear, "I can't do that. It might damage my Porsche."

The officer grinned at me, looked at the car and shouted at the picketers. "Move out of the way. Move, this lady is a pastor, and she needs to get through." The picketers slowly edged aside just enough to allow my small car through. In my rear view mirror I noticed the sheriff giving the quiet car a puzzled look.

My errand did not take long. Mrs. Cole met me at the door, standing back out of sight of the picketers. "Thank you for bringing this." She took the hot pizzas, and I handed her the grocery bag warning her to keep the ice cream frozen. "Oh, you brought ice cream, too. It will be good for the children to have a treat. Excuse me, I don't want to be rude, but...I can't..." She looked at the picketers and closed the door nearly in my face.

I felt sorry for the poor woman. She was trying to do something good by taking in foster children, and her efforts had brought the state, the police, and picketers down around her home. I stopped at the end of the drive and debated trying to talk the picketers into going home. I had no idea what to say, so as soon as they moved out of my way I headed home while praying for wind and rain to send them about their own business.

Back at the church, I thought I'd make another phone call on the off chance that I might get some information. I called the county sheriff. "This is Pastor Maude Henderson from Blackfish United Methodist Church. I am calling to check on the status of Joel Giddens." My call got transferred three times, and I repeated my identity three times, but nobody cut me off. I finally got hold of the person in charge of Joel's case. "He is in custody at Harrison hospital." I shuddered when I discovered how close he was to Shelly and her father.

"I was unaware he was hospitalized. What is his condition?"

"He has some injuries. He was vomiting when we picked him up. That is all I can say. You can visit him." I heard a pleading tone in the officer's voice.

"I planned to visit the hospital later tonight—about eight. Would it be too late for me to see him then."

"Since you were at his house earlier, I think we can give you a few minutes with him. I'll set something up so an officer will be with you."

I got off of the phone and thought, "Well this is turning real interesting. It didn't take long for the message that I visited the family to get through the system. I wonder if they don't realize that these people are not members of my congregation. Why am I doing this? I'm tired. I don't want to drive around at night. I don't get paid to do this. What is the matter with me?"

I thought for a few minutes and realized that by comforting others at this time, I was rewriting my own experience with love. I wished that my parents could have had more support. I wish someone would have assured Hal's parents that they were okay people—that the attack was not their fault. I sighed and went out to pick up the dinner at Timmy's Locker and drive out to Oak Creek again.

Timmy would not let me pay for the dinner. He handed me two dinners--one for the teacher and one for me. I thanked him profusely and headed out to Oak Creek.

I love my GPS. It found the right house for me without any problems. Mrs. Stevenson answered the door. I couldn't help but notice her blotchy face and red swollen eyes.

"I won't keep you long. I just wanted to make sure you had a hot dinner. Timmy made this up for you."

She blew her nose and tucked a strand of hair behind her ear. "Come in if you don't mind the mess. I haven't been feeling well lately so I haven't cleaned.

"If you don't mind, I'll run back to my car and get my dinner. Perhaps we can eat together." She nodded so I ran to my car and grabbed my dinner while she waited for me at the door.

I explained as I entered her house. "Timmy made something for both of us."

Mrs. Stevenson cleared a chair for me and made an effort to talk. "I've never eaten there. I'm surprised the owner would do something like this."

"He gave me dinner last night when he learned I intended to go to the hospital to stay with the Perrys."

She pouted, "He's married. Why are all the good ones taken?"

"It does seem that way." I sighed.

She laughed.

I suddenly realized that I was eating dinner with another single, professional woman. I smiled. She wasn't even a member of my church.

Mrs. Stevenson commented, "This is from Timmy's Locker? It's much better than I expected. But, maybe I'm just hungry. I don't remember the last time I ate real food."

I asked, "I understand that you live alone? Do you have someone who can come stay with you? Can you go home to your parents?"

"No, I'll be all right. This helps. I stayed home today and I'm starting to feel better. I think most of the problem is just the stress of too many students with too many needs."

"I know that some of your students may want to talk to a professional I'll be in my office after school. I am not charging for this. It is just part of my job."

Mrs. Stevenson sounded wary, "I can't tell them about you if you are going to talk about religion to them."

I explained, "This is not the best time to talk about religion unless someone is asking why God lets things like this happen. I don't know the answer to that question so I hope nobody asks. I will do what any other therapist would do in this situation. I try to be client directed."

We finished our dinner while discussing books and gardening. When I asked about the quilt on the back of the sofa, she confessed to being an obsessive quilter. Apparently, the gleam in my eye told her she'd met a kindred, quilting spirit. We made arrangements to meet again in a week or so and go to Timmy's for dinner. I left her house thrilled to the toes about the possibility of making friends with another professional woman in town.

I didn't think I needed my GPS to get me back to my own home so I didn't pause to set it. I made a poor choice. I think I must have forgotten a turn and then turned the wrong way at the next intersection. It took me about five minutes to realize I was lost. I looked for a wide spot to pull off and set the GPS. I drove for a minute or two before I descended a small hill and pulled off in a nice wide spot on the other side of the road. My headlights seemed muffled in the pitch-black night. The dark house in front of me did not help me see. It sat hunkered down away from the road as dark as the night. I set my GPS, and as I turned my car around to retrace my route, the headlights flashed across a realtor's sign. Without really thinking about it, I jumped out and grabbed a flyer. My GPS took me back to the parsonage in about twelve minutes. I asked for a blessing on the machine and those who made it available to me.

I'd been running around in the Porsche all day so I decided to change cars before heading into the hospital in Bremerton. Apparently, Joey had not solved my mud problem. It oozed in, filling half of my garage. I gave thanks for being able to get out of the Porsche, plug it in, and get into the Sentra without getting my feet dirty.

At the hospital, I found Joel Giddens lying down in bed in a secure room. I couldn't see any signs of wounds, but he had an IV drip into his arm and was on oxygen. He had dark circles around his eyes and appeared listless. During my visit, he showed no signs of horror or remorse for what he had done. When he learned I was a pastor, he smiled, sat up a little more, and told me how much he liked church. I glanced at the sheriff sitting by the door. Soon, Joel was chatting happily about his church memories. I sat quiet and let him talk. He used all the right phrases in a knowledgeable way. I could easily tell he had spent years in a church much more conservative than mine. I noticed that he talked about being saved and being baptized. He recited some verses from memory. He seemed to particularly enjoy verses about the blood of the lamb. I wondered who on earth asked children to memorize verses about blood. Perhaps the little ghouls took on this task all by themselves.

After twenty minutes, the sheriff shifted in his chair. I explained, "Joel, it is time for me to go now. Since you believe in Jesus, I want you to remember that Jesus loves you very much. When life gets rough, I want you to remember that someone loves you."

"Huh? Nobody loves me."

"Jesus loves you very much."

"Oh…no…nobody loves me." I got my first glimpse of sadness from this boy.

"Yes, Jesus loves you." I stood to leave. Joel brightened up.

"I know that song. I can even sign it. I'll show you."

"I have to go now." I walked out while Joel sang and signed, *Jesus Loves Me*.

While still puzzling over Joel, I found Shelly's room. She had been transferred out of intensive care. Her parents sat with her. I saw cards and balloons. She held a new plush teddy bear. Her parents introduced me.

"Hi, I see some of your friends have sent gifts." She looked confused. "I talked to Coach Muller and Stan, Dawn, Cerise and Stacy this afternoon." Shelly smiled vaguely, but still did not seem to connect with what I was saying.

Shelly's parents told me that Elaine had come by their house with a Kentucky Fried Chicken dinner for them.

I blinked, "Oh my! She must have driven into Silverdale after I talked to her. How sweet of her."

Inez continued, "She invited our youngest for a sleep over, but I am not sure what goes on at that house. She and Ed aren't married you know, so I told her that he needed to stay with his family just now."

I nodded, "Elaine has a good heart."

I got home shortly before ten. The mud in the garage spread across the floor past the back wheels of my small cars. I figured by morning it would be up to the front doors. I propped the electrical chord for the Porsche up so it wouldn't get wet and went inside. I found a note on the refrigerator door.

You left your garage door open so I came on in and tidied up a bit. The bread in the refrigerator was past its pull date, so I threw it out. – Jean

I read the note, grunted and decided to check phone messages. I had twelve. Joey called and asked me to dinner. Shirley called and said some people didn't believe it was the job of the care committee to cook meals for people outside of the church. The chair of the missions committee called to say his committee should cook meals for people outside the church, but they couldn't do it. The pastor-parish chair needed to talk to me immediately. The firemen wanted to sell me a ticket to something. Daddy called and wanted to know why I was so busy. My real estate agent wanted me to call her ASAP. Shirley called again. Ralph called. I couldn't stop the grin that I felt growing across my face. All my frustration over the other calls disappeared.

I called Ralph back as soon as I got upstairs to my bedroom. He answered on the first ring. "Hi Maude. How are you doing?"

"Oh, I've been frantically busy here. We had an incident at the high school. I am trying to see that all the families involved get the community support they need."

"Um…yeah…about that incident. Is that the one involving Joel Giddens?"

"Yeah, how did you hear about it?"

"I know we talked about being friends and not each others pastor or psychologist, but can we talk as confidential professionals?"

"Sure, what's up?"

"That is what I want to know. Joel has not been formally charged. He does have a public defender, and somebody asked our office to evaluate Joel and the situation. I volunteered because I know you, so I'd have a contact in the community."

"Oh. Good. I think it's a real good idea for someone from your office to be involved. I talked to Joel this evening."

"What? You did? Why? What did you say?"

"I didn't say much of anything. Joel rambled on for about twenty minutes. He used a great many words and phrases that I'm certain he didn't understand. He came across as just another youth except for his naïve air and religious talk."

"He talked to you about religion?"

"Yes, he used pat phrases to tell me that he was saved—washed in the blood of the lamb…"

"Oh God!"

"My thought exactly. As I was leaving, I tried to assure him that Jesus loves him. He didn't get it. He insisted nobody loves him. Ralph, there is something very wrong with that young man. He showed no sense of guilt or remorse over what he had done. His whole agenda seemed to be impressing me with his knowledge of the Bible and salvation."

Ralph grunted, "Good. You've said some things that give me some idea of where to start with this. I'll be out in the morning."

"I plan to check in with Shelly Perry in the morning, and I have to be here after school gets out to meet with any youth who want to talk about this. Otherwise I am free."

"Oh Maudy, you have been busy. Have any youth talked to you?"

"Yes, I probably should not say too much to you about that, but I have talked to some youth and a couple teachers. Mostly, I am dealing with issues of anger and guilt."

"Good girl. Do your best to defuse this issue. The concern is always that the underlying unresolved anger will smolder and break out in more violence or slide into drug and alcohol abuse. I'd rather you didn't talk to Joel again until after I see him. I'll go straight to the jail in the morning."

"Joel is in Harrison hospital."

"What? I was told he was taken to the county jail over there."

"I called the sheriff's office here about that, and they sent me to Harrison to see him. That is where I saw him at eight this evening. They may transfer him in the morning, so you might want to check."

"Thanks, you just saved me a ton of hassle. I'll see you in the morning."

CHAPTER **13**: FRIDAY

*O*n Friday, my day started out as usual until I reached the garage. I had to wade though eight inches of mud. Fortunately, I had the cutest rubber boots. They were pink knee-highs with a yellow and orange calico pattern. I bought them because I thought the pattern would look good in a quilt.

When I got to the church, I finished writing my sermon. I thought it was the best I'd ever written.

At nine, I took special care in dressing to go to the hospital. I wore make-up. At the hospital, Ralph thanked me for meeting with Joel. He looked into my eyes and asked if he could come over later. I told him I might not be home, but he could come over anyway. I gave him a key.

I went about the rest of my day. I moved both cars outside because the mud was almost knee deep. I put towels under the door between the kitchen and garage to keep the mud out of the kitchen.

Finally, I reached the point where I felt so tired I wanted crawl into bed and sleep for days. Ralph had not called or come over. Discouraged, I struggled up the stairs to my room and slid out of my dress. John Wesley sat on the bed looking toward the bedroom door. I thought I saw the figure of a man reflected in the cat's eyes. I turned and there stood Ralph staring at me.

"How...how did you get in?"

Ralph continued to stare at me as he held up the key I'd given him.

I clutched my dress to my front in an attempt at modesty.

Ralph finally spoke. His voice sounded low and soft as his words caressed me. "Maudy, you are beautiful. I...I...I need to touch your skin. I must touch your skin." He still stood in the doorway, looking desirable, and manly. His shirt collar stood open and his tie hung loose around his neck like a clerical stole. This late in the day, I could see a manly stubble on his jaw. I wanted him. As I pretended to modestly lower my eyes, I noticed his obvious desire for me creating a bulge in the front of his pants. He started unbuttoning his shirt. I stood there unable to move, transfixed. My mind clouded over, and my desire for Ralph overwhelmed me. I wanted to make love.

Ralph freed himself from his shirt and took two steps across the room to where I stood. I wanted him to hold my body, but instead his fingers lightly caressed the side of my face before he lowered his lips to mine. If I held any resolve to resist him, it melted away. I wanted him. He wanted me. I forgot about the United Methodist Book of Discipline, or rather, I shoved it under the bed with my bare toe.

Under the magic of Ralph's hands my undergarments melted away. He picked me up and lowered me onto my back on my bed. He bent over me. I reached up and pulled his lips down to mine. I wanted to taste and tease their fullness. I wanted his fullness to fill me. I ran my leg up and down against his naked leg. I felt his erection pressing against me. He kissed me and told me that I am precious, then he started fondling my breast. "Oh Maudy, you are perfect—so beautiful and perfectly feminine. I want you. I want you to be mine."

"Yes, my love, I want us to be together, really together. I shifted under him bringing my private areas closer to his."

His breathing came out raspy as he asked, "Are you sure?"

"I am certain. I want all of you."

"I love you. I have loved you since that first moment you fell into my arms. In my heart and mind you have been mine." He entered me then. He filled me and started moving inside me. I'm certain I'd ever known that sex could be like this. He moved inside me, and my whole existence centered on those movements. His movements became quicker, matching the growing need in me for more. Finally I felt great shattering waves of release, and joy, and peace radiating from between my legs up through my body, flooding my stomach, heart and mind with a feeling of well being. I slept sound feeling safe and loved and completely satisfied.

CHAPTER 14: THE REAL FRIDAY

When I woke up, Friday still stretched before me. I sat up as I realized I hadn't finished my sermon. What I had so far might not be that good. I had yet to get through this day. Most of all there had been no passionate love-making. I smiled. "I still feel pretty good." I shook my head wondering when sex ever became that good. I flopped back down on the bed remembering my dream and thinking that it had been good—fantastic.

As I recalled more of the dream, I thought that perhaps I should move the cars outside to keep them out of the creeping mud. I thought about the mud in my dream and lamented the loss of the cute boots. "Why do I dream about cute shoes that I will never find anywhere?" I thought about the shoes and about Ralph as a lover. "Yeah, I guess I dream about things that I can never have." I sighed and got up to go about my business.

I checked on the mud first thing when I went downstairs. I could not get into either car without getting my feet dirty. Again I lamented the loss of the cute boots. I didn't own any boots. Finally, wearing an old pair of slippers and using towels to protect the floor of the cars, I managed to move both cars to the church parking lot.

I showered, dressed and went to the church to return calls and work on my sermon. I played telephone tag with the real estate agent. I called Shirley about the meals. She finally agreed that since nobody on the mission committee could do the job, the care committee would supply meals...this time.

My bride called me and left a message, "We applied for our license, but we have to wait three days, which is a real bummer because we're both busy all week so we have to wait for the weekend to get married. Can you come out here on Saturday morning?"

I called back and made arrangements to meet with them for a couple hours to plan out the wedding and what they wanted for vows. I recalled part of a different dream I'd had the night before where the bride and groom had exchanged feathers instead of rings. They explained the symbolism as the recognition that love is fleeting. I shook my head remembering that part of that dream.

Finally, I left for the hospital wearing make-up and a nice business suit with a clerical stole. When I found Ralph at the information desk asking questions about how to find his client, I had another flashback to my dream where I met him at the hospital.

I intervened. "Excuse, me I know the way to where he wants to go. I'll walk him up."

Ralph turned toward me, "Hey you look official."

"I try to wear some indication of my status while I am here. Come on. How was your ferry ride over?" I led Ralph toward the elevators.

"Beautiful, I intended to read or study, but I ended up watching the waves, and the sea gulls."

"Good. I still think ferry rides are special. The trip between here and Seattle is especially beautiful."

Ralph sounded as excited as a little boy, "That is what I thought. I don't think I have seen more beautiful scenery anywhere. I saw seals, sea lions, cormorants, and a bald eagle. How cool is that?"

I smiled at Ralph and felt as if I was floating a foot above the floor. Darn that dream! I was mooning like new lover. I blushed and tried to get down to business. "After you see Joel, what will you need to do? Are you going back to Seattle?"

"No, I need to come out to Blackfish and talk to some people. I'll stop at the school to meet his teacher."

"Oh, I know her. We had dinner together the other night." My dream still seemed so real that I was having trouble keeping track of days. "She wasn't feeling well so I took her some dinner. She says she has been sick lately. I think she said it was because she is stressed with too many students." I paused. "Oh dear, I hope I am not saying something I promised not to talk about." I tried to concentrate on who had said what. Ralph stopped walking and turned to face me. He sounded very gentle.

"Maudy, too many students, cannot possibly be confidential information."

I looked at Ralph, horrified. I answered, "It is if somebody says they were not supposed to talk about it." Ralph looked closer at me, and I continued to feel guilty for saying something. "As I think about this I don't recall Mrs. Stevenson confiding that information in a formal counseling session. I was at her house more as a friend."

"I won't ask any more questions on this topic. Well, I might bring it up with Mrs. Stevenson, but I won't let on that you tipped me off." Ralph smiled at me as if maybe he'd had the same dream I had. His voice sounded low and soft, "I'll be in Blackfish a while. When can we meet up again?"

I gave Ralph my schedule. "I will visit Shelly. I don't think I need to stay more than twenty minutes. She is still pretty disoriented. I want to assure her and her parents that it is to be expected and that it is okay. I'll be back at my office by noon. I am keeping my afternoons open from about two forty-five until five for any youth who want to talk."

"Would you mind if I join you this afternoon?"

"Oh yes please! Sometimes I think I am crazy for acting like a counselor when really I don't have any great wisdom."

Ralph laughed. "Honey, I don't have any great wisdom myself. I think the best we can do is point out the options to our clients and let them take it from there. I suppose one reason I like forensic work is that it has more concrete answers. I don't know how you deal with something as immeasurable as the spiritual realm.'

I scowled and pouted. "Okay I confess. My biggest fear is that sooner or later someone will ask why God allowed this to happen. I don't know that answer. We make guesses, but in the end that is all they are. I must have asked God why he let me get hurt a million times. I've never gotten a straight answer."

Ralph smiled and ran his finger down my cheek. "You're okay Maudy. See you later."

I danced or floated off to see Shelly and her parents. I walked into Shelly's room and almost didn't recognize her. "Wow, girl you're looking good. You must be doing much better."

Alex sounded happy. "Yeah she's looking good enough that I might go back to work this afternoon. Do you think that would be okay?"

What on earth? This man asked me if he could go back to work? I turned the responsibility away from me. "What do you think Shelly? Will you be okay without your dad here?"

She looked at her mother and asked, "Mom staying?" Inez assured her that she would stay. Shelly blinked then said, "Okay." Both parents looked so proud of their daughter. I looked at her and my head almost ached remembering the effort that it took me to begin speaking again. We visited a little about what was happening in the outside world.

I had a good idea that Shelly's friends would want to visit her soon. "So, what is the doctor saying about visitors? Can Shelly's friends come visit?" My question was greeted with confusion.

Inez hesitated, "We'll have to check with her doctors."

I sat down by the head of Shelly's bed and started talking to her parents. "Shelly's friends Stan, Cerise, Dawn and Stacy will want to come see her. They are worried and want her to know that they are her friends. Coach Muller may come too. She seems to take good care of her cheerleaders. I'm sure that she will want to take care of Shelly too." I spoke slowly and clearly, trying to give Shelly the hints she would need to remember her life. As I spoke, her parents seemed to realize for the first time how much Shelly had lost in the attack.

Inez murmured, "We'll check with her doctors and let her friends know when they can come. Her best friend is Candy. I think Candy should be the first. Perhaps the other cheerleaders Stan, Dawn, Cerise and Stacy can come later."

I continued, "Perhaps Candy or one of the other cheerleaders can organize visits and carpools." I asked Shelly, "Do you feel up to having your friends visit? They are worried and want you to know that you are loved and that your friends are thinking of you."

Shelly smiled a lopsided smile. "Yes, I want my friends."

"Good we'll speak to the doctor and I can pass the word to Coach Muller." I turned to Inez. "Maybe you could let Candy know when she can visit." After twenty minutes of this line of talk, I felt exhausted from remembering those first few weeks when my brain refused to answer my requests for names, faces, and details. As soon as I left, Alex caught up to me in the hall.

"Do you think she doesn't remember?"

"Yes, she remembers, but right now she may not be able to access her memories. I still have nightmares about not being able to remember names and faces. I could not remember where my own home was. I recovered quick enough, but this is what I meant when I talked about supporting her. It will make things easier for her if you prepare her for who is coming and what is about to happen. I know it depends some on where the damage is as to the long term problems, but right now, I'm guessing she has some pretty general memory problems."

"She keeps repeating the same thing over and over."

I smiled, actually relieved that my estimation appeared correct. "That's normal. It's good to know she is at that stage. I think she might be past that soon enough. Um…I don't know if this would help you, but I have a friend who is a forensic psychologist. He might be able to tell you more--what to expect. I confess I'm working from what I remember from my own incident."

Alex replied firmly, "You've been where Shelly is now. You know what it feels like. I'll trust you before someone who has read about it in a book somewhere."

I nodded, but I really wanted to curl into a ball and scream that I don't know what I'm doing. "I'll try to help you with the supports I remember needing. I think you will learn soon enough what she needs. You'll end up walking a thin line between being adequately supporting and overprotecting."

We stopped at the nurses' station and discussed the rules for visitors for Shelly. I added, "I've also suggested that a friend of mine, Dr. Ralph Graham, stop to see Shelly for a few minutes in hopes that he will have some ideas for supports for Shelly when she gets home."

The nurse gave me a blank stare that told me she didn't understand a word of what I just said. I continued, "Anyway, watch for Dr. Graham. You can't miss him. He's big, bald, and about the sexiest thing you'll see today." The nurses and aids giggled and promised to take real good care of him. Alex looked shocked.

Back at the church, I parked as close to my front door as the parking lot allowed. As usual, I checked my messages first thing. I had one from my realtor saying she had exciting news for me and I should call immediately. I called.

"Oh Maude, Hi, I think I have some good news for you. Your renters have been looking for a new home. They haven't found anything they like as well as they do your house. They are willing to buy, if the price is right."

I wanted to snarl that I didn't like my renters. "Well that is fine, as long as the price is right. I'm not lowering the price for them. I set the price somewhat below top market, and I think I can get that much if they will move out. You might remind them of how much it will cost them to move if they make an offer I don't like."

"We can save some money on my commission since I am both the listing and selling agent."

"Listen, those people will push and shove until they get their way. If they can afford the rent, they can afford to make payments. I'm not budging. I'm selling the house to get people like them out of my life. I've set a fair price and I am not lowering it for those manipulative freeloaders, and you should get your full commission. You deserve it for putting up with them for the past four years."

"Oh…well…if you put it that way…"

"Yeah, I put it that way."

"I'll tell them that the price is firm."

"You might also tell them to start packing because I want to put the house on the market."

"Um…yes, I'll get back to you."

I wasn't done with my rant. "You could tell them, that for them, I will make a special price of ten-thousand more to cover the costs of their harassment."

The agent laughed nervously. "Maude, you have a lot more backbone than when I first met you."

"When you first met me, I was little better than dead. You might also play the poor widow card with those folks. I am a widow, and I am poor, at least my income is below the poverty level. Why should I give them something? Don't they have any self-respect?"

"Maude. Maude, I get the message. I'll deal with it. You have a good day."

I hung up and wondered who had just said all those things. I called the school and asked to talk to Coach Muller. I told her what the rules were for visitations for Shelly. She agreed to talk to the rest of the squad and set a time to visit.

I worked on my sermon for another hour before Ralph arrived. "Hi. There you are. I was beginning to wonder if you were lost in the wilds of the back woods."

Ralph melted into a chair and pulled off his tie.

I remembered my dream and blushed.

"No, I spent most of the morning with the Giddons boy. Wow, what a mess! I don't think he can stand trial. We'll have to think up some sort of appropriate lockup or something."

"What do you think is wrong with him, if it is okay for me to ask?"

"Yeah, I'm calling you a consultant on this one. The kid has brain damage. It seems to be overlaid with delusions and confabulations. He has no sense of consequences or the seriousness of his act. He's manipulative." Ralph paused and ran his hands over his baldhead. "I think you saw that last night. Today, he talked to me in clinical terms and played the counseling client extremely well. People have tried with him. He has been in therapy. He has been in church groups where he was taught the rules. He has no concept that the rules apply to him. I'm not sure he sees himself as human. That is the crux of the matter. He doesn't see himself as subject to the same rules as the rest of humanity." Ralph sat silent for a moment then shrugged and continued, "He's smart enough. If I hadn't talked to you, it might have taken me longer to get past his counseling jargon. He seems to try to be whatever others expect or want him to be."

"Oh dear, what will become of him?"

"I don't know. He could end up spending his life in and out of prison. It depends on the decisions we make now." Ralph's quiet voice conveyed his discouragement. "Or, we may have no control over the direction his life takes. I see some signs that he has had a great deal of loving help, but he doesn't recognize it." Ralph sighed, rubbed his hands over his bald-head again and sat up. "Thanks for paving the way for me to get in to see Shelly. I needed to have some idea of the seriousness of her condition in order to gage my client's reaction."

I swiveled in my chair and debated whether my observations were important enough to mention. I had no idea if they were important. "When I saw him, he seemed totally disconnected from the seriousness of his behavior."

Ralph grunted, "I can believe that. I bet anything that with you he was the perfect little church boy."

I chuckled, "Not perfect. He quoted too many scriptures about blood and none about love."

Ralph stared at me open-mouthed. "I think you just hit something on the head there." We looked at each other in silence for a few moments. Finally Ralph said, "Hey what's for lunch? I'm starving."

"What do you want to do? The closest restaurant is Timmy's Locker. We can walk to Timmy's, or we can go out to the Oak Ridge Country Club. The country club restaurant is open to the public. The food is good at both places. At Timmy's you will have to put up with everybody who comes in asking me about Shelly. The country club will be quieter."

Ralph started to get out of his chair. "Lets go to the country club. I'll drive--your Porsche." I laughed and led Ralph out to my car for a quick driving lesson. When I got in the passenger's seat I found the real estate flyer from the night before. I set the GPS to give us directions, and told Ralph the story of my renters and real estate woes on our drive out to Oak Ridge.

The country club served good food. I liked the company better than the food. I kept remembering my dream and trying not to blush. We talked about his travels. I elaborated on my real estate woes. "Even if I sell in town, I'm not sure I will stay here with the dying church."

"You're staying."

"What?"

"When you took on the Shelly Perry case, you made your decision to stay. Someone who is undecided would not put the effort into this case that you have. Inez told me how helpful you were with Alex. She seemed to have some idea of how hard it was for you to talk about your incident. If you were willing to do that, you will stay with this community until this incident is resolved. I think you may know better than I do how long that will take."

I sighed and leaned back in my chair as I thought about how long it would take. "Thank you for clarifying that for me. I guess I'll be here until Shelly leaves for college. I wonder about trying to buy and sell houses in this market. What if I buy something here and can't sell it when I leave?"

Ralph shrugged. "Why do you have to buy something here?"

I gave Ralph a partial list of my woes. "Oh! And, I haven't told you about the mudslide that is creeping into the garage. That is why my cars are outside. And Jean managed to get in through the garage and threw out my bread that I was going to have for toast with cheese sauce."

Ralph laughed. "Oh God Maude, that is one of the things I like about you. You live."

"What? Anybody can have mudslides. I admit that few people have parishioners who come in and throw out their food."

Ralph chuckled, "Most people would have given up on this church after a month."

I sighed, "Well I need a job."

"And you can walk down the street and get a counseling job any day you want."

"I like counseling well enough, but my passion is in the church."

Ralph looked at me for a moment before he asked, "Or is it in something like we have with Shelly right now?"

"I guess I am passionate about this case, but you know I don't know what I'm doing here. I say things, and then I wonder what do I know?"

Ralph patted my hand. "Alex and Inez seem to think you know a great deal. I suspect you know more than you think. Alex told me about how you tried to tell them what you remember about being hurt so they'd know how to help Shelly. They appreciate that. I know it isn't easy for you going back and living through that experience for them."

I told Ralph my thoughts about rewriting my own story with more love this time. He didn't seem shocked that I was getting something out of this. I felt a little embarrassed over how much I revealed, so I responded happily when my bride came into the restaurant and came up to my table. I introduced her to Ralph and explained to him about the wedding. She told me about how the wedding was growing. They had friends coming. One of her students wanted to sing. I thought it showed a great deal of love that people were willing to come to a wedding at seven on a Saturday morning. I hugged her then she left to go to her own table. Ralph was smiling at me—almost laughing.

I raised my eyebrows. "What?"

"You might as well buy a house. I'm not sure Blackfish has any idea what hit it, but you will stay until you think it is time to leave."

"What makes you say that?"

"That woman has purple and blue hair."

"I know. I almost didn't recognize her. It was green and orange last week."

"And, you, the pastor of a very conventional church, love her in spite of the fact that she dresses funny and is how pregnant?'

"How can you tell? I didn't notice."

"Boobs don't match her frame, but they're not fake either. Her layered clothing disguises the bump, but it is there. She has students?"

I chuckled, "She and her fiancé are a matched set. She teaches modern dance and ballet at the community college. He is a programmer for Willits-Manion. They have a house out here somewhere."

"Willits-Manion? So he went to MIT?"

"Probably, I think they are financially secure. The wedding is at his house at sunrise on Saturday morning."

"I hope the weather is decent for the sunrise."

"I'm just thankful that sunrise is coming at a decent hour these days." We laughed some more, over nothing. I think we both laughed a great deal at lunch. It felt good to laugh with someone again.

After lunch, I again noticed the real estate flyer when I got back in the car. "Do you want to take a few minutes and look at this house with me? We can't get in, but I'd like to see what it looks like in daylight." I set the address into the GPS. It took us less than five minutes to find the tidy brick ranch-style house.

The flyer told us it was a thousand square feet with two bedrooms. We got out and walked through tall grass and weeds to look in the windows. We waded our way around to the back and stopped, amazed. There, stretching out before us sat Oak Lake. I'd never known of its existence until this moment. Its beauty took my breath away.

"Look! You have a dock. Come on." Ralph led the way down to the dock. We walked out onto the lake. Ralph looked down. "You have fish." My eyes followed his pointing finger and saw a small school of tiny fish turn and dart back under the dock. I looked across the lake to the far end and felt peace descend over my whole being.

"I'll take it. I wonder what I just bought."

"A mess."

I turned and looked in the direction Ralph faced and studied the weeds and encroaching blackberries. I sighed. "Shall we look in the windows on this side?"

As we approached the house, Ralph commented that it appeared to be built on a concrete slab.

"Is that a problem?"

"Not if you don't want to remodel, or don't have plumbing problems." We cupped our hands at the windows, looking into the living room. "Nice sized room with a good view. Hardwood floors."

I asked, "Do you think they are laminate? Or hardwood? I wonder if the fireplace is functional?"

"May I help you?" We both jumped startled and turned to look at a man standing knee-deep in weeds in the yard.

Ralph answered. "We are thinking of looking at this house."

"I'm the listing agent. Let me show you inside." We looked at each other, shrugged, and followed the man around to the front where he let us in through the front door. From the entry hall I could see through the house and out the living room window. The bedrooms opened to the right and left off of the entry hall. The main bathroom looked serviceable and in need of remodel or repair. The dining room had French doors out to the concrete patio.

The kitchen, bigger than many modern kitchens, didn't have a dishwasher, stove or refrigerator. It had lots of cabinets, but needed new countertops. I looked around me as the agent talked to Ralph. I liked the utility room. It had a shower and toilet in a small closet. They looked serviceable. The laundry had real laundry sinks and a huge pantry lined most of one wall with its back to the garage. The jumbo-single garage might be big enough to hold both of my cars. I looked for outlets. The outlet at the front of the garage looked serviceable despite being awkwardly located. The garage looked dry. The house felt solid. Ralph asked questions about the heat, wiring, and plumbing. The agent smiled at him and answered questions. I wandered through the house blissfully unaware of the rumors that this little adventure was going to start.

Before we left, I took another look at the lake and paused a moment as a lone duck glided across the surface. I remembered Doctor Dave asking me what I did to nourish my spirituality, and nodded.

When we left, I told the agent that I would call him if I decided to buy. Ralph looked a little confused. When we got in the car, he asked me why I was waiting.

I explained, "The house isn't going anywhere. If it still seems like a good idea in the morning, I'll call him. Maybe I should look at some other houses. I'll do some online research before making an offer. Ralph grunted and started the car.

I had another idea. "Wait, do you want to talk to Joel's teacher? She lives near here. I'll call." Ralph arched his brow at me while I called Mrs. Stevenson and made the appointment.

"Are you always this productive and organized?"

"You think I'm productive and organized? Wow, I've never heard that before. Actually, I think I drift from one thing to the next. We are near Mrs. Stevenson's. You need to talk to her, so I am drifting in her direction."

Mrs. Stevenson looked better than she had when I first met her. I introduced her to Ralph and commented, on her improved health.

Her relaxed tone of voice told me she considered me a friend. "I went in to work this morning and have a sub this afternoon. I'm feeling better, but I still had a headache by the time I got home."

I let Ralph direct the discussion while I thought about my new home. I wondered how long it would take for the repairs and if I really needed to make them. Mrs. Stevenson told Ralph that Joel seemed smart enough, that he acted more disabled than his school-work indicated. Ralph asked her questions about his scores in reading, math and spelling. After forty-minutes Ralph said we needed to leave to get back to the church in case students showed up.

Mrs. Stevenson warned us, "I think several will walk over. I told my class that Pastor Maude was available to talk about anger and guilt."

I muttered, "I hope they don't ask why God allows such things to happen."

Mrs. Stevenson looked at me and asked, "Why do you think?"

I whined, "I don't know. Nobody knows the mind of God, so we don't know why. I just hate the question."

Ralph laughed at my tone of voice.

We got back to the church in time for me to show Ralph the mud. We discovered it oozed from the vacant lot behind the parsonage. Ralph strode off across my lawn. When he turned back, he called out to me, "We can divert the mud into the woods beside the house or onto the church parking lot.

"I guess we better send it into the woods then. I wonder where it is coming from?"

At two forty-five, Candy, Shelly's best friend, arrived at my office. Ralph and I introduced ourselves and sat down to talk. Within five minutes a group of boys from Joel's class showed up followed by the rest of the cheerleading squad. Shelly's friends eyed Joel's friends warily.

Ralph took charge. "Right. This group is getting pretty big. I want all of you who knew Joel to come with me." He led them off to the boardroom. As they left, another girl came in. The boys with Ralph invited her to come with them. I thought they acted a little protective of her—almost as they would a younger sister.

I thought my session went well. Shelly's friends wanted to know how she felt and how to behave when she got home. Once again I searched my brain for how it felt after my beating and what helped me think and remember. "One of the things that other people could not grasp with me was that I really did not remember much of the attack. I was unconscious most of the time. The actual attack was less traumatizing than my problems trying to function afterward. That is not to say I am comfortable talking about it, but the biggest part for me was trying to heal and remember my life. Shelly will need a therapist to talk to about her issues of trust and security. Her friends are for giving her back her life."

"Can she still be part of the cheer-team?"

"I hope so. Right at first her physical limits may mean she won't be able to do anything other than dress up and sit on a bench. She may be too tired for weeks to even do that much."

Candy asked, "Should I take her my ipod with all her favorite songs on it?"

I pounced on the idea. "Yes! Music is going to be one of her strongest memories and will help her access other memories."

Dawn asked, "How soon do you think she will be back to school?"

I sighed, "Weeks and when she returns she won't really be able to learn. I went back to school about nine months after my attack. I took only one class. That much was hard for me. It took me two years to take half time and three before I could handle a full load." I smiled, "But I was older and had two children to raise by myself."

The students continued to ask questions about what to expect. I continued to try to remember how challenging that part of my life had been. We talked about depression, what causes it and how to be friends with someone who is depressed. Shortly after four, Coach Muller arrived with another teacher. The students left. I felt pleased with my session with them.

The teachers asked the same questions as the students. It impressed me that they cared enough to try to learn how they could support this student. I offered what advice I could. "One thing I'd do is be up front with her. Ask her if she is having trouble. Ask her what she needs from you." At five the teachers left.

I went looking for Ralph. I found him out behind my garage with a team of men and boys directing the placement of straw bales. Some boys were shoveling the last of the mud out of the garage. They were talking as they worked. Ralph answered many of the same questions I answered.

By five forty-five a wall of straw bales protected my house from mudslides, or mud-oozes. The men and boys went home. Ralph ran his hands over his baldhead, "That has got to be the best, and strangest, session I have ever had. I got some good information about Joel from his classmates. After an hour, I took the boys outside to look at your mud. That's when the football team showed up. I think having physical labor to do while we talked helped. The two groups of boys talked. Joel's classmates expressed their fear that they might have a meltdown and hurt someone. I think this surprised the other boys. Joel's friends talked about being called retards and spaz. Both groups worked hard on the drainage ditch. We talked about normal sexuality and how to disguise the fact that you have an erection. Man! I need to be taking more male clients out and making them work. They kept me running from spot to spot to do my job, but they talked." As we walked back to my office, I could see that Ralph was high from his success.

I laughed at his happiness then sobered. "I hear you saying something that concerns me. I heard something like it yesterday. Were the other students teasing Joel about having an erection?"

"Yeah, they teased him about his boner whenever he saw Shelly."

"Oh. Did you talk to them about their feelings of guilt?"

"Yes, I didn't let them off easy on that one. One boy's father had arrived and he asked some tough questions about what the boys were learning at home that they could behave that way. The boys admitted that their parents would kill them if they knew that their sons were teasing special ed kids."

"I should hope." I plopped down on my counseling sofa.

Ralph eased himself into a chair. "The problem seems to be that the school does not have a policy on non-harassment or bullying. If they do, it is not being enforced. I told the boys they needed to take the lead in changing behavior at school. I told them to work with you." He ran his hands over his bald head again and appeared to be thinking.

Impure thoughts ran through my head, but I stayed focused on the topic at hand. "I talked to two teachers this afternoon. They were focused on how to support Shelly when she returns to school. I'm concerned that we are not hearing from more teachers. What do you think their role has been?"

Ralph sighed, "At best they have been negligent in not catching or stopping the teasing. Both groups of boys said the teachers don't care about it. Both groups of boys felt that some of the staff supported it."

I held my head and griped, "Prejudice against disabilities is so epidemic--even at a seminary. Some of my teachers were supportive of me. Others took a hard line about deadlines or being late to class. Some came out and said that if I couldn't take a full load and keep up, I shouldn't be in school—that I shouldn't be ordained. Even at seminary, my limp attracted unwanted attention. Some people were helpful and asked if I needed help. Others treated me like a pet, or lesser human in their efforts to minister to the handicapped woman. Ralph I understand the rage. I would get so hurt and angry."

"I think you need a session with the special ed kids. I think it would help them to see a successful adult who struggled against the same things that hurt them."

"I could do that. I admit that there were times that I got depressed, even on medication, and thought about giving up and living the life of a handicapped person. It would be easier than fighting the expectations and my own limits. I had one difference from our school kids. I had a history of being successful, beautiful and popular." Another thought bounced into my brain. "Hey, what was with the girl who joined your group?"

"She has a crush on Joel. He was nice to her. He was her best friend."

"This must be hard on her."

"Yeah, the other boys were supportive. She told me that it was Joel who got them to start including her. Maudy, despite all of his behaviors Joel was a decent guy in some ways. He was the person the special ed kids looked to for friendship and leadership. He was the one who pulled them together as friends."

"Wow." I sat stunned as I considered this dynamic. "I could see how he could become their leader. How is this going to affect the whole prognosis?"

"I'm thinking about that. I think he has a good case for getting off with nothing more than probation until he is twenty-one. He has strong points in his leadership and friendship abilities. His ability to talk the talk is in his favor. He acts like a good kid. He doesn't have a record. He does have brain damage. The teasing was a factor and the lack of supervision by the staff was a factor. Yeah, he could get off."

"That's not right either." I reacted more out of my own history than out of a sense of justice. I thought a moment. "No, his lack of remorse and lack of understanding for what he did still remains a problem. He cannot just be turned loose in society."

"No, you're right." He scowled out my window. "Our society does not have any place for someone like Joel. If he's surrounded by decent people, he will be decent. The problem is that he will always be exposed to an element that seeks to be exploitative. There will always be people who will try to put him down." He shifted his weight forward in his chair. "Well…tomorrow, he will be moved. I requested that he be sent over to Swedish for evaluation. He's not right, and I don't want him in jail." Ralph pushed himself to his feet. "Well I suppose I better get back to the ferry. Sw…Maudy, you've done a good job here. I think we've gone a long way to defusing most of the anger. The fact that you contacted so many people really helped me. I don't usually get this much first person information on a case." He stood up and made motions to leave. "I'll be back Monday before the kids get out of school."

I stood and warned Ralph, "Watch the ferry schedule."

"I'll be on this side early for Joel's court appearance. I'll testify. There won't be any problem getting him assigned somewhere for evaluation. I need to talk to his foster mom."

I remembered the Coles. "Oh! I hope somebody got a dinner out there. Last night people were picketing her house."

Ralph chuckled, "Why didn't I know you had already contacted her?"

"I may have mentioned it and you forgot, or I forgot about her until just now. You go catch your boat. I'll see you Monday." I paused and smiled. I felt my voice soften, "I'm thankful you were here to help with the kids." I would have walked Ralph to his car, but Shirley arrived. She looked like she had been crying.

Ralph looked at her, and looked at me. "Maudy, get some rest. You've put in some long hours and done a great job. Take care of yourself."

I waved Ralph off. "Shirley, what is the problem? Can you come in?"

Shirley sniffed and blew her nose on a tissue retrieved from her sleeve. "No, I have to get home. I tried to take a dinner out to the Coles like you asked, but the neighbors wouldn't let me in. They went so far as to call me names."

"Oh Shirley, I'm so sorry. Wasn't the sheriff there?"

She shook her head.

"Do you have the dinner with you?"

She nodded tearfully.

"I'll take the food out there, and those people will let me through. I think it is about time they went home."

Shirley commented in a tone more coy than watery. "So that was your boyfriend?"

I tried to be firm. "I don't have a boyfriend. If you are referring to Dr. Graham who just left, I know him, yes. He is here on business and to help me with the students who are upset over the incident."

"He's the man you went to the Seahawks game with." She accused.

I confessed. "Yes, that was the closest we've come to dating."

"You had lunch with him today."

I refused to continue the discussion of Ralph. "Shirley let's get that food out of your car so you can go home to your husband."

Shirley giggled. "I'm surprised that a bald man is so attractive."

I had to laugh. "Oh for pity's sake, yes, he's devilish handsome. I think it is because he is so physically fit. He is also a very good forensic psychologist. I really appreciate his help." I finally got the food out of Shirley's car and sent her on her way while she tried to probe for every detail of information about Ralph. I'd made a huge mistake by confessing I found him devilish handsome.

Before I headed out to the Coles', I called the sheriff's office and complained about one of my elderly parishioners being intimidated by the picketers. I took the Sentra when I drove out to the Coles, arriving before the police. The picketers blocked the highway. I put on my clerical stole to show that I belonged there as a professional on business. I knew they could see me, but they still blocked the driveway. I put the car in park, opened my door and got out. I positioned myself so I could get back in the car quickly. "Excuse me, I am here on business."

"You can't go in." A tall, thin, but powerfully built man with thick grey hair snarled at me. His huge hands on his picket sign sent a shiver down my spine. His tone told me he held no respect for the church.

"Well, yes I can. I may have to run over a few of you but that is why I brought my big car." I saw some funny looks when I called the Sentra "my big car." I thought a second, searching for something I could say. "Listen, this behavior is not helpful. Mrs. Cole took in a child because she was trying to do a good thing."

The spokesman snarled, "She only takes those kids for the money."

"Good grief, do you really believe that? The state does not pay enough for anybody to make money. I'm sure this costs her more than you can imagine in time and energy and money. But, the point is that your behavior is not helpful. The problem we had at the high school could happen anywhere. The students—really the children who are most hurt and are closest to the situation are talking together to find constructive solutions so this won't happen again. I've been working all day to bring a helpful resolution to this problem, and I come out here and find a bunch of ignorant busybodies perpetuating the problems that triggered this episode. You know Shelly Perry's parents may have grounds for a lawsuit against everyone who supports the tormenting of special ed students. I will be certain to mention you folks. You are every bit as guilty in this incident as the young man who couldn't take it anymore and lashed out at the first person available." My audience refused to move. I started working myself into a good rage when the sheriff arrived. I smiled at the same officer I'd met last night and started to tell him how these people harassed one of my elderly parishioners.

"Yes, Ma'am. I heard about that." He turned to the people who were still blocking the driveway. "Okay folks, I've about had it with you. Go on home before I think up some excuse to arrest you."

The spokesman turned on the officer and spat. "You can't arrest us. We are practicing our right to assemble and free speech. We don't want these criminals here in our neighborhood. It is just a matter of time before another one hurts somebody."

I turned to the officer. "Dr. Graham who has been investigating the case has found that there was a great deal of bullying that provoked the act. Can these people be cited for accessory for their behavior?" I doubted that they could. The sheriff scratched his shoulder for a moment.

"Yeah, I can get them for inciting violence. Unlawful imprisonment is my first choice. Folks, move along now. I told you before you cannot block people coming in and out. Now, you can go home or I'll call for backup and pull you all in."

The leader again stated his rights to assemble and free speech.

The officer tried for a reasonable tone of voice yet his disgust with this group showed through his professional demeanor. "I told you last night that you do not have the right to trespass or to block this driveway."

We waited. After about a minute, the sheriff got on his radio and called for backup. He walked up to the leader, stepped behind him and handcuffed one hand. Things got a little exciting then. The leader still had his picket sign in one hand and swung it at the officer. The officer twisted away taking the blow on his shoulder. He pulled out his long flashlight and swung it at the picket sign, breaking the handle and knocking the thing out of the older man's hand. Both men kicked up a cloud of dirt as the picketer tried to hit the officer.

I ran around the back of my car to the police car, dove into the front seat, and grabbed his radio. "Help, an officer is being attacked. Help!" I didn't know really how to work the radio, but dispatch got the idea that someone attacked an officer, and an hysterical woman was calling for help.

One smart picketer threw down his sign and ran. The rest of the crowd stood silently watching the scuffle. The officer finally pulled the picket leader's other arm behind his back and handcuffed the struggling offender. I thought I heard more sirens. We were near an exit from the 303, so I hoped help was nearby.

The picket leader threatened lawsuits, and screamed, "My lawyer is going to rake you over the coals! When he gets done with you, you won't be able to get a job anywhere if you don't end up in jail yourself! My lawyer will get you!"

Another picketer asked me, "He can't really arrest Mr. Paulson, can he?"

I felt myself shaking. "Yes, he broke the law and now he's resisted arrest. Fortunately, Mr. Paulson is in serious trouble." I knew I sounded quite gleeful. "I am hoping that since you blocked the driveway and intimidated a senior citizen and are picketing someone who takes in children with disabilities that we can get you on some sort of hate-crime charges. I can assure you that your behavior does not fall into the loving-your-neighbor category."

"Okay, who's next?" The officer had managed to get the uncooperative Mr. Paulson into the back seat of the police car. He stepped forward with another pair of handcuffs. The rest of the people dropped their signs and ran. I saw police cars at both ends of the road now. The officer had back up.

With the driveway clear, I thought this might be a good time to mind my own business. "I think I'll take this food up to the house now before it gets any colder."

The officer was panting from his struggle with Mr. Paulson. "Yeah, thanks. Say was that kid really being bullied at school?"

I nodded. "Apparently it was pretty bad. Most of the kids I've talked with are facing up to the reality of the situation—better than these folks have."

Mr. Paulson continued to threaten and demand his release from the back seat of the sheriff's car. I got in my car and drove up to the house.

Mr. Cole answered the door. "What's happening out on the road?"

"The cops are arresting your picketers. They broke the law when they wouldn't let someone come in. Your dinner would have been here earlier if it wasn't for them. The leader attacked the officer so he is in deep trouble."

"My wife was so upset that I took the day off work to stay with her. Pastor, we are trying to help these kids. I know they have problems. We are sick over what Joel did. I would never have expected something like that out of him."

I nodded. "I talked to Joel last night. He seemed happy to have a pastoral visit. He obviously has had some church background. He struck me as a youth who would be okay in the right environment."

"Yeah, I thought he was a good kid. He has some mental problems."

I nodded. "Dr. Ralph Graham, a forensic psychologist, is working on the case. Would you be willing to talk to him?"

"Oh sure, my wife is the one who called his office. She knows how to get the services our kids need."

"Great! Dr. Graham will be in court with Joel Monday morning. He is trying to get him moved somewhere for evaluation and plans on spending the rest of the day in Blackfish."

"Thanks I'll talk to him there. What does he look like?"

I felt my face grow warm and a smile tugged at my mouth as I gave the basics about Ralph's appearance then I turned to leave, but paused. "Say, when the dust settles a bit, both you and your wife are welcome to come in and talk."

"Thanks, my wife might need another woman to talk to."

"I'm available."

In the car on the way home I thought about inviting the Coles over to talk. I didn't have the same anxiety about feeling inadequate as I had in the morning. I realized that all my anxiety about not knowing anything, or about saying or doing the wrong thing was gone. I wondered why. I thought about it for several minutes before I remembered Ralph thanking me for helping. He treated me as a partner. I wasn't alone in my efforts. He assured me that I said the right things. I thought to myself, "Well, this is interesting. I get a little feedback and I feel much, much better. I'm too isolated."

I thought about what Dr. Dave said about nourishing myself and recognized his wisdom. I needed relationships outside of my parish. I thought again and realized I needed relationships outside of my family. I began to suspect that I felt so vulnerable to Ralph's attractiveness because I didn't have friendships outside of my work. Peace washed over me when I reached this conclusion.

I felt as if I really could solve my problems for several minutes. Then, I started thinking about my own dinner. What I really wanted was a nice cheese sauce over toast. I remembered Jean had thrown out my bread. I thought about stopping at the store for more bread and felt frustrated because it would be fresh and would not make the same kind of toast that I wanted. My good feelings left me. I felt tired beyond belief. I knew I needed food, but I didn't want to take the effort to stop at the grocery store and then go home and make cheese sauce. I just wanted to lie down and never get up.

I drove straight to Timmy's. When I walked in, the hostess greeted me by name. "We have a special table for you. We set it up special so you don't have to sit in the bar. Is your boyfriend with you?"

"Thank you for the table." I felt better. "No, Ralph lives in Seattle. He went home."

The hostess leered. "He's very good looking for a man of his age."

I smiled. "Honey, he's good looking for a man of any age." The hostess led me to a small table just perfect for one.

Timmy came out to say hi. "I thought you might be in tonight. Where is that big boyfriend of yours? Oh boy, does Joey have some tough competition! Although from what I hear, Joey has been locked out, rolled up, and left in the cold. Do you have a wedding date?"

I held my head for a few seconds. "What? What on earth? Where did you get such an idea?"

"Oh don't play coy with me. Everybody in town knows you looked at the Thompson house together today. I heard about talk of a wedding up at the country club."

"Oh for pity's sake! I am a pastor. I perform weddings. I'm doing one next week for a couple with a house in Oak Ridge. Look, I've only dated Ralph once. He is here to work on this case—doing an evaluation on Joel Giddens and helping me work with the school kids." Fortunately, Timmy got called away on business, so I looked at the menu mourning my loss of the cheese sauce over toast.

I finally ordered a ling cod and potato dinner and sat staring at a painting on the wall done by a local artist. The perspective was off, yet I found it strangely beguiling in a modern art sort of way. I wondered if the artist intended this effect.

A strange man suddenly came to stand over my table. He twisted his napkin in his hands. "Pastor Maude, I'm Frank DeRosa, I want to thank you for giving the kids a chance to talk. My son has trouble in school, and I know he gets picked on. When I stopped at the church to pick him up, I was real pleased to see him working side by side with the guys from the football team. My son is a good worker. Maybe those boys could see that he should be respected. That boyfriend of yours is a good man. You marry him and make him live here in Blackfish. We can use more people like him around."

Timmy's wife arrived with my dinner. "Oh, yeah, he's a keeper. I heard about him. Who'd have thought that our quiet little pastor would show up with a man like that? You better marry him right away honey." She set my dinner in front of me.

By this time, speech eluded me. I mumbled my thanks for the complements, but had no idea how to respond to the comments about Ralph. I wondered if I should warn Ralph. I could call him. I wouldn't know what to say and he might think me pushy or angling for a commitment.

Timmy's wife said in a voice that carried through the restaurant. "See that, we mention him, and she drifts off into delightful daydreams."

I laughed. "I was wondering if I should warn him about you people." I picked up my fork hoping my company would take that as a sign to go away. They did.

Joey came in and spotted me almost immediately. "Hey Maude what is this I hear about you being engaged? If you are taken you should have told me." He came in, pulled a chair from the table next to me with a flourish and sat down blocking the aisle. I thought the rest of the diners were getting a real floorshow. I'd never noticed Joey's theatric gestures before. His bearing and the way he turned his vowels made my dining-out even more like a stage play.

I tried to sound sincere. "Joey, I am not engaged. I am not even really dating Ralph, other than the Hawks game. He is here to help with the incident at the high school."

Joey grinned. "Then there is still hope for me?"

I sighed. "No. You are too close to a member of my congregation for me to even think about dating. It would be outside the rules of pastor/parish relations."

"What do I have to do about that? Stop coming to church when I am here."

I held my head. "Oh for pity's sake. Joey, I'm exhausted. I've been working long hours doing things that are personally very hard for me. I just want to eat my dinner in peace. Go away."

Joey's voice softened. "Yeah, I heard about all that. I'm sorry. I can't say I admire anybody more than I do you right now."

"Thank you." I silently praised God when Joey went to sit at the bar. The dinner tasted excellent. The fish was fresh. The sour cream dill sauce added an excellent delicate touch. I knew the fresh vegetables came from a local farm. I ate and focused on my excellent dinner for three minutes.

Another total stranger accosted me. "Hey, pastor, I hear you called the cops on the picketers out at the Coles. Why did you do that? They were within their rights."

Oh dear, I set my fork down and explained. "They broke the law when they blocked one of the members of my church from entering the property. What they were doing was hateful and really part of the problem that led to the whole incident. The Coles are good people trying to do something to help challenged children. She seems to know what she is about. The problem, as I see it, is that she needs more support from the community rather than the prejudice and bigotry displayed by her neighbors."

The stranger sounded offended after publicly interrupting my dinner. "Hey, don't preach at me."

I snapped back. "Then don't interrupt my dinner."

The restaurant went deathly silent. Yup, my dinner out furnished the best live entertainment the town had seen since the senior class play last spring. I needed to buy some groceries and do some serious cooking so I could eat at home. The other diners had just resumed their conversations when the real estate agent who showed us the Thompson house walked in. I eyed the pillar across the table from me and wondered if I could move my chair around so I would be less visible. How did everybody see me among the crowd, anyway?

Lester, the agent called from across the room, "Hey Pastor, where is that nice man of yours."

I wanted to sink into my shoes. "He lives in Seattle. He went home."

Lester continued to approach my table. "Listen, if you are interested in the house, I called the owner. I think they might be willing to deal."

"Thank you, I am thinking about it. I want my daddy to look at it."

"What does Ralph think? He seemed knowledgeable."

"Ralph and I have been too busy to talk about anything other than business." I used a crisp tone that I hoped redefined our relationship as business.

Another voice interrupted, "Woo hoo, honey, you better hold on to that one. If you don't want him, I'd be happy to keep him warm at night." I recognized the new arrival as Mrs. Stevenson. Inspiration struck. I looked at the young hostess who was trying to get Mrs. Stevenson to move along. I couldn't remember her name, but she wore a name-tag.

"Darlene, would you go get Joey Miller, the guy with the curly hair at the bar, and seat him with Mrs. Stevenson."

Darlene giggled.

"No, I'm serious. Joey is fun company. I'm not going to think of dating him because of pastor/parish relations, but he'd like to meet someone to hang out with when he comes to check up on his mom." Darlene seated Mrs. Stevenson at a table and headed off to get Joey.

Other patrons dragged Joey out of his chair and shoved him toward the dining room. At this point, everybody in the restaurant laughed and gave me great round of applause. I couldn't help it. I stood and curtsied to my audience. I think I could have taken a few more curtain calls.

Joey sat with Mrs. Stevenson and acted charming. I finished my dinner. I decided not to wait for my check at the table and went up to the cash register. "How much is my bill?"

Timmy's wife met me. "You can't pay in here."

"What?"

"We can't let you pay for a meal."

"What? Of course I must pay. What do you mean?"

"We're so grateful, for what you are doing for Shelly--teaching her friends what they can do to help her and all that we can't charge you for a meal.'

"You can't afford to feed me for free."

"Here, I'll pay for her dinner." I didn't know the man behind me. "Most of us don't know what to do when something like this happens. I guess I can buy a dinner for the one person who knows what to do." He looked me in the eye and added, "This cannot be easy for you, even with that burly boyfriend to help."

Overwhelmed and humbled, I barely managed to choke out, "Thank you… thank you for the dinner and for understanding." I left before I started to cry. I didn't cry until I got to my bedroom where I could throw myself down on the bed and sob. I must be tired—exhausted. I realized that for the past two days I had been living through the worst part of my life. Apparently, everybody in town knew enough of my history to begin to suspect that my husband beat me. I wondered what to do about their assumptions about Ralph and I. I fell asleep crosswise of the bed with my clothes on. About one, I woke up enough to get undressed and crawl under the covers.

Chapter 15: Saturday

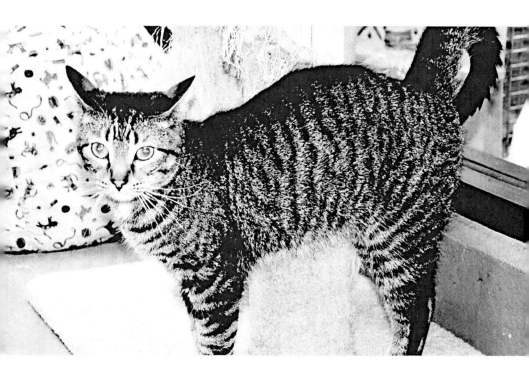

Saturday morning, I woke up wide-awake at five with a full-blown, heart-pounding anxiety attack. I had an appointment to perform a wedding out at Oak Ridge at seven! I ran into the shower and started shampooing my hair then I realized that the wedding was next Saturday. Surely, I wrote next Saturday on my calendar. Okay, I was up, in the shower, and had remembered the wedding. I would be okay even if the wedding was this morning.

Before I finished drying, I pulled on a robe and ran downstairs to my study. I found my appointment book. The wedding wasn't in there. Where had I left my notes on the wedding? I thought some more, and remembered that all my contact with the bride and groom had been at the church. I paused for a moment and thanked God that my hidden congregation showed up at the church for business and never contacted me at home. They never emptied my refrigerator. They said thank you and bought dinner for me.

I walked across the parking lot in my robe and slippers to check my notes in my office. I wondered how many people would see me and comment on me being out in my robe and slippers. I let myself into my office and found my note in a folder in the top drawer of my desk. I sat down and looked at the date for the wedding. Something still seemed off, so I tried to reconstruct my past week. I calculated and recalculated but always came up with the answer that everything I'd done since Wednesday had really happened in the space of three days. I went back to my house feeling relieved. I went upstairs to get dressed and flopped back down on my bed on my back. I think I stared mindlessly at the ceiling while thoughts free-floated through my head. I might have dozed off because at seven I felt much more rested.

While I waited for my coffee to brew, I decided to make waffles for breakfast since I didn't have bread for toast. Before the coffee was ready John Wesley joined me, crying loudly for my attention. He yowled and pranced around his food dish. "Oh sweetie, are you hungry? Do you want some gooshy food?" I hoped Jean had not thrown out my cat food. John Wesley yowled louder. This was strange behavior so I investigated. As I moved closer and looked in his dish, I discovered that John Wesley had caught his own breakfast. He pranced around his dish acting immensely proud of himself. He had the plumpest sleekest dead mouse that I had ever seen. "Oh, you caught a mouse. Oh, you are a mighty hunter. You protected me, and all my stale food from a horrid mouse. You are a mighty hunter and the best cat ever. You're the only male I need in my life. That is a very impressive mouse."

I petted John Wesley while praising him and debated whether or not my life was turning into a horror story with dead animals in the kitchen. I decided to wrap the dead mouse in a paper towel and put it out in the garbage can in the garage. While I tried to get a paper towel without the door to the cupboard under the sink falling off, John Wesley disposed of his kill in three crunchy bites. I went back to making myself some waffles.

I ate my breakfast in the dining room, such as it was. The small room had a small window that looked out on the brambles of the field next door. I could also look at the dreary kitchen or the dark living room. My elegant velvet sectional overpowered the room and looked drab. I thought about the Thompson house. I wondered how to pay for it.

At eight-thirty I called my parents. Mom answered first and told me all about the quilt she was making. It sounded fun. I wondered about going back to quilt making. I told Mom about my renters and the house I looked at. She had some good advice about what to look for in a house. Her thoughts were much the same as mine. If you buy a house that needs a little work, you can have it fixed to your own taste rather than living with someone else's ideas of what is nice. "Don't get granite counter tops if you can help it. You have to keep it treated or it will stain. Delores has a great big ugly stain by her sink. It's not worth the money you will spend."

"This house needs new counter tops. I might go with a resin or a good reliable laminate. I've always lived with laminate. It lasts forever and does the job economically." My father came home from his walk at this point and Mom turned the phone over to him saying that I was thinking of buying a house. He had a thousand questions. We talked about how I might pay for it by taking a mortgage on my Seattle house. Finally, he and Mom agreed to drive up and look at the house with me.

I planned to call the real estate agent at a decent hour, but he called me almost as soon as I got off of the phone with my parents. "Have you thought any more about the house on Oak Lake? I talked to the owners and they are willing to bargain."

I thought about me being willing to bargain with my renters by raising the price just for them. I felt wary of bargains. "My parents are driving up this afternoon. I wanted to make an appointment to see it about one. I don't think it's time to harass the sellers quite yet. I don't have financing lined up. I don't know how much money I can borrow." The agent made more noises about the sellers being eager and about how solid the house was.

"I will need to do more research as to whether or not this is feasible for me. I need to research banks and loans. I want to have the house inspected and certainly find out everything I can about the septic system since it is so close to the lake." I got more information about grandfathered systems than I wanted to hear at this hour. I finally, got rid of the real estate agent and went to my study to review my sermon.

This sermon seemed to lack vitality. I tried to think of ways to make it better. I wondered what my congregation needed to know. I prayed. I didn't get any inspirations other than to include a description of what the word meditate meant in Hebrew. I thought the congregation might like the image of the lion sitting with his half eaten kill, just relaxing and letting lion thoughts float through his brain. I added a few more thoughts about the nature and power of words. There, I finished the thing. Perhaps, at times, I've done better, but for this Sunday, I was finished.

I looked at my calendar and noted our Annual Charge Conference written down for Tuesday. I got irritated over this. I needed to be here for the high school kids not running off to some meeting so the district superintendent could find out that my church was dying. I looked over my attendance and financial reports—not good.

I looked through the annual reports that had come in. Shirley's report had arrived promptly. She reported on how many meals her committee provided and how many cards they sent. She did not have any projections for next year other than to say they would continue as they had in the past. I didn't have a report from missions. My lay leader had not turned in his report. I called him. "Hi, this is Pastor Maude. I am calling about the Charge Conference Tuesday."

"I know it is Tuesday. Are you driving? I don't see so good after dark."

"Of course I will drive. Do you have your report done?"

"No, I don't have it done. I would have it done if you were not so busy running here and there."

"Oh…um…uh…Is there anything you need help with?"

"Yes, how many kids have you and that boyfriend of yours talked to?"

"I don't know. The man you are referring to is Dr. Ralph Graham. He is a forensic psychologist working on the problems with this incident. He is not my boyfriend. Um…as for how many kids we've worked with so far. I don't know. I've spent time with…well…five…no six. I think Ralph talked to more, possibly a dozen. I've also spent time with a couple of the teachers closest to the students involved."

"I heard about you having those picketers out at the Coles' arrested. Picketing that family was a rotten thing to do. I hear Mrs. Paulson hasn't bailed her husband out yet."

"From what I saw of him, I don't blame her. He attacked an officer. She may not be able to bail him out yet."

"What is it that that fellow of yours does?"

I wasn't completely certain what forensic psychologists do, but I explained anyway. My parents arrived interrupting this call.

When my parents came in, Mom ran off to the restroom. Daddy gave me a good hug before he asked about the straw bales and the mess around the garage. I explained about the mud and the volunteers who came to fix it. Mom came back and told me my toilet wasn't working so I ran off to fix the finicky toilet. When I got back Daddy had gone outside to look at the mud problem. Mom and I joined him. Shortly before one, we drove out to Oak Lake Road to meet Lester.

Lester waved at us the minute we pulled up. I really wanted to take my parents around the house to see the lake first, but Lester wanted to enter through the front door. I had to laugh at Daddy compulsively turning and jiggling every door handle to see how they worked. He turned every light on and off several times. He opened and closed every cupboard and closet door. He played with the fireplace. Mom took her shoes off and walked the length and width of each room several times, promising that if anything was not level, her arthritic ankles would know. Daddy pulled out his measuring tape and measured halls, doorways and the garage. Lester seemed surprised that we thought both of my cars would fit in.

I finally got Mom to look out the window at the lake while Daddy inspected the attic. I was explaining that the dock came with the property when Lester started an alarming conversation with Daddy. "Her boyfriend looked the place over yesterday and seemed to know what he was doing." I could tell Daddy was trying for more information and pretending he knew more than he did.

"Which one?"

"Big guy, bald head."

"Oh yeah, that's Ralph."

Mom stopped listening to me talk about fish and ducks, and tuned into the conversation coming from the attic. Daddy wanted more information about Ralph. "What did he think about the place?"

"He asked about the wiring and septic system. I think he liked it. He asked good questions. He seemed to approve of the purchase."

I snorted and said to Mom, "Ralph and I didn't really talk about the house. We just stopped to look before another appointment. He kept Lester out of my way so I could look around."

When Daddy came down from the attic he announced in a tone of triumphal glee, "The attic has paper wasps." He looked at Mom whose eyes glistened as she smiled back happily.

I wondered what Lester thought of my parents' obvious joy over paper wasps. I knew full well that talk of Ralph had brought smiles to their faces.

Lester blithered on about how the sellers would immediately have an exterminator out to deal with the wasps.

I suggested we walk down to the lake. Today, I noticed a little footpath that seemed to follow the edge of the lake. I asked Lester about it.

"Yes there is an easement here so that people can walk all the way around the lake."

"So I could not fence this area off, but I could walk all the way around the lake myself. How far is it?"

"About two and a half miles."

"Does the public have access to the lake?"

"There is a boat ramp further up."

"Does the public use the trail?"

"No. Only members of the homeowners association."

Daddy asked more questions about the HOA and the easement. I stood on my dock and let the beauty and peace of my surroundings calm my soul. We walked around the property some more. Lester talked.

When we reached the cars I told Lester that I would call him when I had done some more research. He tried to set a firm date. "I don't know. Tuesday night I have a big meeting for the church. When I am done with that, I can do some research. I suppose I can call you Thursday. That is the soonest I can deal with this." We left with the sounds of Lester's pleading and promises in our ears.

"It's a well-built home. I'm sure you'll like it." Daddy knew me much better than Lester.

"Won't it be fun to have family picnics out here. The kids can swim in the lake." Mom knew me as well as Daddy.

"I hope I can get the financing together to move-in before Christmas. I'll need a contractor right away. I want the kitchen counters done."

"Why don't you put in new cabinets?"

"Why? Those seem solid. I like them. I might paint them and change the pulls." We continued to discuss repairs and remodels on the drive home. Mom and Daddy dropped me at the parsonage and headed home before it got dark. I spent a quiet evening looking at quilting books and mentally planning my move.

Chapter 16: Sunday

Sunday morning the wind blustered around the church and parsonage. I hoped that the sheets of rain did not make the mud situation worse. I saw some sign of water coming around the garage, but wasn't alarmed.

Before worship I usually took my place early and sat down for a quiet moment of prayer that consisted of begging and pleading with God to help me remember everything during worship. Pastors often forget parts of the service. I hadn't done so yet, but it was one of my greater fears. I used recorded music for the prelude. When I stood up for the invocation, I got a shock that almost knocked me out of the pulpit. I had a new person in church. Mrs. Stevenson sat next to Joey. They looked smug and happy, which was nothing compared to how I felt.

I did my best with the service. I wished I could use recorded accompaniment for the hymns, but the congregation didn't like that. They wanted me to play the piano. The best I could do was try to bring the reality of Gods love as close as possible.

After the service, Joey and Christine Stevenson thanked me for the wonderful service and for introducing them. They drifted away on a happy cloud. I looked at them and thought that I was not in love with Ralph. I knew I didn't look at Ralph the way Christine was looking at Joey. I knew when I was with Ralph the world was not so rosy that I would think the worship service I'd just participated in was that wonderful. Ah love.

As part of coffee hour we held a congregational dinner to discuss the Charge Conference. When I asked my lay leader if he'd finished his report, he snapped that it would not be done until Tuesday because he had to keep changing it. I wondered, "What on earth?"

After the congregational meeting we held a short pastor parish meeting. "Pastor what is this about you getting married and moving out to Oak Lake? We shouldn't have to learn this stuff at the grocery store."

"Then I suggest that you don't believe the stuff you hear at the grocery store. It is mostly rubbish. I asked Ralph Graham to help me with the school kids. He was in the area on other business so he agreed. We had lunch at the country club. I think the talk of marriage got started when I met the bride I'm marrying Saturday, and she told me how the wedding is coming together. I'm not marrying Ralph Graham or anybody else." I'd tried for an outraged tone with a hint of poor widow. I knew I was on trickier ground with the Oak Lake rumor. I hadn't done my research and secured financing so I didn't want to give the impression that more was settled. "As far as the Oak Lake rumor goes, I have looked at a house. I like it. I will have to do more research. Perhaps, I will buy it. Perhaps I will find a reason not to buy it. Please do not get excited over what you hear in the grocery store. If I decide to move, I will give you at least the same notice that I would give any landlord."

The committee refused to let me off so easy. The chair asked in a whiny voice, "Don't you like the house we provided for you?"

I don't know why I humored them. I sighed. "My renters want to buy my Seattle house. My problem is that clergy who have never owned a house are left financially insecure when they retire."

The chairman sat up straight, smiled and nodded. "Oh, so this is part of your retirement plan. Yes, a house will appreciate and is more secure than stock. You are never too young to be planning for retirement. Now, if you need to buy something for your retirement, we will be happy to look it over for you." The committee members looked at each other and nodded sagely.

I had a meeting with my bride and groom at four on Sunday afternoon. At three, I returned to my office and went over the information I had for the Charge Conference. It looked bad. The financial report worried me because I could not see how the congregation could continue to pay my salary. I wasn't sure why I was not being shared between two or three congregations. I wondered, "Am I foolish to even think of buying a house here? Could the bishop find me another congregation within commuting distance? Should I supplement my income by substituting at the public school as I had in Othello?" I'd decided I wanted to stay here, but would the district and the bishop allow this church to stay open? I continued to worry until my couple arrived.

We spent a delightful hour and a half going over their wedding plans. As I got to know them, I became more comfortable with their relationship. They had some good, solid values. In some ways they seemed a little naïve. I recommended a couple books. We talked about budgeting. I tried to get across to them that money mismanagement was one of the biggest problems that destroy marriages. I showed them samples of budget planners. They listened carefully to everything I said, which scared me a little. What if what I said was wrong for them?

When they stood to leave, the bride, Cricket, hugged me and thanked me for taking so much time with them. "You are better than having a Mom."

Skunk added his thanks to that of his bride.

I wondered how I was going to manage to conduct a wedding for Cricket and Skunk with a straight face. "Oh, one more thing, do you want to use your nicknames or your legal names during the ceremony."

Cricket explained, "Um...uh...our legal names are Cricket and Skunk. That's kind of how we met. We were both getting our drivers licenses at the same time. The clerk who waited on him gave him a bad time about nobody legally naming their child Skunk. I felt so bad because I got in trouble over the Cricket thing so often."

I felt embarrassed. "Forgive me for my misunderstanding."

Skunk shrugged, "It's okay, everybody asks. I got used to being called Skunk. It's my name and I never got teased or called worse things."

I grinned, "That works. Have a good evening you two. It is going to be a lovely wedding." Yup, I would need to say, "Do you Skunk take Cricket..."

As soon as the bride and groom-to-be left, I locked the church and walked back across the parking lot. I decided to drive the Porsche into the hospital. I found the whole Perry family spending Sunday evening with Shelly. As soon as I entered the room, I heard their news. "The doctor thinks Shelly will be well enough to come home tomorrow."

"That is good news. I think everybody in Blackfish will be happy to hear how well you are doing. You're doing a great job of getting well."

"What about the bastard who hurt her? Will he be happy she's getting well?" The youngest Perry child shocked everybody with his question.

I hardly knew what to say.

Alex said, "You watch your mouth young man."

I decided to lie. "Joel Giddens will be very happy to hear that she is getting well. He is not right in his head. He got angry, and he attacked the first person he could find. He will not be in Blackfish. He's in jail, but yes, he will be happy to hear she is getting well."

I didn't wish to intrude further on the Perry's family time. I left after only ten minutes. I thought maybe I would go downstairs and see if Joel was still in the building. I never made it down to see Joel. Dr. Davis saw me in the hall.

"Pastor Maude." I stopped and waited for the doctor to catch up to me. "I've heard rumors that you are friends with Dr. Graham."

"Yes." I wanted to say more, but Dr. Davies was not acting coy like everyone else who mentioned Ralph.

"Can you get some information to him before tomorrow morning?"

"Sure. Just a minute." I pulled out my cell phone and dialed Ralph. He answered on the first ring. I explained, "Hi I have information you need to know before tomorrow morning. Here is Dr. Davis. I handed the phone off to Dr. Davis who explained about Joel's medication levels being way off. He said "Yes" a couple times, recited some numbers and passed the phone back to me.

Ralph asked, "How do you do that?"

"What?"

"Get information out of all the most important people. This will make a huge difference tomorrow. I'll let you go. Thanks." Ralph hung up. I went on home.

Chapter 17: Monday

John Wesley woke me up Monday morning. I wanted nothing more than to spend the day in bed, but I had chores to do. I found some stale raisin bran for breakfast. The last of my milk tasted a little bitter. I ate the breakfast and moved going to the grocery store to the top of my priorities. I also needed to visit a bank.

I drove into Silverdale and surveyed the banks in town. The dismal choices included Bank of America, Chase, and Wells Fargo. I started with the Wells Fargo bank. When the loan officer learned that I might not need a loan, she became impatient. "Here are some brochures that explain the process. You can come back when you are ready to get a loan."

I went next door to Bank of America. The loan officer acted much nicer. I remained vague about how much money I would need. I didn't want to commit just yet. She told me more about the process of buying a home.

After the bank, I went to Trader Joes. I bought some fresh fruit and vegetables. I wandered the aisles thinking about what I wanted to eat. I bought some day old bread for toast. I found a selection of cheeses. I spent an hour in the store reading labels, looking for fair trade items and things without corn or soy. I am opposed to supporting the Monsanto Company.

By the time I got home and put away my groceries, I needed to go to the church to meet the students. Candy and the rest of the cheerleaders came. Ralph arrived just in time to change roles and ask me to work with the special ed kids and he would take the cheerleaders. My session went okay. The students got off topic talking about Dr. Who and Firefly. I talked to them about the fact that having brain damage or a learning disability does not mean you are a failure or will fail. I talked about everybody having trouble controlling their anger and what they could do when being teased. I felt I preached more than counseled.

Finally, the kids went home and Ralph stopped by my office to say goodnight. "Maudy, I think I'll run for the ferry now. I had a good session. Hey babe, you look tired. He came the rest of the way into my *office. You need to go home and get some rest. " He stroked the side of my face with his finger and looked into my eyes. "You are a very special lady." He kissed me lightly on the end of my nose.*

"Thank you. I am tired." I leaned closer to him and he pulled me into a hug. I rested my head on his shoulder. It felt unbelievably good to be held in his arms.

"Pastor Maude, how many kids did you talk to today? Did we send out more meals? Remember you are not supposed to be doing that." Larry Bruce, my lay leader interrupted our hug. Larry's last remark referred to me resting my head on Ralph's shoulder.

Jean followed her husband into my office. "Never mind that. Did you know that you bought day old bread? I fed it to the ducks in your back yard."

I knew that I should step away from Ralph but his arms held me tight. I wanted to stay in his warm embrace. Instead I struggled away from his security and warmth. The struggle to free myself caused me to wake up.

I opened my eyes and stared into the darkness trying to remember what day it was. I struggled to separate dream from reality. I had a horrible feeling that the part about Trader Joes was a dream, and I would have to go grocery shopping tomorrow. In my dream I had spent so much time and energy shopping that I hated to have to do it again for real.

I could still feel the warmth of Ralph's arm around me. I tried to puzzle out my confusion for a moment until I realized John Wesley was sleeping across me. I sighed, shoved John Wesley off of me, and curled up in a ball, feeling confused and sad.

Chapter 18: Community Action

When I got up for real on Monday morning, I remembered that on my day off I'd promised to meet students in the afternoon. "Perhaps nobody will come." As I showered, I realized that my dream had at least planned out my day. I spent several pleasant minutes thinking about whether or not I wanted Ralph to hug me. I recognized the problems of getting a hug anywhere within ten miles of Blackfish.

I did go to the bank, and remembering my dream, I remained vague on the exact numbers question and asked lots of questions about inspections. At the end of the interview, I explained my circumstances. The loan officer looked up how much it would cost to get a loan on my Seattle house until it sold. She explained that I couldn't qualify for a loan on the lake house without a huge down payment, because of my low income. I left feeling discouraged about the costs of getting a loan. I didn't want to spend that much of my only asset just so I could buy a house sooner. I resolved to stay in the parsonage until I had the cash from my Seattle house.

My trip to Trader Joes turned out to be much less stressful than in my dream. I know what brands I like. I realized that I rather looked forward to having some fresh food. I thought about the quality of my life as a pastor. I couldn't qualify for a mortgage because my income was too low. I was getting excited over buying fresh food. Then, I remembered that I had been eating most of my meals at Timmy's. I also remembered that I had not paid for those meals. I decided that my life was pretty darn good because people are good.

Ralph called shortly after I got home. "Maudy, hi. We just got out of court. It went real well. They are transferring Joel over to the psych unit at Swedish. I'll evaluate him there when he recovers from his injuries and his meds are balanced."

"You mean he is still showing symptoms from his injuries?"

"It's not bad, but his liver enzymes were still off enough that I think the situation might influence the validity of my test results."

"So you think the information from Dr. Davies made a difference?"

"Yes! It gives us enough to hope for a better outcome for this young man. I can't tell you how much I appreciate you putting him through to me."

"It was nothing on my part. He wanted you to know."

"That's what I love about you. Without trying, you manage to put all the right people together to make good things happen."

When I got off of the phone, I felt shaken to the core. Ralph had not said he loved me. He said he loved something about me. That came close enough for my poor heart and soul. Stunned and shaken, I went to my living room, sat down and tried to think. I took slow shallow breaths. I closed my eyes. I relaxed my arms and legs. I asked God to help me be sensible. I'm not certain that I heard God's answer. I thought and remembered Dr. Dave telling me not to harbor negative thoughts. All the things I wanted to tell myself to dismiss Ralph's words were negative thoughts. Ralph said something that meant that he approved of me—of my behavior. I could accept approval. There, I could accept Ralph's words as a sign of approval. I continued my breathing exercises and fell asleep on my sofa.

The doorbell woke me up. I jumped up without thinking. A quick glance at the clock told me that it was only a few minutes past one. I hadn't slept long. I opened the door.

Ralph stood on my porch holding two cups of coffee. "I woke you up."

"Yeah, thanks. I would hate to miss my appointments this afternoon."

"I must be psychic. I picked up a coffee for you when I came through town. It's a mocha."

I smiled and something inside me melted. Ralph remembered how I like my coffee. I took the offered coffee as Ralph came through the door. I motioned toward the sofa and said, "Sit." I tasted my coffee. "This is good. Where did you find this?"

"The little kiosk in the IGA parking lot."

"Oh? I would never have guessed they had something so good." We continued to sit and chat about unimportant things. I felt more energized by the companionship than by the coffee. I wondered if I was awake or asleep. Ralph was sitting at least five feet away on the other leg of my sectional sofa. I must be awake.

He asked, "How are you coming on your house purchase?"

"Not very good. I don't make enough money to qualify for a loan so I have to wait for my Seattle house to sell. I haven't even solidified an offer on the lake house. I do have some idea of what inspections are needed. I need to find a contractor."

"I thought you planned to wait until your Seattle house sold, anyway."

"Well, yes, then I fell in love with the lake house. I worry that I'm not thinking of everything I need to know before buying." The phone rang.

"Pastor Maude, why did you schedule a big meeting at the church and not tell the trustees?" Alva Brinks whined at me.

"I'm not aware of any big meeting at the church. When is this supposed to happen?"

"Right after school lets out."

"Oh, that's nothing. I've been meeting with about five of Shelly Perry's friends to talk about their issues with the attack." I looked at Ralph. "Dr. Graham has met with about a dozen boys to talk about the same thing."

"No. That is not what this is about. There is a big meeting today."

"Um…where did you hear about this?"

"Elaine at IGA told me, first. When I went to the hardware store everybody there told me they were coming. They're shutting down the hardware store so everybody can come to the meeting."

"Oh for pity's sakes. Mr. Brinks, I didn't call a meeting. It is my day off. I was napping on my sofa. Um…let me call Timmy, and see if he heard anything. People could have decided to show up here without notice." I got off the phone and told Ralph the story. He laughed and enjoyed the whole story as if it was a play. I teased, "If you think this is amusing, I should tell you about dinner at Timmy's. I could have had three curtain calls the other night." The sound of Ralph's laugher in my house made my toes want to curl.

I called Timmy. He hadn't heard anything about a meeting so I didn't worry. This time, the Timmy's Locker news source failed me. There was a meeting. Ralph and I walked over to the church about two-thirty. We decided that I would take Joel's friends, and he would take the other students. Our plans proved to be useless. I later thought we should have spent the time before the meeting kissing, since that is what everybody in town thought we had been doing anyway.

Shortly before three, the special education students arrived in a group. The girl who liked Joel huddled in the middle of the group. Three other girls lagged behind the other seven students. "Oh welcome. I'm so glad to see you. Please come in."

"My parents are coming. They want to talk to you because the jocks call me a retard." I saw ten other heads nodding up and down.

"Um…sure…that is a good idea. They will be welcome. We will

need to use a bigger room." I prepared to lead the students into the boardroom. A couple parents came through the door and held it open for another group of girls I'd never seen before. Fortunately, Ralph moved quickly to hold the door and got a good look into the parking lot.

"Maude, what is the biggest room you have?"

"Oh...oh...Oh! Um." By now about thirty people had gathered in the hall outside my office. "Um...please come with me to the social hall." I led them back to the door and around the corner to the left and into the social hall. More people poured through the door. I thought I spotted Alva Brinks. "Um...Alva?" He hobbled up to me, looking important. "Can you put some coffee on? This is looking bigger than I expected." I invited my waiting parents and students to sit down at the tables that are always set up for coffee.

Another wave of parents and students surged through the door. I tried to collect my wits and pretend I knew what was happening or was in charge. "We need more chairs." Jean appeared before me out of the mess of people filing into the social hall. I turned to her. "Help, we need more chairs and a greeter to get people to sit down." Without my supervision, someone found the extra chairs and the students formed an amiable bucket line to pass chairs from the supply closet to the parents who set them up. By three-fifteen I estimated that about one hundred-fifty people filled our social hall. I looked around for the fire chief. I worried about being over capacity. While I was occupied with greeting and getting people settled, Ralph started talking to people and organizing. He took charge of the meeting.

"Right, from what I understand, you folks are here because you want to do something about the teasing and bullying at the school." I heard a few angry responses among the general affirmations. I looked toward the door when some latecomers arrived. I tried to slip quietly to the back of the room to greet the Coles and seat them where they could make a hasty exit to my office.

Ralph continued. "Since you are here, I assume you don't want your children involved as perpetrators or victims."

"Is Joel Giddens really going to be set free?"

Ralph remained calm. He sounded almost bored. "Probably not, I will be evaluating him to determine appropriate placement when he recovers from his injuries. I very much doubt that he will return to Blackfish." I thought I heard a collective sigh of relief. I noticed Jean and Larry Bruce edging through the crowd to set out cups, coffee and plates of cookies. Shirley stayed out in the kitchen. They made me so proud of them at that moment. There is something about sharing a meal—even coffee and cookies—that brings people together with a sense of community.

I looked the situation over and decided to let Ralph lead the meeting for now. I would stand in the back of the room near the Coles and silently ask God what she thought she was doing now, and would he please give me some guidance, and thank her for the way my congregation silently passed out food. "You know, God, I have no idea how to handle this situation, but with your help I am willing to love these people. They are really being amazing. They want to be good parents. Look how they are trying to solve this problem. Can you be with them and give them the inspiration to solve this problem?"

The meeting went well. At one point, I found a large tablet of paper so the parents could write down their action plan. It surprised me when part of that plan included drafting me to talk to the students about the feelings that cause them to bully other students.

The football team came with their coach. The football players insisted that they should take the lead in treating others with respect. The student body president suggested that the students make a non-bullying pact. I wasn't too sure how that would really work out.

The parents wanted to monitor the halls. They made a plan to approach the district superintendent and make the proposal at the next school board meeting. The only member of the school board present opposed the plan because of the insurance liability of having parents on the premises. At this point, I talked about the need for background checks on all adults who are on the school ground as volunteers. Mrs. Muller and the cheerleaders had some concrete ideas of things they could do to solve the problem. I saw workable suggestions offered. I saw adults taking responsibility, and adults and students working together to solve a problem.

I sat down quietly on the edge of the crowd. "You know God, this is going pretty good. I see some good community here. What I don't see are the teachers and school administration. Is that going to be a problem? These kids are talking about red slips for people who break the no-bullying rule. Um…is that going to work? Help us walk the line between teaching awareness and punishment. Help us to teach without judgment." I wondered what people would think if they knew I was praying. "Oh, and please guide me in how to make your love real to those who have suffered spiritual abuse."

The meeting adjourned at five. The student body president took a copy of the action plan with him to post on the student bulletin board the next day. I felt exhausted. I thought maybe Ralph was tired. I asked,

"How are you doing?"

His sigh sounded weary.

I tried to sound encouraging. "You did a great job with the meeting. You kept it from descending into a gripe and whine fest."

The Bruces interrupted us to say goodnight and tell me Alva Brinks and Elma Miller were cleaning up and would lock up. I nodded, "Thanks." I rubbed my aching back.

Ralph continued our conversation. "Yeah, that was pretty amazing. I've never seen anything like it. I wonder if something like that could happen in the city? Say, I'm starving. Can we get something to eat before I get on the ferry? I need something more than ferry food."

"I have tons of food in my house, but it would take some time to cook. Timmy's Locker is just a block and a half. The food is good, and there is plenty of it. The biggest problem is the floor show."

Ralph sounded half amused. "What? They have a restaurant with a floor show in a town this small? What is it Country Western?"

"No. It is called The Love Life of Pastor Maude."

He chuckled. "This I have to see. Come on." We walked over to the restaurant. I hoped that everybody would be appropriate. The noise of a large crowd hit us when we walked in. Roberta met us at the door and prepared to seat me. Her eyes grew big when she looked at Ralph. She asked us to wait while she checked on a table.

She came back almost immediately. "All right, your table is ready. It's a little small for two, but I don't think you'll mind." She giggled.

I rolled my eyes, and Ralph looked clueless. Actually, dinner went reasonably well, all considered. People stared. Two parents came over to our table to thank Ralph for spending time with the boys.

He answered warmly. "Oh, hey, I enjoyed it. I don't usually get to have this much fun when I am working. The kids were great—all of them."

Aside from watching Ralph and I as we ate, nobody said anything embarrassing.

Ralph became a little unsettled when he found out that we couldn't pay for our dinner, but he accepted the gift with good grace when he learned that people had taken a collection to pay for our meals at Timmy's. We walked back to the parsonage in the dark. He took my hand. "I see what you mean about being the floor show. I think eyes followed every bite I took."

"I thought they were remarkably good tonight, but then perhaps our performance was a bit tame. There is not much excitement to be had out of watching two tired, hungry people eat."

When we reached my door Ralph took both of my shoulders in his hands. I almost panicked wondering what he intended to do. He squeezed my shoulders gently with his fingers. It felt good. "Goodnight Maudy. Thanks for all your help. You did a good job here, which made my job easier." Then he dropped his hands and turned to leave.

"Thanks for the encouraging words. Goodnight." I turned and unlocked my door while Ralph walked away. I fumbled with the lock, but managed to get the door open and get inside to my sofa before my knees gave out.

I crashed onto my sofa and wondered what was wrong with me. Was I disappointed that Ralph didn't kiss me? Was I afraid that he would? A tear escaped my eye. Did I even want a romantic relationship with Ralph? What did I want? I wanted my next appointment with Dr. Dave to be better than my last. I wanted to talk to someone about Ralph. "Well, God, what do you think? I have no idea what to think about Ralph. Do you think I should have a relationship with Ralph? Um…how far would that go? I think he's attractive, but I…well…I… um. I'm not ready to marry him. I'm not sure that if I have a romantic relationship with him…well…I'm afraid…I might…but I'm not supposed to do that." As I drifted off to sleep, I though that perhaps I had been alone long enough.

CHAPTER 19: CHARGE CONFERENCE

Tuesday morning didn't dawn. The day remained dark and dreary. I woke up still on my sofa and instantly remembered that I had fallen asleep after dinner without brushing my teeth. "Ewwwwww!" I almost ran for my bathroom and my toothbrush. I hopped into the shower then remembered that I had Charge Conference this afternoon. Small churches like Blackfish did not warrant the honor of a visit from the district superintendent. I'd have to drive into Tacoma.

As soon as I got to my office, I called my lay leader. "Larry, hi, this is Pastor Maude. I thought I'd go over the schedule for the Charge Conference. I think if we leave here at three, we can get there soon enough. I think the whole process is supposed to run until about eight tonight. My idea is to get there early enough to listen to the report before ours, give our report, maybe listen to the people after us and leave. I think they are serving a soup dinner. Do you want to stay for dinner?"

"Well, yes, we should stay for dinner."

My heart sank. I didn't really feel like socializing after reporting how much trouble we were in. I knew others were in exactly the same position. I didn't want to hear their woes. I wasn't excited to hear about how well other churches in richer, bigger communities were doing. I inherited the problems in Blackfish, but I didn't want either sympathy or judgment. I reluctantly agreed. "I suppose we can stay. I'm taking my big car so driving the freeways in the dark won't be a problem. It looks as if it may rain hard later in the day."

"Yes, I hear a pineapple express is supposed to blow in about four."

"Charming. I hope the freeway doesn't flood at Gig Harbor."

"Oh they got that fixed."

"Is your report ready?"

"Jean is typing it up. I can add more notes on the drive down."

"Oh…uh…um…I guess. Do you want me to pick you up at your house at three or do you want to meet at the church."

"I don't see well enough after dark to drive home in the rain. Better pick me up about two forty-five then we can pick up Alva on our way out of town. Shirley said she could help you out by meeting you here."

Oh dear, I hadn't expected Alva to want to go.

"Just a minute Pastor. What was that?" I wondered if I'd just spoken my thoughts out loud. "Oh okay, I'll tell her. Jean says she is coming with us too."

"Ah...right...um...so that will make five in my Sentra." Larry sounded quite cheerful just before we ended the call. My heart sank and I wanted to hold my head. I didn't want more people than absolutely necessary to witness our dismal report. I just felt generally grumpy. I didn't want to drive four elderly people through the rain to Tacoma to announce to another group of people that the church was dying, then sit and smile and chat through a dinner only to turn around and drive back through a downpour. I wondered if I would feel so grumpy if Ralph had kissed me last night. I smiled. The little increase in my heart rate told me that, no, I wouldn't feel so grumpy if Ralph had kissed me. I thought a few seconds and admitted that I would feel stark terror if he had kissed me. I checked my calendar for my next appointment with Dr. Dave.

The wind came up about two. I texted the students to remind them not to come over this afternoon. I also warned them that it was not safe to be walking around outside. Douglas Firs have a nasty habit of dropping bits and pieces of themselves during windstorms. I hoped it would be safe to drive. I spent five minutes wondering if I could cancel due to wind. I finally decided that if we cancelled, we would just have to face this meeting later.

The day continued to be dark. I turned on the Sentra's headlights when I left the church. I grumbled about it being too dark to see safely at two in the afternoon. The first raindrops hit my car at two forty-five when I pulled into Larry's driveway. By the time I picked up Alva, the rain hit the pavement briskly.

The real deluge held off until just before I reached Bremerton. The sky opened up and poured water. My wipers could not begin to keep up with the rain. I crept through the dark hoping that I didn't run into a stalled car in front of me or that some fool who thought he could see didn't run into the back of me. I debated which lane was the least flooded. Every muscle in my body tensed as I guided my car though the downpour.

"Oh, this feels just like driving through a waterfall." Shirley sounded delighted with the experience. I spared half a second to wonder if Shirley was senile.

"Yep, I haven't seen it rain this hard for maybe ten years. Remember when Pine Creek flooded into the IGA?" For the next few minutes my passengers cheerfully argued over which year Pine Creek flooded the

IGA.

When I reached Highway 16, a new horror added to the challenge of finding the road. Large trucks began to pass me as I struggled along in the right hand lane. They threw more water onto my windshield. They threw up a wake of wind and water that knocked my Sentra sideways. I wondered if I could just get off of the freeway and have a good cry.

My passengers had stopped discussing the rain and moved on to an animated reminiscence of a pinochle game. I thought, "They could at least pray." I was too busy trying to stay on the road to do anything other than think, "Oh God. Oh God. Oh God." Perhaps that was prayer enough. I saw taillights in front of me. I gauged my distance as best I could and followed the lights. At about Purdy, I thought perhaps the rain let up a little. I figured we would still get about six inches of rain in an hour, but it seemed a little lighter. I tried to relax.

By the time we reached the Narrows Bridge, we had outrun the worst of the rain, but the high wind warnings were posted for the bridge. I made it over the bridge with nothing worse than the car shuddering constantly, and realizing that I was steering into the wind and needed to correct at the towers so that I didn't drive off of the bridge and plunge two hundred sixty feet to a watery grave. We arrived at the meeting later than I originally expected.

The district superintendent greeted us, "Oh there you are. I was sure you would cancel because of the wind and rain."

Shirley answered cheerfully, "Oh no, we didn't have any trouble. Pastor Maude is a good driver. She took it a little slow, but we didn't have any trouble."

Our host pastor speculated, "Maybe it isn't raining as hard up where you are."

I grumped. "I think it is lighter here." The meeting continued while I sat and shivered from nerves. We took a short restroom break before my congregation presented their reports.

I still don't know what to think about those reports. At first I debated on the necessity of a sermon series on bearing false witness. At some point, I drifted into a surreal twilight zone as my members gave their reports.

Shirley started our reports. "The care committee has served two-hundred sixteen meals. This fall we combined with the mission committee to start an outreach program to serve the rest of the community by bringing meals to un-churched families in need."

I sat up and looked at Shirley. Huh? That sounded okay.

Alva gave his report next. "The trustees are opening our buildings to more community events. We recently sponsored a community forum to create a plan to stop bullying in the schools and throughout the community. We have opened the buildings for youth activities and school related meetings."

Huh? What?

Jean gave a short financial report. "The financial committee reports a budget surplus this fall."

I thought, "Oh. My. Goodness. Am I going to get paid?"

Jean continued. "We've had a seventy percent increase in contributions earmarked for salaries, missions, and community ministry."

Ah, I wondered who gave us a couple hundred dollars?

After Shirley, Jean's and Alva's reports, I should have been prepared for Larry. "We have sixteen youth meeting with Pastor Maude. We've been expanding our ministries through volunteer opportunities for the constituent congregation."

I wasn't sure what that meant.

"The volunteers have met with the youth, worked on the parsonage landscape and assisted with the meals program."

I wondered what Elaine would think of being called a constituent. I remembered the man who paid for my dinner at Timmy's. He must be a constituent too. I wanted to hold my head.

Larry continued, "The church is taking the lead in the community to deal with the problems with our youth. One hundred fifty-six constituents attended the meeting on bullying. At the request of those parents, Pastor Maude has specific plans for starting Sunday School classes for school children. We plan to hold the same classes mid-week for children who have sports conflicts Sunday morning."

I tried to figure out if we were really doing as good as we sounded or if Jean, Shirley, Alva and Larry were part of the senile fifty-percent of my congregation.

Larry hadn't finished his report. "Sunday worship is increasing with two middle aged professional people attending regularly."

Wha…Oh. Joel and Christine. I felt numb from nerves and shock when the meeting took a break for dinner.

I needed the soup and bread. I think the district superintendent gave me a sideways hug and congratulated me on how we were doing in Blackfish. I smiled vaguely at the lay people and found a seat near another pastor. I knew the conference was talking about combining her church with two others. She said, "It is good to hear you are growing out there, but then suburban churches are growing. It is the city churches that are struggling."

I grumbled back. "We're all struggling. Let's face it. Most churches have not adapted their schedules and worship to meet the needs of contemporary communities. Apparently, some children do not attend Sunday School because they have soccer practice on Sunday. I'm told that is due to a shortage of play fields. Anyway, Blackfish is a small community. We may still go under. I wouldn't be surprised if we do."

From behind me I heard Jean's voice, "Yes, she is very busy. She doesn't have time to cook or shop for herself. I try to help out by throwing out her food that is past the pull date so she doesn't get sick. Our local restaurant owner has made it his ministry to see she gets healthy meals whenever she will stop to eat." I thought perhaps I needed to do a sermon on words like ministry and mission. I wondered what I would call Timmy's kindness to me about my bill. I smiled. I'd call it love.

Shortly after seven, with the rain still blowing in sideways in great sheets, I herded my congregation's representatives out the door. I almost hated to drag them away from the meeting early. They were having so much fun—out of touch with reality, but they were having fun. Before we left for home, someone announced that we had gotten sixteen inches since the rain started at two. I knew I needed to be careful to look for water on the roadway.

I finally made it home shortly after nine. I'd made one detour for water on the freeway and one for a down tree on Blackfish road. The second detour proved to be the most challenging because Pine Creek flooded over the road at one point, but I could avoid it by driving through parking lots and over the curb to get back on the road.

I ached all over as I started to get ready for bed. I still felt grumpy so I decided to wake up my cat. "Well, John Wesley, I hope you had a warm snug evening." He opened one eye and gazed at me from the bed where he was sleeping wedged between two pillows. "I'm glad that is over. Who on earth came up with this ridiculous idea for charge conferences?" John Wesley purred.

Chapter 20: Pineapple Express

After the charge conference, I thought my life would return to some sort of quiet, normal routine. On Wednesday, I called the Perry's. Shelly had started getting up and dressed. Her speech continued to improve between morning and night. She confessed to needing a nap.

I met with a group of students after school. I hadn't met two of the girls. They didn't know Shelly well but wanted to talk about being snubbed. Candy and Stan came. Three of Joel's friends came. I wanted to check to see if Larry was lurking around a corner counting to see how many students came to my youth group today.

Shortly after the students arrived, Elma knocked on the door and asked to come in. She wheeled in a kitchen cart with cookies, cut-up fruit and a half-gallon of fruit punch. I hadn't expected this, but the students cleaned up the snacks in a manner that gratified Elma. I wondered why I ever thought that there was something wrong with my congregation. We settled down to talk about the student's issues.

One of Joel's friends complained bitterly. "I got tagged for bullying today. That's not fair."

"Why not?"

"Because that's only supposed to be for popular kids." This produced a general outcry from the other students that the tagging was for everybody who bullied others.

Mary, the girl who had a crush on Joel spoke up. "I know….um… uh…let me say this." I liked the way the whole group waited for her to try to say what she had trouble getting out. "No…you popular…you and Sandy…and…and…and red…um."

"Darin with the red hair?"

"Uh huh…uh…and Darin…are friends. I…no…don't have any friends. I've never been to a birthday party. I eat lunch by myself… uh…"

Candy reached over and patted Mary's hand. "You can eat lunch with me. You're okay. She's right, if you want to say the rule is only for popular kids then you are popular in a way because you have friends you hang out with. If you broke the rules, you deserve to be tagged the same as anybody else."

I decided to referee. "Candy and Mary are right. If you break the no bullying rule, you should be tagged. This is not about being punished. It's about reminding you to treat others as you want them to treat you."

After the students left, I spent an hour going over what I would include on a class on how to prevent bullying. I reviewed my material on mirror neurons and decided to include it as a demonstration of how you hurt yourself when you hurt others. I made myself a healthy stir-fry for dinner and read a trashy novel until bedtime.

On Thursday morning my dream of a peaceful routine got delayed for weeks to come. John Wesley alerted me to the first problem. When I got out of the shower he was sitting on the windowsill between the blinds and the window. He yowled fit to bring the curtains down.

"What is it sweetie? Is there a dog in the yard? Is it a squirrel?" He stuck his head through the blinds and looked at me with disgust written clearly on his furry face. "Oh okay, I'll come look. Don't mess with the blinds." He started having a battle with the blinds as he tried to free his head. I disengaged my cat from the blinds and pulled them up enough for me to look out. My back yard had turned into a lake or rather a wide stream. From the second floor I could see that the drainage ditch and straw bales failed to contain the water that poured out of the vacant lot and ran through my back yard. I knew it must be coming around and into the garage. I prepared to run downstairs and make certain the electrical cords for the Porsche were not in water.

I spent the next two hours protecting my cars and house from the water that was flowing in from the vacant lot and from Blackfish road. The church sat on slightly higher ground so I moved the Porsche up there and parked it on the covered sidewalk leading to the building. I knew that I would be in trouble with the trustees, but perhaps they wouldn't come out in this miserable weather to discover that I used the sidewalk as a carport. The sturdy Sentra had to brave the storm and flood in the parking lot.

I was soaked through and had ruined my walking shoes by the time I got into the Sentra to go to the hardware store. I had no idea what I was looking for. I thought maybe I needed sand bags. The hardware store was crowded with people stocking up for a power outage. Everybody wanted to hear the story of my flood. They suggested tarps, duct tape, batteries, bottled propane, flashlights and a good supply of food. I was reasonably prepared for a disaster so I wandered the store looking for inspiration. Finally, I found the thing I needed most--boots. I found ugly black knee-high rubber boots—how exciting!

Back at my office, I made a few phone calls to the county about my water problem. Nobody expressed interest in one more story of flooding. They took my name and location, and said they might have a crew out in a day or two. I pulled on my new boots and went outside to explore the river of water coming off of Blackfish road. I walked a half block before I found the source of the water. It came bubbling up out of the storm drain almost like a small fountain. I looked around and saw the truck of a construction company parked down by Timmy's. I went back and called them and explained about the problem and my theory that something was blocked up somewhere. "I know. I already called the county. They are swamped and may not get here until tomorrow or Saturday. This sounds like a small problem to them. You can't work in this wet mess. I wondered if perhaps some of your workers could look for the source of the problem and see if it is easily fixed. I'm afraid we are going to loose the parsonage if this gets any worse. What is happening at the IGA?"

The contractor grunted, "I'll see if anybody wants to go out, but it isn't our job to fix this."

"I know it isn't, but you are part of the community."

"I'll see what I can do." He grunted.

I didn't know it, but I'd just furnished the male population of Blackfish with the most fun they had had in ages.

I checked my messages and found one from my real estate agent asking me to call immediately. I called. "Hi, this is Maude Henderson. I got a message that you wanted me to call."

The receptionist transferred me immediately to my agent. "Maude, I think I have good news for you."

I wandered out toward the doors to watch the growing flood in the parking lot.

"Your renters have made a cash offer. They can close early next week. I think it is a great offer—no contingencies."

"How much?"

"Maude, you know the market is not good. Nobody is selling houses this time of year. Even in the spring you may not get an offer this good."

The renters were making a low offer. The flood in the parking lot was growing. I wondered if I could even get back into the parsonage. I wondered if straw bales outside the garage door would keep the garage from flooding. I asked the agent again, "How much?"

"It is a good offer Maude. They cashed out their 401K's and she has a small inheritance. They are putting everything they've got into this. For this reason they don't want a mortgage."

"How much?"

"Maude, I'm serious that you really need to accept this offer. It's five hundred eighteen thousand. It is a good offer. I know it is not what you wanted, but this time of year in a shaky market it is a good offer. They're not asking anything from you."

"Okay…um…what do I have to do? I am flooded in so I can't come to Seattle to sign papers today. Can you FAX the offer to the church and I'll FAX it back?"

"You will? Oh, thank you. You won't regret this Maude. It is a wise decision." I thought the water in the parking lot was starting to creep toward the covered sidewalk and my Porsche. I watched the water swirling around the Sentra, almost up to its doors. I wondered if I could find higher ground for the Sentra.

The voice on the phone remained oblivious to my immediate problems. "What is your FAX number there? I can FAX the offer over for your signature right now."

I went back to my office as I recited the FAX number for the church.

She repeated it back to me. "Oh Maude, your renters will be so happy. This will mean a lot to them. Do you need to hang up before I hit send?"

"No."

"Good, now you will have to furnish them with proof of clear title. There will be excise tax and my commission is five percent since I'm representing both parties."

I must have been in shock at this point. The FAX machine came to life, and I watched as the papers came through. The agent issued more instructions, but I didn't understand them. I was selling my house on the hill in Seattle while a flood engulfed me in Blackfish.

The voice on the phone asked, "Do you have the papers? I marked the place where you sign with an X. Just sign your name and send them right back to me."

"Oh, okay, I can read them and send them back within ten minutes if the power doesn't go out."

"I'll stay on the line and go over them with you. They're pretty straight forward the first paragraph…" She did stay on the line and talk about each line of the offer. I probably made the correct noises because she seemed to think I knew what I was doing. "Okay, now sign where I marked that with an X and put the papers back in your FAX machine." Perhaps she did know that I wasn't functioning at full capacity. She was talking to me as if I were a small child. I vaguely recognized that this might be appropriate. I was selling my house in Seattle for fifty thousand dollars less than I really wanted. My heart pounded as I put the papers back in the machine punched in the agent's FAX number and hit send.

As I waded back to the parsonage, I tried to rationalize that the difference between my asking price and my selling price was not as big as it seemed because of the lower commission, and I didn't need to do any repairs, and I wouldn't be paying taxes and insurance. I'd just sold the last link to my husband, Hal. I amended that thought to exclude my children. They would always be a link to Hal, but a good link. The house was a dark memory.

I entered the parsonage to find water creeping under the door from the garage and spreading across the kitchen floor. I didn't know if shoving a towel up against the door would help, but I thought it worth a try. I found my cotton picnic blanket and shoved it tightly up to the bottom of the door. I spent the next half hour moving everything I could up from floor level. While I was busy with moving stuff up from the floor, the power went out.

By one o'clock, I felt cold, tired and hungry. I wondered if Timmy had a generator. I tried calling and reached a message saying the restaurant was closed while he dealt with a personal problem. I pulled on my boots and waded back to the church carrying a carton of homemade soup to warm up on the church's gas stove.

As I ate my lunch alone in the church social hall, I decided to call

Daddy. Nobody answered at my parents' house. I left a message for my daughter, Patty and tried to reach my son, Trevor. I wondered if my children would be upset that I sold the home where they had their only memories of their father. He had been a good father—an excellent father, until he wasn't. I called Ralph.

He sounded cheerful. "Hi, are you okay? We have flooding everywhere over here."

"How can there be flooding in a city that is all hills?"

"The cross streets are full of water from higher up. Fifth and Denny is a mess with a stopped up storm drain. The biggest problem is that the storm drains are full of debris."

"That may be our problem out here. I have water on the kitchen floor in the parsonage and Blackfish road is flooded from a storm drain that is flowing backward onto the road. The church parking lot is awash with about eight inches of water."

"Are you okay?"

"Well, I'm dry, sort of. The power is out. I suppose things will get cold soon. On top of all of this I accepted an offer on my Seattle house."

"Good."

"I'm not sure it was good. They offered fifty-thousand less than I was asking, but it was 'as is' and I know I would have needed to spend several thousand to get the house in show condition."

"Maudy, any reasonable offer is good right now. I think it will be good for you to get rid of the thing. I can hear the distress in your voice every time you mention that house. Now, you can buy your lake place." I think at this moment an elephant of anxiety got up and walked out of my life. I was rid of that house. I was free to buy something I loved.

"Oh, I'm so glad I called you. I do feel better to be rid of the thing. Yes, I think I will buy the lake house." We went on to talk about when I expected to close and how soon I could move.

"I know, when you come over to sign escrow papers, let me know. If I can clear my schedule, we'll go out for lunch or dinner and celebrate."

"Oh what a wonderful idea! You might be the only person who will celebrate with me. Daddy has always insisted the house was a great investment. My children have good memories of the house. Yes. I do want to celebrate. I have good memories of the place, but that is my past and I want to live in my present."

"Good, I'll think up someplace fun for either lunch or dinner." Ralph's voice sounded warm and enthusiastic.

I hung up quite pleased with the fact that I was rid of my Seattle house, and I had a date with Ralph.

I looked at the clock and mentally outlined the rest of my day. I needed to work on my sermon. I wasn't expecting students to show up before three, if they braved the floods at all. As soon as I got off of the phone, I heard voices in the hall. "Hey it smells good in here. I'm hungry." I greeted two boys. I hadn't met the one who declared himself hungry.

"I think there is some leftover soup. I can get more from my house. Why are you out of school?"

"They let us out early because the power is out. Who's Porsche is that parked out there?"

"Mine…Oh dear…is it flooding at the school too?"

"The parking lot is full of water. See I got my pants wet." He dripped seriously. "We were supposed to go home, but nobody is there and the power is out so I wanted to stay in town and see what is happening." I divided the soup between the two boys. The hungry one, Darin, looked a little disappointed.

I thought out loud more than talking to the boys, "You know, Timmy's is closed. I think I should make up some more soup in case people can't get something hot anywhere else."

"Great. We'll go over to the IGA and get some bread and something for salad." The boys bolted for the door before I could ask them if they had enough money. I left the church unlocked while I waded down to my house and emptied my refrigerator. I carried my laundry basket full of food back to the church--so much for stocking up. When I got back to the church, I headed for the kitchen.

"Pastor Maude is that you? The door was unlocked so we came in. We were supposed to go home, but the buses can't come down this street and we were supposed to walk, but it's too wet. What are you doing?" Candy came around the corner from my office with about eight other students including one I took to be about first grade.

I looked at the youngest. "How old are you?"

"Seven."

I asked slightly horrified, "Did the school really release first graders to walk half-way home in this mess?"

Eight heads nodded.

"Oh dear. That wasn't the wisest choice. Listen, can one of you come out this other door and watch for other students and tell them they can come in. The rest of you come with me to the kitchen. We'll make some hot soup."

We made soup. Candy invited some children in. We worried about a couple younger children who were determined to wade home. I gave the kids in the church my cell phone to call their parents and tell them where they were, and why, and what they were doing.

"Hallooo, Pastor Maude? Are you here?" I left the kitchen to see a couple men--total strangers carrying children on their shoulders. The kids were soaking and shivering.

"The kitchen is warm, bring them in here."

"They were trying to walk home, but Blackfish road is totally blocked off below Timmy's. The water is running way too fast for them to try to wade."

The littlest one cried loudly and hiccoughed. The other boy wailed. "We were told to go straight home."

"Come into the kitchen. You can call your parents and get something hot to eat." I looked at the rescuers. Tears of terror filled my eyes. I felt an anxiety attack coming on. I tried to stay focused on the present danger. "Apparently, the school let the children out because the power was off. I'm concerned because the parents may be at work and not realize their children are walking home in a flood." I think my voice rose with near hysteria. "Some children may be locked out and they won't have electricity if they do get home."

One of the men pulled out his cell phone and called the fire department relaying my concerns. Both men left promising to look for more children. I called Candy in from the front porch. Four more high school students had joined her. We were becoming quite crowded in the kitchen. We were warm enough and the students started steaming as their clothes began to dry. I put water on to boil for hot cocoa. I remembered to ask God to bless the person who installed the huge, eight burner, gas stove in the church kitchen. The thing was ugly and hard to clean. Right now it was keeping us warm and heating food for a crowd.

Another voice called, "Hey where is everybody?"

Joel's friends came in with a sobbing, soaking-wet Mary. She didn't have a coat and was soaked to the skin. "What happened to you?"

One of the boys answered, "Our bus got stuck in the water in the dip by Timmy's, so we had to get out and walk."

I was horrified at Mary's condition. "Candy, can you take Mary over to the parsonage. Go upstairs to my bedroom and find her some dry clothes to put on. Get her one of my coats too. Oh, and, there are towels in the bathroom. She needs to dry off."

The boy who was speaking for the group sounded quite thrilled about Mary's mishap. "Yeah, she tripped and fell and the water went all the way over her head. We had to pull her back up or she would have drowned."

Candy took Mary by the hand and led her off toward the parsonage. I returned to my cooking duties, "Okay, who is ready for hot cocoa?"

They all wanted the cocoa. The kitchen had gotten hot enough that I opened the doors into the social hall and had the children sit at tables as I served cocoa. I'd found boxed soup in the church kitchen that I heated up while my homemade soup cooked. I started sweating from the high humidity in the church kitchen.

"Oh hi Pastor. We heard on the radio that you were running a shelter here." I was so thrilled to see Shirley with Larry and Jean that tears filled my eyes. I explained about the flooding and school being let out.

Jean scolded, "You're not feeding them anything past its pull date are you?"

I sighed, "Thanks for coming. The adult/student ratio here was getting a little skewed. I'm making more soup. I wonder if I need to make some sort of bread?" The afternoon continued. Twice, firemen brought in wet children who had been unable to get home. A man with a high, four-wheel drive truck brought over ten children who had sheltered in the hardware store. I'd never seen him before, but he stayed to help. Shirley knew her way around the church kitchen. She took responsibility for opening the freezer door and pulled out cookies and bread.

"I like your cat. What's his name?" Mary returned wearing several layers of my clothing. It fit too tight, but at least it was dry except around her ankles and feet where she had waded back to the church.

I made it a point to make time for Mary. "His name is John Wesley. What was he doing?"

"Sleeping, I petted him and he purred."

Candy informed me, "Pastor, there is water all over your kitchen floor."

"Oh dear, that can't be helped."

"Hey everybody! Guess what! We found the problem with the water." Our newcomers, Cary and Andrew, grabbed everybody's attention. "We climbed down into the gully where Pine Creek comes under the road. The bottom half of the culvert is blocked up with a landslide. Some water is getting through so it looks okay from up above." The boys looked triumphant and muddy.

Daren and Bill who'd left for the IGA an hour and a half earlier returned with five more boys, all soaking wet. They carried wet grocery bags filled with groceries. I estimated about two hundred dollars worth of food was soaking in those bags. Shirley greedily took charge of the food as soon as I ushered the boys into the kitchen to get warmed up.

My grocery messengers were excited about their adventure and talked loudly. Daren began the story of their adventure. "Yeah, we had to come around the long way because the intersection between Timmy's and the IGA is about five feet deep now."

Bill disagreed. "No, you idiot, it's only about three feet deep."

The adventurers who had found the blocked culvert talked equally loud, "That's because the culvert under Blackfish road is blocked up. We climbed down there."

One of the seventh graders told Bill, "You're tagged for calling him an idiot."

Daren argued, "Nah ha, it is way more than three feet deep because it was over the scotch broom on the corner."

I lost track of who said what as the boys argued about the depth of the water at the intersection. I tried to distract them from their argument. "Have some hot chocolate and get warmed up."

Bill wasn't giving up the argument. "Yeah, but the scotch broom is downhill from the rest of the intersection so it is not that deep right at the intersection."

I interrupted the argument again. "Who paid for the groceries? Did you charge them?"

Bill answered, "Mr. Stanley said they were free."

Daren explained, "He was the one who told us to come back through the alley."

Bill bounced in his chair. His voice grew louder and higher. "The alley was blocked with a school bus so we climbed over the bus."

I became frantic, "Were there children in the bus?"

Daren's eyes danced as he loudly answered, "Yeah, the driver had walked out for help."

I looked around helplessly and spotted one of the firemen drinking hot coffee and eating a sandwich. Praise Shirley for thinking of coffee for workers.

I decided to organize the youth. "Four of you at a time may go to the kitchen and make sandwiches. When you have made up one loaf of bread into sandwiches, come out and four more can go make sandwiches." I hoped taking turns working in the steamy kitchen would give all the children a chance to keep warm. I approached the fireman. "The older boys tell me that there is a school bus full of children in the alley between here and the IGA. They will be dry enough, but I worry about them getting too cold.

My fireman didn't answer me. He got on his radio and relayed the information to dispatch.

The man with the four-wheel drive truck got up and headed for the door. "If some of you bigger guys are warm, come with me."

I saw Larry sitting in the corner talking on a cell phone. I wondered what happened to my phone and went to search for it. I finally found out that Larry was using my phone. The kitchen soon grew roaring hot with all the burners on the stove being used. Shirley was doing something in both ovens. I opened both doors into the social hall. All the windows in the kitchen ran with steam and the ones in the social hall quickly fogged over. The room was growing dark. I went in search of emergency lighting. When I came out of the supply room, I noticed more adults had arrived. I recognized Lester, the real estate agent. "Lester when you get a chance, write up an offer for the house on Oak Lake for…" here I paused and used a lesson from my renters. "…for two-hundred eighteen thousand, as is, closing to be in two weeks." I thought again as more wet people surged through the door. "Um, that is unless Oak Lake is over its banks and creeping into my kitchen."

"Oh no, Oak Lake never floods. It overflows into Oak slough, which has acres of wetlands. It would take much more than this little bit of rain for Oak Lake to overflow." Lester exaggerated.

I surveyed the situation in the social hall. We had food. We had enough adults to help out. Forty children from the school bus poured through the door. They had firemen with them. Four children came from the kitchen with sandwiches and four more ran in the other door giggling. The children were starting to get rowdy. I knew how to put a stop to that. I stood at the end of the room and bellowed in my best stage voice, "Have. You. Done. Your. Homework?" The room grew quiet except for some moans and groans.

The four-wheel drive man said, "Okay kids you heard her. Get to it." The students obeyed. They had enough parents to help. I slipped off to my office. I thought I should pray. I couldn't think of a thing to say to God. I sat and stared at the wall without a thought in my head. Finally, the rising tide of voices in the social hall recalled me to my duties. I left my cold office for the steamy heat of the social hall.

Daren called out to me. "Hey Pastor Maude, come watch. They have a backhoe on Blackfish road and are going to try to open the culvert." I looked outside to find the world dripping but not really raining. I thought a walk might be a good idea. I looked at the people inside. Adults sat visiting with each other. Some students were still doing schoolwork. Larry directed a group of younger children as they put tablecloths on the tables.

A fireman said, "Go ahead Pastor, you were the one who suggested someone local can do the job."

Cary begged. "It should be cool to watch how much water shoots out of the culvert when the slide is cleared." I went back to my office for my coat and changed back into my boots. As I walked down the sidewalk, I saw a woman wading toward the church with a huge roasting pan in her hands. I hoped she carried food. Two to three inches of water flowed down the sidewalk at the church. I found it a challenge to wade in the swirling water because I couldn't see bumps and cracks in the sidewalk.

"Be careful Pastor, we are at the curb. Step down." I smiled at the considerate warning. We crossed the intersection at the alley. In the ambient light, I could see the school bus wedged between a fence and a tree. As we passed the dark Timmy's Locker, I saw that only a tithe of the population of Blackfish had found its way to the church. Everybody else had gone to the intersection.

People stood in the water watching as the construction company backhoe maneuvered for the best position. The backhoe driver planned to reach over the guardrail and try to dig out the slide at the culvert. Bright construction lights running on generators created a festive scene. The fire truck with its red lights flashing pumped water from the intersection back into Pine Creek's bed. On the far side of the intersection, I saw the street blocked both lanes with cars. Spectators sat on the hoods of the cars or stood in the back of trucks. The bright lights at the intersection blinded me, making it hard to look at the scene.

After several minutes, the backhoe operator seemed to think he was ready. He uncurled the backhoe and raised it up to go over the rail. I noticed the power lines above him and experienced a moment of anxiety, but he seemed to be aware of them, too. He slipped the bucket of the hoe between the rail and the lines. It seemed to take him forever before he had a load to bring up. Again he carefully maneuvered the bucket, now dripping mud, between the power line and the railing. He dumped his load of mud in a waiting dump truck. I watched as the load of mud slid and oozed out of the dump truck as if seeking to return to its comfy home in Pine Creek. The crowd waited silently as the backhoe went back for another load of mud. The second time the bucket came up, I could see bits of brush and debris among the mud.

For the third time, the operator eased the bucket and arm between the rail and power lines down to where he thought the end of the culvert must be. I watched as more mud oozed out of the dump truck and wondered if he made any progress. The cold and damp seeped through my layers of clothing. I thought I should get back to the church. It seemed a little insane to be standing in water up past my ankles, in the cold and dark, watching someone fishing with a backhoe for the end of a culvert. I watched as the operator seemed to be wiggling the bucket back and forth down in the gully. Suddenly, the backhoe tipped forward. I thought for sure it would fly over the rail. Next, it settled back, but the arm to the bucket flew upward and hit the power line creating a shower of sparks. As the backhoe settled back onto all four wheels it sent up a spray of muddy water that soaked everybody nearby. The wave of cold water slopped against my legs and splashed me up to mid thigh.

I heard a loud roaring as the water trapped in the culvert burst free. It shot straight out from the culvert, hitting the trees and brush on the far side of the ravine. With all the lights in the intersection reflecting back off of its muddy glory, the water leapt into the air to be dispersed among the branches of the trees overhead. The display lasted at least three minutes before the water stopped hitting the far side of the ravine with enough force to leap into the tree branches over head. The crowd around me cheered and honked car horns. I looked down and thought that perhaps the water around my feet was not so deep. I announced to the people nearest me, "Pass the word that there is hot coffee, soup and sandwiches at the Methodist Church."

I turned my back on the bright scene. I couldn't see well walking away from the lights. When I came to the curb at the alley, I knew the water was shallower because I could see the curb in the dark. I looked up the street toward the church with its stained glass windows glowing like a multicolored beacon in the dark. In that moment my heart ached for all the things that people have done, in the name of God and the church, that have turned people off to the beauty of Gods love, and the community of a church family. I thought to myself that surely the sin of erecting barriers between people and God's love is a far worse sin than the things that lonely, desperate people do in their search for love and community. I recognized that it has been the church leaders through the ages that are guilty of this sin. "Please God grant me the wisdom to know my own ignorance. Help me to make your love real to everyone I meet."

I returned to the church to find tables set for about a hundred people. The children and youth had started a dance and game of musical chairs in the hall outside my office. By running my laptop on battery power they had music for their game and dance. As the younger children lost their chairs, they joined the older students in the dance. I knew my computer battery would be drained soon, but maybe the parents would come to take their children home before long.

At nine-thirty, the last parent left with their child. I looked around and saw Elaine cleaning up. We'd used up all the church's china and started using plastic and paper. Elaine had a large garbage bag and wandered from table to table filling it with paper products.

"Oh, Elaine thank you for staying to help. Where are your children?"

"Oh they went to Mom's because they knew I was at work."

"Then you just came by to help out? Thank you."

"I wasn't going to leave you here alone with my boyfriend. He was too impressed with you."

I laughed. "Oh Elaine, I've been so busy since one o'clock, I haven't had time to notice anyone's boyfriend." She made several attempts to describe him.

"Wait a minute, does he drive a four-wheel truck? And he drove around town rescuing school kids?"

"Yeah, that's him." Elaine smiled.

I thought she'd found someone to love. "I think he is a good one. He was good with the kids."

Elaine smiled at me again and looked a little dreamy.

I said softly. "Hey, I don't poach."

We finished picking up the garbage. I looked in the kitchen. "There isn't much that can be done in here until the power comes back on for the dishwasher." We said goodnight. Elaine went home to her man, and I returned to the cold damp parsonage and a very unhappy John Wesley.

CHAPTER 21: COMMUNITY SHELTER

Friday morning I thought about going home to Mom and Daddy. I didn't have power so my house was cold, the kitchen floor was still wet, the garage was still flooded, and I didn't have any food in the house. Then I remembered that Timmy's was closed for a personal crisis.

I gave John Wesley a breakfast of canned food in my bedroom. I couldn't blame him for not wanting to walk on the kitchen floor. After dressing in the cold, I hiked through two inches of standing water to the Sentra and went looking for food and news. I found the IGA open. I bought bacon, milk, cocoa mix, and a pancake mix. The owner worked at the checkout.

I asked him about the bill from yesterday. "Hey, a couple boys came in here last night and got food for the people who came to the church for shelter. I want to see that you get paid."

"Oh no, that's okay. I wasn't sure they were really taking the food to the church, but they weren't getting the things kids want when they are on a food binge."

"It was a lot of food. I hate for you to be out the money."

"I hear you fed a lot of people last night."

"Only about two-hundred and fifty. I'm sure Larry Bruce will have an accurate head count."

"That is a lot of people."

"What is going on with Timmy?"

"His dad is in Harrison hospital and not expected to live. He had a massive stroke."

"Oh that is sad. Thanks for the information. I thought I might have to call all over town to find out what was happening. It must be hurting him financially to have the restaurant shut down."

"He might be accusing you of stealing his customers."

I pulled the hair away from my face. "I don't think we will want to go through another day like yesterday. What was the school admin thinking to let the school kids out early?"

"I haven't heard the whole story. Apparently, that is the policy if the power is out. They must send the kids home because they can't keep them warm."

I started working up to a good outrage. "It is a policy that doesn't make sense. I suppose it would be fine if the children had a parent at home, but most of the families in Blackfish are two income families. I suppose my congregation needs to make a policy that we will serve as a shelter anytime there is an emergency early release."

"I think most of the time, most children can make it home fine. The problem yesterday was the flood at the intersection. All the children east of the intersection couldn't get home. Is the school bus still stuck in the alley?"

"Yeah, I would have liked to use the alley to get here. The intersection is still muddy."

"The fire department spent half of the night cleaning that up."

I finished paying for my groceries and went back through the mud in the parking lot to my car. I wondered how long I was going to be wearing my black, rubber boots as a regular fashion item. Much to my surprise, the coffee Kiosk in the parking lot was operating on generator power. I got a nice, hot, mocha with whip and went back to the church.

I have no idea what was running through my head that I thought I could use the only gas stove in town to fix myself a solitary breakfast. When I entered the church kitchen Elma stood at the stove making scrambled eggs for herself and the grandkids.

"I have pancake mix."

She pointed with her spatula. "The griddle is in that cabinet."

And so, my day began. We were not as busy as yesterday. Most of my congregation arrived to get a hot meal. I left at ten in the morning to visit Timmy at the hospital.

Timmy has four brothers. They are all what I call beefy. They'd crowded into their father's hospital room. One brother gave me his chair. He didn't have much space to stand in. We talked about general things. The youngest of the boys had flown home from Alaska. I sat with them for about a half hour. I could tell from their father's breathing that he would be gone in a few hours.

"Timmy, I should get back to the church. Blackfish is a mess. The power is out, and you probably know the road flooded by your place last night."

"Yeah, I hear my entry hall had a couple inches of water. The wife is cleaning that up today. Hey don't run me out of business with your soup kitchen."

"Believe me, I have no intention of feeding all of Blackfish one moment longer than necessary. I hope the power comes back on soon."

The power did not come back on soon. When I got back to the church, I decided to do something about the phone system. All the church phones were on a system that needed electricity to run. I sloshed through the mud and standing water to the parsonage to get a regular telephone. John Wesley stood at the top of the stairs yowling at me. I felt sorry for him alone in the cold damp house. I took time to put him in his carrier and take him back to the church. It seemed to be marginally warmer in my office than in the parsonage. I thought the cat might be happier with me nearby.

I was hot enough by the time I had moved my desk to plug in the landline. I nearly jumped out of my skin when the phone started ringing in my hand. At first I thought it must be broken, but I answered anyway. "Pastor Maude."

My bishop identified himself. Until this moment I hadn't been sure he knew I existed. He continued, "I see on the news that your church is serving as the community shelter. How are you doing? Do you have what you need? I can get someone to bring over supplies from Bremerton."

I confessed, "I don't know how we are doing. I seem to be doing what needs to be done at any given moment, but I don't have a plan. Yes, I could use supplies. We have a gas stove in the kitchen, but our heat is off."

"What kind of heat do you have? Would it work if you had a generator for the fan?"

"It is a propane furnace, but I wouldn't have any idea how to plug in its fan."

"I'll see if I can find someone to help with that. Save all your bills and turn them in to the conference office. I just heard from Nashville that we can get some Committee On Relief funds. They are sending a team out to try to help out the churches like yours that have opened their doors."

Tears filled my eyes. I knew Nashville would not be involved for a minor power outage. "I admit that I am happy for any help I can get. I keep hoping that the power will be back on before help arrives.'

"It doesn't sound good. Chehalis is under water. I-5 is closed in four places. We have massive flooding in six counties. I'm afraid you are on your own until help arrives." After these encouraging words, the bishop assured me he was praying for us and hung up.

I hung up and turned around to see Lester at my office door with papers in his hand. "I had to type up your offer on my mom's old manual typewriter, but it is ready for you to sign. Are you sure you can't go higher than two eighteen? I left the amount blank. That is a lovely piece of property and worth more than you are offering."

"Yes, and I just sold a much bigger lovelier piece of property in Seattle for fifty-thousand less than I wanted. Those are the realities of this time of year and the market." Larry wrote in two hundred eighteen thousand and I signed the offer. After he left, I sat and held my head for a few minutes before I went to the kitchen to make soup.

In the early afternoon, the firemen started bringing elderly people to the church to get hot food. The first floor low-income apartments along Pine Creek had two inches of water on the floor. The apartments were cold, and the elderly residents had no way to cook. I ran back to the cold parsonage and brought back every blanket I owned. We served hot coffee and soup, but the people were still cold. One tiny frail woman sat and silently cried. I wanted to be reassuring, but I had no idea what I could say to her. "God, here I am again in the middle of something that I don't know how to handle. I don't know how or if we can heat this place. I am exhausted from cooking and cleaning up. These people are cold and I don't know how to warm them up. What am I doing here? Are you sure I shouldn't go back to teaching school? I know how to teach reading. This is beyond me."

I sat down beside the crying woman and held both of her tiny cold hands in mine. "Is there anything I can do for you?"

She could hardly speak above a whisper. "I never thought I would come to this—forced to eat charity food in a shelter. I always provided for others. I started cooking for my family when I was eleven. I cooked for my parents and the farm workers. I worked all my life, and I am forced to take charity." She paused and sobbed. "It isn't right. I married a good man. He worked hard and made good money working in the woods." Her breath came in shallow raspy gulps. I worried that she might be on the verge of pneumonia. "He bought me a nice house. We had five kids." She sat silent so long I thought she'd forgotten what she was going to say. "They didn't turn out good—worthless every one of them. They thought they were smarter than their parents." She paused to get her breath. I started becoming alarmed. "They got into drugs and alcohol. My youngest is in jail. Who would have thought that I'd end up in a shelter and my son is in prison." She sat and sighed. I passed her a box of tissues for her nose. "My cat ran off in the flood."

"Oh dear, I'm so sorry about your cat. My cat doesn't like having the house flooded either."

"Is your house flooded?"

"Yes, the first floor is soaked. I brought my cat over here. Would you like to hold him?" The woman nodded. I went off to my office where John Wesley scowled at me, totally disgusted with being in his crate. "Okay, big fellow, it is time for you to do some work around here." I opened the door of the crate and picked up the big animal. "I want you to come out here and comfort an old woman. Can you do that? Sure you can."

John Wesley did his job well. He gave the old woman a hug, so she wrapped her arms around him and fell asleep in the folding chair. John Wesley stayed at his post. I hoped he would help the woman warm up. I listened to her breathing and thought about her falling asleep in that uncomfortable chair. I pulled a chair to each side of her, in case she fell over. I stood and looked the situation over then I went back to my office and called the fire department.

"This is Pastor Maude. Can one of the paramedics come over to the shelter at the Methodist Church and check out an old woman. Her breathing doesn't sound good. I'm worried. She might need hospital care." I gave the dispatch all the information they needed then went back out and looked at the woman. She'd slumped over but still breathed audibly.

A commotion at the door distracted me from my fear for the old woman. Three men came in carrying boxes. I went to greet them. "I'm Pastor Maude."

"We're from Bremerton First. We have food, and emergency blankets and flood buckets." I wondered what a flood bucket was. I invited them in. Larry and Alva appeared from the supply closet. I wondered what they had been doing in there. Alva asked, "Do you have the generator?"

The men looked confused.

Alva explained, "We are supposed to get a generator. We are almost ready for it."

"No, no generator, just supplies." I started looking through the boxes. The first box contained food. The second box had the emergency blankets. These were the reflective type that would help hold in body heat.

"Thank you for the supplies. We need them. Can you take the food into the kitchen." I pulled one of the blankets out of its plastic packaging. One of the men showed me which side went in. He helped me wrap up the old woman. She woke up and startled John Wesley so he hopped down. She made a few sounds as we wrapped her up. I could see that the woman's ragged breathing distressed my assistant.

I was looking around me wondering, "What next?" when the paramedics came through the doors. I waved at them. They checked the woman's pulse and listened to her chest. I recognized their grim expressions as bad news. "There isn't much we can do here. Do you want us to transport?"

"Yeah, I think that would be best. I think a doctor should be in attendance if at all possible."

"I'm not sure she'll make it, but we'll do what we can." The EMT looked around. "This doesn't look like a bad place to go."

I smiled. "It is probably a very good place, but this woman--or at least her family, will need some medical opinion." It took some time for the EMTs to maneuver their stretcher into the social hall and transfer the frail body to the stretcher. I stood outside the door and watched as they loaded her in the ambulance and pulled away from the curb. I wanted to go to my office and pray.

Loud screams came from the kitchen. I rushed back into the social hall expecting to find dead bodies. I almost collided with John Wesley as he raced toward my office. He lost traction a little as he turned the corner, but he kept moving and ran into my office. I was irritated with the screaming person for scaring my cat. I detected sounds of agitation coming from the kitchen so I rushed in expecting to find that someone had been scalded. Mr. Cole stood at the sink laughing. Shirley held a large knife and looked as if she was debating whether or not it was safe to laugh. I didn't know the red woman who stood by the stove sputtering about something jumping right at her. "It was a wild animal. It attacked me. I was attacked by a wild animal."

"Oh dear, what color was it?"

The red woman's coloring began to fade to something more normal, but her eyes still bulged. "Grey with black beady eyes and big fangs." I suspected the grey part was correct.

"Are you hurt? Did it hurt you?"

Mr. Cole snorted, "It was a big grey cat, and he jumped on the countertop beside her."

"Ah, he's harmless and very social. I suppose he was attracted by the smell of food and came in to talk to you."

"Well….well…well."

I returned to my office. "John Wesley? Are you in here? Sweetie, were you scared?" I closed the door trusting that the cat was hiding under the furniture. I folded my arms on the desk and put my head down on my arms. "*God, are you here? I am sad about that old woman. Please take care of her.*" I fell asleep.

I woke up just a few minutes later when I thought a truck must be driving through the church. I heard a loud engine close to the building. I looked out my window, but didn't see anything. I went back out to the social hall to be surprised when the lights came on. We all cheered. I thought the electricity was back and everybody could go home. I soon learned that we had a generator.

Alva took me through the supply closet to the furnace room. I heard the wonderful sound of the furnace coming to life. He showed me the new electrical box that a local electrician installed for us and explained how we had one circuit for lights, one for the refrigerator and one for the furnace fan. What luxury!

More people arrived. The buckets crowded the entry hall. "Alva, what are all those buckets doing in the entry hall?"

"The people in Bremerton made those and brought them over. They're flood buckets."

"What on earth is a flood bucket?" I went to investigate. I found thirty-five five-gallon buckets. Each bucket contained bleach, cleaning solution, and dish soap, cleaning cloths, and sponges and rubber gloves—everything I needed to clean the parsonage. This gift overwhelmed me. I sat down on the floor and cried. Someone, who did not know me, put together this bucket of things I needed to clean up the mess in my house.

Shirley put her hand on my shoulder, "Um, Pastor, maybe you better go to your office and lie down."

I sniffed and tried to smile at Shirley. "Yeah, I think so. Say can you take one of these down to Timmy's? His wife is supposed to be cleaning up there. She might appreciate this. "

Shirley nodded. "I'll see that it gets done right away."

I picked up one of my comforters that had been discarded and went to my office. I curled up in my blanket on the too-short loveseat. John Wesley crawled out of his hiding place and snuggled up next to me. I slept.

I woke up when my cell phone in my pocket came to life. "Maudy? It's Ralph. How are you doing? Your church was mentioned on the news as a shelter in Kitsap County."

"Oh, you woke me up."

"Sorry."

"No that's okay. What I meant was that I have enough help that I was able to take a nap. I didn't sleep well last night because of the cold. John Wesley and I have set ourselves up in my office."

"Do I hear a generator running?"

"Yes, volunteers got that going sometime this afternoon. I think I am beginning to get warm."

"Are the kids tiring you out?"

"No. The kids aren't here today. Most of the people are elderly. The fire department evacuated the low-income housing and brought people here. Oh Ralph, I think one of the women was dying. Her breathing was raspy and she was so frail and cold."

"That must have been hard on you."

"Yeah, I called the EMTs and they transported her. I think that is really why I started crying and got sent to my room."

"Oh ho—the truth comes out. You got sent to your room. I thought perhaps you really do have enough sense of self-preservation to take a nap."

"What? Self-preservation? Where did you get the idea that I don't have a good sense of self-preservation?"

"From watching you work."

I felt sheepish, "Oh, I thought you'd been talking to Daddy."

Ralph chuckled. "Maudy, take care of yourself. Stay in your office as much as you need. Running a shelter is a huge responsibility, and your congregation is too old to be much help."

"Oh but, this is a wonderful volunteer opportunity for my constituent congregation." I giggled. "Did I tell you about our meeting with the district superintendent?" I stayed on the phone with Ralph for a half hour. He laughed over the charge conference and praised me for offering less than the asking price on the Oak Lake house.

Finally, I knew I needed to return to my duties. "Hey, thanks for calling. I needed to laugh and hear some encouraging words. I should go. The noise level in the social hall is rising. I should go check on my elderly people. It sounds like families with children have arrived. Oh it's good to feel warm again. It is a miracle that only one person went to the hospital." We said goodbye. I left for the social hall to check on our elderly guests.

We ate a good dinner of roast turkey and ham with mashed potatoes, carrots and green beans. We had two kinds of gravy and bread stuffing. I went in search of the cook. I found Mr. Cole in the kitchen commanding a bevy of helpers to get things on the tables while it was hot.

"What? Have you been here all day? Did you cook all this food? What a lot of work."

"I was a cook in the navy. You have good equipment here. It was pretty easy. People have been coming in and helping all day."

"I appreciate this more than I can say. How can I ever thank you enough."

"I guess it's my wife and I who still owe the debt of thanks."

I almost started to cry again. Instead, I decided to get people seated. The older people were slow finding a place to sit. They seemed a little confused to be warm and about to eat a hot dinner. As I worked, I began to worry about how much these folks got out.

An old women bent almost double over her walker argued, "Who me? Am I supposed to sit down? You're not feeding me again are you?"

An elderly man picked at the skin on the back of his hand and fretted, "Who are all these people? I don't know any of these people. I should go home and eat. The electricity is on. I should go home."

Another man who still stood straight asked, "Is this charity? I got money. I want to pay for my dinner. I don't want charity." This man proudly gave me fifty-cents to pay for his dinner. I found a donations basket on the dessert table and added the fifty-cents.

I didn't know what to think of the donations basket. I recognized that some people like the man I'd just seated, would be more comfortable making a donation toward the food. I didn't want these poor people to feel like they had to pay. I planned to bill the conference for the food. In the end, I ignored what I had no idea how to handle.

After the dessert dishes had been cleared away, I began to worry about where people would sleep. I didn't have much time to worry. Once again our doors opened and strangers entered. These men were clearly in the navy. They came in carrying cots and more blankets. I did a quick check and decided to use the sanctuary and some unused classrooms for sleeping. The sanctuary with its rows of pews provided a fair amount of privacy for sleeping.

In no time at all, the sailors set up the cots with blankets and small pillows. A woman who said she was from Helpline placed a hygiene pack on each cot. The pack contained a toothbrush, toothpaste, soap and a washcloth. I really didn't know what to say, the best I could do was say, "I'm so thankful for your help."

As people got ready for bed, I learned that the firemen had done a great job of making sure each person brought their medication with them. I got most of the elderly tucked into bed by nine. I found a kitchen crew finishing washing dishes with water heated on the stove. Finally, the kitchen looked clean and the children and elderly were in bed. The few adults still awake sat and talked about when the power might come back on, and speculated on how their neighbors were getting along. A middle-aged man who walked with a limp had mopped the social hall floor for us before he left to go home to his wife and a house with a wood stove. I wondered if Larry was keeping an accurate count of the number of people in my constituent congregation. Maybe I did need to write a sermon…

"Oh shit!" I clapped my hand over my mouth.

Everybody looked at me and giggled or snickered.

"I forgot to write my sermon and it is Friday night." I got up to go to work on it with everybody laughing nervously--probably because the preacher said a swear word.

I realized I felt too tired to work on my sermon so I went across the parking lot to the cold-wet parsonage. I thought I might change clothes there but it was so cold. I got everything I needed plus some cat food and John Wesley's traveling litter tray. I hoped the poor cat had not improvised without a litter box all day.

Finally, we turned the lights out. The quiet settled down around us. I got into bed on the sofa in my office. I wondered, "Have I ever been this tired before?" I immediately knew the answer. For two and a half years, I had been much more tired on a daily basis.

The memory of my injuries or perhaps my fatigue triggered a mild anxiety attack. Suddenly, I sat up wide-awake. I sat feeling the fatigue on my body, but my heart raced as adrenalin poured through my veins. I decided to get up and try to walk off the anxiety. I walked the hall outside my office, down past the classrooms. I walked back up the hall and through the social hall to the kitchen. Everything looked so clean nobody would ever know we fed over a hundred people again tonight. Finally, I entered the sanctuary. I could hear the sounds of people sleeping. The center aisle was mostly clear so I carefully walked the length of the sanctuary. I climbed two steps and sat down in my chair by the pulpit. *"Well, here I am God. I am exhausted and I can't sleep. I haven't written a sermon for Sunday and it is Friday night. I may still be running a shelter on Sunday morning. Please send your spirit to be with all of the people in this building tonight. They are away from their homes and worried about their pets. Please protect the road and power crews who are working to restore our lives to normal. Thank you for each volunteer who came through those doors today. I can open the doors to the building, but I know that you are the one who calls the volunteers."* I sat a while longer listening to the sounds of sleeping people. A child whimpered. Several people snored. *"Father, may each of these people have a night of sleep that restores them body, mind and soul."* I finally felt at peace and went back to my office to sleep on my too-short sofa with John Wesley sleeping above me on the sofa back.

I started breakfast early Saturday morning. I wasn't quite certain how to make coffee in the old fashioned percolator on a stove burner. I made the coffee too strong, but I watered it down. I did a better job with the pancakes. By the time people were ready to eat, I had a respectable breakfast buffet with ham, bacon, applesauce, and pancakes with syrup. I wished for orange juice, but I didn't have any. I found a bag of chocolate chips and made hot chocolate.

At eleven-fifteen A. M. the power came back on in Blackfish. My refugees were ready to go home. I worried about people returning to cold houses with damp floors, but they wanted to go home to their own homes. Some gathered their things and began to walk home. I offered rides to those who looked too frail to walk two and a half blocks. People came to pick up their elderly neighbors. By two in the afternoon, I stood in the totally empty church. One lone flood bucket sat by the door. It reminded me that I still needed to clean the parsonage. I took John Wesley and went back to my own house wondering what I would do for a sermon.

CHAPTER 22: FIRST KISS

On Tuesday before I went to Seattle to sign the papers on my house, I spent my morning researching my next sermon. I knew I couldn't pull out something I'd used before two weeks in a row. I read the lectionary passage in two English translations then went back and read it in the ancient Hebrew, then ancient Greek. I wondered how much I could get into the ancient writings as compared to the contemporary understanding of the passage. I sat back in my chair to let my mind wander around the passages and see what bubbled up.

I did some deep breathing. Nothing bubbled. I repeated the words that challenged me. My eyes roamed the walls looking for inspiration. I thought I might think better if I took a walk. My eyes fell on a series of notebooks on the top shelf of the bookcases. I knew they were the minutes of the past church counsel meetings. My free-floating mind became curious about the big stove in the kitchen. I vaguely remembered someone saying something about the furnace being twenty years old. I wondered if the propane furnace and stove arrived at the same time. I got up and pulled down three years of reports and thumbed through them. The bills were filed in the back. I realized that I could tell when the furnace arrived by when the Suburban Propane bills started. I put the notebooks back and pulled down two, more recent years. I found the propane bills. I felt quite excited by my discovery until I remembered that this was not writing a sermon. I could leave my hobby reading for another time.

I sat back down in my chair and thought about the old-testament reading for this week--another prophet telling the people to be prepared for the coming of the Lord. My mind drifted over the idea of being prepared to serve God. "Hm, it is a stretch, but I wonder if it would work? Would the congregation like the analogy of being prepared to serve. I could talk about how the congregation prepared seventeen years ago to serve last week." My understanding may have been closer to what the prophet meant than some contemporary interpretations. Would people see it as stretching the words? I could talk about waiting. It would be another opportunity to make the congregation feel useful and valuable. I could do it. I reread my scriptures in English and Hebrew. I looked up what others had to say about the "Day of the Lord." Yeah, I could do it. I hoped the congregation would catch my understanding that the "Day of the Lord" is the day that God asks something of you, rather than a specific day of second coming, or exclusively Sunday. I could work with that idea. I put the church counsel minutes in my bag to take with me and read on the ferry.

I took extra care when I dressed to go to Seattle. I chose a basic black dress with a scarf for color. It would be appropriate if the restaurant Ralph chose was fancy, or more casual. I smiled at myself in the mirror as I put on make-up. Part of me chided myself for getting fancied up for Ralph. The rest of me answered, "Why not? He is a successful, attractive man. Yes, I have a date with him. I can date. I am a widow. I am not going to feel guilty for wanting to look pretty on a date with an attractive man." I surprised myself by feeling self-conscious about dressing up for Ralph.

When I got on the Seattle ferry, I decided to take the notebooks upstairs to read. I got out of the car and smiled at being tucked into the middle lane of the boat between two large trucks. My little Porsche could almost drive under them, which was good because parts of the big trucks seemed to be hanging over into my lane. I smiled remembering my dream where I parked my Porsche on the back of the boat outside the safety nets. I remembered kissing Ralph in that dream. I remembered how I felt about it then. I concluded that I wasn't ready to kiss him then. I smiled. I was ready to kiss him now—you know, just a little thank you or goodnight kiss. I wasn't sure where I wanted the kissing to lead. I decided to read the church counsel minutes.

I discovered the beginning of the discussion about the furnace. For a full year, the counsel debated about remodeling or just replacing the furnace. I laughed over the minutes as I read between the lines on church process. I saw some familiar names, but most of the people, on the church counsel from seventeen years ago, had moved away or died. The second book of minutes started with the same debate. This was where I found the first mention of the stove. They could get it at a good price at the navy surplus outlet. The debate raged over why they needed the big stove.

Finally, I saw the minutes of the meeting where they voted. The record showed fifty-two members showed up to vote. They presented the question: Shall Blackfish United Methodist Church remodel the kitchen, side entry, and choir room to: 1) convert the choir room into a closet and furnace room with a propane furnace. 2) remodel the kitchen to install a propane stove. 3) remodel the room where the present furnace is into a large entry to the social hall so that people using the social hall do not need to enter through the sanctuary. They presented a second measure that surprised me. Shall Blackfish United Methodist Church, serve as the community shelter in case of power outages or disasters. Both measures passed forty-seven to five. I shrugged and gave thanks that without knowing I was official, I followed through on the church decision.

I felt nervous during the signing of the escrow papers. As the seller, it didn't take long for me to sign. I filled out the necessary papers to have the money paid directly into my checking account. I think I was a little dazed when I got back into my car. I had just signed papers to sell my house. I hadn't told Daddy I was doing this today. I hadn't told Patty and Trevor that I was even close to selling. I hoped they would be so enchanted with the lake house that they wouldn't mind losing the house in town. I called Patty and left a message for her. Next, I called Trevor.

"Hi mom."

"Hmm, I think I am beginning to figure out why Daddy always complains when I say, 'Hi Daddy" when I answer his calls."

Trevor laughed.

I took a deep breath and plunged in with my news. "Anyway, I am calling with exciting news. I just sold the house here in Seattle, and I'm buying a cute little place on a lake near Blackfish."

"Cool."

I had been worrying about how my kids would take this news and all Trevor had to say was, cool. "I hope you are not disappointed about me selling the house in town."

"No, I don't really like it. It's your house so do what you want."

Relief washed over me. "I think that was always part of my problem with that house. I couldn't do what I wanted with it. When we bought it, we didn't have money to fix it up and modernize. We didn't even look for something we might like better. Your dad's folks knew it was for sale before it came on the market. We got a good deal on it, but it was never quite right for us. Anyway, I love the house I'm buying. It's a thousand square feet and the garage is big enough for both cars. The view…oh Trev the view is so peaceful. When Ralph and I first looked at it, he knew I was in love with the lake, and the view, and the dock before I even looked at the house."

"Who's Ralph?"

Oops, damn, I hadn't intended to mention Ralph. I thought, Well, maybe I can slip this one through in the house excitement. "Oh he's a friend. He was working on a case in Blackfish when I first found the house so he looked at the house with me. I actually have two lots on the lake so I have seventy feet of lakefront. I can't decide what kind of boat to get."

"What about a jet ski?" Ah, I had successfully diverted my son.

"I'll have to check with the homeowners association to see if motors are allowed on the lake. I was debating between a canoe or a rowboat."

"Mom, canoes and rowboats are out of fashion. You at least want a Kayak. They are more efficient. Maybe I'll get a jet ski and keep it there."

"I'll check on the motor issue, and do you have enough money for school? Shouldn't you be saving money for school instead of getting expensive toys?"

"How is the Porsche running?"

"The Porsche is not an expensive toy. It was just a little over twenty-thousand. It doesn't use gas and it is running just fine." We sparred for a few more minutes and I hung up.

After I talked to Trevor I called Lester, "Hi, this is Maude Henderson. I just closed on my Seattle house. The money should be in my account by Thursday afternoon. How are we coming on the Oak Lake house?"

"That was fast. The structural inspection came back clean this morning. If you have cash, all we need is the title insurance. We've applied for that. I guess we can close whenever you can get a certified check from your bank."

"Okay, I'll check with them. Uh, who needs to check on the status of the title insurance?"

"I'll take care of that right now and make sure it's ready as soon as possible."

I started getting excited about my new home. I realized that I didn't want to wait to remodel before I moved in. I could remodel as I went along.

I called Patty, but she still didn't answer her phone. I decided to go shopping before my date with Ralph. I went to Nordstroms and wandered around looking at clothes. I saw some cute shoes, but didn't buy them because I remembered that in Blackfish, the most practical footwear was black knee-high, rubber boots. I bought five pairs of tights. The saleswoman promised me that these would not roll down around mid-thigh.

"Are you sure? I mean…I'm a pastor. After the sermon, I need to move quickly from the pulpit, down two steps and to the back of the church. More than once I've had to do this while unable to move at mid-thigh because my tights have rolled down and are hobbling me." I demonstrated hobbling with my thighs stuck tight together. The other female customers laughed at my story. We had a wonderful time laughing over the perils of tights. I'm not certain our clerk appreciated our trials or our humor.

I called Ralph at four. "Hi, I'm done with my signing and shopping. Are you free?"

"Yeah, I'm just now leaving the office. Can you meet me at my place in fifteen minutes and we'll walk from there."

"Sure, I'm in my car now so give me your address, and I'll program in into my GPS."

"Maudy, if you are at Nordy's it is only a few blocks. You hardly need a GPS."

"In Seattle I do. I get confused when the streets start running at angles." He gave me the address and I punched it into my GPS.

I probably could have walked the six and a half blocks to Ralph's condo faster than I could drive. Most of the time I sat in downtown Seattle gridlock. I started singing praises about my electric car. I inched my way through town until my GPS told me that my destination was on the right. I recognized Ralph's condo from half a block away because I could see him standing out front waving to me. I pulled in and parked. Ralph came to my car door to help me out.

I looked up as Ralph approached my car. I couldn't see his face. In fact, I couldn't see much above his waist. What I could see was… well…in the vernacular…happy to see me. I think I blushed and looked away. I know I smiled. I felt very flattered that he obviously found me exciting. I hoped it was me, and not my Porsche, that he found exciting. I still smiled when I got out of the car.

He spoke softly. "You have a charming smile."

"Thank you." This date was starting off in good form. "I think I am having a good day. I sold that house. I found tights in Nordy's and the sales woman insists they will not roll down around my knees hobbling me. Where are we going?"

"A place in the market. I think we might have a sunset. This early we should get a table where we can see it." The rain had gone to Portland for the day, so our clouds made great grey streaks across the sky, which did look promising for seeing the sunset.

I told Ralph about the closing. "I called Trevor. He sounded cool with me selling the house. I was worried because both grandparents have said that I should save the house in case the kids wanted to buy it from me. Trevor said that he doesn't like the house. That is probably because it is not grand, with illogical stairways, and flat roofs that are totally impractical in Seattle. He is majoring in architecture. I'm afraid he will be disappointed with my prosaic little lake house." I went on to laugh about Trevor thinking of a jet ski.

Ralph is bigger than I am and accustomed to walking in the city. I needed to hurry to keep up with him. I started to limp. He didn't say anything about my limp. He just slowed down and continued talking about his new client. "…so the man's children want to overturn the will. I'm not sure what I can do about it. This happens often enough, and it is hard to overturn a will. It is possible if the new will was made late enough, and does not really make sense. Sometimes leaving the estate to the caregiver makes sense if there is not enough cash to cover the cost of care before death, or the children are provided for. I leave in the morning for Missoula and will see what I can find. I doubt this will be as much fun as the Blackfish case. I really enjoyed working with you."

I smiled at Ralph. "You know, I enjoyed having you there. I felt so unsure that I was on the right track. You gave me courage to do what I guess I knew how to do in the first place." We continued to talk about our work until we reached the restaurant.

Nobody met us at the reception desk when we arrived. We stood with our backs to the market waiting for the receptionist. We could hear voices so I assumed that someone would be along in a minute. While I was waiting and thinking about dinner, someone attacked Ralph. He was standing right beside me when suddenly a great, big young-man grabbed Ralph in a chokehold and around the middle and shook him back and forth.

Ralph stayed calm. "Rich! Cut it out! You are not too old to thrash, but I'm not going to do it right here. You know you are not suppose to do this indoors." The young man grinned, and Ralph smiled back at him. Ralph turned to me, "Maude Henderson may I present my son Richard. Rich, this is a friend of mine Maude Henderson."

We both said something appropriate before Rich reacted honestly. "Oh, right, I know, now. You're the woman he took to the Seahawks game. Oh maaaaan," he whined, "I just ran into my dad and he's on a date—weird. Dad, why didn't you warn me that you had a date and where you were going so I could avoid this place like the plague?" He ended this rant in tones of total angst.

I laughed.

Ralph acted ready to butt heads with his son. "What is so weird about me having a date? I am an adult. I've been widowed almost four years. Maybe you should apologize to Maude for being rude."

Poor Ralph. I laughed too hard to be any help to him.

He grumped, "I don't see what you find so funny. He was rude."

Rich grinned at his father. "I like her."

"Oh…oh my…oh my gosh…" Perhaps the stress of the day had given me the giggles.

Ralph started to smile. Rich looked like he wanted to run and started backing away.

Finally, I recovered enough to explain. "Oh remember, the first time we went to lunch and my daughter called and I refused to answer?"

Ralph smiled, then grinned. "Surely, your daughter is not as bad as Rich."

"I'm afraid so, in a different sort of way. I'm sure she would find it weird to think of me dating. She might also be defensive." I smiled at Rich. "I have a daughter Patty and a son, Trevor, ages twenty-three and twenty-one."

"Does your daughter look like you?"

"Well, she's taller, but yes."

"That's cool."

Our hostess arrived so we said goodbye to Rich and followed our hostess to the table. I chuckled again.

"He was rude. I'm sorry."

"He was normal. It's okay. I prefer honesty."

Ralph held my chair for me. "He's a good kid."

"He appears to be fond of you so I'm assuming he's a very good kid." I tried to smile reassuringly at Ralph. We talked about our children as we decided what to eat for dinner. I think I smiled a great deal more. Ralph smiled and laughed during dinner. I was vaguely aware that we both did a great deal of smiling and laughing when we were together. The setting sun put on a lovely display.

I snorted.

"What?"

"I was just thinking the sunset is a much nicer floor-show than my love life."

Ralph laughed. "I admit they did make me slightly uncomfortable, but they seemed to be good people. I liked Blackfish. There are hundreds of people who work with the inner city youth here for much less than they deserve. I doubt very much that they can walk into a restaurant and get a great dinner free because the owner appreciates their work."

"That is very true. We don't have the problems that people have here either. Our situation was bad. It was a terrible thing, but the community responded appropriately. I think they may make some progress with the bullying issue. The kids have starting calling out the adults who bully. I hope the adults start thinking about what kind of role models they are. Of course we will always have some bullies, but I hope the type of mindless thing that was happening at the school will die out."

Ralph played with his spoon. "I think it already has changed dramatically. People are conscious of what they're doing."

After dinner Ralph asked me if I wanted to go to a movie or visit a club. "Do you go to movies? I guess I should have asked. Some churches don't allow…"

"I love movies. Ralph haven't I ever told you that I worked in theater in college? I've been in movies, too. I guess knowing something about how they go together helps me enjoy them more."

"What movies were you in? I'll have to watch them."

"You'll never notice me. I did extra parts. All you see of me is my back or the side of my head. I think one scene near the space needle shows me eating an ice cream cone. Anyway, I better get home. I'm doing the funeral for Timmy's dad tomorrow. I want to spend some time with the family in the morning." We talked about Timmy on our way back to my car. Ralph finally convinced me to tell him the names of the movies I appeared in. "Oh, in that one my cousin Amanda came with me. We looked enough alike that we dressed exactly alike and did our make up and hair the same so you can probably pick me out as one of the identical twins." We reached my car.

Ralph took my hand. "Hey, thanks for having dinner with me." He stood close to me.

"Thanks for celebrating with me. Having dinner with you made today seem special."

He smiled. He still held my hand. With his free hand he lightly touched the side of my face and lowered his lips to mine. I turned my face up to meet his kiss.

Ralph did kiss me. I liked the feel of his fingers on the side of my face. His lips felt warm on mine. I think my soul centered on the feel of Ralph's lips on mine. I loved the feel of those lips. They were warm and full, yet firm. I know I leaned toward him, seeking to know more of him through our bodies. This kiss turned into a long, slow, like-in-the-movies kiss. As our bodies pulled apart to break off the kiss, our lips stayed together rejoicing in the feel of the other. I slid one hand up his strong arm to the back of his neck. I relished the feel of his muscles. The feel of his skin against my fingers warmed my hand and my heart.

I knew I should be getting into my car but my lips totally rebelled—demanding that I satisfy their need to be kissed.

We did eventually break off the kiss. We smiled at each other, satisfied with the success of our first kiss. My voice sounded shy as I said goodnight. Somehow I found my car. I'd been leaning against it all the time. Ralph held the door for me. I smiled up at him. He grinned. I told my GPS to take me home. I wasn't sure I could find my own feet without help just then. I pulled away from my parking space. Before I pulled out onto the street, I looked into my rear view mirror. Ralph was on the sidewalk behind me. I watched him jumping up and down in a circle and punching the air above his head. I settled down in my seat and pulled out into the evening traffic. I giggled and grinned. "Yeah Maude, I think you have yourself one fine man."

CHAPTER 23: CHURCH COUNCIL

I finally, caught up with Patty on Wednesday morning. "Hi, I tried to call you yesterday."

"Yeah, I saw you called twice. You didn't answer when I called back, so I called Trevor. He told me you sold our old house and that you have a boyfriend." Patty didn't sound like she completely believed her brother or liked his news. I decided to distract her from the house thing.

"Trevor told you I have a boyfriend? Yeah, I kinda said something I didn't mean to with him. I thought I distracted him with talk about the lake house I'm buying."

"Mom, we're not kids anymore. You can't distract us with a different toy anymore. Why did you decide to sell the house in Seattle?"

"Oh several things set me off, like being tired of dealing with renters. The house needed repairs." I paused and thought about the question for a second or two. "Um…you know… I think the real thing is that I'm done living in limbo—neither here nor there. I want a real house—not a parsonage. I want to paint it the color I want. I want to decide whether or not to repair or remodel. I want to live like a grown-up."

Patty laughed. "Oh if that is your reason—that you want to live like a grown-up, then that's okay. I understand that. Is the boyfriend part of being a grown-up too?"

"I don't know…perhaps…but not on a conscious level. I think maybe I'm ready for a relationship. Maybe, I just met a great guy, and ready or not, I want to spend time with him."

"What if he turns out to be a jerk?"

"Then I'll dump him the same as any other sensible woman would do. I don't think he'll turn out to be a jerk. The people he works with respect him. He's a widower. He is considerate. Honey, I've met enough jerks in my life to recognize them. I'd be very surprised if he turned out to be a jerk."

"Was Daddy a jerk?" Patty had never asked about my relationship with Hal before. I knew she needed to know some things. I instantly decided to be completely honest.

"What? Good heavens no! Your daddy got hurt. He had an infection in his brain. He would never have done what he did if he hadn't been hurt. He was most probably hallucinating when he attacked me. Your daddy was a fine man."

Patty made a few noises that sounded as if she wasn't convinced then asked, "So what is your new house like?"

I'm no more likely to be distracted from something that concerns me than my children are. I was concerned that Patty felt upset over her father. I figured the truth would come out sooner or later, so I told her about my new house.

I'd scheduled Timmy's father's service for the late afternoon. He and his older brother met me in my office in the morning. We discussed the service. I remembered to write in my notes, "Remind the Bateses to move the communion table forward."

The day passed off smoothly. The special ed students came by after school. They seemed more interested in some new game than in talking about being bullied, or the problems of being in special ed, or their fears about being like Joel and hurting someone. Mary had a grocery sack full of the clothes I'd loaned her. Eventually, I sent the kids home saying I needed to do a funeral. I assumed they left when I went to let the Bateses in with the casket and flowers. The sanctuary looked lovely. I put a cassette tape into our sound system for the prelude.

"Pastor Maude, what is that thing?" Bill, one of the students, surprised me by staying at the church.

I tried not to laugh. "It is a tape player for playing music. And, yes, it is old fashioned, but not that old. It works." The care committee arrived and started setting up in the social hall. I thought Mary must be waiting for a ride. I watched her carry a tray of cookies from the kitchen and set them on a table. She handled the plate gingerly. I thought it made her feel good to be helping. Timmy arrived by the sanctuary door so I went to greet him.

The service went well. I always enjoy learning about the amazing things people have done. Timmy's dad had been in the marines. A fellow serviceman told the story of their landing on some Pacific island. They were hesitant to land because of snipers on the small hill above them. They didn't have any trenches to hide in so they would be completely exposed. Timmy's dad fired up a tractor they had with them. Against direct orders from his superior officer, he took the tractor ashore. He put the blade down opened up the engine and dug a nice long trench for the others to come ashore. The man laughed at how Timmy's dad had hid down by the foot peddles and watched where he was going through a small crack in the cab housing. The tractor looked as if nobody was driving. The snipers fired a few shots at the thing, but when it made a three point turn and came back up the beach, the snipers stopped firing at the driverless tractor. Timmy's dad got busted for disobeying an order, but nobody died in that landing.

I locked the church up about six-thirty and went home for dinner. I'd finally completely given up the idea of remodeling my new house before moving, so I started packing. By eleven PM, I had most of my packing done. John Wesley sniffed the boxes. He'd moved enough times that he knew what the boxes meant. I talked to him telling him about our new home.

I had hopes that Thursday would be as nice as Wednesday. I liked my job. I thought some funerals were sad, but even with the sad services, I felt that I was making a difference in others' lives by bringing love into a sad situation. The morning started off excellently with a phone call from Ralph. "Hi, how are you doing?"

"Good actually, the funeral yesterday went well. What are you doing?"

"I'm in some God-forsaken place about thirty miles from Missoula. I'm not the best person in my office for this type of work, but I am the only one willing to travel. I had time to look over the paperwork yesterday afternoon. The kids might have a good case. Their father set aside a fairly typical will made when he was well in order to leave one and a half-million to his care attendant. I need to see what the situation with the care attendant was—how long she worked for him, what she gave up to work for him. I'd like to get some better information on the father's condition. I hope my clients have better information than what I've been able to get so far." We ended this conversation by talking about our last dinner together and planning for him to come out to the lake when he got home.

I flopped onto my back on my bed. "John Wesley, this is an excellent start to the day. I hope you won't mind sharing me a little bit with Ralph. I like him. You will just have to get used to it."

John Wesley groomed his privates.

The day continued in excellent form. I worked on my sermon. I liked it and thought it was coming together nicely. Lester called at ten. "Kitsap Escrow called. They have the title insurance. They can have the paperwork ready this afternoon, if you have the money." We talked back and forth about how much the check needed to be. I promised to call my bank to find out how soon I could have the money. I called the bank. My money could be withdrawn. I could buy my little house on Oak Lake.

I did buy my house on Oak Lake. I drove into Bremerton and spent a half hour signing papers. I really didn't have to do much to buy the house. I've spent more time buying a pair of shoes. While in town, I stopped at the nursing home and visited some parishioners. I got home about five-thirty, fixed myself a dinner, and ate it while I tracked down a rental truck for my move.

After dinner, I finally called my parents and told them about buying the lake house. "Oh I suppose I should mention that I could do it because I sold the house in Seattle."

"Trevor called and told us about that. Patty called and told us that you finally confessed that Ralph is your boyfriend."

"Oh good grief." I thought to myself that this was the reason I felt reluctant to tell any of my family anything. "Well, I guess that about covers all of my news. I'm picking up a moving truck in the morning. It has a lift on the back so I figure I can do the work myself if I have two days."

"Your mother and I will come up and help. Aren't you going to clean the new place before you move in?"

"Oh, I looked it over. Nobody has lived there for over a year. It's clean enough except for dust and spiders. I don't want my moving to run into Sunday if I can help it." John Wesley came downstairs for the first time since the flood. I smiled, happy to see that he gave up being such a wimp. "Anyway, my plan is to store everything…"

John Wesley ran at the front door and jumped up on it.

"…everything in the spare…John Wesley what on earth do you want? Daddy, I think I'll go. My cat is acting really weird and jumping at the front door." I hung up and offered the cat food. He wasn't interested in food. He sat down and stared at the front door. Finally, I opened it and looked out. I discovered cars in the church parking lot and people going into the church. I thought I better go check.

I found shoes and a sweater to walk over to the church. The door to the social hall was locked. I looked around. Six cars still sat in the parking lot and I could see lights on inside. I unlocked the door and stepped inside. The social hall sat dark and deserted. I headed for the classroom wing. I heard a voice whining, "…no respect for the property of others." I pushed open the door to the boardroom and stood looking at my church counsel. Horror washed over me as I realized I'd totally forgotten a church meeting. Fortunately, I wasn't too terribly late.

"Excuse me for being late." I found a chair and sat down. This suddenly looked interesting. Nobody said a word. I'd expected them to continue with their agenda. The group remained mute. It took me a minute to calm down from being flustered before I realized that something was wrong here. "Would somebody please tell me what the problem is?"

Larry looked down at his hands folded on the table in front of him. I saw his lower jaw trembling. I wondered if he was going to start crying. His flushed face revealed his discomfort. I worried about his blood pressure. He stammered, "Ahem, yes, this meeting was called to discuss the use of this building as a shelter."

I nodded.

Larry looked at the table in front of him and continued. "We have some concerns about the building being used as a daycare."

I nodded. "What are the specific questions before the council?" I kept searching my brain trying to remember something about this meeting. I kept drawing a blank. I could not remember who told me about it, probably Larry. I worried I might have to confess that I'd forgotten all about it.

"Well…ahem…first…uh…the first question is about using the church as a shelter." I knew that Larry had finally wrapped his brain around the problem and I would get an interesting reconstruction of reality. "Well, the matter of whether or not the church is to be used for a shelter is an issue to be decided by the church council."

I nodded.

Larry's voice shook, "We didn't vote to use the church as a shelter before you took in all those children." Larry looked at his hands again.

I relaxed. I now felt at least eighty percent certain that I had not been told about this meeting. I looked around the table. "Oh, sure, didn't Margery tell you? Surely, you remember when the vote was taken. Some of you weren't here then. Just a minute I did research this. The minutes of the meeting are in my office." I got up and limped across the hall to my office and picked up the two notebooks I'd left on my desk when I got home Tuesday. I limped back to the meeting.

"Here we are. Let me see…" I flipped through the pages. Here it is." I read the date and names of the people attending the meeting. I read the minutes, including exactly how the questions were worded.

Margery wailed, "But that's not binding on us now."

I looked up from my reading. "Yes, it is."

"No, that was so long ago." She persisted.

I took a firm tone of voice. "Margery you were at that meeting. You were one of the fifty-two people who voted on this. Yes, it is binding." I began to suspect that Margery was one of the five people who voted "no."

Margery asked, "Well, how do we change this?

Larry explained, "We'd have to repeal it through election."

I started getting disgusted with this line of talk. I had just written a beautiful sermon about how this congregation had been ready when God called and here they were lamenting their good deed. I explained, "Actually, it's not as easy as that. The gas furnace and stove were purchased with donations with the intent that they would be used for a shelter. In fact part of the entry hall was remodeled also for that purpose. You are just going to have to live with the reality of being the community shelter until that equipment wears out. You might pray that we will not have any more disasters before then. I haven't read all the minutes. Is this the first time we have used the church as a shelter?" The church counsel members began to remind me to of a group of guilty children. I heard a few mutterings. They refused to look at me.

Larry spoke up. "Oh no, the electricity goes off every winter. We all come down here and use the stove. It was just worse this time because the power went off during the day and the school children were sent home."

I picked up on Larry's comment. "Yes, I understand that it is a school policy to send the children home when the power goes out. That's one reason why a shelter is needed."

Shirley explained, "I don't mind the church being used for a shelter for the members, but we don't have to include strangers. Some of those people are sinners." I went back and read out loud the question the church voted on emphasizing the word "community."

I came close to losing patience. "I'm going to be blunt about this. This church will continue to be a community shelter. It was voted on and changes were made, equipment was brought in. We will honor our commitments. I want to make one more thing perfectly clear." I heard my voice growing very stern. "God loves every single person who steps through our doors. We will love them as God loves them. To do anything less places us lower than any person who makes unwise choices to solve their problems or in looking for love."

"Amen." Larry sounded equally firm.

Margery remained unsatisfied. "What about those retarded kids who were here today. They stayed all during the funeral."

"So? What did they do? I saw Mary helping set up refreshments."

"She also ate a dozen cookies. During the service they all sat in the social hall and ate cookies." I saw a half dozen heads nodding and a half dozen faces set in a scowl of disapproval.

I wanted to laugh. "Yes, I suppose that was socially incorrect. It did no real harm. Hey, we have a group of adolescents who want to be at the church after school and you would rather, what?"

"We're not a daycare." Shirley pouted.

"They are too old for daycare. The state law cuts off at age eight."

Aza asked, "What about our liability?"

I tried to sound slightly bored to hide my anger. "We're insured. If I'm not going to be here, I'll lock the church and make certain nobody is inside. Is there any other business on the agenda?"

Nobody said anything.

I continued. "I have a bit of new business then. I am buying a house on Oak Lake. This is officially my thirty-days notice. I plan to move sooner, but I said I would give you thirty-days and this is it. I will have more to discuss with the pastor/parish committee. Perhaps the trustees would consider renting out the parsonage for a source of income for the church."

My mention of a source of income started a lively round of delighted discussion. I shook my head. I should have distracted them with talk of the parsonage earlier. I felt heartsick about the discussion of the shelter. "If there is no further business, Larry would you adjourn the meeting so we can all go home to bed."

Larry adjourned the meeting. It seemed to take forever for the counsel to assemble their canes and walkers. Jean came up beside me and gave me a sideways hug. "You handled that real well. I was so upset when I heard about this meeting. We went over this stuff seventeen years ago. I didn't want to go through it again. We worked so hard to raise the money for that stove. I didn't know the minutes of those meetings still existed."

Curious, I asked, "Did people outside the church contribute to the stove?"

Jean smiled, "Oh, yes, the firemen held a dance to raise money. People put money in a jar at the IGA and Timmy gave us a big donation— five hundred dollars."

I held my head. "Jean, this meeting should never have been held. We cannot go back on those commitments." She looked so distressed I hugged her. "People get crazy ideas sometimes and when they do it is hard to stop them. I read those minutes for the year before the vote. I suspect that some people haven't changed their minds." Jean and Larry left the building and locked the doors behind them. They still looked sick over the whole meeting thing. They were good people with good hearts.

CHAPTER 24: MOVING DAY

Friday morning I got up early to go pick up a truck to move my belongings to my new home. I arrived at the truck rental outlet at eight. I got stuck in commute traffic on my way home so I sat and worried about backing up the big, unfamiliar vehicle. I didn't get back to the church until after nine-thirty. I saw a truck in the parking lot and a couple guys in navy uniforms standing around. I didn't park properly. I just stopped to see what the men wanted.

"May I help you?"

"We are supposed to pick up the cots we left here."

"Oh yes, those were so helpful. Thank you." I took the sailors inside and showed them where the cots had been stacked. We chatted briefly while they picked them up. I checked phone messages in my office. In just a few minutes they had the cots safely stored in their truck.

The leader of the two asked, "What are you doing with the moving truck?"

"Oh, I bought a house out on Oak Lake and I am moving out there today."

"Do you have help?"

"Not really. My parents threatened to come up, which will mean I will run around trying to keep Dad from lifting too heavy and Mom will ask a thousand questions, then question my answers."

They chuckled. "We are not going to try to get back until the accident on Kitsap Way gets cleared up."

"Is that what that was?"

"Come on, show us what needs to be done. We can get the heavy pieces before your dad gets here."

"I don't have much furniture. My mattress is the heaviest piece." I watched as these two physically fit men tossed my mattress around as if it was light.

My parents arrived at ten to find my bedroom furniture, the sectional sofa and the TV safely stored in my truck. By ten thirty we had all the boxes stored.. I wondered if I could get the back of the truck closed with my sailors inside so they could help me unload. I decided that abducting sailors might be a crime so I waved them off with my thanks and blessing.

The three of us went through the parsonage looking for any forgotten items. I debated driving the truck myself, but that would mean letting one of my parents drive the Porsche. I decided to drive the Porsche and let Daddy drive the truck. With half the job done with very little effort, I was not so worried about the second half of the job.

For some reason, I felt extremely proud to drive up to my own house. The yard looked a mess with the un-mowed lawn, and blackberries creeping in from both sides. Unloading went much slower than loading the truck.

Mom called out the minute she stepped into the kitchen. "Honey, where are your appliances?"

"I haven't had time to buy any. I thought I'd eat out and store the refrigerator food in my cooler on the back porch. It will stay below forty-degrees. I want to think about what I really need for a few days."

Mom stated firmly, "You need a stove and refrigerator."

"I have the microwave and what little food I have will stay cool in the cooler. I think I want a side by side refrigerator/freezer." We debated the merits of refrigerators while we finished unloading boxes. Finally, I rubbed my lower back where it ached. "I'm hungry. Let's leave the big stuff and get some lunch. The country club is just up the street."

Mom said, "The country club, how fancy. Can we eat there?"

I answered, "The restaurant is open to the public. Can we take your car?"

Dad grumbled about the size of the Porsche, but he drove the three of us up to the restaurant in his Subaru sedan. As I rode in the back seat, I had an opportunity to look around. I admired the landscaping of the golf course. "Wha…?" The dark, muddy, exposed earth on a green shocked me more than what it looked like.

Dad stopped the car. His voice dripped disapproval. "Now who would do such a senseless thing to a golf course? There is no reason for that."

Mom leaned over so she could see out Dad's window. "What is that? It looks like someone dug a picture of a large…." Mom shut up and both parents looked at me.

I cracked up laughing. "I am a mother. That is how you got grandkids. I didn't forget that male genitals exist when I went to seminary. If you like, I could tell you a great deal about scripture and male genitals." I laughed some more. My parents appeared shocked by my frankness.

Dad drove on.

The hostess kept us waiting for lunch. She didn't have a smaller table ready yet. It would be just a few minutes. We waited long enough for another couple to come in. "Cricket! Skunk! How good to see you."

Skunk asked, "Pastor we saw the truck down at that house did you buy it?"

"Yes, I closed yesterday. I'm so excited about owning my own home at last. Oh excuse me." I introduced my parents. The hostess returned and told Cricket and Skunk they would need to wait. "Wait! Do you have a table for a party of five? We can eat together." I turned to Cricket and Skunk for their affirmation. Cricket looked happy. Skunk nodded.

I thought I picked up an air of sadness about him. Cricket hovered and clung to him. Daddy made a few general comments to try to make the young couple feel more comfortable. I wondered if there was something wrong with me when our waiter seemed nervous as he seated us.

I finally uncovered the problem. "Skunk, why are you home in the middle of the day? Are you taking the day off?"

Cricket put her hand on his leg and looked anxiously up at her husband.

"No, my house was broken into last night. The police want an inventory of everything in the house and of anything that might be missing. I have a video of the house contents so we are comparing that to what is in the house now."

We expressed our sorrow for their shock.

I offered, "Listen, if there is anything I can do, let me know."

Cricket volunteered, "Someone mentioned bringing in Ralph to see if he can get a make on the reasoning of the person behind this."

I smiled, "I think Ralph likes more to go on than a list of missing things."

Skunk growled, "Have you seen the sixth hole?"

My Dad perked up at the hint of mystery, "Ah, the authorities think the two incidences are related?"

Cricket explained, "They happened about the same time. My students had a dance recital last night. I had to be there and Skunk came with me. We were gone from home from about five until after ten. We discovered our robbery as soon as we got home. The vandalism was discovered while the police were investigating our robbery."

We continued to talk about the robbery for a few minutes more. I thought I understood the wait staff a little better. It must be a shock to come to work and have your workplace defaced in such a manner. I moved the conversation on to how lovely Skunk and Cricket's wedding had been. Then we talked about my house.

Skunk asked, "Do you have everything out of the truck?"

"No, the bed and sofa need to come in…well…all the big stuff I have is still in the truck. We did the boxes first."

Skunk volunteered, "Okay, I'll come down and help you right after lunch. I don't feel like working on that project at home."

Skunk's obvious reluctance to stay home distressed me. "Oh dear, it is not good to feel that way about going home. Um…uh…well…I do know some rituals for spiritually cleansing a house."

"Maudy!" My father sounded as shocked as I suspected he was.

Cricket clapped her hands. "Oh, that sounds wonderful. The place has bad vibes now. Would you come clean our house?"

"Sure, perhaps you can help with expressive dance. Would you want to smudge with sage?"

Daddy's tone turned severe. "Maudy, does your bishop know you do things like this?"

"Oh, not specifically, but it is part of our church history. We've thrown out too many church customs that reach people's hearts. If they think the house feels bad, we will do something to make it feel right again."

Cricket started smiling happily. "I think this will be fun."

"Can we do it so we finish right at sunset?" Skunk seemed to time his life to the sunrise and sunset.

I wondered if he would insist on the baby being born at sunrise. "Sure, I'll gather some things this afternoon and be to your house about a half hour before sunset. What time does the sun set today?"

Of course Skunk knew down to the second when the sun would set today. We finished our meal and went down to my house.

Cricket and I wandered my yard and planned the house-cleansing while Skunk and Daddy unloaded the rest of the truck. Mom followed us around and told us the names of the plants in the yard. We stood admiring the view from the back patio when Mom drew our attention to another plant.

"Maudy, did you say you wanted sage? This is a culinary sage. Would it work for your aromatic herb?" I appreciated the fact that mom did not judge the method I'd found to reach out to this young couple to nourish their spirits. The plant was big, which turned out to be good because today was the first of several such ceremonies.

My parents wanted to be on the road by two-thirty in order to avoid commute traffic. I waved them off and decided I had time to return the truck before getting to Skunk and Cricket's at four. I stopped at the church on my way home and checked my messages. I called Inez Perry back and set up a time for counseling with Shelly. In the mail, I found the information from the conference on submitting our bills for the shelter expenses. I called Jean and made arrangements to drop the information by her house on the way out to Oak Lake.

I stopped at my house before going to Skunk and Cricket's. I admit that I ran my fingers along the walls and repeated the words, my house several times before I got down to the business of feeding John Wesley and telling him I wouldn't be home for a while. I took a moment to watch the breeze rippling the lake. I stood and did nothing but breathe in the peace of the moment. I thought I needed to be filled with peace in order to bring peace into Skunk and Cricket's home. I found my guitar and picked up the bundled sage Mom had made for us. I smiled at the sage. The church had used holy water or salt for this in the past. Other cultures used sage. Aromatic herbs have multiple roles in the Judeo-Christian heritage. I thought the fact that my mom found this and bundled it for us added a blessing in itself.

Skunk and Cricket's house smelled of tomatoes, garlic, wine and a blend of other delicate herbs. The owners seemed curious about what I intended. Cricket and I had worked out how we would proceed. She prepared by wearing her ballet shoes. Skunk started the stereo for us. We used the music from the opera "Ruth."

We opened all the doors and windows downstairs, then went upstairs opening windows as we went. I ignored the dirty laundry on the floor. When we reached the farthest back bedroom we started retracing our steps. Skunk took charge of the smoking sage. I noted that Mom had done a great job of mixing enough dry wood to burn with greens to make a little smoke.

I made a guess at the key of the stereo music and started playing a quiet Alleluia on the guitar. Cricket started her dance. Sometimes, I thought she was chasing the evil out of her home. Sometimes she looked as if she was sweeping under the furniture. I had a thought that evil would find a strong opponent in this woman. I smiled and began to pray silently. "Yes, God, I will nurture this one for you. I think she sees more with her heart than most do with their minds. Let your spirit flow through this house. Bind any lingering thoughts of evil and remove them from us. Thank you for bringing these wonderful people into my life." I stumbled in my guitar playing. I stepped out of my shoe and left it in that spot on a landing above the living room and went on with our ritual. We played and smudged and danced in every room of that three-story house. When we finished, I felt exhausted.

Skunk and Cricket seemed energized. Cricket hugged me saying, "I feel as if my house is mine again."

As we went back through to close all the windows, I stopped where I left my shoe. "There is something about this spot. Can you look around and see anything out of place?"

We stood silent for a minute before Skunk spoke, "The picture that hung here is gone. My great aunt sent it to us for a wedding gift. She painted it herself. It was kinda weird, but the colors looked good right here."

I looked around some more. "You should mention that to the police. Your stereo system appears untouched, but an original painting is gone. You know what else I see from here? Isn't that the sixth green?" We could see construction lights at the green as the workers tried to repair the damage. "I think I will call Ralph when I get home. There is more here than just a few missing items."

Cricket interrupted our thoughts. "Let's get some dinner. I'm hungry. You're staying, Pastor. Your mother thinks you need to eat better." Both Skunk and Cricket seemed to think this was a great joke. With a baby on the way, she'd soon learn how mothers worry. As I thought about our ceremony, I wanted to laugh at Skunk calling a painting weird when we had just done the most far-out thing I'd ever encountered in ministry. Perhaps there is some hope for our younger generation if they can see the importance of ritual for their spiritual lives. I thought my congregation would faint if they knew what I had done. I debated within myself whether they would faint before or after they wrote to the bishop.

Cricket is an excellent cook. The dinner tasted delicious. The stimulating conversation convinced me that I wanted to spend more time with these two people.

Just before eight o'clock I went out to get in my car. "Oh it's windy!"

Skunk replied, "Yeah, we are supposed to get a big windstorm tonight. I heard a report of winds out on the ocean of over a hundred miles per hour."

I pulled my coat on. "Charming. I suppose the power will go out and I'll be running a shelter at the church again."

Cricket asked, "Does your church have a shelter?"

"Yes, we have a gas stove, gas heat, and now we have a generator to run the furnace fan." I went on to tell Skunk and Cricket about the school children and the elderly.

"And you cooked for all those people? Someone else should volunteer to cook."

"When I cooked they got soup, salad and bread. We had a navy cook come in the second day and everybody got roast ham, and turkey, and dressing, and all the trimmings." I made a face. We were laughing when I said goodnight.

It took me just minutes to get home. I found John Wesley sleeping as soundly as only a cat can on the sofa back. I wondered if I should start a fire in my fireplace with the sticks Mom and I had picked up and left outside the door to the laundry room. I decided to bring the sticks inside so they wouldn't get any wetter than they already were. I wandered through my house and thought about where to put things away. I looked at the jumbled mess and unmade bed in my bedroom and decided to sleep on the sofa.

By ten, I'd snuggled down on my sectional, wrapped up in a comforter. I thought about lighting a fire and resolved to buy presto logs tomorrow. With my lights out I sat and stared out my window. I loved this house and the view. The weeping willow tree by the lake thrashed wildly about in the wind. I saw the white of waves breaking on my dock. I didn't feel any drafts. The doors and windows didn't rattle with the gusting wind. I felt snug. I settled down in my comforter and slept soundly despite the storm.

CHAPTER 25: DEATH OF THE PARSONAGE

The chill in the house woke me earlier Saturday morning than I liked. It took me several minutes to figure out that the power had gone off. I told John Wesley, "Oh dear, it is most likely off at the church too. Well, I don't have hot water for a shower or anything to cook with so I guess I'll go to the church and start breakfast there."

I managed to figure out how to open the garage door without electricity. I still decided to take the Porsche because its smaller size would help me maneuver around down trees and branches. It took me almost twenty minutes to make the twelve-minute trip to the church. Once, I stopped in the middle of the road, got out of the car and pulled a limb out of the road. I thought about renaming the Douglas Firs, zombie trees, because they dropped parts of themselves at the slightest breeze. They are not at all like the cottonwood, who had just given up the fight with the wind and fell over blocking the road. I drove around the tree on the opposite shoulder.

People and cars filled the church parking lot when I arrived. Because I was anxious about being late, and needing to feed people, I didn't immediately notice something wrong. I'd parked and gotten out of my car before noisy people descended on me. I thought they must be hungry. I remembered my earlier thoughts about zombies as they attacked. Jean pulled me into a hug and praised God.

Confusion reigned. "What? What is going on here?" Silently, the people parted and looked toward the tree resting on top of a very flattened parsonage. I couldn't believe my eyes. I had to look at the trees on the lot behind where the parsonage once stood. I stared at the broken glass gleaming in the morning sun. People hugged me and told me how thankful they were that I had not been in the house. I felt sad for the big leaf maple that had commit suicide by toppling over on my former home. Maybe Doug Firs are not so bad after all. I stared and stared.

A voice asked, "Was your stuff still in there?"

"No. No, everything was out."

Someone else asked, "Your cat? Is he okay?"

"Oh yes, he went with me when I took the furniture. He's moved so many times, he's used to it." I smiled. I didn't intend for John Wesley to move again for a long time. "Um, well, I guess we better get something to eat. There is nothing to do here. The house was insured. This is not a disaster."

I turned around to be caught up in a big hug by Timmy. "I just heard the house went down. I'd hoped you spent the night at your new place."

"Yeah, I'm okay. My power is out so I haven't had a shower or any coffee. We do need to get the coffee going."

Timmy volunteered, "I don't do breakfast at the restaurant so I might as well cook over here. My stove works, but I don't have lights or heat." Larry had to show Timmy the gen-set before any cooking got done. Timmy's wife came over and gave me a hug. I went to my office and looked over my schedule and checked messages while Timmy organized the kitchen. After fifteen minutes, my stomach knotted up and I started to shake. My heart started pounding. I hadn't had an anxiety attack this bad for years. I hoped I had some pills in my desk or purse. I tried practicing my slow, shallow breaths—very slow, shallow breaths. I found a Valium in my desk drawer. I'd kept it for several years it in a small pillbox in with my personal office supplies that I'd taken from job to job. I took the pill then thought being with others might help. I walked out to the social hall.

"Pastor Maude are you all right? You don't look so good." This gem of tact came from Stan, the male cheerleader.

I shook my head. "I was in my office when the shock of losing the parsonage finally hit."

Stan pulled a chair out for me and stood beside me looking helpless.

I tried to assure him. "I'll be all right in a few minutes." I decided not to confess that I took a pill.

"Here Pastor, drink this." Jean shoved a cup of hot chocolate under my nose.

I took it with shaking hands.

Jean continued, "You've had a shock. You need to get your blood sugar up."

"Thanks, I'm afraid you had a bigger shock than I did."

"You know, I just felt in here…" Jean placed her hand near her heart. "…that you were okay."

I nodded and tried to smile reassuringly. I made a mental connection between the denial stage of grieving and the fact that most of the time when we fear something bad has happened—nothing really has happened. I recognized my disconnected, theoretical thinking as sign of my own shock. I wondered if Jean saying she felt in her heart that I was okay was any less weird than Cricket, Skunk and I spiritually cleansing their house.

"Here Maude, eat this. It will help you feel better. You do look a little pale." Timmy set a plate of ham and eggs down in front of me. "The potatoes will be done in a few minutes."

Jean sat beside me as I ate. Larry brought her a plate of food and sat down with us. Another thought floated through my head. "You know there is something profoundly sad about losing a house. They seem to hold memories. I don't know what it is, but losing that house feels like losing a friend."

Jean agreed and talked about some of her memories of the house. We held a little informal memorial for the parsonage there in the corner of the social hall. I drank coffee to keep me awake. The Valium had hit on an empty stomach. I wondered if being aged made it more potent, or if I was just so unsettled that my metabolism was running like a yo-yo.

Shortly before ten, Cricket greeted me from the entrance. "Oh Pastor Maude that poor parsonage. I'm sure that it was God's work that someone helped you move out yesterday so you were safe in your new house."

I thought about the sailors, and my parents and Skunk and realized that I had not asked for help, but it came when needed to move me out of the parsonage.

"I'm sure you are right. Everything worked out okay, in God's time." I felt better. "Is your electricity out too?"

"Yeah, Skunk dropped me off here. He's going in to work today. The police and the FBI are going over our house again today. I wanted to stay out of their way, and we knew you were here because one of our officers told us where you went."

"Why is the FBI at your house?" Alva's eyes grew huge as he asked this question. I introduced Cricket to those members of the congregation nearby.

Cricket explained, "My husband works for Willits-Manion. Our house was broken into Thursday night. They want to be certain nothing sensitive was taken and they are looking for possible DNA samples. Of course, my husband does not bring anything from work home with him."

I almost laughed at the way Cricket said her husband worked for Willits-Manion. No grand dame could have communicated her pride in her important husband better than Cricket had done.

She wore hiking boots with her leggings and a bright colored cotton skirt that seemed to emphasize her baby bump. Her bright blue and green hair matched her skirt. On her top half, she wore an assortment of items including two tees, scarves, a sweater and a jacket.

I thought my congregation could be more accepting of Cricket if they knew more about her. "Cricket teaches dance at Olympic. Her students had a recital Thursday night. While she and her husband were at the recital, someone broke into their house. The thieves left obvious valuable stuff and took some rather distinctive things."

A discussion started about the number of break-ins around town and the vandalism at the country club. I got up and returned my plates to the kitchen. Cricket followed me. I thought to ask, "Have you had breakfast? Get yourself a plate of food."

Cricket sounded cheerful enough. "Oh I can't eat yet. I just finished throwing up before we left the house. I won't be able to eat for a couple hours yet."

This statement overpowered the other women in the kitchen. They made Cricket sit down, and they gave her a lesson on defeating morning sickness.

She sounded grateful and naïve. "Oh, I didn't know any of that stuff. My mom is not much help. Pastor Maude has been really helpful, but I hadn't told her about the morning sickness before. I thought it was just something you had to put up with."

Late in the morning, Joey came in with Christine Peterson. "Mom said you had food down here. We came to see if you needed help."

"Oh thanks. Is your mom okay at her house?"

"Yeah, she has a wood stove she can cook on. She likes it, really. I'm glad I got home in time to get in some emergency supplies and firewood for her."

"When did you get here?"

"Late Thursday."

Christine moved possessively closer to him. "I was so surprised when he showed up on my doorstep at ten-thirty at night." Christine and Joey dissolved into a discussion of how he didn't want to wait until morning to see her. This conversation could only be interesting to the lovers so I went out to clear tables. I remembered to thank God that Elma's son had gotten home in time to make certain her house was secure before another power outage.

The rest of the day passed without any drama. I finished all my paperwork and decided to leave my sermon as I'd written it. The electricity came on about one. After I saw that everything was cleaned up, I locked up the church and gave Cricket a ride back to her house.

The police and FBI were just finishing up. She seemed happy to stay home and cook dinner.

At bedtime Ralph called. All my anxiety from earlier in the day melted at the sound of his voice. "Hi, I'm home. How have you been?"

"Oh I'm glad to hear from you. How was your trip?"

"I think I could have driven between here and there faster than I could fly. The small town where I was working was quaint enough—not as friendly as Blackfish."

"You mean that everybody there doesn't know everybody else's business?"

"Maybe they do, but I never got the insider scoop."

"Do you think your clients have a case?"

"Yeah, it looked pretty clear that the old man had severe dementia by the time he made the last will. The medications he was on indicated a fairly advanced stage. The medical examiner discovered that the care attendant had not been giving the guy all his meds. We suspect she was stealing the pain medications and selling them. His kids did a good job in ordering an autopsy. He had been to the doctor two weeks before he died, and his blood-levels for his pain medications and one psychotropic were almost non-existent. Yeah, they'll win the case. I hope the care attendant ends up in prison. What have you been up to?"

"I moved into the lake house yesterday." We talked for almost two hours as I told him about moving and Skunk and Cricket's house. We made plans for Ralph to come over after church in the morning.

CHAPTER 26: SUNDAY ON THE LAKE

Sunday morning, Christine showed up early for church. She told me that Joey would be bringing his mom later. "Would you like me to play the piano this morning?"

"Would you? I'd be so thankful."

"Sure, this instrument is really nice. Of course it needs tuning, but Joey says he'll see that it gets done. I'm sorry about the parsonage. Did you get all your stuff out?"

I nodded and told her a little about my move. "Christine, I probably shouldn't say this, but having that tree fall on the house was a blessing. We are insured. The house was eighty years old. It had been lovingly cared for, but the wiring was old. The plumbing was old. It had ants and mice. I'm sure the congregation is heartsick, but I lived there. The place was not sound."

We chatted for a couple minutes about music for the service then Christine went off to practice. I went to my office. "*Wow…a musician… oh thank you God. I suspect that you were tired of my playing or all the recorded music, but I thank you for Christine.*"

I preached my sermon as I had originally written it. I gave thanks that I hadn't changed it when I noticed a couple people crying. They gave me hugs afterward and thanked me for the sermon.

Church let out at eleven. Just after twelve I pulled my Porsche into my yard. I saw a pickup truck parked out front. "What now?" I went inside and looked out my living room window. A man stood on my dock, fishing. He turned slightly and I recognized Ralph without really seeing him. I could tell by his build. I sighed. Then, I ran out to meet him. I still wore my church shoes and needed to wade a stretch of water between the dock and me. That little stretch of water, housed a boat—a ten-foot aluminum rowboat.

"Just climb through the boat." Ralph reeled in his fishing line. I saw that he had the dock covered with an extra pole, a fishing box, and one of those mesh things for dead fish. I climbed into the boat and took off my shoes. I still needed to wade through the water that was over the top of my dock where it was anchored at the shore. I reached the dock just as Ralph put down his fishing pole. He pulled me into his arms for a hug and a kiss. I melted. I slid my hands up his chest and around his neck. I think I kissed him as eagerly as he kissed me.

When he broke off the kiss, I still leaned against him with my arms around his neck. "You know, it's really nice to come home and find someone I like here."

He smiled. "Did you see what else is here?" He indicated the rowboat.

"Where did that come from?"

"West Marine. I got it for you for a housewarming gift."

"For me? Oh it's wonderful! Oh wow—a housewarming gift. I can hardly wait to go rowing. Thank you."

"Let's eat first. I had a little luck for our brunch." He showed me three nice sized trout in the creel. I put my shoes back on in the boat, and we walked up to the house together.

"Um…I just remembered something. I don't have a stove. Well, I do have a small propane burner thing that I use for picnicking. While I changed clothes, Ralph set up the propane burner on the patio. He'd brought bread and potato salad from the deli. He fried the fish for me.

Ralph cooked my first meal in my new house for me. It was a little cold on the patio, but neither of us complained. It didn't take long for the fish to cook. We ate our fish at my dining table in my dining room. I used my best china for my first meal in my new house. I left the dishes by the sink in the kitchen saying I would do them later. "Like maybe when I buy a dishwasher. See, this is one of my problems. I could store a portable dishwasher here." I indicated an open space under the counter across the kitchen from the sink. "I'd have to remodel to put in a regular dishwasher. I want to think about this and live with it longer before I remodel."

"Buy a portable. It can be stripped down and installed by the sink when you remodel."

"Can I really do that—convert a portable to installed?"

"Yes, they are made to do that." Ralph grinned and chuckled, "I can't believe the woman who converted a Porsche to an electric car couldn't figure that out. Now I want to take my favorite gal rowing."

I grinned. I think I smiled more over being called his favorite gal than over the rowing, but I wanted to get out on the lake.

A chill breeze blew out on the water. Ralph rowed. I sat on the back seat facing him. The breeze seemed stronger than I expected on the small lake. "You know, if someone had a wet suit they could possibly wind surf here. I wonder if Trevor has a wet suit that fits? Speaking of our kids, did Rich recover from meeting up with us Tuesday night?"

Ralph sighed, "Rich described how weird he found the situation on Facebook."

"Oh dear, is that a public enough announcement that we are seeing each other?"

"I'm not sure how it could get more public."

I demanded that Ralph let me row on the way back. I got warm quickly enough while rowing. I worried about leaving the boat on the dock so we carried it up to the house and turned it upside down under the living room window.

We warmed up by making hot chocolate in the microwave. I think I smiled all afternoon. We spent most of the day talking. We toured the house and talked about where to put shelves and books.

"Your laundry room has great potential as a bonus room. It's big, has its own bath, and an outside entrance."

"Yeah, I looked at all that space and wondered about the best way to use it. I'm seriously thinking about a stackable washer and dryer despite the fact that they would be expensive. That would leave me more room for a study or whatever."

About four, Cricket called and invited me over for dinner. I explained that Ralph was visiting. "Oh good, bring him over too. I know you don't have a refrigerator or stove."

I turned to Ralph, "Would you like to have dinner with my friends Skunk and Cricket?"

He nodded so we made the arrangements. On the drive up to Skunk and Cricket's, we talked about their break-in. I told Ralph about the vandalism and the picture that was stolen from the only spot in the house that had a view of the sixth green. He laughed when I told him about my parents' reaction to the vandalism, and how I laughed over their thinking I would be more shocked by the figure of the vandalism than by the fact that it happened.

I helped Cricket get the food on the table while Skunk showed Ralph around the house and talked about the robbery.

As Ralph sat down at the table, he commented. "I think it was more than one person. You probably had someone looking for something specific. Some of the things you describe are easily sold, the DVD's and the laptop computer. They left some of the stuff that could pose a problem. Your stereo is unique and hard to move. Your TV is heavy. The second thief is probably the one with the mental disorder who did the vandalism."

Later, when I remembered this conversation, I was amazed that

Ralph had come so close to describing the thieves.

We returned to my house for a few minutes before Ralph needed to leave to catch his ferry. He'd left his fishing gear on my porch. "Can I put this away in your garage? I won't need it anywhere else until spring." After he put his things away, we spent the last few minutes before he left, kissing. I rediscovered that I like kissing very much. He whispered, "You taste good. When is the next boat after this one?"

"Eleven, and it's an hour crossing."

He nuzzled my neck. "I need to go to work in the morning. Maudy, we have something good going here."

"Yeah, I think so, but I don't want to rush anything."

"I don't think we are rushing to share a few kisses."

"I…I've been widowed so long that a few kisses are very special to me." I smiled and giggled. I really liked being in Ralph's arms. I didn't allow my anxiety to reach the conscious level, but I think Ralph saw it.

He asked, "What is it?"

I was confused. "What?"

"You seem afraid of something."

"I do? I don't know. I suppose I'm just afraid of making a mistake with our relationship. I want to do things right."

He looked into my eyes. "I have to catch a ferry. I'll call you."

My life finally fell into the routine I had been trying to establish all fall. I managed to take Mondays off simply by not driving into the church. I spent the day shopping for my new house, cooking for myself and planning my gardens. I started making new curtains for all the windows. I decided to use the second bedroom for my sewing room for now. I really wanted it for a guest room for my kids.

I had four counseling clients now, which brought in some extra pennies. Most of my time seemed to be spent in committee meetings. I wrote my sermons. I visited the parishioners. I learned that the woman who had been so sick during the flood had survived. I visited her when she returned home. Joel's friend, Mary, started coming to worship service regularly. I hoped that she recognized that God loved her.

Several people mentioned how much they enjoyed the community dinners when the power was out. I convinced the church to start community lunches once a week to help out our low-income seniors. Sometimes I cooked. Mr. Cole agreed to cook once a month. His lunches were fantastic.

I joined a choir in Silverdale just to get a chance to really sing and meet people outside my church. I finally bought new appliances for the house. Patty and Trevor visited me on Saturdays. Trevor developed a passion for turning my large laundry room into his hang out. He decided to make a sleeping loft above the garage. I ignored him.

I devoted my Sunday afternoons to Ralph. I lived for Sunday afternoon when I got home to find Ralph there before me. He cooked me lunch, and we spent the day puttering around my house. We went to a couple matinees at the theater in Silverdale. Ralph bought me gardening books, and we spent hours planning my landscaping.

CHAPTER 27: THANKSGIVING BREAK-IN

Ralph's family lived in California so when Thanksgiving arrived he was at loose ends. I invited him and his children to eat dinner with my family. We finally agreed that he would arrive at my house early Thursday with his kids, and we would have breakfast before we went to dinner with my parents. I invited Skunk and Cricket as a buffer.

The minute Ralph arrived and began to introduce his children to mine, Rich exclaimed, "Dad this is still weird."

Ralph asked, "What is so weird?"

I tried to say something normal. "Welcome. Come in. Hang your coats in this closet."

"Amen, it is weird." This surprised me coming from Trevor.

Ralph commented, "That is a cute window in your closet."

"There is a window there? I hadn't noticed." Patty had to go back outside and look at the closet window from the porch. She met Skunk and Cricket on the porch. Cricket had died her hair russet and orange. Ralph and I did not get a chance to kiss among all the confusion.

I asked, "What have you got there, Cricket?"

Rich asked. "Do you go rowing much?"

Trevor answered Rich. "I want to get a kayak, there is a huge swamp further up…"

Cricket answered my question. "Oh this is ravioli with sausage. My grandmother always made this for Thanksgiving."

Skunk asked, "Can we go out on the dock?"

April, Ralph's daughter, asked, "Has Dad been poaching your fish?"

Ralph answered, "No, we eat them fried usually."

I took Cricket's dish. "Let's put this in the warming oven until we are ready to sit down."

"Daddy!" April sounded disgusted with her father's sense of humor. "What …?"

And so, the morning went. Our children got along with each other reasonably well. I thought Patty seemed friendlier with Cricket than April, but they were closer in age. Trevor led the others on a tour of his renovations in my laundry room. Skunk seemed to know something about carpentry. Breakfast included a discussion as to whether I should work toward a Prairie Style or Asian for my landscaping. Cricket spoke so knowledgeably on the topic that she amazed my children. When I noticed Patty revising her opinion of Cricket's intelligence, I gave her *the look* for judging others. She rolled her eyes at me. Cricket and Skunk left right after breakfast so she could cook something for a party in the afternoon.

On the way out the door, Cricket paused, "Oh, before I go. I should tell you that Mary and I want to cook a meal for the weekly community lunches. She can get school credit for it." Skunk shifted his weight. "Skunk, I'll be fine. I'm healthy. Mary can do the heavy stuff."

In the afternoon, we went to my parents' house for dinner. My parents were thrilled to meet Ralph. I had some aunts and uncles there. My uncle's wife has a rather loud voice and felt the need to comment, "Well, it's about time you brought home a man. You've been widowed too long—a pretty little thing like you should have remarried long ago."

"I'm glad she waited for me." I gave thanks for Ralph's graceful handling of the situation.

"It's still weird." This message arrived in stereo from Trevor and Rich.

"They're not engaged or anything." Patty announced.

"Yeah." Patty and April had found something to agree on. Patty liked Ralph. I wasn't sure why she had a problem with April. I sincerely hoped that she was not going to be upset that April had not talked about anything except sports all day. On the other hand, April could exercise some social skills.

The day passed smoothly with a few exceptions. My cousin, Amanda came with her husband and daughter, Fay. Mandy is six months younger than I am. We've always been close, which was why it hurt my feelings when her husband volunteered, "Women should keep silent in church. Any church that ordains women is not following the Bible and therefore is not Christian." I'm not sure what appalled me more--his rudeness, or his ignorance. He upset Ralph more than he did me. Ralph didn't say anything. He just stood up and came up to me and put his arm around me. I remembered that I hadn't been kissed today so I led Ralph off to my parents' walk-in closet. I felt much better after about five minutes.

"Maudy, I'm so sorry about Harve." Mandy whispered when she cornered me where nobody else could hear. "Harve has been a good husband for twenty years...well...for fifteen anyway. He has gotten on this kick where he is the head of the household and Fay and I can't do anything. She is an honor student, but he will not let her out of the house to do things with her friends. I can't spend any money without his approval and he doesn't approve of any expenses. He wouldn't even let me buy new shoes this fall when my black ones burst out at the side. He said I could wear out my brown ones first." I thought Mandy might start to cry. "He gets so angry when I try to stand up to him. I have no idea what he does with the money he earns. He demands that I give him my paycheck. I used to have automatic deposit, but he yelled and fussed until I stopped that and now I have to show him the check."

Harve's behavior toward Mandy disgusted me more than his comment to me. "He needs to be tagged for bullying. Has he forgotten the part about husbands love your wives or about do not vex your children?" I got angry with Harve all over again.

Mandy continued to whisper her woes to me. "I don't have any idea what is running through his head. Perhaps he is worried about retirement. I've gone to counseling. I even talked to an attorney. I'm giving him until Fay graduates to change." We got interrupted when Mom announced dinner. Daddy asked me to say the blessing. Harvey whispered audibly his own blessing much to the amusement of the rest of the family. I worried that Fay might be embarrassed. She seemed to be in her own little world.

I didn't learn of any problems in Blackfish until Friday afternoon following Thanksgiving. I got a call at my office. "Pastor Maude, Jon Archer here. I am a member of the Jewish Fellowship. Um…say… uh…we had a break-in at our meeting hall."

"Oh no, I'm so sorry. Is there any thing I can do to help?"

"Well that's why I called you. Officer Ryan suggested that you are the best person to talk to. We need someplace to meet. I wondered if we could use one of your rooms."

"How many people do you have and what time do you need the room?" We made arrangements for me to talk to the chair of the trustees and get back to him.

I hated to call Alva Brinks. His wife sounded cross, but she let me talk to him. I outlined the details. "They've offered to pay rent. They have insurance that covers renting another place while theirs is unusable. His offer is generous. What I need from the trustees is someone to show the people around and lock up when they leave. Some help with set up for them would be nice. They must be heartsick over being vandalized."

"Maude we haven't voted on this."

"Alva, this is part of being prepared to help others. We already voted to open the church to those in need."

"Pastor I think you are stretching this. Jon Archer is a decent enough man. I didn't know he was Jewish. I'll make some calls and be there in a half hour." I called Jon back and made the arrangements.

My people arrived shortly before four to clean out a room big enough for eighteen adults. I didn't know what they needed. When the equivalent of a worship committee arrived from the Jewish Fellowship, I was glad we were prepared for them.

They acted distraught. "It is a shame that people are still so narrow minded. They are filthy beasts."

I wanted to be comforting. "I am so sorry this happened. What supplies do you need to get set up here? We have cloths, and banners, and candles."

An elderly man just needed to talk. "It was horrible—just horrible. I was the one to discover it."

"Oh dear, how distressing for you. Can I get you anything? Would you like some coffee?" I soothed.

Alva asked the question our guests wanted to hear. "What did the thieves take?"

"They took some cups. We don't have anything of value. It is what they left. They smeared shit all over everything then drew swastikas in it. They even defaced our Torah."

I sat down in shock. "Oh, how horrible! Oh this is terrible! I am so sorry for you. I wonder if this is the same group that broke into Skunk's house and vandalized the country club. I want to talk to somebody about this."

Alva said, "Aw, Pastor you'll use any excuse to talk to that boyfriend of yours."

I smiled at Alva, laughed and blushed.

One of the women asked, "You are not married then?"

"Widowed, and I just started seeing a man who just might be the right kind of man. He's a forensic psychologist and was interested in another break-in associated with the vandalism at the country club. Do you need another Torah for your worship?"

One of the men grumped, "It is a little hard to get on without one. One of the men might bring something from home."

"Just a minute. I might have something suitable." I limped off to the supply room that I had cleaned earlier. I found the scrolls and their stand and carried them back to the waiting worship committee. "Will these help? Are they the right thing?"

Jon Archer looked over the scrolls that I brought out. "Yes, these are perfect. They are beautiful. What is a Christian Church doing with such a magnificent, traditional, copy of the Torah?"

"Well, it is the same God. Beyond that I don't know how these came to be here, but please use them. I want you to feel welcome and cherished here. Come I have banners and cloths in the back of the sanctuary too."

When we finished, we had constructed a lovely Jewish meeting place. I think the stress of witnessing the others' grief tired me out. I wanted nothing more than to go home and curl up on my sofa.

CHAPTER 28: FAMILY TIME

On Sunday morning, I cornered Jean before worship and asked her to call a meeting of the finance committee to discuss some surplus funds. I figured the best way to head off complaints about letting the Jewish Fellowship use our classroom was to distract the congregation with something else. This trick worked better with my congregation than it did with my kids.

After church, I went home to a yard full of cars. One belonged to Ralph, of course. I recognized the other two cars as belonging to Patty and Trevor. I went in to find Ralph fixing my lunch and my kids nowhere to be seen. "Are we really alone?" Ralph greeted me by pulling me into his arms for a long kiss then kissing me quickly all over my face. He punctuated the kisses with his explanation.

"Trevor and Rich…" kiss "…are working on the loft…" kiss "April took the boat out." Kiss. "And, Patty is in the sewing room." Kiss.

"Mmm…" I kissed Ralph back. "Do you suppose…" kiss "that they will think…" kiss "that we are weird…" kiss "if they…" kiss "catch us at this?"

"Mmm…" kiss "probably."

"Okay, that's enough you two. Mom, how do I get this seam to turn right?" I gave up hugging Ralph to help Patty with her sewing. Ralph went back to his cooking with a big grin on his face.

I looked at him. "What?"

Ralph explained, "I like this. When the kids said they wanted to come over, I was frustrated because I wanted to be alone with you. They don't often ask to do things with me so I brought them along. Your two were here when we arrived. This feels good to me. It feels good to have both sets of kids here with us." I smiled and slid into Ralph's arms for another hug.

"Weird." Trevor and Rich came into the kitchen. "When do we eat?"

I laughed at the boys. "I'll go get changed. How will we tell April, it is time for lunch."

"I told her when to be back." Ralph seemed to be at peace with his children.

When I finished changing. I looked out the living room window to see April carrying the rowboat up the lawn. Instead of dragging it across the grass like I do, she had turned the thing over and was carrying it over her head. I saw that she had left the oars by the water.

"I'll help April with the boat." I volunteered.

"No. She can manage." I looked at Ralph. He looked me in the eye. I nodded and wondered about April's issues.

It felt a little weird sitting down to a Sunday dinner in a family of six. We all praised Ralph for his cooking. The conversation flowed around Trevor's progress on his loft. Rich sounded enthusiastic about Trevor's skills. We discussed Patty's work in accounting and the others' schoolwork. April's major was in pre-law. Rich had not decided what he wanted to do. He was thinking of some sort of pre-med program. It impressed me that both Ralph's children attended Seattle University. It is an expensive school.

When the topic of my work came up I mentioned that the Blackfish United Methodist Church was now also a meeting place for a Jewish Fellowship. I told everyone about the break-in and mentioned vandalism that involved swastikas. The local crime didn't sound very exciting to young adults who live in the city. They were not impressed that I had found an appropriate Torah in our supply room.

"Do you have a Qur'an too?" April sounded a little belligerent.

"You know, I don't know. I'll have to look in the church library. We probably should have one."

April asked, "What about copies of the ancient Hebrew and Greek?"

My kids laughed and Patty answered, "Certainly," in the Greek while Trevor said the same thing in Hebrew.

I laughed. "As you can see they suffered when I had to learn the Hebrew and Greek. I have copies of both that float around here wherever I sit down to study or write a sermon."

April seemed a trifle more accepting. "I didn't know a preacher had to know all that stuff."

"It depends on your church. Some churches ordain people who have never been to seminary. Ours has a long process for ordination." I could have gone on for a long time describing who does what for ordination.

Trevor intervened. "Don't get her started. In fact, I should warn you never to get in a theological discussion with my mom. She knows her stuff. I'm surprised Uncle Harvey got off so easily."

"It was a family gathering and I didn't want to embarrass Mandy and Fay."

Patty volunteered. "Fay has a serious boyfriend. I don't think she knew we existed."

This news surprised me. "Oh? Mandy says her father won't let her go out."

"Yeah, she was texting him from my phone. She doesn't have a cell phone." We finished our lunch with a discussion of how barbaric and primitive it would be to live without a cell phone. Uncle Harve was denounced as a zombie. I wondered if Fay had caused her parents problems or if, as Mandy suggested, Harvey was in deep spiritual trouble.

Trevor suggested, "Hey let's go into Silverdale and watch a movie." All four young adults headed for the door leaving their plates on the table. I didn't move. Patty remembered first.

"Oops we forgot to clean the table." She came back and gathered up her plate and carried it to the kitchen.

"Are you two done with the potatoes and green beans?" Trevor didn't seem to think much of clearing away his dishes. Rich watched Trevor and did as Trevor did. April narrowed her eyes and appeared to be debating whether or not to conform. She decided to conform, for now, and cleaned away her dishes.

Our offspring finally went out the door leaving Ralph and I alone to kiss or talk. We did both. I told Ralph about feces being used to deface the Jewish Fellowship.

Ralph grunted, "That fits with my estimation of the second thief. He is probably borderline intelligent. He probably participates in the break-ins to self-stimulate. The fecalphillia would fit with this description. The bigger question is, what does his partner want and why is he hanging out with his low functioning sidekick." We changed our topic of conversation to more pleasant topics. He didn't talk about April's issues today.

I didn't learn about a break-in at the local welding shop on Thanksgiving night until I went to breakfast at Timmy's. "It looks like we have a real crime wave here in Blackfish. It doesn't happen often. The sheriff will eventually get the kid. Out here crime is rare enough that when it happens, the criminal is easy enough to spot—just look for some troubled kid in his early twenties."

"Ralph thinks it is two young adults. One has borderline intelligence and the other is after something specific with each break-in. The smarter one may be working for someone else and comes out with a shopping list. Ralph wonders why the smarter one hangs out with the low functioning one."

"Oh we produce a regular crop of low functioning kids who hang around in Blackfish until they end up in jail. The smarter one might want someone to stand guard. If it is a homegrown kid, he'll know who has what and how to get into places. The local kids regularly go swimming in the country club pool after the place closes down. They all know how to get in there. Most of them know how to get into most places they shouldn't be. Be sure and lock up the church real tight. It won't keep out anybody who knows what they are doing, but you won't feel guilty if they do break in."

CHAPTER 29: ADVENT

I forgot about our crime wave as I prepared for Christmas. The choir I sang in had extra rehearsals for our concert. I needed to shop for my family. I sent out Christmas cards. I prepared special events for Advent and the Christmas Eve service. The congregation decorated the church the same as it always had with a few notable exceptions. Cricket and Mary helped with the decorations. Cricket took home all the tatty, broken and worn-out bits of balls, and angels and worked magic with them. She brought them back more beautiful than when they were new. She and Mary placed these in strategic places among the old things. They brightened up what would have been a drab display.

Just before the third Sunday in Advent, I got a call from the Deacon at the Catholic church. Pastor Maude? Brian Kelly here. I just discovered that we had a break-in last night. The church is a mess."

"Oh, I am so sorry. Would your people like to come here? We could do a blended service. I'm flexible. It isn't a Communion Sunday for us so we won't have a conflict there. Oh, I am just sick for you."

"We don't have Mass until eleven and you start earlier."

"Oh. Oh, of course, you can come at eleven if you like. It won't hurt our people to greet each other as one congregation leaves and the other enters. Of course I will hold your congregation in my prayers. This is so shocking and heartbreaking." I knew I was gushing a bit, but decided that gushing at a time like this might be acceptable.

On Sunday, I got home from church late because I stayed and greeted each of the fifteen members of the Catholic Church. I found that Trevor and Ralph had carpooled. As soon as I got home, I went immediately to Ralph for a kiss. "I'm sorry I'm late. We had another break-in. This time the Catholic Church was vandalized."

"Was there anything significantly different this time?"

"No, instead of swastikas they got the word, pedophiles. Usually, there is a home or business broken into at the same time. Everybody is assuming they break into the business or home for money then when they are high from the break-in or drugs, they vandalize something. Anyway, the Catholics think they can get it cleaned up soon enough.

I've committed to joining them for a cleansing ceremony and mass on Wednesday." We discussed other happenings in our lives for most of the meal.

"Um Mom?" I looked at Trevor. "Uh…Bret and Steve are moving out of the apartment because Derik is such a slob. I don't want to try to get more roommates because I don't want to live with Derik either. I think I'll stay here next quarter."

I nearly jumped out of my seat. "What about classes?"

Trevor explained, "That is the other part of it. Most of my classes are seminars with labs. I needed a Shakespeare class for humanities credit, but I couldn't get it on campus. I can take it online. I can take my "History of Design" in Tacoma. My other classes are on Wednesday, Thursday and Friday. I think I'll commute-in three days. Go to Tacoma one day and stay home three days."

I worried, "I'm afraid you'll miss out on campus life."

Ralph laughed, "Trevor your mom is a gem. I wish my mom had been like that." He changed his tone to a falsetto, "Oh son, I want you to have fun at college."

I slapped Ralph's arm. "Oh shut up. I was thinking of guest lectures and visiting with friends between classes."

Trevor sounded happy with his plan. "I'll still meet my friends when I'm there. Staying here will save me five hundred a month after commuting costs."

I smiled and thought of the joys of having my son close by. "Of course you are welcome to stay here. I can clean my sewing out of the spare bedroom."

"I'll stay in the loft."

"It isn't finished. It doesn't have stairs."

"Oh I'll finish it next weekend. Skunk has offered to help me."

I looked at Ralph and felt a little sad. I liked being alone with Ralph, but maybe with Trevor in his loft he wouldn't be too intrusive. I had a brilliant idea. "One other item of business is that I need to be in Seattle next week for an appointment with Doctor Dave. Do you want me to bring back a load of your stuff? I suppose I could even bring the big car."

"Yeah, thanks."

Ralph asked, "Do you have other errands in town? Can we get together?"

"Sure, I can always do more Christmas shopping. I don't know. Let's do something Christmassy."

Ralph leered at me. "Okay I'll think something up. Perhaps I'll take you to sit on Santa's lap."

"Keep it clean you two. Sheesh, what do you call this? Inappropriate role reversals?" Trevor chided.

I laughed at Trevor.

He paused, looked at me then looked at Ralph and spoke to him. "You know, I vaguely remember seeing her really happy when we were little. She has been sad so long that I'd forgotten what she was like. Take care of her."

Trevor's observation left me speechless.

Ralph assured my son. "I intend to Trevor. She is a special lady. I'll be real careful with her."

Wow! I was going to have something to say to Doctor Dave.

Ralph had decided that he needed to take his children to California for Christmas. "Maybe I should have made more effort for them to get to know their cousins. They were impressed with the generations at your parents' house and how much fun the cousins and second cousins had together."

"I'd like to see you during the holidays, but to be honest, I am so busy, then I am tired. I have my family parties and a party with my college friends. You go enjoy yourself and we'll do something special when you return—maybe something like a twelfth-night party or date."

"The twelfth-night it is." Before Ralph left, we spent some time necking. I liked rubbing my hands on his body—just feeling him. I giggled and he whispered, "What?" his breath hot in my ear.

"You know, when we met, and you were feeling my leg as you tried to get my shoe off..."

"I wasn't feeling your leg."

"Yes, you were and I was feeling your shoulders and arms."

"Well maybe I was feeling your leg a little. Okay I really enjoyed feeling your leg."

"How naughty I was to be carrying on like that with a total stranger."

"It turned out good, Maudy, very good."

"I think so too." The twelfth night was two and a half weeks away. We would see each other again next week. I needed to talk to Doctor Dave.

CHAPTER 30: UNFINISHED BUSINESS

On Wednesday I went to Seattle for my appointment with Doctor Dave. I drove over early in the morning to meet Trevor at his apartment near the University, and picked up a Sentra-load of stuff. I planned to meet Patty after my appointment.

I arrived a wee bit early for my appointment, but Doctor Dave told me to come on in. "How have you been?"

"Surprisingly good. I'm busy."

"How is your church?"

"You know, right now we are doing okay. A few new people are coming. We have had some donations for our shelter work. The Jewish fellowship rented out part of the building for three weeks. We are serving free meals to low-income people once a week. I have huge community support for the meals. It started with me cooking all of the lunches, but I keep getting more volunteers. The Catholics are cooking one week and the Jewish fellowship another week. I have volunteers for the other two weeks. Of course, when Cricket gets close to having that baby she may not be able to cook, but I can always make soup."

"Good. What do you think the prognosis is for the church?"

"Realistically, it could still go under. Most of the activity is being generated from my counseling or the shelter. If I leave, the volunteers will leave too."

"Are you planning on leaving?"

"Oh no. I solved most of the problems I had when I started. I'm getting some counseling income. I love my little house. Trevor is moving home and commuting next quarter. That will cramp my relationship with Ralph some." There I had worked the conversation around to Ralph and continued on this topic. "Rich and Trevor get along quite well. He is only nineteen and seems to hero worship Trevor. April is Trevor's age. She is going through a feminist stage. I suspect that she is having trouble with her sexual identity. I haven't talked to Ralph about it. With her, we just take things as they come. Anyway, Ralph says that April doesn't know what to make of me. I am in a non-traditional profession, which she thinks is good. I dress like a woman, which confuses her. She has the same problem with Patty being an accountant and dressing like a woman. Ralph just chuckles over this. He seems to think that April will get things sorted out."

"Sounds like you are getting along with Ralph just fine. Are you sleeping with him?"

"No, I'm afraid that if I got into bed with Ralph neither of us would get any sleep. We are not having intercourse either."

Doctor Dave laughed. "You always were one to go for the heart of the matter."

"You know, I think you are right. I want to know the heart of a matter—what drives behavior. That is why I am here. I think there is some unfinished business between me and Hal and I don't know what it is."

"Don't push the memories Maude, you are under a great deal of stress with buying a house, and trying to grow a church, and starting a relationship with Ralph. If you push it, you will just end up confabulating. Your memories of the beating are just fragments. If you push the fragments, the brain will weave them into a story that may be worse than the truth."

"That's interesting. Perhaps that is what the brain is trying to do, because I still have a sense that there is some big shadowy thing out there that I don't know about. I think it has something to do with why my in-laws blamed me for Hal's death. I have the autopsy report. I understand Hal's injury and death. I don't know, do his parents think I pushed him or something that he got the second hit on the head? The report said that he hit his head getting into his truck."

"Maude. You're pushing for something that may not be there. Anger is a necessary part of grieving. Hal's parents seem stuck there— possibly because they took their anger out on you. They don't admit the truth so they can't move on."

"Trevor and Patty have agreed to spend Christmas Eve with them. I'm really hurt all over again that they wanted the children to come, but told me to stay home."

"Aren't you busy Christmas Eve?"

"Yes, I have a service to do. It's not this year I'm sad about. It's when the children were little. That very first Christmas after I got hurt, and I was still living with Mom and Daddy, and they invited the children to come for Christmas Eve and told me to just drop them off at four and I could pick them up at ten."

"That was an unrealistic expectation. You didn't drop the children off. Perhaps that's what they wanted. Hal was gone. It may have seemed easier to cut off his whole family. You were easy to cut off. They could manipulate you into refusing to bring the children."

"You think they got what they wanted?"

"They're successful in other ways. People generally get what they want. They don't always get what they need or what is best for them. In a case like this, the best you can do is look at the outcome and conclude they got what they wanted."

"They wanted to cut off Hal's wife and children because of their own hurt. I can buy that. People do that often enough. Perhaps they're starting to get past that anger and have invited the kids over for Christmas because they need to reconnect." I felt quite happy with this explanation. As it turned out, I was wrong, but at the time I liked the explanation.

Doctor Dave said that I could work from that premise and see how it fit. I left his office happy. We'd talked about something that puzzled me and might be part of my hesitation with Ralph. Dr. Dave's explanation of my in-law's behavior fit with what I knew about grieving, death and dying.

I met Patty. We had lunch and did a little shopping. "What do you think? If you and Trevor are spending Christmas Eve with Grandma Henderson, should I send along a little something to indicate that I am willing to mend the relationship?" We were standing next to some Christmas candles. I thought about them as an appropriate peace offering. "I talked to Doctor Dave about them. I want them to know that I understand their rejection and want to love them as Hal's parents."

"Um…maybe not this year. Let me check the situation out and see where they are emotionally. If they seem open, I'll tell them that you send your love and would like to see them."

I smiled, relieved. "Good. I think you're right. I don't want to intrude if they are not ready to accept me, and well, I have moved on with my life."

"What are you and Ralph doing tonight?"

"He got us tickets to a concert at the Opera House. It should be good."

"I think he is trying hard to impress you."

"He doesn't need to try hard. I was impressed when we first met. I think he does like doing things that make me happy." Patty needed to return to work so we parted and I returned to my car. I had trouble finding someplace to put my purchases with all Trevor's stuff in my car.

Ralph and I ate dinner at a small Thai place near the Opera House and talked about my visit with Doctor Dave. He thought our understanding of Hal's parents sounded plausible. "Death and dying studies are not my area of expertise, but that explanation fits okay. For them to drag this out for ten years seems excessive to me."

"Well Patty said she would look at the situation from that perspective and see if she thinks it fits."

We enjoyed the performance. Ralph was a little crowded into his seat. The Seattle Opera house is the only place I've been where the seating is more cramped than on a Boeing 737. We snuggled up to each other and didn't mind being so close at all. I didn't have time for much kissing when he took me back to my car. I had just a few minutes to catch my ferry. However, I did risk missing my boat to make certain I got a thorough goodnight kiss. After all, I wasn't going to get kissed again until Twelfth Night.

CHAPTER 31: CHRISTMAS EVE

During the ferry ride home, I got out of my car and sat upstairs to watch the lights on the water. I became aware of a gnawing dissatisfaction. I liked kissing Ralph when I was with him, but now I felt a constraint about my relationship to him. I wanted a relationship without barriers, but I sensed barriers and I suspected they came from me. I thought about what could be troubling me. It felt connected to the whole ball of grief over Hal. I sat looking out at the water and not really seeing the beauty of the night.

I still had unresolved issues with Hal. but I had no idea what they were. I had worked and worked in counseling. I knew my memory problems hampered my healing because I could not recall events at the time. Too much happened while I was in the hospital. Hal had died, was cremated and had his ashes buried with his grandfather, and I had not been present.

At seminary, some other students and I had made a memorial worship service for un-grieved deaths. It was a big project for me, and the service turned out beautiful. I felt better after that. I had mourned his death. I wondered what bound me to the past? I remembered Trevor telling Ralph that he had not seen me happy for a long time. Did I have survivor's guilt? Was I just tired? I knew I needed routines to keep me from getting exhausted. I thought about how I felt. Exhausted, pretty much described how I felt. I think I drifted off to sleep for a couple minutes. The announcement that we'd arrived at our destination woke me up. I limped down to my car.

I pulled my carload of Trevor's stuff into the garage and left it for him to unload. I didn't have any obligations at any distance from Blackfish until Christmas day. Trevor would be home in time to unload my car.

On the fourth Sunday in Advent I sang in the concert with my Silverdale choir. Both Trevor and Patty came. Ralph acted disappointed to miss the concert. He had left for California Saturday. He sent flowers that arrived late in the day on Saturday. I was thrilled about the flowers, but worried that he sensed the constraint I was feeling about our relationship.

The concert came off very well. Trevor and Patty presented me with roses after the performance. Their thoughtfulness gratified me. I thought maybe we were feeling closer—more like a family. Perhaps it had been my depression that made me feel distanced from my children, and they were really normal adolescents. We chatted happily on the way home. Trevor had seen Skunk and Cricket at the concert. "They left as soon as it was over because she was tired. "She's starting to look real preggers."

"Oh I'm glad they came. Yeah, I'm not sure when she is due. Perhaps I should have a baby shower for her. I think they have enough money to outfit their child, but the gesture would be meaningful."

Patty pounced on the idea. "Hey, let's do that. You and I can come, and we'll invite April. If we have an afternoon tea at your house, it will be perfect."

"I could invite the women from my congregation. She is getting to know some of them. Mary Carter would be thrilled. Let's do it. I'll ask Cricket when her due date is and we'll schedule it for about a month earlier." I suddenly felt optimistic again with something to look forward to.

I went to my office early in the morning on Christmas Eve. I needed to print out the bulletins for this evening's service. Trevor and Patty had gone to Seattle, planning to visit their Grandparents later, so I wouldn't see them until Christmas Day at my parent's house. I decided not to mope about my kids not being home for tonight and Christmas morning. *"I will just focus on making God's love real to my congregation."* I'd picked up a few hints that I would have more people attending than just my regular congregation. I thought the service would be beautiful. I thanked God that Christine had agreed to play the piano.

I drove home for lunch and wrapped Trevor's and Patty's presents for their stockings. I wondered what to do Christmas morning if they weren't here. I unloaded the last of Trevor's belongings from the trunk of the Sentra. Why did I think my son would get this done on time? I wondered if this was just part of the mother-child relationship. He did most of the job and intended to do the rest, but mom finished the job. I smiled. I liked being Trevor's mom and looked forward to having him home with me.

I sat for a few minutes looking out at the lake. It shone silver. The sky was just plain gray, but the lake reflected silver. I sat and stared at it. I needed to go back to the church in a few minutes, but I made my plans for Christmas morning. I would get up early and dress real warm then I would take the rowboat out. I imagined myself sitting in the middle of the silver surrounded by the lacy shrubbery around the lake. Maybe I could take some pictures. Perhaps I could even take the boat out after the worship service tonight and look at all the Christmas lights around the lake. I had a plan that made me happy.

I arrived at church early to open the doors and start the coffee. I unlocked the supply closet in case we needed more chairs. The worship committee arrived to hand out bulletins and serve as ushers on this special day. Madge whined, "You made too many bulletins. You don't want to waste paper. We have to think of the environment."

I smiled. "I hope we will need all of them." I continued to smile despite my grumpy parishioners. We did need all the bulletins. Mary Carter arrived early with her parents. More students from the high school came. I recognized some people from the shelter. The man who bought my dinner at Timmy's came. The people filled the pews and the hastily set up chairs. I gave thanks that I had put together a lovely service. Usually, people are fairly easy to please on Christmas Eve if you just let them sing the old Christmas carols. The challenge of Christmas Eve is making the experience fresh and exciting for them. I used contemporary issues in the old stories as my theme. I mixed the old with the new. I noticed a delighted Larry counting heads.

After the service, Mary's parents made it a point to talk to me. "Thank you for including Mary. She doesn't have many places she can go other than home."

"I'm planning a baby shower later next month would it be okay with you if I send Mary an invitation. She and Cricket are cooking together once a month."

Cricket arrived at this moment so I made the introduction. She'd dyed her hair green and red for the occasion. As Trevor noticed, she looked quite pregnant.

Shirley stood beside me as an official greeter. She asked, "Cricket when are you due."

"Late February."

"Oh we should have a baby shower for you. Do you know if the baby is a boy or a girl?"

"No, I don't want to know. We'll love whichever it is."

I intervened "About the baby shower thing, Patty and I were talking about it. I'd love to have it at my house."

Shirley looked a little surprised.

I continued, "We have plenty of time to make the plans, but I was thinking of an afternoon tea." I tried to include Mary's parents in this conversation. They were looking a little uncomfortable. I thought

Cricket looked tired. "Where's Skunk?"

"Oh he is putting away chairs. He wanted me to tell you that we really enjoyed the service. This is the way we want to celebrate Christmas every year."

"What are you doing tomorrow?"

"Having dinner with some of the Willets-Manion people who don't have family out here either."

"You look tired. Take it easy."

"Yeah, I wasn't sure I'd survive finals week. Each of my students needs an independent evaluation. I worked long hours, but I am done."

"Come on babe let's get you and the kid home to bed." Skunk led his family away. He called over his shoulder. "That was a great service. Thanks Maudy." I smiled.

I turned to the Carters. "I think Cricket is a great person for Mary to be friends with. She is very responsible."

"How old is she?"

"I have no idea. She teaches at Olympic so I am guessing she has at least her Masters Degree."

"She looks young. Was that her husband?"

"Yes, they are the nicest young couple. He helped me move in, and she feeds me."

"I'm glad I came. I had no idea that Mary's new friend was an adult." The press of people who wanted to speak to me was starting to pile up at the door to the sanctuary so the Carters moved on.

I enjoyed the social hour after the service. I don't usually circulate and visit after a service, but tonight everybody seemed to be mellow and having fun. I introduced myself to the parents of the students I recognized. The whole Parry family came. Shelly looked good. She still seemed to have a little trouble processing language.

Finally, everybody went home. It had been the kind of service I would like to have every week. I was thankful that Jean Bruce had handed Christine Stevenson a little gift for playing the piano for us. Actually, I'd gotten an envelope too. I felt good as I walked through the empty church making certain all the doors were locked and the lights were out. I double-checked the lock on the file cabinet where I kept the money from the collection. I checked my locked window and the grid we'd made for security. I locked my office behind me. *"Well God, it is your birthday. You ought to have the day off, so do you want to send a couple angels to protect this building? I've done all I can to protect us from the thieves. I suppose I should ask for healing for both of them."*

As I pulled my car into my garage at home, car lights pulled into the parking strip in front of the house. I didn't get a good look at the car. I just saw the lights. I was curious and a little anxious about who it might be. I heard my children's voices in the front hall when I came in from the garage.

"What are you two doing here?"

"Thanks Mom, we're happy to see you too." Patty's tone sounded teasing, but I saw a profound sadness in her eyes.

"I wasn't expecting you. You told me you were going to stay in town. Is anything wrong."

Patty answered quick enough. "Uh...no."

I know when my children are not telling me the truth. "Uh...yes there is. You are not happy after visiting your grandparents. What is it?"

"Oh nothing really." Patty sighed, plopped down on the sofa, and looked at Trevor. "I guess the big thing was that we missed being with you and going to church."

Trevor smiled encouragingly at his sister as he sprawled on the other end of the sectional.

I looked intently at Trevor. "I doubt that church and mom are the big problem."

Trevor squirmed in his seat.

Patty explained somewhat. "Yeah, it was kind of the whole thing. They were so focused on presents, and there was more drinking that I am used to, and you know I just graduated eighteen months ago. I'm used to other students drinking."

Trevor nodded, "Yeah I am used to roommates getting drunk and stuff, but this was different—dark—not like a party."

"That must have been weird for you."

My two grown-up children looked at each other, and I recognized their silent communication. I'm surprised they hadn't figured out by now that they couldn't fool me.

"You know you two are grown up now, but you are still my babies. I have spent more hours than you will ever know staring into your faces. You might as well tell me what upset you, and what you are trying to hide from your mother." I'd decided to go for honesty. "I am picking up something from the two of you that I sometimes get from Daddy when the Henderson's are mentioned. It distresses me, what is going on?"

My babies descended to looking guilty.

I pushed harder. "You know, I think I need to know the truth in order to heal. There is something here. What upset you? Remember the truth will set you free, and maybe help me."

They looked at each other. I fixed my eyes on Trevor as the one most likely to cave. Patty decided to protect her brother.

"The story is that…Mom I so don't want you to be hurt." I heard the strain in Patty's voice.

"Then give me the keys to healing."

"Dad had an affair." Trevor blurted out as he slouched lower on the sofa.

I felt the blood draining from my face but resolved to be calm. "Um…well…first of all, he's been dead for ten years. Uh…second… what makes you think that?"

"He got his TA pregnant. She was there with her kid." Patty had decided to share the unsavory details with me.

I felt myself recovering from my momentary shock. "Um, how old is this kid?"

"Ten. Gramma Henderson…"

"Oh no, no, no…no…" I gasped.

Trevor and Patty looked ready to pounce on me if I did anything else more strange.

I was almost laughing with relief. "He most certainly did not get Cerise Barnes pregnant ten years ago."

"Who is Cerise? Who?"

"She is the only TA he ever had. We've kept in touch. She is married with a family, but none of her kids are his. On top of which, your daddy had a vasectomy right after Trevor was born. He was upset over the C-section and didn't want to put me through that again."

"Vasectomies sometimes fail." Patty tried to sound certain.

"And if your father's had failed I would have been the first woman pregnant. You know, I can't say for certain that your father never cheated on me. I don't think he did, but I can be as certain as anybody that he does not have a ten year-old son. So, did Gramma Henderson really tell you this kid was your half brother?"

"Yes, she dotes on him, which was rather sickening." Trevor sneered.

"I think that is one reason we wanted to leave early. Mom! This isn't funny." Patty sounded distressed so I tried not to laugh any harder.

"I am sorry you are distressed. I wonder if Daddy knows this story?" I snorted and my children scowled at me. "Okay…okay, I confess that I think it is hysterically funny that Gramma Henderson has been doting on the illegitimate son of some lying strumpet who cannot name the father of her baby. I suppose the real father abandoned her, and she decided to name someone who was conveniently dead."

"You are not upset?" Patty sounded relieved by my assurances that her father was innocent in this affair.

"No, the child is not your dad's. If she lied about that, she probably lied about having an affair with him. I do suppose that I feel somewhat sorry for the girl. She was probably desperate, and dead men cannot deny paternity."

"Yes, they can. DNA testing can determine paternity."

"I'm not sure I have any of your dad's DNA."

"I do." Trevor stuck out his tongue.

"Of course, but it is not necessary. Please don't be upset about this. Your dad loved me. We had a good life together. I wish our time together had lasted longer. That's been my biggest grief. I wish my last memory of him was not of him looking so ill just before he attacked me."

CHAPTER 32: CHRISTMAS DAY

P atty, Trevor and I did whatever we wanted on Christmas morning. I took my early morning row on the quiet lake before my two sleepyheads got up. By the time I got back, Trevor and Patty were up preparing breakfast. After breakfast, we shared our Christmas stockings. Patty had made me a new stole for worship. Trevor bought me the book of Robert Louis Stevenson's poems that I'd been wanting.

When we got to my parent's house, we had one disappointment. Mandy and Fay were not joining us. Apparently, Harve decided not to celebrate Christmas because Jesus was born in the spring. I became more than angry with him. "Who cares what month Jesus was born! Celebrating that birth is what is important. Having family celebrations is almost more important. What is that ignorant ass thinking to deny his wife the opportunity to have dinner with her family?" I shut up then because I could see I was distressing Mandy's parents.

I gave my Aunt Phyllis a hug. "I think I will go visit Mandy on Monday. I assume Harve will be at work then?"

My aunt retuned the hug. "I think Mandy could use a sensible friend just now. He wouldn't let her receive gifts from us either."

I snorted, "I fear we may need to save our gifts to help her out later."

Later, I interrupted Trevor telling Daddy about the accusation that Hal had a love-child by some woman I'd never heard of. Again I laughed it off. "I suppose I should feel sorry for my in-laws being duped by some desperate woman, but I am angry over their rejection of me."

Daddy's tone was terse. I could tell he hated any mention of my in-laws. "They didn't make life easy for you at a time when you needed all the assurance you could get. I suspect this business started before you got out of the hospital."

I tried to be reasonable. "People do crazy things when they are grieving. I can see why they might want to cling to a new baby, but I don't really understand them rejecting the family Hal left behind." The topic was treated as a curiosity for several minutes before we moved on to another topic.

At ten on Christmas night, Ralph called me. We talked a little about the weather in California and how we each spent the day. I told him about the accusations that Hal had a love child. "I am concerned because Trevor seems distressed. He wants to prove that the child is not his half-brother."

"I can understand his point."

"Oh? I'm certain the child is not Hal's so I find the whole thing only mildly annoying when I am not laughing about my in-laws being duped, so I have no desire to enlighten my in-laws."

"Trevor's position is different from yours. His father's reputation is at stake."

"Hal's parents don't seem to condemn him. They've embraced the woman and her child."

"And rejected Trevor and Patty?"

"Well, they've always blamed me for not dropping the children off at their house for visits. They even got an attorney to stop me from moving to California. I don't understand them."

"People do strange things when they are grieving." We left the conversation there.

CHAPTER 33: MANDY AND FAY

I drove to Port Angeles to visit Mandy on Monday, her day off from the library. Harve was at work and Fay stayed home with her mother. As soon as I arrived, Fay started nagging wildly for us to leave immediately for Victoria.

Mandy laughed at her daughter, "Do you have any intention at all of shopping with your poor mother and aunt?"

"No."

I raised my eyebrows.

Mandy explained, "Her boyfriend lives in Victoria. Those two have been back and forth ever since middle school. Jeremy is a nice enough young man. His mistake was asking Harve if he could ask Fay to marry him."

"He asked Harve?"

"Can you two talk about this on the boat? We have to get in the ferry line." Fay handed her mother her purse and pulled her by the coat sleeve toward the door.

As soon as we were settled on the ferry, Fay asked to borrow my cell phone to call Jeremy. I wanted to meet the young man who had my niece so wound up, but Fay walked off of the boat to meet him, and we didn't see her again until we were back on the boat to go home.

On the way home, I asked Mandy, "What did she need us for?"

"I think she is afraid to take the ferry alone for fear someone will see her and tell Harve. At least if I am nearby, people are less likely to talk."

I took a deep breath and let it out. "Mandy, I'm not going to address the idea that people tell your husband what you and Fay do."

Mandy interrupted me. "Don't worry. They do."

"How much longer are you going to let this go on?" I expected Mandy to make excuses for Harve.

Mandy's answer surprised me. "Until March. Fay graduates in March. Harve doesn't know she is finishing early. He won't be expecting us to leave."

"Do you know where you are going?"

"No. I thought about going home to Mom and Dad. They'd take

us, but I am afraid that Harve would make trouble for them. Fay wants to go to Victoria, but I want to give her some time and space away from Jeremy."

"You best come stay with me." I sighed wondering if I would ever have the opportunity to be alone with Ralph. "I doubt that Harve could even find Blackfish, and he certainly could not find my house."

"It will just be until I find a job or Fay gets married."

"What? Jeremy is not respecting Harve's wishes?"

Mandy chuckled. "No, Jeremy is a middle child. He wants his own family. His mum, Jane, is sweet in a distracted sort of way. Jeremy's older sister married very well. All Jane talks about is Sarah and Jacob. I feel sorry for Jeremy. I'm not certain his mum knows he exists. The father is a likable, sensible man."

I whispered to Mandy, "Um…so…these two are determined to get married?"

Mandy nodded.

I grinned. "That must mean we get to plan a wedding! I have tons of ideas. What shall we do? Will they want me to officiate?"

Mandy laughed and hugged me and burst into tears.

Mandy sent the few things she bought in Victoria home with me. Harve was not home yet so she ran in the house and brought out several cold packages wrapped in butcher paper. "Here are some of my important papers and some money. Keep these safe for me."

I looked at the printing on the wrappers. "Liver, soup bones, liver… Mandy, what on earth?"

"I hid these at the back of the freezer. Harve hates liver. You better go now. Harve comes home early sometimes."

"Cousin, don't stay a moment longer than you think necessary. If things get worse, call me. I'm only an hour and a half away." I left Mandy standing on the steps of her bungalow.

I used the drive home to sort out how I felt about Mandy's situation. On one hand, I felt thankful Mandy was making decisions and taking action. On the other hand, Mandy was planning on leaving her husband of twenty years. I didn't blame her. I decided leaving was sad but necessary. I hoped he didn't turn physically violent.

At home, I circled March twenty-third as the date Fay finished school. I would not schedule anything for that day in case I needed to fetch Fay and Mandy.

When Ralph called, I told him about Mandy. We talked for about an hour. Finally, Ralph started to chuckle.

"What?"

"Sweetheart, you continue to surprise me. You are planning on helping your cousin escape an abusive marriage. That surprises me."

"Why? I know the danger of staying with a man who is not quite right. Hal, had a biking accident and cracked his head into a tree a week before the incident. I knew something was wrong with him. I stayed, not believing that my husband who suddenly turned angry and belligerent could get worse."

"How did a bike accident a week earlier change his behavior?"

"He cracked open a sinus, and it drained into his brain. The autopsy report said that the infection was encapsulated for about five days before the capsule burst and the infection spread through his brain. He died from the infection just a few hours after he left me."

"Thank you, I didn't know that. I didn't know that you had only a short time to know something was wrong with him."

"Ralph, don't try to be my doctor. Yes, I knew something was terribly wrong for a couple days. I tried to get him to go to the doctor. He wouldn't go. Perhaps I should have packed up the children and gone home to my parents. I didn't."

"No. You had no way to know what would happen. It could have just as easily gone a different direction, and Hal would have needed you to get him medical help. I'm not being your doctor. As your close friend, I think I need to know what happened just as I need to know why you converted a Porsche to electric and what you studied in school."

"I don't mind talking about it. It just seems to me that this one incident has defined my relationships ever since. I just want to be me, not the poor woman whose husband almost killed her."

"I'll take you as you are."

I smiled into my semi-dark room, and we talked of more lover-like things until I was ready to drift off to sleep.

CHAPTER 34: BLENDING THE FAMILY

In early January, the church finally received the payoff for the destroyed parsonage. An advisor from the district office worked with the administrative board to decide what to do with the money. I knew they were supposed to pay me for housing and looked forward to the added income. Feeding Trevor was putting a strain on my budget. He refused to eat food past the pull date. Jean loved him.

Trevor did a fantastic job remodeling in my laundry room. He had opened up the ceiling and the wall into the attic over the garage. He told me he would install a skylight in the ceiling when the weather dried up. I worried about where he would put stairs to get into the attic. He built a ladder into the wall.

It hadn't taken him long to insulate and sheet rock a narrow room above the garage. The ceiling was only seven feet in the middle and quickly sloped down to six feet, then four. Ralph had very little room to move up there. Rich was almost as tall as his father and complained about bumping his head regularly. He also talked about where he was going to put his bed, which amused me and annoyed his father.

After the third time Rich announced his new location for his bed, Ralph snarled at his son, "This isn't your house you know."

"Sweetheart," I came up behind Ralph and wrapped my arms around his middle. "What is distressing you with Rich? I don't mind if he wants to make himself a place to call his own when he visits."

"I don't want him imposing."

"He's not. I can set limits."

Ralph squirmed. "I'd like more time alone with you."

"Ah. Now that is something I can relate to. Perhaps I need to build a little summer gazebo down by the lake and turn this house into a motel."

"It's not summer. Damnit Maudy, I want more time alone with you." Ralph raised his voice.

The house became deadly still after Ralph's outburst. Finally, I heard Rich say, "This is weird."

Trevor took charge, "Come on."

I heard scrambling and then the door into the garage opened and closed. I heard more scrambling as April and Patty ran out the front door. I assumed the young people would go to a movie.

Ralph grinned, "That is much better." He pulled me into his arms and just held me. Finally, he started to chuckle. "Sweetheart, I am certain there is nothing like our situation in psychology books. Do your pastoral classes tell you how two adults with grown children manage to date without all the kids tagging along?"

I thought a minute. "No. We get information on how to blend families when the children are small but nothing on grown-up children."

"I think our children are blending quite well. It's you and I who are having trouble getting time to ourselves." He chuckled.

"Do I need to point out that they are gone?" I smiled at Ralph. He picked me up and carried me off to my bedroom.

We snuggled and kissed for a good portion of the afternoon. Since, I am a pastor, I will note that we kept our clothes on. I knew I wanted to make love to Ralph. For the first time, I sensed that Ralph wasn't quite certain about what he wanted. "Ralph, aside from our children being underfoot, and my church book of discipline being as it is, is there some other reason we are not lovers?"

He rose up on his elbows and looked at me. "Do you want to be lovers?"

I avoided his eyes. My first glance into them told me they didn't hold the excited passion of a man who thinks he is about to get laid. "Yes, I think I do, when the time is right. Something tells me that the time isn't right today, but yes, I want an intimate relationship."

Ralph blew out a long breath and inhaled deeply then he smiled. "Maudy, one of these days, I will take you to bed, and it will be wonderful. However, that day will be one when we can think about each other exclusively. It will be a day when you are not half frantic from the antics of your congregation, or your cousin leaving her husband. It will be a day when our children will not come bursting through the door in another hour. It will be a day when half of my mind is not mulling over another case."

"Ah, you have a new big case?"

"Yeah, a minor politician in Colombia. His enemies seem to disappear mysteriously, yet he seems intent on equality and justice for his people. He makes great speeches. I don't know. I may end up going to Colombia to see what I can learn about him."

"Ralph are you in the CIA or something?"

"Huh?"

"Well, the FBI and the CIA fall into the category of things I should know about."

"I do get contracts from the state department. I occasionally travel to other countries to lecture on forensic psychology and to find out what the locals say about an individual. I get information from the state department. I assist foreign police agencies in the best methods to use with someone with diminished mental capacity. I don't carry any sort of weapon. I've never been in a position that I would class as remotely dangerous." Ralph rolled over on his back on the bed. "Sweetie, we are close to something that bothers me. I love my work. I like seeing how culture influences certain behaviors. I like traveling."

I looked at him and waited for him to get to the point. I waited. Finally, I asked, "It sounds like this is a good thing. Why does liking your job bother you?"

Ralph came back from wherever his mind had wandered. "Huh? What? Oh! Well, I like to travel, and I like to spend time with you. I'm not certain it's fair to you to enter into an intimate relationship when you have ties here and cannot travel with me."

"Ralph I'm not some hot house flower that needs constant attention. We can work around your schedule. I'm really pretty independent. Less than a year after the attack, I packed up my children and moved to California for almost five years. I'll confess that when I did that, I was still unbelievably weak. I survived and I raised my children alone. I will survive if you are gone for a few weeks."

Ralph rolled onto his side and propped his head up on his hand. He sighed. "Your attitude is strange to me. My father has never spent a night away from mom. My wife, Karen, was…well…she was strong in her own way. She was insecure. She was afraid to be alone in the house. Don't get me wrong. I adored her. I still love her, but I could not have the job I do now with her."

"I'm not Karen."

"I know. You are like her in some ways. She was tough in some ways. She survived. You may have dealt with your hurts better, but then your parents love you. Her parents kicked her out of the house."

"Oh no! What happened?"

"She was seventeen when she fell in love with a guy who was twenty. She got pregnant. When she told him about the baby, he told her to get rid of it. He didn't want anything to do with a baby. She was heartbroken and turned to her parents with the whole story. They let her take one suitcase of belongings and kicked her out of the house. Her boyfriend wouldn't have anything to do with her so she went to a shelter. I think the shock of the rejection from the man she thought loved her and from her parents caused her to lose the baby. The social workers at the shelter helped her get a job and a place to stay. She worked her way through college." Ralph sighed and looked at the wall for several minutes.

He coughed and cleared his throat. "I don't think she ever recovered from that rejection."

Ralph looked so sad, I stroked the side of his face and tried to think of something comforting to say. "Did she ever reconcile with her parents?"

"No. The shelter called them and talked to them after she lost the baby. Whatever those people said to the social worker may have motivated the social worker to try extra hard for Karen."

"So she never reconciled. Do they know about your children?"

"Yes, when she died I had a detective track them down. I sent them a copy of the obituary and a small picture of our whole family. They never responded."

I felt sad. "There was something wrong with those people. No wonder Karen looked for love with someone exploitive."

"Yeah, there is a great deal of ugliness in this world. They hurt their daughter deeply. I think April's issues are related. I suppose that if April has children they will suffer from not knowing their grandmother, and any identity issues April has."

"...down to the third generation. Oh what evil people do! The worst part is that those who are most evil seem to think they are acting for God."

"Like Harve?"

"Like Harve. I wonder if Fay would be so eager to marry Jeremy if her father were more loving?"

"We'll never know the answer to that. Maudy, when the time comes, I want to be part of making Fay feel that she is accepted and loved. I want to do this for Karen."

I smiled and wondered if I really wanted to share my life with Karen. I thought for a few moments and realized that Ralph was sharing his life with Hal. I decided we are who we have become and that is partially determined by the people we love. On this thought I realized I was preaching to myself. "Shall we take a walk around the lake? It's gone down enough that the trail is passable."

CHAPTER 35: HAL JUNIOR

In mid-February I found a message on the house phone, "This is the Pacific-Cascade Lab calling for Trevor Henderson. His test report is ready. Please call at …" I immediately went into an anxiety attack. What kind of study could Trevor be having? Was he sick?

I didn't have much time to devote to an anxiety attack. I did some breathing exercises while I stared at the lake then got into my car and went back to the church. I had a meeting with Mrs. Brinks at one.

When Mrs. Brinks arrived, she looked saggy and her skin appeared grey. Her hair hung in strings. Her appearance shocked me and told me something very serious had happened. My heart started to pound, but I ignored it.

"Please Mrs. Brinks sit here. Can I get you some hot tea?" The poor woman wiped at her nose with a used tissue and nodded. I set a box of fresh tissues beside her and quickly fixed some tea.

As soon as we were settled, I opened the discussion. "Mrs. Brinks I can see that you are sick with distress. What is happening?"

"Alva's run off with another woman!"

I sat stunned. I'd heard this story many, many times before but never when the man was well over eighty.

Fortunately, Mrs. Brinks was willing to continue without prompting. "I got suspicious when he came home from working on the shelter. He acted too happy. You know what I mean?"

I nodded not knowing anything at all.

"Well on Christmas day I knew something was up. Earlier, I thought he must have bought me something expensive for Christmas because half of the money was missing from the Christmas savings envelope." She glanced up at me and her eyes narrowed with anger. "He spent half of our money on that trollop and left me with half what I'd saved to buy something for the grandkids. Kids these days want expensive things. Well I knew something was really wrong on Christmas morning. He bought me a box of chocolates. That's all he got me with half of our savings—a cheap box of chocolates. He knows I'm not supposed to have sweets. I gave them to my daughter." Mrs. Brink's voice sounded thin and watery.

I was becoming increasingly convinced that Alva Brinks had really run off with another woman. I wondered if that was really a bad thing for his wife. I asked, "So the affair has been going on for several months. What prompted you to come in now?"

"Well I didn't know who it was. It could have been you. He's always running down here to clean and fix things."

I shook my head. "First of all, I'd never poach. Secondly, Alva has not been here. I haven't seen much of him for months."

Mrs. Brinks nodded, "He was running off to see his hussy. I know that now."

I found myself disconnecting from reality. I thought I should try to master the floating feeling and focus on my client. That little voice inside my head laughed and said, '*You're not going to grasp this problem by clinging to your silly notions of reality.*'

Mrs. Brinks tucked her soggy tissue up her sleeve, took a fresh one from the box and blew her nose. She sobbed and gulped. "Anyway, yesterday when I got home from Gig Harbor, he was gone. I opened our closet to put away the new clothes I got at Chicos and his clothes were gone. I'd gone out and got myself some new clothes and even got a fancy nightgown at that Soma place. I was too late. He was gone."

The floating feeling deepened. The little voice inside me gloated, '*See. You don't need your reality to talk to an eighty year old woman who has just bought a fancy nightgown to try to entice her eighty something husband back into her bed.*'

I worried that I might start seeing spots. "Mrs. Brinks, I confess that I am shocked and surprised. After so many years of marriage, to have something like this happen is beyond my comprehension."

"Oh Alva's always been a flirt, but he never left me. His clothes are gone and he didn't come home last night."

"Have you talked to your children?"

"No. I can't tell them. I just can't."

I smiled, "Ah, perhaps that should be Alva's job."

"If you are thinking that man will do an unpleasant job, forget it. He never did a damn thing that didn't suit him!"

She was getting angry, which I considered good. "Mrs. Brinks, I know you are in shock. Part of my job as your pastor is to see that you are physically cared for during this crisis. Do you need help with food? Do you have enough money to get you through the next few weeks?" I hoped focusing on the things she could control would help her manage her shock.

She nodded, "I worked at the navy yard for forty years. I have a good pension. I inherited my house from my parents. That is part of what I don't understand. Alva doesn't have much money, he's lazy, and irresponsible. Why would Elma want him?"

I began to see the wisdom of floating disconnected from reality. "Elma? Not Elma Miller."

Mrs. Brinks nodded.

I sat and stared at her, stunned. "Let me get this straight. Alva has moved out of your house and moved in with Elma Miller."

Mrs. Brinks nodded.

"Mrs. Brinks, I…"

"Call me Trisha, I don't want his name. Should I take back my maiden name, Smith? That is what the young women are doing now days."

I wanted to weep, not so much for Trisha and Elma, but for myself, and the loss of my nice, comfy notions of the world.

"Trisha, I think you are going to be okay. You have money, which is the most important thing for your physical well-being. You are getting angry, which is emotionally appropriate."

"Is it really okay for me to be angry? Isn't that a sin?"

"No it isn't a sin. The Bible talks about how to manage anger and warns us not to let anger ruin our lives, but it is not a sin to be angry. Remember how angry Jesus got at the money changers in the temple?"

"But he was God. It was okay for him to get angry."

"We're created in the image of God. It is good for you to be angry. It is part of taking care of yourself and healing."

Trisha smiled at me then. We went on to discuss her anger over Alva taking the Christmas money and all the little things he had done that irritated her.

Our session was almost over when I asked another question. "I know you are angry with him now, but you two were married for a long time."

"Ever since I was seventeen."

"That is a long time. Forgive me for asking, but do you love him?" I expected immediate reassurance.

Tricia sat for perhaps three minutes staring at the wall. "Alva is good in bed. I'll give him that. I'm not certain I love him. I was crazy wild about him when we got married, but he has not been a good provider, and he is such a flirt. He is my husband and the father of my children. I would have stayed beside him no matter what. Do I love him? I suppose I do, in a way. Maybe he left because Elma could love him in a way that I can't. His laziness, and flirting, and irresponsibility have killed much of my love for him." She sighed and began to collect herself. She stuffed another soggy tissue up her sleeve and shifted her weight to get up off of the sofa.

I shoved the wastebasket closer to her with my toe and prepared to stand. "My door is open any time. You are going to need friends through this, but I have no idea how this will affect your relationships in the church. Be prepared for people to take sides."

Tricia looked at me with her head at an angle then stood up. "Thank you pastor. This was real helpful. People in town said you are good at this. I feel much better."

After the old woman left, I made my way to the sanctuary. I still felt disconnected and disoriented when I knelt at the communion rail to pray. I couldn't find any words. "Lord, you must know what these people are doing. I don't know what to say or think, or how to guide them."

The voice inside me said, '*Didn't I tell you the story of Abraham, Sarah, and Hagar?*'

After Trisha left, I had a surprisingly quiet afternoon. I made excellent progress on my sermon. I left work a little early and picked up a couple items at the IGA for dinner and Trevor's sack lunch.

Trevor came home shortly after six. He came in through the garage and went straight to his room. I waited. I started worrying about the call from the lab. When dinner was ready Trevor came in with a piece of paper in his shirt pocket.

He waited until we were eating our dinner before he unburdened himself. "Mom, I think you are going to find this hysterical."

I raised my eyebrows.

"Well...um...you know about Grandpa and Grandma Henderson and the kid who is supposed to be Dad's?"

I nodded and smiled.

"Well, I think part of the whole introduce-Trevor-and-Patty-to-Hal Junior."

"She didn't! She didn't name her baby Hal!"

"Oh Mom, this is better than you could ever imagine." Trevor grinned gleefully. "Anyway, I think part of the idea was that Patty and I are supposed to help take care of the kid. Grandma called me in early January to pick Junior up at school. She didn't want to drive in the snow."

I sat and stared dumbfounded as I began to get the same floating feeling I'd gotten when talking to Trisha.

Trevor continued, "When Grandma called, I was a bit pissed because it wasn't freezing and not really snowing, but she whined and begged so I agreed to pick the kid up. He goes to school down by Greenlake. By the time I got the kid, I knew I couldn't get back on the freeway so I decided to take Denny. Anyway, I had to go right past Ralph's office and he'd told me about a lab in his building that does genetic testing. I had the kid with me so I decided to stop."

I was curious now. "Was that Pacific-Cascade Labs?"

Trevor nodded and pulled the paper out of his pocket. "I got the results back today. I stopped by on my way home because I didn't understand this. The short story is that Junior and I do not have the same father."

I smiled and nodded.

"We are however, closely related."

I dropped my fork. I immediately thought of long lost relatives.

"Junior is probably not my half-brother. He is very likely my uncle." Trevor smirked.

I stood up and stared at my son. I breathed in and out a couple times. I sat down again.

Trevor leaned back in his chair and started laughing. "That one surprised you didn't it?"

"I...Oh My God...I wonder if Grandma Henderson knows? How on earth could that slimy bastard bring his mistress and illegitimate son into his wife's home? Oh I am so thankful I took you children to California so you were away from all of that." I forgot to eat my dinner. I thought that God must surely have been protecting me, and my children, in calling me to California. I sat and stared.

"Mom you're not upset are you?"

I smiled at Trevor's alarm. "I am shocked that people could behave in such an underhanded manner. All this time, I thought I should have tried harder to keep in contact." I snorted. "Contact with me was probably the last thing the old man wanted." I thought some more. "You know Dr. Dave is not as incompetent as I often think. He told me that Hal's parents didn't want to be close to me. They got what they wanted. We assumed it was because they didn't want the responsibility. Huh." I sat and thought.

Trevor volunteered his thoughts. "Yeah, I can see why Grandpa didn't want you to know about Junior." He chuckled. "What a slime. Yeah, I grew up thinking that my grandparents didn't like me. Sometimes I thought there was something about Dad's death that people were hiding from me."

I smiled at my son. "I got the hidden secrets idea too. I worried that there was something I didn't know and couldn't remember. I guess there was something, but it had nothing to do with us. I am going to call Daddy."

Daddy answered, "Hello Maudy, I got caller ID."

"Good."

He chuckled, "How did you like me knowing who called before you told me?"

"I'm used to it. Now, I want to know something." I launched right into my issue. "Trevor just had genetic testing done on himself and the kid who was supposed to be Hal's. The kid is not Hal's. He is most likely Grandpa Henderson's son." I couldn't hear anything on the other end of the line. "Daddy? Daddy are you there?"

"I'm here. So the old man had an affair and passed the kid off as Hal's. That explains a few things."

"So you didn't know anything about this?"

"No. I had some arguments with the man. You know that. Huh. I wonder if this is why he came up with that wild story that you had killed Hal?"

"What? The autopsy report was clear."

"Yeah, I went over that report with him, but he insisted Hal's death was your fault. Huh. That whole charade was to cover up his own sins."

"Ugh, yeah. Some days I wonder about why God puts up with us. I had a case at church where a man in his eighties left his wife of sixty-five years for another woman in her eighties."

Daddy laughed, "You do run into some interesting cases. What are you going to do about the Hendersons?"

"Huh? Nothing. Well I think I will rejoice that the weight of guilt I've felt about not being closer to them has left. I feel quite free when I think of them." I giggled. "Yeah, this is much better. And there is no big secret, other than Junior, about Hal's death?"

"Honey, we told you everything we knew. Well I didn't mention the lawsuit to have Hal's estate put into a trust for his children. That seemed so silly at the time and boiled down to him not having an estate."

"Oh, I do remember a big fuss being made about Hal's estate, but everything passed to me and the house wasn't worth more than the mortgage." I shrugged.

We got off of the phone and I waited until almost ten to call Ralph. We spent a half hour marveling over the strangeness of my day. Finally I asked, "What about you? How was your day?"

"Not near as interesting as yours. I think I'm close to having what

I need for the case in Colombia. I don't see anything in the paperwork so far that should be a cause for alarm with this man. I'm not certain why our government is investigating him. In fact, this case looks boring compared to your life. Why did I ever think my life was exciting?"

"Because you travel?"

"That is part of it. I get to see new and interesting places. I get to meet new people. I get paid a good salary. Look at you. You stay in that small town. You don't get paid a tenth of what you are worth, and yet you are at the center of the most bizarre circumstances I've encountered in years."

CHAPTER 36: CRICKET'S SHOWER

I invited the women from the church to my house for Cricket's baby shower. Everybody admired the view. A few of the older women sighed over the loss of the parsonage. Finally Trisha quoted, "For everything there is a season…. Perhaps it was time for the parsonage to fall down."

I wondered if she was thinking about her marriage with that quote. "I'm certain it was time for it to go. My purchase of this house fell together so easy, and the sailors came that day and helped me move the heavy stuff."

When Cricket arrived, the melancholy for the parsonage passed. I'll say one thing for those old women. They knew how to have a baby shower. They presented Cricket with homemade blankets, crocheted sweaters, booties and nifty diaper bags. They laughed and told stories about old-fashioned beliefs about childbirth like putting a knife under the bed to cut the pain.

I felt profoundly thankful for the wisdom those women brought into my home. I gave thanks that they surrounded Cricket and her baby with love, community, and stability. I could not escape seeing the example that was set for the younger women.

Mary Carter acted excited to be at a party and watched to see how others behaved. She'd bought the baby a cloth book about kittens, and a beautifully illustrated copy of Robert L. Stevensons's "A Child's Garden of Verses." I wondered if the book of poems had been her own idea. She answered my unasked question by reciting Who Has Seen the Wind.

April came with Patty and helped us set up for the formal tea. She had a little trouble with the idea of a formal table setting. On the other hand, she brought some marvelous little pastries that she'd made herself. "My mom used to make these. Grandma Graham showed me how at Christmas." I noticed that, like Mary, April watched the older women's behavior.

At one point poor April was shocked to tears and had to leave the room. The dear sweet old ladies started talking about their first pregnancies. "I got knocked-up in the back seat of a thirty-four Ford. Back then most babies were started in the back seat of a Ford or Chevy."

"Oh do I remember my first love! He was a Mexican who came to help Daddy with the haying. Oh my, he was the most beautiful man I've ever seen with his brown skin and muscled body. Course, when Daddy found out what we'd been doing, he paid Carlos to leave, and I was whisked off to the doctor to have the evidence taken care of. Oh I cried. But that was how things were then. Girls like me didn't marry Mexican men, and nobody talked about abortion. Everybody had them, but we didn't talk about it."

"I should have known there was something wrong with Ed, my first husband. I was the only girl I knew who was a virgin on her wedding night. 'Course I was still a virgin three months later when I stole some money out of his wallet and took the bus home to Mama."

Cricket choked at this point. I thought she was going to have an upset stomach, but she insisted she would be fine as soon as she had some water. Patty assisted her to the kitchen. April ran after them. "We have some ginger ale in the refrigerator if you need something for your stomach." The younger women hid out in the kitchen for a few minutes before beginning to set out our tea.

The formal tea Patty and I had prepared was a hit except for Jean asking if all the ingredients were fresh. Jean seemed to think it was vastly amusing to entertain my guests with horror stories of the things she'd found in my refrigerator.

I discovered that I thought her stories were really rather funny. "Please, don't be afraid to eat the refreshments. Trevor eats up all my groceries every week. You won't get sick."

After Cricket had been bundled into her car with her gifts, and the other women shuffled off to their cars, Shirley and Jean filled me in on the details of another break-in as they helped me clean up.

"This time it was a house off of Dusty Road. I heard they broke into a shed and stole a boat motor. It wasn't a big thing, but they left a big pile of dung on the picnic table on the patio. That is why the police think it was the same person."

"Have the police made any progress in recovering any of the stolen items. It seems like a boat motor would show up at a garage sale or something."

Jean changed the subject. "I heard that Alva and Elma got home from the Holy Land last Monday. I wonder if they will come to church."

I sighed, "I hope they do, but I'd hate for Trisha to be hurt any more than she is."

"Pastor do you think they are going to repent of their sin?" Shirley sounded genuinely curious.

"No. No, I don't expect much in the way of a consciousness of sinning at this point. Frankly, I expect Elma to get tired of Alva and kick the bum out."

"Do you think Trisha will take him back?"

"At this point, she probably will. They've been married a long time. He is the father of her children. I think she'll take him back, but maybe his life won't be quite so comfortable."

"I heard that Alva won't let Joey into his mother's house. Or at least that's the story. Maybe Joey would just rather stay with Christine Stevenson when he visits his mother." Jean hissed.

I sighed and chuckled, "Poor Joey has tried to do the good-son thing. He's made the trip back and forth every month. The poor man tries to do what he thinks is right, and his mother is just not cooperating with him. She's off having the time of her life."

Shirley again sounded puzzled. "What I really don't understand is why she would want to take up with Alva in the first place."

I said the same thing I'd been saying a great deal lately, "People do strange things when they are grieving. Perhaps she is particularly confused because she enjoys the freedom of visiting friends and family, but is still distressed by the death of the man she was married to for all of her adult life."

As soon as the house looked half-way presentable again, Patty and April needed to run for the ferry. As they were headed for the car, I heard April commenting. "You know people are always talking about the morals of our generation, but did you hear those women!"

Patty snorted, "Yeah things don't change that much."

CHAPTER 37: MANDY LEAVES HARVE

I was home alone on a Thursday night in the middle of March. Ralph had left for Colombia a week earlier, promising to be home before Mandy and Fay arrived on the twenty-third. My laundry room sat in a state of construction mess. Trevor had stopped working on his bedroom in order to study. On Sunday evening he went into town intending to stay with Patty until finals were over.

I hadn't seen either of my children for over a week. Patty was busy preparing documents for income tax. She'd left her latest quilt project spread around my spare room. "Mom, don't worry about the mess. I can clean it up Sunday when I come over." Sunday had come and gone. Patty had gotten free lift tickets so she went skiing. I stopped feeling resentful when she told me she took April with her.

I looked around my house and tried to tidy up. I shut the doors to the laundry room and spare bedroom and the house looked quite presentable, especially after I hung up the coats and sweaters hanging on chairs and doorknobs. I decided I needed a shoe holder by each door.

Finally about nine o'clock, I turned out the lights and snuggled up in a comforter on the sofa. I sat and listened to the quiet. I loved the absolute quiet. The clouds had cleared away so I watched the starlight dancing on the lake. It felt good to just sit and breathe in the silence.

My mind drifted from topic to topic. John Wesley came and snuggled next to me. I ran my fingers into his thick fur. The vibration of his purring caused my fingers to relax. The warmth and vibration spread up my arm and across my shoulders. My eyes drifted closed.

Far away, I heard a car door slam, then another. John Wesley stopped purring and sat up. I didn't want to open my eyes. The cat jumped to the back of the sofa and stared intently toward the wall between the living room and my bedroom. "You silly cat. It is nothing. The neighbors just came home. That's all."

My doorbell rang. I jumped up and started turning on lights as I made my way to the front door. I could hear voices now. I opened the door. "Mandy! Fay! Are you okay? Come in. What happened?"

Fay snapped. "Daddy turned seriously creepy."

"Oh baby I am so sorry." I tried to hug both women at once. "Come in."

I focused on Mandy. "Sweetheart you're shaking. Are you okay?"

Mandy nodded, but she hadn't said anything since coming through the door. I looked at Fay and raised my eyebrows.

She explained. "She's been like this ever since Squim."

I hated to talk about Mandy in front of her. "Did he hit her or do anything physical?"

Mandy shook her head and tried to talk but no sound came out of her mouth. I decided to put her on the sofa and wrap her in my blanket.

Fay volunteered, "I'll go unload the car. We managed to bring a fair amount of stuff."

While Fay unloaded the car and put their things in the spare room, I made Mandy some hot cocoa, built a fire and sat down next to her.

Finally, Mandy got out a few words. "I don't know what came over me. I've known for the past six or seven months that this day would come. I don't know." She sat and stared out the dark window.

The moon had risen making the lake almost as bright as day. I sat and looked at the moonlight on the water and waited for Mandy to speak. A tear running down my face surprised me. I had no idea why I was crying.

While we were getting organized for bed, Fay explained what had precipitated their flight. "I think what set him off was three advertisements from colleges that came for me in the mail. I didn't send for them, and I told him so. He yelled at me and shook the ads in my face and told me that it was a waste of time and money for me to go to school more. He called me a liar and told me I would get a job and pay him back for raising me. I didn't say anything because he was so angry. Mom tried to tell him that those were just advertisements that all graduates get this time of year. He ripped up the papers and started jumping up and down on them. He was so angry he was spitting. Finally he called me a stupid cow and sent me to my room." Fay helped me carry sheets and blankets to the spare bed and continued her story. "I knew we were leaving as soon as we could get away so I packed what I could without making noise."

It was Fay's turn to use the bathroom. Mandy finally managed to talk as we moved quilt pieces and made up the bed in the spare room. "It was the strangest thing I've ever seen. There was no warning. He just came through the door with this handful of papers. I had no idea where they came from. First, he asked me what I thought I was doing. He shook the papers in my face and called me a whore. Then he saw

Fay and turned on her." Mandy shook her head. "I was able to figure out what the papers were, but I'm not certain they came in our mail." She sighed. "Anyway he had a meeting for his church tonight. He left shortly before seven. We knew he wouldn't be home until nine, so we took some time to pack the car. I've got everything we'll need immediately with us. I just don't know what happened to set him off."

I tried to sound calm and reassuring. "He was probably upset over something else and used the advertisements as an excuse to take his anger out on you." I sat down on the bed we'd just made. Fay joined us. I wasn't really planning what I said. It just came out of my mouth. "You know from the few things Harve said to me, I can piece together a good idea of the theology of his church. It's more common than I'd like. The basic theology is based on the idea that people are basically bad."

Fay nodded her head and sat on the sewing stool.

I continued. "This is a strange perversion from my perspective, since we are created in the image of God who is good. However, I'm not certain how good their image of God is. The only hope for people who follow this belief is in death, because they are bad and all of creation is bad. The theology focuses on the law rather than love and grace. I met many in seminary who seemed to follow this theology, and it didn't bother them. I cannot accept it. It would make me desperately depressed. I need to be loved by God. I need to be told there is hope in this world. I need to love others without reservation. This theology operates a great deal on the fear of going to hell, or worse, missing out on the rapture. They talk about repudiating evil and everything is evil. Perhaps poor Harve is a bit like me. The theology has made him desperately depressed. Anger and depression go together. This would account for his behavior tonight especially if he had a meeting."

Mandy gave me a hug. "That helps to understand what went wrong. I'm having trouble believing that I am really leaving him. I would not stay and allow him to call us names, but it all seems so strange."

Fay volunteered to sleep on the sofa because I didn't have enough beds. As I crossed the hall from the bathroom to my bedroom I heard her on the phone talking to her Jeremy. She sounded excited about being able to see him freely.

CHAPTER 38: CHURCH BREAK-IN

F riday morning, Fay came dancing into the kitchen for breakfast. Mandy was still sleeping. Fay helped herself to some coffee, took the spatula away from me and poked at the bacon I was cooking. "Jeremy says he will catch the first ferry after work and be down here as soon as he can. Can I keep your phone to stay in touch with him today?"

"I guess." I was too stunned by the whole incident to think rationally. I forgot that my boyfriend might call me on that phone. I guess I was partially in sympathy-shock with Mandy. Harve had been my cousin for over twenty years. "Uh, Fay, I'm going to have to go into work this morning. Be sure and stay by your mom today. I'm worried about her."

"Yeah, she seemed okay, at first. She was so prepared. She'd been wrapping packages and putting them in the freezer for months. I was surprised when she pulled off the road in Squim and let me drive. She just sat there shaking and staring."

I nodded. "She seemed as okay as one can be with the idea of leaving when I talked to her in December."

Fay slid the bacon onto a plate. "She assured me that we would leave at least a hundred times. I wonder now, if that was more a fantasy for her than a reality. I don't think she's been really in touch with the reality of Daddy's behavior these past several months."

I went to my office. I finished writing my sermon, thankful to have it done on time. I printed out the bulletin. At noon, I went to the kitchen and heated some soup. Just as I finished my soup, two men in black suits came into the social hall. I recognized them as outsiders, since nobody in Blackfish wore suits other than to funerals. I spent a half-hour with them.

I met with the worship committee at one, then sorted through the church mail and answered e-mails until time to go home. I'd had a peaceful day at work, but felt totally exhausted by the stress around Mandy.

My house smelled divine when I walked though the door from the garage. My path took me through the kitchen. I found Poulet Marango simmering on the stove. I looked around and saw a pile of fresh veggies chopped up in a roasting pan. I didn't see Fay or Mandy. The dining table was set with a lace cloth and my best china. I raised my eyebrows. I heard the sound of my sewing machine working away in the back bedroom.

I found Mandy sewing quilt blocks together. She appeared to be in full, frantic, quilt production. I called over the sound of the machine, "Where's Fay?"

"She's cooking dinner." Mandy fed more quilt pieces into the machine.

I again raised my voice over the sound of the machine, "Dinner smells good and I see you are making progress on the disarray in this room."

Mandy nodded.

I decided that she was not really okay, but lost in the land of quilt pieces. I went to my room and changed clothes. When I came back to the dining room, Fey was coming in through the French doors with herbs in her hand.

"Ah, I take it that you are the one who is cooking dinner."

"Yes, Jeremy was able to get on a four o'clock boat. He should be here before seven."

I glanced at the table. It was set for four. "Trevor is done with finals. He'll be here too. What can I help you with?"

"Have you talked to Mom?"

"Um…well…she was sewing quilt pieces."

"The way she is going at that, I'm surprised she hasn't finished yet. I hope Patty doesn't mind too much. Mom didn't like the arrangement of colors that Patty laid out. She redid the design. I don't think it is as pretty as Patty's plan."

I asked dryly, "Uh…how did your mom arrange the colors?"

"Monochromatic. Each block is to be shades of all one color."

I moaned, "We may have to write this quilt off as therapy. Oh, thanks for starting dinner and cleaning house." I looked around. Everything looked gleaming and tidy. I thought Fay had been doing some therapeutic housecleaning.

Fay sighed. "I wanted to cook dinner for Jeremy. I also want him to know that the rest of my family lives in something other than former company bungalows." She wrinkled her nose when she referred to her home.

I smiled vaguely, "Will Jeremy be spending the night?"

Fay's face lit up. "He's spending the whole weekend."

I excused myself to go make up Rich's bed for Jeremy. I wondered where we would put everybody when Ralph got home. Trevor interrupted me while I was tidying his room. "What are you doing here?"

"You're getting a roommate this weekend."

"That's okay. Tell him not to wake me. You can call me for dinner. Trevor dropped down on his bed and fell asleep before I finished making up Jeremy's bed."

Jeremy arrived a few minutes before seven, which meant he hadn't obeyed speed limits on the trip down. He smiled happily at Fay, praised everything about my small house and answered our questions politely without taking his eyes off of Fay.

As soon as she had eaten some of her dinner, Mandy excused herself to go work on the most boring quilt I'd ever seen. She loved it and looked at her handiwork with the same gleam that shone in Fay's eyes when she looked at Jeremy.

After clearing away the dishes, I excused myself to go to my room to make some phone calls. I called Patty first and told her about Mandy and Fay.

Patty sounded compassionate, "I guess we are not surprised, but it is still sad. How is Mandy taking it?"

"Bad. I hope you are not going to be too upset about this, but you know that quilt you were making?" I gave thanks when Patty laughed about her quilting project being hijacked. "I should add...and...well... it's bad...really ugly."

"Mom, if piecing something together in what feels right to her, helps Mandy, I will consider it money well spent. I hope it does help." Patty paused, "It sounds like you have your hands full with three extra people in the house. I'll come over Sunday morning and have dinner ready for you when you get home from church."

"Thanks." I felt that my thanks sounded somewhat weak. I doubted that another person in my small house would help.

After talking to Patty, I called my mom and told her what was happening with Mandy.

Mom sounded relieved. "She's at your house then. Harve showed up at her folk's house and searched the house for some sign of her then he called her a whore and declared she had run off with another man."

"Oh no! How are Aunt Phyllis and John?"

"Worried. They had no idea she had left or where she might have gone."

"I would think they might know she would come here. Shall I call them?"

"I think that is Mandy's job."

"Um…well…I don't think Mandy can do that. She isn't talking yet."

"What is she doing?"

"Sitting in my sewing room making an ugly quilt."

"Oh! Oh dear. I'll call her parents and let them know that she is safe but too upset to talk just now."

After I got off of the phone with Mom, John Wesley came and snuggled up to me. I fell asleep crosswise of my bed. The phone woke me up at eleven-thirty. I grabbed it before it could wake the rest of the household.

"Pastor Henderson? This is Officer Kindle with the Kitsap County Sheriff's office. There has been a break-in at the Methodist Church. Can you come down and look things over for us?"

I tried to pretend I was awake. I wasn't sure I wasn't asleep and dreaming. I heard the whirr of my sewing machine from across the hall. "Yeah, it will take me about fifteen minutes to get there."

On my way to the garage, I found Fay and Jeremy in the living room with the lights down low. They explained they were watching the moonlight on the lake. I mumbled something about submarine races and continued to the garage. I unplugged the Porsche, opened the garage door and prepared to get into the car.

"Mom, what are you doing going out so late." Trevor stood in the door to the laundry room in his slippers.

"Break-in at the church. The police want me to check for anything missing."

"Wait for me!" Trevor ran off toward the main house. He returned in less than a minute with Jeremy. "Fay will stay with Mandy. We're coming with you."

I closed up the Porsche and got into the Sentra. Trevor rode shotgun, and Jeremy took the back seat.

My heart started pounding again when I found the church parking lot was filled with the fire trucks and firemen, and it looked as if every sheriff's car in Kitsap County had responded to the call at the church. An officer greeted me and instructed me not to touch anything on my way through the building. The boys were not allowed in. Trevor protested loudly, "I came down here because I don't like mom being alone in that building even if half of your force is here. If this is the same people, they do ugly things. I don't want my mom surprised by something ugly."

Trevor was right of course. I checked my office first. I found a mess. The file cabinet made a hole in the wall when it had fallen. The chairs were overturned and a sofa cushion was slashed.

"Ma'am do you see anything missing here?"

"Not really. I've been keeping things locked pretty tight. Um…the phones and FAX seem to be okay." I didn't realize until I entered the sanctuary that the bulletins that had been sitting on my desk were gone.

We found the bulletins in the Sanctuary. They were wadded up and thrown in a pile with Bibles and hymnals. The room smelled of smoke and something much worse. One side of the pile was blackened and dripping foam. I sat down in shock as I stared at the charred stack of torn Bibles, hymnals and bulletins. I just sat and couldn't think anything rational. The only thought floating through my brain was the idea that I should go home and make ugly quilts with Mandy.

I couldn't go home immediately. I stayed and answered questions about what time I'd left and what measures I'd taken to secure the building. I didn't get any information from the police other than someone leaving Timmy's had noticed a flickering light in the church when my car wasn't in the lot. They called in the fire alarm.

Finally, my brain began to work. I remembered something I hadn't given any thought to earlier. "You know, two FBI agents were here this morning doing a security check. I wasn't much help, but some members of my congregation do have classified jobs for the navy. Would you notify them about this break-in? I think it might be important." I looked again at the stack of Bibles and paper at the front of the sanctuary. I assumed that it was excrement that covered some of them. I felt a tear rolling down my face. The police immediately escorted me back to my son. I wondered if they thought I was going to be hysterical. I was too tired for hysterics.

On Saturday morning, I woke up late to the sound of laughter and the smell of bacon. I stirred and John Wesley moved his paw off of my forehead. I wondered if the cat knew I felt distressed and slept with his paw on me to comfort me, or to reassure himself that all was well.

I slipped out of bed without waking Mandy who had joined me. John Wesley followed me into the kitchen where Patty was making breakfast and the other young adults were having a party.

I kissed Patty. "I thought you weren't coming until tomorrow."

"Trevor called last night and told me about the break-in."

My congregation began to call me at about nine. I assured each person that I knew about the break-in and that I had seen the damage and that nothing valuable had been taken.

After the fifth phone call Trevor answered the phone. He listened for a moment, "This is Trevor Henderson, her son. She was down at the church half of the night talking to the police and verifying that not much was taken. She is in shock. My sister and I will not allow her to take anymore phone calls." He hung up.

I sighed, "Thanks."

Mandy got up at noon, fussed at us for letting her sleep so long, and went off to work on her quilt.

Patty held her head and giggled.

The police called at four to tell me that we could get back into the church. I called Larry Bruce and relayed the news.

I announced to my household. "We can get back into the church. I want to see if we can possibly hold a worship service in there."

Trevor took charge again, "Wait. We'll all come with you."

It took longer than I liked for everybody to get into cars. Some of the congregation had arrived by the time I got there. They waited for me to unlock the doors.

The poor elderly people were overcome with shock and grief when they realized how close their beloved church had come to being burned. Mandy recognized grief. She cooed, and soothed, and ushered people into the social hall where she helped Shirley make coffee.

Trevor, Patty, Jeremy and Fay pulled on rubber gloves and set to work cleaning up the piled papers in the sanctuary. I ran to the IGA for more garbage bags and disinfectant. When I got back to the church, Timmy came over and left fried chicken, mashed potatoes and coleslaw for those who gathered at the church. Kelly Brian arrived with a crew of Catholics to help with the clean-up. By seven, I could see that we would be able to use our sanctuary in the morning. It would still smell of smoke, but I was determined to carry on as normally as possible. By eight, the freshly cleaned carpets were drying so I locked up again and headed back to my house.

Sunday morning we had thirty-some people in worship. The largest group of guests came from my house, but the Carters came with Mary, and Skunk and Cricket came to be supportive. Before the other worshipers arrived, Cricket and I shocked my family by doing a cleansing ceremony for the church.

CHAPTER 39: PARENTHOOD

On Monday I came down with a vicious cold. I wanted to stay in bed, but the insurance company wanted to talk to me. The police had more papers for me to sign. The FBI stopped by my house to demand that I tell them why I had not notified them of the break-in immediately. They grumbled about the local sheriff not calling them until this morning.

Patty and Jeremy had left on Sunday night. After her spell of acting responsible, Fay turned useless. Jeremy had affirmed that he still wanted to marry her and they made plans for her to spend the next weekend in Victoria to pick out a ring.

Mandy had almost finished her ugly quilt, but still was not as much help as her daughter.

Trevor planned his spring break to include visiting friends and working on finishing the loft. He manfully took over the job of cooking and keeping the household running.

In the afternoon, he took a break and went rowing. When he'd been gone two hours, I began to worry about him. I finally went out and tried to see where he might be. I couldn't see him on the lake. I went in and got my binoculars and tried again to find him on the lake. I couldn't see him or the boat. I searched the whole lake with the glasses twice before got so scared I peed my pants. I stood on my dock in my wet pants and debated whom to call. My heart pounded, but I was too frightened to cry. I turned to return to the house and call for help when I saw movement at the far corner of the lake. With the binoculars, I could tell it was someone in a black coat with a rowboat. I went in, showered and changed, thoroughly ashamed of myself for getting so upset because my son had gone exploring.

Trevor acted energized by his explorations. "I took the boat all the way into the swamp. There are some really big fish in there. The reeds are too thick to row, but most of the time I was able to pole the boat." He grinned and laughed and patted Fay on the rear as he helped her fix dinner.

Trevor finally set off my mom radar. He'd rushed us through dinner and announced that I was to go to bed immediately after dinner and stay there. I tried to clear the table, but he sent me to my room. I popped out again to use the bathroom and caught Trevor having an intense, whispered conversation with Fay. On my way back to my room, I bumped into Trevor going out the front door. "I'm going to run up and see Skunk about some work." He ducked out the door. I went to bed determined to find out what Trevor was up to tomorrow.

I woke up shortly before noon on Tuesday, horrified at sleeping when I should be in my office. Nobody was home except for John Wesley. I would have liked to wander through my empty rooms and breathe in air that nobody else was breathing, but I rushed off to my office.

After I got to the office, Tuesday turned into a totally quiet day. I researched the scriptures for my sermon and easily outlined what I wanted to do. Nobody came in. I went home at five and found Trevor nailing more sheetrock in the loft. Fay and Mandy were gone. I started dinner, soup and bread.

For the next few days, I was aware of feeling a certain numb melancholy despite being surrounded by family and decisions to make. I went through the motions of visiting my congregation, preparing my sermon and attending committee meetings. The staff parish committee expressed some concern that my family obligations would interfere with my church obligations. I held my head and wondered if any of these people had a life other than running mine.

I finished the last of my classes on bullying on Wednesday evening. I would miss the students. Most of them had put the incident with Joel Giddens behind them. The tagging for bullying had died a natural death.

On Thursday, I learned that an auto-body repair shop had been broken into while the police were busy at our church. Some equipment was stolen. Everybody had a great deal to say about the brake-in and nobody knew anything.

On Friday I had a bit of excitement that pulled me out of my melancholy for the whole weekend. At about ten in the morning, I got a phone call from a very uncomfortable and overdue Cricket. "This is it. Skunk is at his office. Can you drive me in?"

"I'll be there in less than five minutes." Just before I ran out the door, I called to my household, "Cricket's in labor. I don't know when I'll be back."

I was very proud of myself for getting Cricket into the hospital with no anxieties or mishaps. Skunk met us in admitting. Skunk went into the labor room with Cricket so I sat down in a waiting room to silently pray. *"God, please be with Cricket and each person helping her bring this new soul into the world. Keep them safe during this passage and ease her pain."*

"Pastor Maude? Pastor Maude? Why are you still here?" I woke up to the sound of Skunk's voice. He grinned. "It's a girl. Do you want to come see her? She's wrinkled and all red but has a good healthy set of lungs."

The baby did indeed have a healthy set of lungs and in addition to being wrinkled and red, her head was slightly lopsided. She was beautiful. I asked, "What are you going to name her?"

"Clarissa LeeAnn." Both parents seemed particularly proud of the name.

"Then, I will leave you alone."

"Pastor Maude, thanks for waiting." Cricket looked away from me. "Having you here helps me feel better about not having a mom who could come and stay."

I smiled, "I am happy to be here and share this miracle with you." I refused to confess that I had stayed all afternoon simply because I'd fallen asleep. I decided God knew Cricket needed me here and let me sleep.

As I sat in traffic waiting through two cycles at each light before I could get through, I thought about my lethargy. I finally snorted, "I know what this is. I miss Ralph." I felt better instantly. "I miss Ralph. I'm becoming pathetically dependent on him. I just miss him." I smiled. He would be home soon.

CHAPTER 40: DISTRICT EVALUATION

When I got home from taking Cricket to the hospital, I found a message on the phone from the district superintendent. "Maude give me a call as soon as you get this message. My cell phone is…"

I figured if the DS was leaving his cell number, I should call immediately. "This is Maude Henderson. You wanted me to call."

"Yes, I've been going over appointments and some budget figures with some of our committees."

This was it. They wanted to close Blackfish. I sat down. "And."

"Well, we have to consolidate several churches. They're not self-supporting and…well…we just do not have enough clergy to serve everybody."

"Uh." I wasn't going to make this easy for the DS. I hadn't indicated that I wanted to move. I hadn't complained. We were up to date on our payments to the conference, thanks to our unexpected income.

"Well you know how this is. We have three North Kitsap congregations we want to combine. The church at North Point has five members, but they have money and pay a half-time salary. The church at Cutt's Bay will officially close and the summer people who attend there can drive into North Point. That leaves Thompson Creek and Blackfish. If we combine you with North Point and Thompson Creek, you could have what we consider at least three-quarters salary plus your housing allowance."

"Um, thank you for calling about this. North Point and Thompson Creek are not particularly close to Blackfish. I would think the congregations would want to merge with someone closer."

"Oh…um…well…yes. The people will not be moving to a new church. We would expect you to drive between the churches."

"No. I don't think that will work." I panicked wondering where that decisive answer came from. I knew I should be more diplomatic. "Um…there are some other issues here. "I just bought a house out here, and I love it so I don't want to relocate to a central location. Also, and this is my main concern, I have an idea for how to serve this church. It has strong community support." I smiled knowing what I was telling the truth. "I think Blackfish United Methodist Church will survive. We may not look like a regular church, but we're doing the right things. We're going to make the transition to serving the whole community, and I want to devote my full attention to being part of that transition."

"Oh. Oh! Well if you think so. Your numbers haven't been real strong."

"What numbers?"

"Well for the past five years."

I smiled again. It might have been a slightly feral smile so I was thankful my district superintendant couldn't see me. "That was before my time. Just leave us alone and we'll make it, but it's going to take consistent leadership, and my vision for what a contemporary suburban church looks like."

"I'm happy to hear this. Can I send someone out to see what you are doing?

"I suppose." I wondered if I should let the delegation from the district office experience one of our cleansing ceremonies complete with the Catholics sprinkling holy water, the Jewish leaders carrying the Torah, me with my smudging or guitar and Cricket with her baby strapped to her back chasing the evil out of our houses of worship. "Come on out."

I got off of the phone, surprised at the recent conversation. I'd suspected the conference wanted to make changes in Blackfish. The district superintendent hadn't really surprised me. My side of the conversation stunned me. I hadn't really thought about having a plan for the church. I wouldn't really call anything a plan, but I had a sense that I was doing the right thing.

The DS called me back on Tuesday morning saying he would be out with his committee about one-thirty to meet with me and go over our numbers. I tried to sound gracious. I didn't want to see these people. I didn't want to make changes. I called Larry and told him the whole problem. "Can you call everybody else who needs to know what is happening so they can answer questions. I'm afraid the conference is trying to elbow us out of existence."

Larry grunted, "I'll call the others. What time are they coming again?"

Larry, Jean, Shirley, and Ben Cooper our new chair of the trustees arrived at one-fifteen. Ben greeted me, "Pastor Maude can we hold our meeting in the social hall? I told my granddaughter that the cheerleaders can use our kitchen to bake cookies for their bake sale."

"That's fine." I was too distressed to care one way or the other.

One-thirty came and went without the delegation from the district office appearing on our doorstep. I smiled thanking God for traffic and hoping the committee was hopelessly lost in the wilds of Kitsap County. Our good fortune didn't last for long. The committee arrived at ten minutes before two. They acted eager to get down to business.

"Right, what have you got that can show us some growth. Who is your membership chair?"

"Oh, that's 'Trisha. She couldn't make it on such short notice."

"Well in a church this size you must know how many new members you have."

Larry is shrewd. "Do you want them divided by constituents and confirmed members? I can't tell you who joined by confession and who joined by transfer."

Shirley piped up. "Joey joined by confession. I was his sponsor. What about Christine?"

I knew the answer to that question. "She's still a constituent."

"Wasn't Timmy in Joey's membership class?" Shirley sounded as if she was talking about last month instead of forty years ago.

"No, Timmy was in a different class. I was his sponsor." Mr. Cooper's voice lost some of his frail edge.

"Well, we didn't have classes for a couple years. Does anybody remember who else was in that first class?" Jean ignored the committee and looked at her friends as their tired, old brains tried to remember who was in what class. They argued. "No, no, all of that class joined in October."

"But we had a class during advent."

"The advent class joined at twelfth night."

"I thought Timmy joined in October."

I sat back and smiled as my members dithered and debated over who joined when. The poor dear committee member from Port Orchard tried to move the conversation on. "So you've had some membership classes and people have joined the church?"

Jean looked down her nose at the poor man. "Of course, what did you think we were doing out here?"

"Well, that is what we are trying to piece together."

"Hey Timmy, when you joined the church, was it October or Twelfth night?" Mr. Cooper called out to Timmy who had just come through the door with a fifty-pound sack of flour over one shoulder and a crate full of groceries.

Timmy was slightly red in the face and puffed as he replied, "It was Twelfth Night. Pastor Maude, these things are for the girl's bake sale."

He sauntered off to the kitchen with his burdens.

I called after him, "Thanks, for bringing that by." I hadn't known he'd joined our church. It must have been when he was about twelve or thirteen.

Mr. Cooper wheezed, "Course his wife was brought up Catholic, but we've been making it a point to do more things with the Catholics. It makes it easier for mixed families like that."

Timmy nodded again as he went back out. "Tell the kids I'll pick up anything left over, but they can use what they need."

"Thanks again." I called to Timmy's retreating back.

He stopped to hold the door for someone else.

I immediately recognized four people from the Jewish fellowship. "Pastor, we've come to return the Torah. We finally have one of our own we can use."

I jumped out of my chair and went to greet my guests. "Oh come in. I am so thankful you have a Torah."

The rest of my congregation's representatives hobbled forward to greet the new guests. Mr. Cooper took charge of the placement of the Torah. "Bring that in here. We will set it up front next to the communion table. Here, bring it this way."

Mrs. Shellhauser needed to give me a big kiss on the cheek. "When you are marrying that nice man of yours? I hope you stay in Blackfish. He was so good with the boys, showing them how to clean your garage and all."

The Jewish delegation carried the torah with much flourishing and a few prayers to the front of the church and placed it beside the communion table. The leader of the Jewish delegation came prepared with a prayer for the occasion. When he was finished, I added my words of praise and thanksgiving.

As we all filed back to the social hall, I began to wonder just who Larry had called to come to this meeting. The whole returning-of-the-Torah had looked somewhat staged to me, but then it was important to do the chore with reverence.

We returned to our guests, "I apologize for the disruption. The Torah is so important to them that I thought we should follow their lead in how they wanted to treat its return."

"Ah, yes, of course. Uh…moving along here. Do you have a current treasurers report?" The poor DS tried to keep my congregation on track. I was ready to sit back and watch the show.

"Oh yes, I updated this before I came down here. See, I have it all on Quicken now. My grandson gave me his old computer and showed me how to make these nice graphs." Jean passed out lovely printed copies of her report. With the money from the parsonage insurance sitting in our accounts the numbers at first glance looked impressive and my salary had been paid on time every month for five months in a row."

"Hi, everybody." Stan, the male cheerleader, led the girls into the social hall. "Look we have a surprise for you." He reached behind his back and pulled Mary out from behind himself by her arm. He announced in triumphant tones, "She made the team with her interpretive dance."

Mary pulled at the front of her cheerleading sweater and grinned. I responded appropriately to the occasion. I jumped out of my chair and jumped up and down and squealed like a chirpy cheerleader. This was the response Mary needed so she jumped then did a little dance step.

Larry and Ben jumped to their feet and shook hands with the girls. Shirley screeched. "You are not going to make cookies in those clothes are you?"

The students looked dismayed.

Shirley admonished. "You come with me. We have some big aprons. If you get dough in your letters, it will leave a spot that will never look right. And you will need to use the plastic gloves while working in the kitchen." Shirley led the students off toward the kitchen while reciting health department regulations.

Ben mumbled something about "fundraiser" and "camperships."

"Oh! Do you have some kids going to camp this summer?" Again, the poor delegate from Port Orchard tried to organize this meeting. I wanted to hug the poor man knowing he was destined to fail.

Coach Muller came in before the discussion about camperships got beyond a befuddled argument about who had that information and were Elaine's children going and how many of the Cole's children had signed up.

The organized delegate from the district committee wrote a note, "Several families sending kids to camp and congregation sponsoring camperships. That's good. What else have you got?"

I was too busy hugging Coach Muller for putting Mary on the squad to pay much attention to the official meeting I was supposed to be in. She explained. "We are having Mary do interpretive dance. Evidently she's been taking private lessons and is really quite good."

Larry cleared his throat. "Yes, one of our congregation teaches ballet and modern dance at Olympic. She's been giving some of the youth classes. Her husband is a programmer for Willets-Manion and he is helping us update our computer equipment. We'd like to see him reaching-out to the youth through computer work. That is what all the kids are into now-days."

I shook my head and turned toward the door. "Pastor Maude. Pastor Maude." Andrew one of the boys who'd worked with Ralph was yelling and excited about something. "Hey, guess what! You know that mud that was sliding into your garage? Well, Cary and me saw it was still oozing so we crawled back under the blackberries and Scots broom and found where it is coming from."

I glanced at Cary and recognized him as one of the boys who had discovered the blocked culvert on Pine Creek last winter. I smiled eager for his report.

Cary continued, "Yeah, it was really cool under all the blackberries and things. There's all these neat animal trails. You could hide a dead body under there and nobody would ever know."

I raised my eyebrows. "Oh? Elaine Miller and I had always considered dumping the bodies off Hunters Point at high tide the best choice."

Cary did not disappoint me. He sighed and explained, "No, if you dump a body off there, the current will carry it right around to the beach at the state park. It'll wash up in an hour or so." He flicked his long hair out of his eyes.

"Anyway Pastor, we found the source of the water. There is a great big leaking water pipe about three feet down." Andrew my first informant told me.

Stan came out of the kitchen. "What did you find?"

"A great big leaky pipe in the field next door."

The DS suggested, "Can we move this meeting to another room so we don't get interrupted."

I responded from my years as a teacher, "Can't. Adult to student ratio." I sat back down in my chair.

Ben Cooper spoke up. "I'd forgotten all about that water pipe. It runs out to the new high school."

I knew the new high school to be at least forty years old.

"We fought over them running that under church property, but it would save them so much money to run it under our old parking lot. Course the old log parsonage was still standing then and we used it for classrooms, but they never should have put that there. They agreed to pay for the demolition…"

"Pastor Maude can I use your phone?"

"Who are you going to call, Cary?"

"My mom. She works for the water district. She's in billing, but if I tell her about the leak, she'll get someone out here to look at it."

Andrew suggested, "Hey, lets call Mark too. His dad has a brush hog." The boys took my phone and went off to a corner to make calls.

I looked back at my guests. I enjoyed seeing who looked shocked by my discussion of where to hide bodies. I figured the man from Port Orchard knew kids. He plugged on with the meeting. "Okay, we don't have real accurate figures here, but the finance report," he shrugged, "shows that you have enough money to stay open, and you are up to date on your apportionments."

I knew this was an important factor in our favor.

The boys returned my phone.

The DS asked, "Do you have any other plans for expansion?

"What kind of expansion?" Cary asked.

"Community outreach, classes, expanding Sunday School."

Cary answered. "I came here for classes on Sunday for a couple weeks after Christmas, but then soccer practice started again. You know Pastor, if we turned that vacant lot into a soccer field the teams wouldn't have to practice on Sunday morning, and we could have classes." He flicked his hair out of his eyes and continued in a totally innocent tone. "That stuff you taught us was real interesting." He didn't sound rehearsed. I wondered if someone was hiding out back catching children and telling them what to say.

Mr. Cooper spoke up, "We'd have to vote on it. I think it would be a better use of the property than letting it sit. I'll tell you what Cary..." The old man turned to face the boy. "...you and your friends figure out how you would get the work done then you come tell me how you are going to do the job. I'll take your idea to my committee and we'll vote to make your play field."

I thought Mr. Cooper made a grand trustee. I pulled my hair off of my forehead and looked at the clock. "Oh dear, you folks are going to hit rush hour traffic. Do you know how to take the back road past the airport so you don't get stuck in Gorst?" I stood up knowing the committee didn't have enough information to make a decision about this church, but they had enough to keep them from making any big changes before annual conference in two months.

I walked our guests to the door and tried to add some more details to our case. "I am starting a support group for divorced women in our community, and I need to start a bereavement group." I waved as the committee headed to their cars.

Larry and Jean came up behind me. "They're gone. Do you think they will close us down?"

"No." I was exhausted.

"Pastor, you look beat. Go on home and rest. We'll close up here."

I felt a little weak and wobbly when I got in my car. I debated going back inside and helping myself to a handful of cookies. I started the car and drove home wondering why I felt so drained.

When I got home, I crashed on my bed and thought I don't know if I am so tired because of the meeting itself, or the chaos, or well... Again I wondered about the need for a sermon on bearing false witness. I puzzled over what could have been dishonest about the meeting. I stayed on my bed trying to understand what had just happened until Mandy came to tell me dinner was ready.

CHAPTER **41**: RALPH COMES HOME

Ralph finally returned home from Colombia. He called me as soon as he came in from the airport. "How's my Maudy?" I decided I liked being his Maudy. "Things are hectic here." I told him about Mandy and Fay moving in and the break-in at the church. "I am concerned that Trevor is up to something. He disappears for hours, comes in excited and then runs off to see Skunk." It felt good to dump my small nagging worry onto Ralph.

He said, "He left me a message to call him as soon as I get in. Do you have any idea what he is up to?"

"No."

"It can't be too bad if Skunk is involved. I'll see if I can get him to open up to me. What else is happening?"

"I've decided to start a support group for divorced women. This is really Trisha and Mandy's idea. I think they are bonding over their shock and grief. On the other end of the scale, Fay's fiancé's family is hosting a meet the family engagement party for her and Jeremy in a few weeks."

"Maude stop! I was gone only ten days. How can so much happen to you in ten days?"

I laughed, "It was because you were gone, I got lonely." I tried to sound pouty. "I missed you."

"I missed you too. Life is just brighter when I'm with you."

My toes curled at his assurance that he missed me. I sighed and we spent the next few minutes talking about us. I smiled as I listened to his voice.

I debated whether or not I needed to make a full confession to Mandy when she confronted me on Saturday afternoon. "Maudy, I can't believe you. Look how excited you are for Sunday. You're fussing over your hair and nails and what to wear. I've never heard of clergy getting so worked up over worship services before."

"Huh? What? Who? Me?"

"Yes. That is the fourth time in the past hour that you've mentioned that we have to be ready for Sunday. We have to have food in the house for Sunday. We won't be able to paint the bedroom until after Sunday. I don't know what to think."

Trevor walked in on this conversation and told her what to think. "Aunt Mandy, all this means is that Ralph got home from South America. Ignore her. Well, it might be a good idea to make yourself scarce after church. Ralph gets grumpy if he doesn't get time alone with her."

Fay danced and floated about the room. "Oh is your boyfriend coming on Sunday?" She floated in a circle. "Oh! We must clean the house. Trevor, get outside and run the string trimmer around those flower-beds by the east border! What shall we have for lunch—something simple and elegant. What are you going to wear?"

I wondered when Fay grew up to be such a mature responsible young woman.

"Oh, I forgot that you have someone. And here I am in the way." Cousin Mandy burst into tears and ran off to throw herself down on the ugly quilt she had finished and put on the bed in the spare room.

Trevor looked at the door where Mandy had disappeared then looked at Fay scowling at him then at me. "Right, the weed trimmer." He slouched off shaking his head.

Fay and I spent a couple hours tidying the house, converting the garage into a dining room, and evaluating my wardrobe. I occasionally remembered to give thanks that in the middle of my chaos, I had a companion who understood my need to appear beautiful and feminine.

Sunday arrived. We all went to church. Fay and Mandy sent me home shortly after the service was over. Mandy had recruited Larry and Jean to lock up. Fay would make certain her mother loitered long enough for me to have quiet time with Ralph.

I came home from church to find Trevor and Ralph in the living room apparently engaged in a serious conversation. "Mom! You're early." Trevor leapt to his feet and almost raced from the room.

I watched my son leave the room and asked, "Why is he acting guilty?"

Ralph laughed, "We were talking about the break-ins you've been having in Blackfish."

I raised my eyebrows as I floated toward Ralph.

He opened his arms to hold me. "Trevor did a little checking on things. He's built a good case for someone making a major attempt to break into the submarine base by accessing it through the slough."

I rested my head on Ralph's shoulder and slid my arms around him. His warmth and scent overpowered my senses.

From far away, Ralph's voice continued the story, "I've agreed to push his theory and information with the FBI. He makes sense."

"Ralph, that's nice. Now, kiss me." We didn't talk for another ten minutes until Darling Fay fumbled loudly at the front door alerting us to immanent interruption.

When the rest of the family arrived, Trevor came down from his loft and took Ralph on a tour of his remodeling projects. Ralph laughed at our conversion of the garage into a dining room, "Hey, this looks great."

Trevor grabbed Ralph's arm when he reached out to touch the glossy wall. "Don't touch the paint! Fay and I didn't finish painting until one this morning."

Ralph turned in a circle and chuckled. "I'd hardly recognize this as a garage. Nice work. It's still usable as a garage, but the whole family will fit for Sunday dinner until the weather turns nice enough to eat outside."

My toes curled when Ralph talked about our combined families as one. It was easy enough to imagine us as one family when his children came in with Patty and dropped their belongings on my furniture. April gave Fay a snotty look when Fay told her where to put her coat away. Fay didn't back down.

The look on Patty's face was priceless when Mandy showed her the completed quilt. "Oh. Mandy. I hadn't thought about combining the colors that way."

"Well…yes. When you mix the colors all up you can't see the design as well. This way the structure of the design is much stronger." Mandy smiled fondly upon her handiwork.

Patty stood with her mouth open.

April redeemed herself with Fay for a few moments. "Hey, I like that. I couldn't see what Patty was doing with it, but that makes sense."

Fay and Mandy smiled at April. When I got a chance, I hugged Patty. "Yes, it is hideous. It's what Mandy needed right now."

Patty shook her head. "You warned me. Really, if it helped Mandy through some rough days, I'm thankful." She started to giggle. "It also tells me why April and I don't get along better if she likes that."

"I suppose it does say something about a preference for structure over color."

Trevor and Rich wanted to rush through dinner so they could take the rowboat out. Ralph's voice nearly shook the rafters when he learned of their plan. "Listen you two, and you listen real good. Do not take that rowboat anywhere near the slough. Stay away from the submarine base. Stay away from this case. Trevor, if you are right, the people involved are not to be messed with. Rich, any hint of my son being anywhere near these crimes can cost me my job. I have half a notion to ground the rowboat." He glared at both boys.

Trevor and Rich looked at each other and shrugged. Trevor spoke first. "Common before he gets any more weird ideas."

Rich pouted, "I thought we gave him time to kiss your mom before we got here. What's he so grumpy about now?"

"I don't know. He's your dad." They went out the door leaving the women in shocked silence.

Ralph stared after the boys for a couple minutes before he shook his head, "They are either growing up or innocent." He paused and looked at the women. "That admonition goes for all of you. Trevor had some good insights into this case. Avoid it as much as possible."

Mandy struggled to show an interest in our troubles. "What is the problem?" Her tone told us she didn't care.

April's cheeks sported red flags that told me that she felt upset by her father's outburst. She soon found a target for her discomfort. Fay began to float around the room clearing the table. The activity directed April's attention to Fay. Ralph and I were in for a rough afternoon.

April snorted, "I don't believe in all this falling in love crap."

Her father grumbled, "Believe in it. It's how you came to be." He melted into obviously happy memories.

Fay seemed unaware that April was deliberately baiting her. "I suppose love is different for everybody. Jeremy and I have known each other since the seventh grade. We just kinda have always been there for each other." She drifted out of the room carrying three platters that had formerly contained food.

April waited until Fay floated back in. "I can only hope that I don't meet some guy and suddenly become infected with some gross desire to be a domestic goddess." She sneered.

Fay almost didn't respond then mused, "I doubt that will happen. I also hope you are never in a position of being dependent on a relative for food and housing, which is a far more compelling reason to do everything possible to make your relative comfortable."

Ralph sat back, folded his arms across his chest and allowed a smug expression to flow over his face. April cast him a disgusted look. He grinned back at her.

Mandy and Patty got up to help Fay clear up after dinner and Ralph asked me if I'd go for a walk with him.

We intended to walk the perimeter of the lake. This took a great deal of time because we needed to stop and do a great deal of kissing. Ralph did chuckle at one point. "Honey, I don't know how I would have ever managed to get April raised into a responsible adult without you and your girls." He shook his head. "That Fay is something else. I wonder if young Jeremy knows he's found a winner."

"You can tell him so next week."

"I will. It's unusual for someone her age to acknowledge that her needs are a burden on a family member. Do you need help with your grocery bill? I mean you fed us this weekend and have Mandy and Fay all week."

"Mandy has been buying the groceries. Fay made certain Trevor contributed his share."

"I meant what I said earlier about wanting to help that girl feel accepted." He chuckled again. "She is something else."

I smiled at Ralph and agreed that he could at least be my date for the wedding activities. "I assume you will have enough other opportunities to be the alpha male if you hang around here."

My smug remark caused him to threaten to throw me in the lake. I ran. He caught me and picked me up and swung me around. It felt delightful to be picked up as if I was a young girl instead of a middle-aged woman.

CHAPTER 42: DIVORCE SUPPORT GROUP

Tuesday night, we held our first support group for divorced women. I had no idea who would come. Mandy had printed up notices and Trisha put them up at the grocery and hardware stores. She surprised me when she told me she put them on the mirrors in the women's restroom at Timmys and at Four Corner Tavern out by the highway.

At seven in the evening, Mandy and I opened the church. I didn't know what to think when Elaine came in. I wondered what Trisha would think about Elma's daughter being in the group. Really, group members shouldn't know all the details of the other's situation.

Finally, I took my seat next to Christine Stevenson and asked the women to introduce themselves. Mrs. Stevenson concluded her basic information with the thought, "I'm here because I think I want to remarry again someday, and I want to put my past behind me."

"Well, if you are thinking that remarrying again involves my brother, think again. He is all talk and no commitment." Elaine seemed a bit hard on her brother.

"He may not have been given the best principles at home." Trisha added.

I silently praised God that Trisha didn't say anything about his mother being a trollop in front of Elaine. *'God, this isn't supposed to be how these things go. All these people except Mandy know all about each other. They are not supposed to know who has done what.'* I nodded at each speaker and silently prayed.

I heard an answer, *'Don't worry, sweetheart. This should be more entertaining than the movies, and they might even learn something from each other. Enjoy yourself.'* I wondered if I was getting cynical or if God was.

Elaine's tone softened when she concluded her introduction. "I think I'm like Mrs. Stevenson. I've met a good man. I don't want my past to destroy my future. Oh, and I want you all to know that I never, as the pastor says, poached. Men have left me, but I was never the reason a man left another woman." Elaine looked toward Trisha. "I don't approve of women taking a man who belongs to someone else."

Trisha concluded her introduction, "I'm not really divorced yet, if that bothers any of you." She picked at the fringe on her scarf. "He left me. Maybe I should file. I don't know."

I intervened, "How you decide to relate to your husband is your own business. He left you. You are alone, hurt and confused. You need to be here. Perhaps we can help you sort out some of your issues over time."

After Trisha, Darlene the waitress from Timmy's told her story. She concluded, "So, I mean, I never even lived with the man, but I'm divorced. We had a kid. Is it okay for me to be here?"

Elaine sighed, "Honey, that is exactly what got all of us in trouble—some smooth talking man convinced us that he would love us forever. Shit. They all make promises. Do any of them keep promises?"

Our sixth member, Janette, was a librarian from Bremerton. "…so after the divorce was final the branch library where I worked was closed due to budget cuts, and I moved to this side of the mountains to be closer to my family. I needed an inexpensive place to live so I'm renting out here. I don't have a real boyfriend or anything. I'm still in shock over the whole thing with his pregnant girlfriend."

By the time Mandy and I got home from the session, I needed to go to bed and sleep. I didn't know what to make of the group. They seemed to get along fine. The session energized Mandy. "Maudy, thank you for helping with this. I can see myself in each of those women. Who would have thought that women who are so different in background could have so much in common? Do you think Harve could be cheating?"

I ached all over and wanted to go to bed, so I sighed as I answered Mandy. "Probably not with his penis. He certainly is cheating emotionally by giving his friends the emotional energy that should be reserved for you. What do you think of the possibility of him having a crush on another woman?"

"Harve has been so emotionally dead that I can't imagine him even having a crush." Mandy sighed and looked incredibly sad.

I realized that I felt sorry for Harve. "Harve is in such deep spiritual trouble. It is hard to know what is going on with the rest of him."

CHAPTER 43: JOHN WESLEY

O ur lives settled into a pattern of frantic chaos. Fay enrolled in classes at Olympic Community College. Her abrupt departure from her home disrupted her graduation. Still, she would finish on time.

In early April, someone broke into a video store at the crossroads. I didn't hear anything about vandalism. The rumor mill had it that some computer equipment was stolen.

Ralph admonished Trevor, Rich, April, and Skunk to ignore the break-ins. "Yes. You're probably right that this is some sort of attempt to break into the submarine base. Lord knows what they think they are going to go after. If the base is the target, there may be a bigger organization behind this." Ralph neglected to admonish John Wesley.

Our Maundy Thursday service went particularly well. The whole congregation showed up for the soup dinner and short worship service. Trevor and Fay had served as ushers. Jean and Larry helped serve communion.

In addition to my old congregation, the whole Cole family came. Mary Carter rode with the Coles. A few of the elderly from the low-income apartments came for dinner and went home to bed. The elderly woman who had almost died of pneumonia during the flood came for dinner and stayed for the service.

We decorated the sanctuary in the faded palm branches from Palm Sunday morning and used low lighting. I used recorded music for our gathering time. Mrs. Stevenson managed to wring a majestic Bach prelude out of the old pump organ that sat at the back of the chancel.

I stood to give my sermon and noticed that Ralph had slipped into the back of the sanctuary in time to hear me speak. I looked at the small gathering of people who came honestly seeking to know God, and I was overwhelmed with love for them--for all of them. Perhaps being so centered in love made my sermon so special. I knew it was one of the best I'd ever preached.

I talked about being betrayed by someone you love. "We've all been betrayed by loved ones. As children our parents are occasionally busy when our hearts are bruised. Friends and family don't always understand the power of their words to hurt us. As we get older we find a mate and fall in love." Here I raised my eyes from my script and looked into Ralph's eyes. "This year many of us have had our lives torn apart by betrayal. Alva betrayed Trisha. Harve betrayed Mandy and Fay. Sometimes the betrayal is something everyone can see. Sometimes the betrayal isn't really a betrayal. Everybody said that Hal betrayed me when he beat me. He didn't betray me. He was sick. I saw he was sick and it was knowing how sick he was that made me sad. Yes, he beat me as Christ was beaten, but I came back, just as Christ came back."

After I sat down, I noticed several people crying as we sang "Are Ye Able." When I spoke the words to prepare us for Communion, I added, "Maundy Thursday is a sad time. It's a time for us to examine our hurts our imperfections, our betrayal, and it is a time to confess that we have betrayed others. Maundy Thursday is sad, but it is the beginning of our new joy. Healing starts here. Healing from those betrayals real or perceived starts now as we accept the elements of Holy Communion."

My poor old congregation shuffled slowly forward to take the bread and dip it in the cup. I remembered we'd had a huge argument about the common cup, intinction, and serving separate cups in the pews. I smiled when Ralph appeared before me. Instead of immediately dipping his bread in the cup, he whispered, "This is the wine I need." He bent his head and kissed me on the lips. I smiled. His hair tickled my face when he bent down to kiss me.

The old woman behind Ralph patted my cheek and gave me a knowing smile as she dipped her bread in the cup. A child came next. The little boy had picked up a discarded palm branch and tickled my face with it. He said, "Don't be sad. Smile." And he tickled me again.

After the little boy moved on, an old woman poked me in the stomach with her cane four times. She moved on quickly to be replaced by a bewhiskered old man who started tapping on my forehead.

I opened my eyes. First, I realized that John Wesley was standing on my chest and hitting my forehead with his paw. I had a moment of confusion before I realized that Easter came late this year and it wasn't even Palm Sunday yet. Good, that was really a terrible sermon I'd just preached. John Wesley looked into my open eyes, patted my face, yowled cat breath in my nose, and hopped off of the bed. He ran to the bedroom door, turned and yowled again.

I got up to let the cat out. "Sh, I'm coming. I'm coming. Don't wake the whole household."

John Wesley ran to the French door to be let out onto the patio. I shuffled along behind him in the dark. "Sh, cat. You'll wake the whole neighborhood."

I finally unlatched the door and opened it just far enough to let the beastie out.

In the infuriating manner of cats, John Wesley didn't go out. He sat down smack in the middle of the open door. I contemplated pushing the animal the rest of the way out. I looked closer at my cat and noticed his ears laying flat back against his skull. I froze and listened.

At first, I wasn't certain I heard something. The night was extremely dark with the moon and stars hidden behind a cover of clouds. I couldn't see anything. Just as it occurred to me that the electricity had gone off all over the house, I heard a ripple of sound out on the lake. I knelt down to pull my cat back inside and made out the sound of an oar pulling in its metal lock. Now I could identify the sounds of a rowboat moving through the still lake. I pulled John Wesley inside and silently shut the door. As I quietly turned the deadbolt on the French doors, I thought I saw a slight glow as if someone was shielding a light inside the boat then all went black again.

My heart pounded as I tried to think of one, blessed, legitimate reason for anyone to be out rowing in the pitch black at one in the morning. Any romantic reasons I could think of wouldn't require trying to be so quiet. I thought romance might produce more sound. As I tried to puzzle out what to do, I double-checked the locks on the front door and all the windows.

I gave thanks that I knew my way around my house. I moved easily to the laundry room to lock the doors. Once the doors were secure I thought about my son asleep in his loft. I quickly scaled his ladder thinking, "That boy better be in his bed." I found him sound asleep and whispered, "Trevor. Trevor wake up." I patted his sleeping form.

"Huh? What? Mom? What is it?" He groped on the table beside his bed then flipped open his cell phone.

I almost pounced on the bright light of his phone. "Sh. No lights. The power is out and someone is out on the lake trying to be very quiet, but John Wesley heard them and woke me."

Trevor grunted. "Shit." He pulled his covers over his head. Within a few seconds I heard him whispering, "Wake up, man. Come on wake up and answer the damn phone." He paused, "Cricket? I'm sorry to

wake you up. Wake up Skunk. Yeah, there is trouble out on the lake."
His conversation with Skunk lasted only a minute or less, a few grunts
and assurances then he hung up. He popped his head out of his covers.
"Skunk knows who to call if this is the same people involved in his
break-in."

I sat beside Trevor's bed until his even breathing told me that he had
gone back to sleep. I climbed back down the ladder and made my way
to my sofa. I recognized the ugly comforter by its feel. The thing was
warm enough to wrap up in if I didn't run into a pin. I wrapped in the
blanket and waited knowing I'd feel extremely foolish if the rowers out
on the lake turned out to be innocent lovers. I stared and stared thinking
I could see a wake rippling behind something far out on the lake.

The night remained absolutely silent. I thought the rowers must
have reached the slough by now. John Wesley sat staring intently out
the window. I wondered if he could see anything. "Do you hear them?
What do you hear?" I whispered. The cat ignored me.

Suddenly, the night exploded with light and sound. Helicopters
arose from behind the trees in the distance. Their bright lights lit up
everything between the lake and the overhead clouds. A boat motor
burst into life out on the lake. I thought I could hear police sirens
coming from the direction of Oak Creek Road.

The helicopters' lights scanned the lake. I saw a small boat racing
across the lake from the direction of the slough. I couldn't see anybody
in the boat. The lights followed the boat momentarily. The two machines
in the air, turned and one headed toward the slough. The other turned
toward my house, playing its light along the edge of the lake. A dog
barked in the distance.

I could hear voices now. I saw more lights down at the county lake-
access. A car raced by on Oak Lake road. The noise of the helicopter
began to shake the house.

Mandy and Fay emerged from their room. "What's happening?"
Trevor answered for me. "Intruders on the lake."

A voice came out of the clouds, "This is the coast guard. Give
yourselves up. We have you blocked in. Give yourselves up." Nothing
happened. A couple more cars raced up the road and then came back.
We huddled on the sectional and waited, while the bright lights from the
sky continued to search the lake and surrounding yards.

After about thirty-five minutes six men in navy uniforms came
running along the perimeter trail from the direction of the county
access. They carried guns and moved in a nice formation. I found
myself slipping into a surreal state as I sat in my dark house watching

the activity outside my windows as if watching a live play on a brightly lit stage.

The helicopter continued to light the perimeter path as it made its way around the lake. When the light reached my house it played all over my yard then came through the front window blinding us as we sat dumbly huddled together on my sofa.

Five minutes after the helicopter passed my house, we got a knock at the door. Trevor bounced up. "I'll get this mom." He led a couple agents in plain clothes into the living room.

Agent, Dwight, produced his identification and asked. "What are you people doing up in the middle of the night?"

I blinked and looked out my front window at the bright light. A couple more sailors ran across my lawn. I could see the vibration from the helicopter shaking my big front window. The whole house shook and rattled.

Mandy found her voice first. "It is a little hard to sleep what with the lights and the noise and all."

As if to prove her point, the voice from the clouds once again admonished us all, "Give yourselves up. You cannot escape."

Fay collapsed on the sofa in a fit of giggles.

Agent number two, Donald, chuckled, "Have you seen…" he looked at my giggling cousin in her skimpy nightwear and caught himself before saying anything inane, "um.. any signs of the intruders?"

I gave thanks that he didn't ask if I'd seen anything unusual. I explained about John Wesley wanting out then not going out and about hearing noises on the lake. "So I finally woke Trevor and he called Skunk who knew how to call you."

"Why did you think there might be something wrong?"

I explained about the series of break-ins and the vandalism. "And well, the day agents can probably fill you in on the rest. Anyway, everybody in Blackfish figures the submarine base is the ultimate target."

"Thank you ma'am. So other than the rumors of break-ins and the local gossip you don't have anything more to go on?"

"Yeow." John Wesley gave the agent a disgusted look.

"Well there was someone out there rowing a boat in that direction and they were trying to be quiet and were not shining a light." I looked at my cat sitting in a pose that radiated offended dignity. "And John Wesley did wake me up, and he has been watching the lake intently."

"Who?" Agent Dwight asked.

I indicated the cat.

Trevor asked, "What happened to our power?"

"We're looking into that." Agent Donald grunted without making any effort to satisfy our curiosity.

The voice in the clouds proved to be incorrect. After hours of searching from the sky and on ground, the combined federal, state and county forces didn't catch anybody. They confiscated the empty boat when it lodged itself in some willows with the motor still running. After two and a half hours I went back to bed, thinking I might be able to get back to sleep. As I drifted off to sleep I had a moment of regret that the planning for Easter week was still before me.

Of course I had a full schedule at work the day after I spent half the night awake waiting for the navy to capture saboteurs in my front yard. As soon as I got to work, I called the members of the worship committee and requested a meeting to plan Holy Week.

I'd just gotten off of the phone with the worship committee when a tap on my door interrupted me. I opened the door. "Joey! I didn't know you were in town. Come in."

"Hi, I'm home for only a few days to try to straighten out this mess with Mom and Alva."

"Sit." I waited for him to get as comfortable as he was going to. "What do you have in mind?"

"Well, I don't know. It isn't right. Him leaving his wife and moving in there and sponging off of Mom."

I rubbed my forehead. "I confess, I am at a loss over the topic. The whole congregation is. Do you have a game plan?"

"Well, I thought I'd talk to Mom—see if I can get her to come back to Hollywood with me. She'd like the sun. Uh, beyond trying to get Mom to see reason, I can't think of a thing." Joey shifted in his seat. "Actually, I'm pretty angry with Mom. The whole story is…we argued when I got home yesterday. I'm not sure she is still talking to me. Can you talk to her? Tell her that her behavior is a sin?"

"She knows what her behavior is and at this point, I don't think she cares. Well, I think she knows. One of my problems here is that half the congregation is senile, and I cannot always tell which half is which. Most of the time, I end up concluding that I'm the one who is stark raving bonkers."

Joey shifted his weight and said in a pouty tone, "I talked to Alva a little—told him he was being foolish. I tried to convince him that his wife was a good woman and he should go back to her. He just laughed and told me he was tired of good women and wanted one that was a bit naughty. He was disgusting."

I ran my fingers through my hair.

Joey leaned forward. "Is there any sort of disciplinary action your congregation can take?

"Not really. The administrative board replaced Alva as the chair of the trustees. Truthfully, they did it mostly because he left for the Holy Land and some decisions about investing the money from the parsonage came up." I sighed and felt bad that I wasn't more help. "Perhaps when the novelty wears off those two will come to their senses." I shook my head. "The best I can do is see if I can find some research on how other congregations handle these situations. Of course, I will keep all your family in my prayers."

Joey tapped his foot, cleared his throat and shifted in his chair. I raised my eyebrows and waited for him to speak. He looked away and cleared his throat. I waited. "The thing of it is pastor, how am I to hold my head up in this town when my mother behaves like a trollop? I don't know why, but I never was popular in school—maybe because I'm no athlete. Anyway, I went away and have made something of myself. I'm not the richest man in Hollywood, but I've worked steady. I'm respectable. I'd like the people where I grew up to respect me instead of seeing me as the kid who goofed off in school." Joey hung his head.

"Ah, you are concerned how this will effect your reputation and your relationship with Christine Stevenson?"

He lifted his head. "Yeah, well she's a school teacher, has an education. I know she had some trouble with her first marriage, but she's respectable. She's supported herself and is helping others. How am I supposed to get a woman like that to look at me when all this town sees is Joey the goof-off son of the town trollop." He sunk his head almost into his lap.

"I think the only opinion you need to worry about is that of Christine Stevenson."

"Do you think she likes me?"

"I'm certain she does." I tried to smile reassuringly at Joey. He sounded so much like a little boy wanting to know if his first crush liked him.

Eventually, Joey went away and I settled down to outline some ideas for Holy Week. I liked the idea from my dream where we'd left the withered palm branches from Palm Sunday in place for Maundy Thursday.

I went to Timmy's for lunch where I earned my food by relating the high points of what everybody all ready knew about the raid at Oak Lake. They enjoyed the part about the agents wondering why we were awake in the middle of the night. I left out the parts about who called whom and John Wesley waking me up. "Anyway, I figure a few more nights like last night and my silly cousin will stop moping about what she doesn't have and notice that I have a yard full of sailors, and she can take her pick."

"Ah, so the truth behind the raid comes out. You were trying to find a new man for your cousin so you can get her out of your refrigerator."

Darlene was waiting tables. "That isn't a bad idea. Next time you have one of these parties can I come over in my nightie?"

I chuckled, "The more the merrier."

I spent the afternoon calling on people in the nursing home and found a few minutes to work on my sermon before I went home.

CHAPTER 44: NAMES

L ate in the week after the raid, Christine Stevenson called and made an appointment to see me after school. I agreed and worried about more troubles with the special ed students.

Christine arrived and we took a few minutes getting settled. Knowing how I like to get right down to business with Dr. Dave, I didn't engage in much chit-chat. "Now what is happening with you?"

"Well…um…I don't know. This will be confidential won't it?"

I nodded.

"I mean really confidential like if I were talking to a priest or an attorney."

"Yes, I am covered with the same level of confidentiality." By this time I felt really curious. I confess all sorts of horrid thoughts started to form in my head.

"Well…I don't want you saying anything to anybody official like, but I need some guidance."

I nodded.

"It's about Joey."

"Joey?" This topic took me by surprise. I sighed, relieved that she was not concerned about troubles up at the school. I would have to report child abuse and I gave thanks she was not going to tell me that a child was being molested.

"Yes, well…I've been thinking pretty serious about him. Oh I know he's not the brightest bulb in the pack and that he talks bigger than he is sometimes—like he likes to talk about Hollywood parties as if he attends parties with famous people."

I nodded. "As a production manager, I'm sure he does meet various celebrities. When Mandy and I were doing movies, we both met Kevin Costner. He treated us courteously. So, yes, I suspect that Joey's name dropping is somewhat legitimate and perhaps more of a cultural thing than we realize here."

She raised her eyebrows and cocked her head so I continued. "I worked in some movies in Seattle when I was in high school and college. Mandy and I met several famous people but we didn't talk about it much. When I moved to Pasadena," I sighed and tried to put something into words. "Well people down there realize that the movie industry pays their bills, just like Boing or the shipyard here. Here, people get excited and comment if a ship like the Nimitz or the Enterprise comes in. I remember Daddy calling me on the phone the first time he saw the Boing 777. In Pasadena, people talk the same way only they mention celebrities they've seen. I've never taken Joey's talk to be any different than someone mentioning a plane or a ship."

"Oh! Do you really think that is what it is?"

I nodded. "He's been pretty straight with me about his job and everybody, even at the seminary, mentions if they have a celebrity sighting. Um…kinda like we mention if we see the whales on our way to Seattle."

Christine doubled over laughing. "I bet that is the first time that Sharon Stone has ever been compared to a whale."

We both laughed. "Did you really come in here to talk about Joey's name dropping?"

"Well…no. But, it helps to understand that, so I don't feel so alarmed about the other. Well… you won't say anything?"

I shook my head hoping we were not going to get into child abuse.

"It's these break-ins." Again Christine took me by surprise. "Have you ever noticed that every, single time we've had a break-in Joey has been home?"

"Oh God," I moaned.

"So you think he is involved?"

"I'm not sure how he would fit the profile Ralph uses to describe our perpetrators."

"Well, I don't know what Ralph has said. But, the night they had the big raid out by your house, Joey let himself into my house and got in bed with me just after the helicopters woke me up."

I nodded.

"He was cold and wet. I asked him where he had been. He told me there was some sort of big police raid down at the county access to the lake. He claimed he walked down there from my house and stood and watched them prepare for the raid." Christine paused.

"Is there some reason you don't believe him?"

She shook her head. "Not specifically for this time. But it is the same every time. He comes in at odd hours and claims he was at his mothers, or his plane was late getting in, or he walked out from town because the shuttle wouldn't come out to my place. I don't know what to think."

"Certainly what you've said could be suspicious, but it could be said about many people. I think there are still people in town who think Trevor is the perpetrator simply because he is new in town and worse, is a preacher's kid. Is there anything about Joey that you find odd at these times? Is he high? Does he smell bad or has he used extra cologne? Has he shown you anything that could be stolen?"

She shook her head to all my questions.

"Christine, I don't know. Ralph describes one perpetrator as very low functioning with some level of brain damage. It seems to me you would recognize brain damage."

She nodded. "Well, like I've said, he isn't the brightest bulb in the pack, but he's good with numbers, and he can organize things. He's very organized. Uh...that doesn't sound very low functioning or brain damaged. I don't think I've ever had a student who could organize."

"Ah, so we've eliminated Joey as the low functioning one. What about being the brains of the outfit?"

She shook her head again. "Well, I don't know. There is one thing, and this is something he mentioned. He said in Hollywood these break-ins would be somebody researching a script."

I nodded. "Do you think he could be researching a script?"

Christine sat and stared at me for a full minute. "No, that doesn't fit either." She shifted in her chair. "Did Ralph really describe one of the perpetrators as low functioning with possible brain damage?"

I nodded. "Yeah, our best guess is that he is between twenty and twenty-two." I tried to avoid giving Christine any details about the crimes that she wouldn't know about.

"Huh. I didn't know that. Well I feel better about Joey. Um...twenty to twenty-two, still in Blackfish and brain damage...." She looked into the middle distance and scowled. "That would most probably be Cliff Morgan. Mom died of alcoholism when he was eighteen. His dad's been in prison forever. He was a real messed up kid—liked to play in his poop."

"Oh, that sounds like a sad story." I tried not to jump out of my chair.

Christine started making motions to leave, and I was still bound by client confidentiality.

"Oh, you know...um...about this Cliff Morgan, well, the FBI or the police might think that is a lead. I mean you must know every brain damaged kid in Blackfish who is the right age. I know you wouldn't want to talk about Joey, and really there is no need, but I can't understand why you haven't had agents on your doorstep before now. Would you mind telling them what you told me? This kid is in serious trouble only he doesn't know he's being used."

Christine shrugged. "I'd rather not get involved."

"But. In a way, I see you as an expert consultant. Would you hate me forever or think it's a violation of our discussion if I sent some agents over to talk to you about the special ed kids."

"I can't talk about my students that way. I don't want to talk to the cops. I shouldn't have said anything to you."

"Okay. The matter stays in this office."

Christine left and I sat at my desk and held my head. Finally, I realized there was someone I could tell. "God, The laws of my country and my profession forbid me from telling the authorities that Cliff Morgan may be in very serious trouble. He sounds like a lost soul who never had much of a chance in this world. Will you watch over him and shine your light in his life. Guard him from committing more crimes, and protect him from those who are using him."

I went home and forgot the conversation.

CHAPTER 45: HOLY WEEK

T he Bremerton Sun ran a full page on Holy Week services in our area. They listed our Palm Sunday, Maundy Thursday, and Easter Sunday services. They also mentioned the soup and bread dinner before the Maundy Thursday Service. I decided we better be prepared for our usual elderly to show up for the dinner.

We did have a big turn out for the dinner. Two of the people who usually came to our free lunches asked to stay for worship service so I found someone to drive them home after the service. I thought we were going to have to ask one belligerent young man to leave when he started complaining loudly about us having worship after dinner. He claimed we had lured him into the building under false pretences, and now we were going to preach at him. Just at the moment he became the loudest, Ralph arrived. I floated off to see Ralph. The man disappeared.

Everybody commented that the withered palm branches added a nice touch for telling the whole story of Holy Week. We all remembered singing, Blessed Is He Who comes in the Name of the Lord just a few days earlier.

I decided my sermon on betrayal that I preached in my dream wasn't a bad idea, so I cleaned it up, left out names of individuals and preached on being betrayed and betraying others. I left in the part about communion being the beginning of healing from the betrayal.

I served communion, but Ralph didn't kiss me. I remembered my dream about this service and gave thanks for the reality.

Easter Sunday, my family held the official house warming for my new home. Ralph bought me a monster barbeque. My parents bought patio furniture. I suspected Mandy had made suggestions for what I needed for an outdoor kitchen including a large awning to cover the patio and a chimenea for heat.

Ralph took Friday off and helped get the house and gardens pristine for company. I came home from Easter Sunday services and found the party just getting under way.

Of course, the first official order of business was an Easter Egg hunt. We found both plastic and hard boiled eggs. Apparently, several people brought eggs and hid them, so we had no idea how many eggs were hidden around my gardens. I thought I would probably find Easter Eggs for the next few months.

I'd not expected Jeremy's younger brother and parents to accompany him, but they arrived with apologies from their daughter for not coming to meet Fay's family. I soon discovered Jeremy's mother's agenda was to plan an official engagement party. I left her and Mandy to that delightful project.

I hadn't known my family owned as many boats as they appeared to. No less than six kayaks came to the party. We had three rowboats counting mine, and two canoes. Daddy organized boat races with prizes of extra cake for the winners.

I sat in my new patio chase wrapped up in the ugly comforter and enjoyed letting the party swirl around me. I felt unbelievably tired. Ralph did most of the cooking. Aunt Phyllis organized the buffet. April pleased me by being exceptionally good at helping the younger children find Easter eggs. Trevor conducted the grand tour of the house.

John Wesley ventured outside when he smelled food on the grill. He twisted himself around Ralph's legs. "Oh ho, so when I have food you will be my friend. I'm not giving you any. You can sit with Maudy now, but I get my turn later."

The cat hopped up on the chaise and groomed his privates in Ralph's general direction.

The whole party moved inside when it started to rain about four. Everybody declared my house big enough for family parties especially if we used the garage as a family room. Planning a real two-car garage for me became a new game for the family.

Finally, my family went home. Jeremy's parents declared themselves happy to meet us and invited us for the engagement party in two weeks. Jane continued, "I doubt that my sister will be able to be there, which is a shame, but her duties as first lady and Jake's international obligations take up all their time."

Mandy sounded gracious. "I look forward to meeting your sister whenever her schedule permits. Until then, thank you so much for planning this party. I look forward to meeting the rest of Jeremy's family." Jane's anxieties and Mandy's gracious assurances continued for several minutes. Finally they left.

"Come here woman." Ralph grabbed me around the middle and swung me up off of my feet. He strode off into my bedroom kicking the door closed behind us.

I thought I heard one of the boys say, "weird." But that may have been my imagination.

Ralph dumped me down on my bed then sat down on the foot of the bed to take off my shoes. "You look beat. Do you get this tired doing Easter every year?"

"Oh some years I've been more tired. This year had some added stresses with Mandy being here and," I moaned when Ralph began to rub my feet, "...and the divorced women's support group."

He chuckled and we talked about the support group as much as I was able. As Ralph rubbed my feet, my eyes wanted to roll back in my head, and I moaned some more.

The phone rang and I pounced on it without stopping to think. "Pastor Maude? This is Margery Sidell."

"Uh,"

"I'm calling about those people who came to dinner Thursday. That dinner was not supposed to be one of your charity meals. That was supposed to be for us."

"Well, uh, yes."

"And then you had to go and ruin it all by letting just anybody in. That Cliff Morgan is a no good and he doesn't belong in church."

"Huh? What? Who?" I sat straight up and waved at Ralph that something important happened.

"See that's the problem. You don't have any idea what kind of people you are letting in. That's why I'm opposed to the idea of a shelter where just anybody off of the street can walk in."

I wanted to get her back to the subject that interested me without alerting her that I was interested in someone specific. "Uh, what happened that upset you? Uh, did anything go wrong?"

"Yes. Well you heard him shouting and calling names and out and out saying he didn't want anything to do with church, after he'd eaten his fill."

"Okay, I remember something about that. What was his name?"

"Cliff Morgan."

"How do you know him?"

"He was in my grandson's grade at school, always pinching the other children and causing trouble. They couldn't have anything nice, because he would mess it up for the other kids. Every class party they had, he would tantrum and throw food and push the other children down and laugh when they cried. Even their prom, he left a big pile of shit by the refreshment table. He ruined prom for the whole class, and all the girls were dressed up pretty, and my grandson looked so nice in his tuxedo."

"Margery, I'm sorry that having this person show up at church upset you, and marred what I intended to be a special time for those who did want to worship. I will make you a promise. I promise that I will do everything in my power to see that this young man does not have the opportunity to upset you again. Is that fair enough?" My voice was firm.

"Well this is why I don't want just anybody coming into the church."

"I made you an offer for this one person. Are you going to take it? I'm not offering for anybody else, but for this person, your concerns are valid."

"You'll see that Cliff Morgan doesn't come to church again?"

"I can't promise for other churches and for all time, but for the immediate future, I'll do my best. Do you accept my offer?"

She sniffed, "Well I guess that is something."

"Good, I have to get off of the phone and take care of the matter immediately." I hung up and smiled at Ralph. "That was one of the old women from my church. I think she may have identified our low functioning young-adult with brain damage and a penchant for leaving poop in odd places."

Ralph raised his eyebrows. After I explained, he called Skunk. By the time he got off of the phone, I'd started feeling guilty about getting Margery to agree that we would allow other needy people to come to the church if I kept this one person out. It was a bad bargain on my part, but I expected Cliff to go to jail.

The system of relays from me to Ralph to Skunk to the FBI or whomever Skunk worked with didn't produce results until shortly after one on Monday. Agent Dwight and Agent Evens came out to question me. I looked them over and decided both men appeared presentable. I called to Mandy, "Hey cousin, will you come out here and be a witness to what I have to say."

Mandy dutifully came out and sat beside me. She didn't notice that the men in my living room were physically fit and well groomed. I thought of Harve who had been looking decidedly seedy the past few times I'd seen him. I shook my head over Mandy and began my story.

"Now, when I tell you to write something down, I want you to write it down." I gave both agents a stern look. They pulled out notebooks. Mandy looked through a stack of magazines and found one of Fay's school notebooks. "Good. Now write this down. A parishioner named Margery Sidell called..." I told the whole story making them write down the things that Ralph told me. I wanted to make certain that they had a clear trail to Cliff Morgan that did not come near Christine Stevenson.

CHAPTER 46: THE CAPTURE

Skunk learned about the capture of Cliff Morgan and an older man known to the FBI as an anarchist and called me with the news. Cliff made a full confession. From what I heard, he laughed over how he had fooled the police for so long. He stated revenge as part of his motive for the vandalism. He bragged about sneaking into the submarine base through the slough. He bragged about the camp they were setting up inside the base. He maintained that they were planning on using it as a hunting camp.

The older man requested an attorney and wouldn't say anything. That is all I ever learned about the case that had caused us so much worry and trouble over the past six months. I never heard any more facts or rumors. The paper didn't print anything about the arrests. The level of complete secrecy around the incident told me that there had most probably been a breach of security at the submarine base. We had been right to be concerned. I was very proud of John Wesley for his role in the whole incident.

On Monday afternoon, I sat out on the end of my dock and thought about how much trouble the case had really caused. Cricket and Skunk had been upset at the violation of their personal space. I'd done the cleansing ceremony. That ceremony changed our relationship. I helped them, and we bonded.

I thought about the Jewish fellowship. Yes, their experience had been horrific. Still, they had volunteered cooking one day a month for the community kitchen. They'd learned more about their history in this community when we discovered that our church housed a traditional copy of the Torah.

The Catholics seemed closer to us too. The Catholic women invited the women from our congregation to their spring tea. They bought food for the community kitchen. They helped us clean up after the fire.

I drank in the tranquility of the lake. I thought about Ralph and I. The break-ins had been part of our courtship time. We talked about it. Ralph treated my ideas and Trevor's with respect. He'd also been protective. The memory of his comforting words when he learned about the break-in at the church brought a smile to my whole face. I remembered the sound of his laughter when I told him how I thought about going home and making ugly quilts with Mandy.

I thought about Mandy. She was deeply unhappy. I didn't really blame her. She didn't want to leave her husband. I realized she remembered the young man she married and she loved that man. "God, you see how unhappy poor Mandy is. Is there anything I can say or do to help her heal?" I sat on the end of the dock and thought some more. It finally occurred to me that really what Mandy needed was Harve. "Well God, for reasons I may never fully understand, Mandy wants Harve. He is her husband. I see no reason she can't have him except for the fact that he is being a total ass. Can you do something about that? Why can't he see that he has been learning spiritual lies? Why can't he see that those lies have cost him the woman who loves him and the joy of seeing his wonderful daughter growing up and finding someone to love?"

Finally, the wind turned chilly so I got up and slowly walked back to the house. My heart was almost breaking for Mandy.

CHAPTER 47: ENGAGEMENT PARTY

In mid-May Ralph met us in Seattle to catch the boat to Victoria for the engagement party. Fay had gone up two days earlier to help prepare for the party.

Mandy felt anxious about meeting all of Jeremy's family. Fay had assured her regularly that they were very successful and well connected. Fay agonized over the difference between her position as the daughter of a dockworker and Jeremy's family. His father was an attorney, and his mother was related to some foreign dignitary.

Mandy made her parents nervous. Ralph's calm common sense comforted me. I thought between the two of us we would be hard pressed to keep Mandy and Aunt Phyllis from descending into hysterics. Ralph confided that my uncle wasn't much better. "They're taking the divorce hard, and this wedding on top of it is stressful for them." Ralph took my hand and kissed it. "Maudy, I hope this isn't off limits, but your family knows the reality of what can happen when a man loses touch with reality. They are terrified Harve will find Mandy."

I smiled at Ralph. "No. That wasn't off limits." I thought for a few minutes. "You know, I'm not certain why that isn't off limits. It doesn't bother me to talk about how my experience affects others. I'm glad you told me. It helps to know what we are dealing with." I sighed. "The other part of the story is that Mandy would like for the old Harve to find her. She is so sad."

Fay met us when we got off of the boat. She introduced us to Jeremy's sister Sarah who agreed to drive half of our party to the country club. As we left town, Sarah started a running commentary on her family. "Please don't let my mum make you crazy. I've all ready told Fay to set her wedding date whenever she wants and our family will work around it. And, for God's sakes, don't let mum get started on the international obligation thing." Without pausing for breath, she changed subjects. "I didn't tell Mum I was getting married. We had a small wedding at Aunt Celia's house and Mum didn't know I was getting married until I walked down the aisle, still she reduced me to tears. Grandmum Jones is always vague, she doesn't mean to ignore people or hurt their feelings. Grandpa Jones probably means to hurt their feelings, but he has mellowed out ever since Aunt Celia got married."

I looked at Ralph, smiled and said. "Sarah don't worry so. One of my jobs as a pastor is to smooth over relationships when two families come together at a wedding. I think people worry more than they need over how others will get along."

Sarah looked at me and snorted. "That is an understatement for my family. I'm afraid my mum is so bad Fay will dump Jeremy, and she is perfect for him. He's so much in love, he doesn't know if he is coming or going."

"Ah. Would it be better if Fay and Jeremy saw each other in Seattle or at my place rather than in Victoria?"

"Yes! Believe me. Yes. Jacob and I will want to spend more time in Seattle too. His sister and brother in-law just moved to Seattle. Edward is doing a residency in oncology." Sarah was quiet for a few minutes while she negotiated a traffic jam. "Oh, I hope Mum doesn't upset Fay by insisting Fay buy a second hand wedding dress or by trying to get Fay to wear Daisy's dress."

I laughed outright. "Tell your mother that my daughter, Patty, will kill anybody who interferes in the production of the perfect wedding dress for Fay. Oh, Patty sends her greetings, but she couldn't get off work for this party."

Ralph whispered to me, "This is shaping up to be better than a stage play."

I responded dryly from my position of superior experience. "Weddings often do."

Dinner passed off reasonably well. I sat between the young doctor who was newly arrived in our country, and Ralph. Ralph's eyes danced as he followed the conversation. Occasionally I could feel him shaking with laughter beside me, especially when Jeremy's mother mentioned her sister, the first lady, more than was tolerable.

Sarah's husband seemed more interested in his sister, who had arrived days earlier, than he was in the rest of the party. He acted amiable enough and talked to Ralph for several minutes before dinner.

Ralph chuckled a great deal over that conversation then grabbed me around the waist, swung me around, and kissed me soundly.

In an effort to keep the conversation flowing at dinner I addressed the young doctor next to me. "Sarah said something about you going to medical school."

"Yes, I am excited to be able to study beyond what is available in our country." He turned and smiled at his beautiful wife. "I worry about my wife. She is having trouble finding food to buy. You do not have the type of stores here that we have at home. Everything is strange here."

His wife leaned around him. "He worries needlessly. We are still eating out for all our meals, which is almost like home." She looked at her brother, grimaced, and the two of them both broke into giggles.

I volunteered, "Would you like me to come over to Seattle and take you around? Or Fay can show you the market."

Ralph intervened, "As soon as we get back, I will take you by the market. I think you will find it more like what you are accustomed to. Where are you staying?"

Dr. Edward's accent seemed thicker than his wife's or Jacob's. "Thank you. We have a condo on Lake Union where I can walk or bicycle to my office or the hospital. I admit that we are hoping that Fay will treat us like family until she moves up here."

I tried to be reassuring, "You will meet my children tomorrow. My son attends classes at the U. Patty works in the city."

We experienced a moment of confusion as we explained the relationship between my children and Fay. When she understood the relationship, Mary Anne jumped out of her chair and ran around the table to hug and kiss Fay and Jeremy. "You are bringing us cousins in our new home. Oh bless you. We will have cousins." She smiled, danced and tears formed in her eyes.

Ralph bounced in his chair, laughed, and hugged and kissed me on the cheek. I laughed at Ralph's behavior and wondered what he was so excited about.

Jacob exclaimed, "The world is a wonderful place when we can find family in a place as far away and exotic as the United States."

I noticed a great deal of kissing at dinner. Most of it centered on our end of the table and a good deal of it originated with Ralph. I'd never seen this side of him. He acted lighthearted and affectionate. He kissed me again and assured Dr. Edward and Mary Anne, "Trevor will be very happy to meet you."

Ralph continued with his cheerful affectionate behavior through dinner and back to our hotel. When we reached our rooms, he took my hand. "Maudy may I come in? There is something very important I want to talk to you about."

I felt my eyes growing larger. I couldn't speak to save my life at that moment. I nodded and opened the door.

Ralph led me to the small sofa at one end of my room. He made certain I was comfortable then he took both my hands in his. His eyes looked deep into mine. He took a deep breath. "First, I missed you when I was in Colombia. I missed talking to you and seeing you, but there was something else I missed." He looked out the window at the harbor. "I missed the peace and joy, mixed with a sense of adventure that surrounds you. I missed being part of how your life flows peacefully even in the middle of disaster."

I nodded to let him know I heard him.

He took another deep breath. "I thought about your life. I wasn't brought up in the church. I've never thought much about God or religion, but as I thought about you, I realized that you have something I want."

This conversation, while very important, was not going where I realized I hoped it was going. I tried to stifle the disappointment that threatened to overwhelm me.

"I want faith in God to be part of my life."

I forced a smile to my face. This was an important moment for Ralph. Why wasn't I more excited for him? "Sweetheart, you are a good man created in the image of God. God has always been part of your life. I think what has been missing is the faith part, knowing that God will provide by bringing the people and things you need into your life."

"Yes! That is what God has been trying to tell me. It took me a while to learn that lesson. Tonight I see it so clearly." He smiled triumphantly at me.

I struggled to return the smile.

"I've been traveling all over the world, investigating this person or that. I've loved my work. I think it's important. It is important. I admit that I have held back in loving you. I know you've said I can travel and still be part of your life. I've still been reluctant to commit."

I suddenly started feeling much happier. Ralph said the word commit.

He continued, "Does God really hit people upside the head with a two-by-four? That is how I feel tonight."

I laughed, "Yeah God can come down on us pretty hard, but it is usually in a good way. What?"

Ralph shook his head and laughed. "I have another assignment. I had no idea how to tackle it."

I stifled disappointment and frustration while he told me the background on a case where our state department heard rumors that the elected president of some country was trying to overthrow their democracy, and set himself up as the dictator.

Ralph laughed some more and announced in tones of triumph. "The president I am to investigate is Mary Anne's and Jacob's father. His wife is Jane's sister." He chuckled again. "From the few things his children said about their father and their whole behavior, I doubt very much that President Jaconovich intends to become a dictator. Jacob seems to think his father is counting the days and hours until the end of his second term." Ralph grinned triumphantly.

My heart sank and part of me called myself foolish for thinking Ralph had made the decision to propose. Another part of me tried to believe that I wasn't ready for a proposal. Still I was disappointed.

Ralph sobered and looked into my eyes again. "Tonight God has shown me that I can continue to do my work and still be free to love and have time for a family."

My hopes shot upward again.

"Maudy, I want you to be the other half of my family. Will you marry me?"

I nodded vigorously and moved toward Ralph for a kiss.

He refused to shut up and get down to business. "I will still have to travel. I want to be able to take you with me sometimes. I can't believe how people want to tell you all their deepest secrets. I know you have your commitment to your congregation. Together, we will keep that commitment as long as you need to stay there."

I knew I was ready for a proposal. I almost snorted thinking, "I'm way past ready for a proposal." I nodded and maneuvered into position for a kiss.

Other Books by Delinda McCann

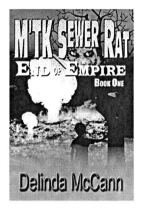

M'TK Sewer Rat - End of Empire

Jake was born the son of a common laborer and grew up on the mean streets of the Empire's worst slum, M'TK. Despite that, his father was able to instill a sense of worth and integrity within Jake that the streets could never beat out of him. M'TK did teach Jake when to fight and when to run and when he learned the army was coming to burn the city, together with his father, they saved the people of the slum.

ISBN: 978-1-938586-32-3 Paperback

ISBN: 978-1-938586-33-0 eBook

M'TK Sewer Rat - Birth of Nation

The new president's first act is to appoint a Supervisor over the Federal Attorney's office, a man loyal to him. Jake quickly discovers his new boss is one of the most notorious professional assassins in the country, an opponent worthy of extreme caution. It plunges Jake into a raging firestorm of corruption and greed among the highest levels of the fledgling democracy.

ISBN: 978-1-938586-34-7 Paperback

ISBN: 978-1-938586-35-4 eBook

Lies That Bind

Jake Jaconovich is the second president elected under the new national constitution. In *Lies That Bind*, he struggles to establish rule of law in a country long accustomed to corruption. Celia McKinsey stands beside him and barely survives an assassination attempt for her role in helping him fight the powerful ruling class.

ISBN 978-1-462898-39-8 Paperback

ISBN 978-1-462898-31-1 eBook

Symbiont

by Melissa McCann (Delinda's Daughter)

Mega-star holo-play personality Emma Sloan teeters on the edge of death after a freak studio accident burns over eighty percent of her body. In a last-ditch effort to save her life, desperate doctors implant her burned skin with a bioengineered symbiotic organism.

ISBN: 978-1-938586-30-9 Paperback

ISBN: 978-1-938586-31-6 eBook

Meet Delinda McCann

Delinda McCann is a social psychologist who has worked in the field of developmental disabilities for over twenty years. She has served on committees for the state of Washington and been an educational advisor to other governments. Her work has earned her the praise of doctors, government officials and families all over the world. She has published numerous articles on disability issues, education, and adoption. Her unique perspective and sense of humor have delighted her readers even when she has been writing about the reality of caring for a loved one who has a severe disability. When the world turns crazy, as it frequently does for the disability community, her friends say there is nobody they would rather laugh and cry with.

Delinda lives a on a small farm near Seattle, WA where she raised her daughters and now runs a small organic flower business with the help of her husband and two giant poodles. She enjoys singing with her church choir and playing the piano-poorly. A brush with cancer made her realize that she needed to slow down, so she turned to writing fiction inspired by her behind-the-scenes experiences of advocating for and loving the people who are just a little bit different.

Visit Delinda's blog at:
http://delindalmccann.weebly.com/index.html

Connect with her on Facebook:
https://www.facebook.com/delinda.mccann?fref=ts

And on Twitter:
@CalicoGardens

WRITERS CRAMP PUBLISHING

http://www.writerscramp.us
editor@writerscramp.us
Amazon, Barnes&Noble, Google, Espresso

CPSIA information can be obtained at www.ICGtesting.com
Printed in the USA
BVOW020411130613

323191BV00006B/58/P